A Decent BOMBER

Alexander McNabb

Copyright © Alexander McNabb 2015

The moral right of the author has been asserted.

All rights reserved.
No part of this publication may be
reproduced, stored in a retrieval system, or
transmitted, in any form or by any means,
without the prior permission in writing of the
author, nor be otherwise circulated in any
form of binding or cover other than that in
which it is published and without a similar
condition including this condition being
imposed on the subsequent publisher.

*All characters in this publication are fictitious and
any resemblance to real persons, living or dead, is
purely coincidental.*

Set in Linotype Palatino and Gill Perpetua

International Edition

ISBN-13: 978-1517679552

The 'troubles' were still a big deal back in 1990, when I first visited Ireland and the homeplace of my wife to be. I was a nervous first timer, I can tell you. I soon found myself in the kitchen with her mum, washing up.
'How are you liking it so far, Alex?' She asked.
Callow Brit me replied, 'I think Eire's just lovely.'
'Oh, *we* don't call it *that*,' she said, all soft Tipperary. 'We call it *Ireland* and we prefer to think of it,' a pause to smile sweetly at me, 'as a *whole* Ireland.'

This, 'the Irish book', is for Brigid and Robert Webster, AKA Ma and Pa Kettle.

Chapter One

Quinlan passed out; a merciful release.

He should have expected them, should have seen the signs of quickening interest in his daily movements. The tailing moped; the sallow, bearded fellow he never saw before and then glimpsed all too often.

They came when Deirdre took the girls for a sleepover with their wee cousins. He had just poured a whiskey when the doorbell rang. His hand flew back from the latch as the door burst open. Their silent, brutal assault buried him under a flurry of expertly dealt blows. They pinioned his hands with nylon ties.

The torture was methodical. Quinlan shrieked himself hoarse, flailing around tied to the kitchen chair until he hurled himself to the floor. They righted him and beat him as dispassionately as they'd pulled out his thumbnails.

And not one word. Not a question. It made it all worse, to think there was nothing they wanted he could give them to make it stop.

They started on his fingers. He called to God, he called to his dear, dead mother. He begged them. Dear Jesus, how he begged. They beat him again to shut him up. His mind slammed down to buy him respite.

A gentle tapping on his cheek. A wipe of wet cloth on his forehead. The awareness of light though his swollen lids. An insistent voice, deep, repeated his name. 'Mister Quinlan, Mister Quinlan.' Accented, the title sounded more like *mist air*.

He took a deep, juddering breath and tried to focus. His hands flared pain. He tasted blood, his mouth dry.

A Decent Bomber

Cool ceramic touched his lips and he leaned forwards to sip gratefully at the icy water. His shattered ribs grated and forced him to cry out, bubbling the water. He spilled a pink dribble down his sodden, spattered shirt.

'Can you hear me Mister Quinlan?' *Mist Air Queen Larne* 'There has been a mistake. These men have been foolish. Do you understand?'

Quinlan nodded. He could just make out the face peering into his own, a look of concern on the dark-skinned features. He tried to speak, his fat lips throbbed and tore, a stab of pain. 'W-who?'

'My name doesn't matter, Mister Quinlan. Some call me The Accountant. It is but a conceit. You are safe, now. Tell me, who is the bomb maker, please? The one who made the big bombs?'

Quinlan groaned. He tried to raise his head. 'Big?' He saw stars, felt a deep lassitude. The cold cloth was pressed to his brow again.

'You remember? The bombs your people made for London and Manchester. People still talk of them. The very, very big bombs. Boom.'

Christ, but that was twenty year and more ago! Quinlan wanted to say. But the cat had his tongue.

'Come. You know who made them. Tell me his name, Mister Quinlan.'

It came to him. Of course it did. *Jesus, but that was Pat. Dear old Pat.*

'Pat,' Quinlan croaked. 'Pat O'Carolan.'

'Where is he?'

He tried to grin. *Ah, these people. Stop, now.* 'Tipp. South Tipp.' Another beautiful sip of water offered to his beaten lips.

Bliss.

'Where is tip, please?'

'Tipperary. The-the Republic.' He was drooling, sloppy-mouthed. The pain clamoured, in and out of focus in waves, his battered nerves shrieked every time he moved his broken body.

'And what is his code word?'

'I-I don't know any c-code—'

The blow to his cheek came fast and with the hard edge of the man's hand. Quinlan's jaw crunched. Pain blossomed in his mouth, both old ache and new sharp. His tied arms stiffened and his bloody hands pulsed agony. He moaned and spat out a tooth.

He sagged against his restraints, snivelling as he tried to breathe through the bloody mucus filling his nose and mouth. 'Dan.' He moaned. 'Breen. Code word. Dan Breen. Danbreen.'

A black leatherette covered notebook was waved in front of his face. The word 'telephone' was picked out in gold, worn where Quinlan's thumb had rubbed it over the years. 'This is yours?'

He wondered how they had found it. He dipped his head.

'Very good, Mister Quinlan. Very good. You can sleep now.'

Quinlan's head was wrenched back. Pain burst from his smashed chest. He opened his mouth to scream but the sound never came. A swift, raw trail scorched across his neck. His hair released, he fell forwards and started to heave for breath that wouldn't come. Blood-stench filled his nostrils. From some other place, dimming, he calmly watched carmine waves pumping down his shirt.

Soon, he stilled.

The milking shed gate clanged shut. The motion sensor

kicked in and floodlight brightened the yard. Patrick O'Carolan had been three days calibrating that thing. At first it had gone off at the slightest whiff of a breeze, then even the herd's scrummaging wouldn't switch it on. Now he'd got it down to a tee. A fine drizzle hung in the air.

The phone rang. Pat squelched across to the house, calling out to his collie, Kirstie. He held open the door for the dog and wiped her paws with the cloth he kept hanging for that very purpose. She padded over to drop on the rug by the warmth of the range. He grumbled at the clangour, 'Alright, I'm on my way. Jesus wept.'

He shrugged off his spattered greatcoat and hoisted it behind the door. The light in the yard clicked off. He pulled up the handset, his skin red from the cold of another harsh winter and spotted with age. Craning out of the window above the sink into the still night, Pat pressed the cold plastic to his ear.

'O'Carolan.' His features softened. 'Well, Mikey. How are you, boy? No, fair enough. And Orla? Still coming? Yes, day after tomorrow is what I had down for her, too. The five fifteen you say? I'll be there, no worry. I'll have that filter coffee she likes, tell her.' He reached for paper and scratched the time, tapping the reluctant biro. 'Not at all. You know yourself I'll only be delighted to have her around the place.'

The yard light snapped on. Pat peered out, but the yard was empty. The dog was still by the range, her long snout on her paws. Her steady brown eyes regarded him.

'Sure, Mikey. No, nothing at all, I have everything I need. Sure I will, of course. Take it handy now, will you? Give my love to Anne. I will, I will. Goodbye, Mikey.'

Pat replaced the handset. Motioning the dog to stay, he lifted his coat from the hook and stepped outside. The harsh light glittered on the puddled ground. Pat stood on the threshold, scanning the yard but nothing moved in the hazy wetness of the South Tipperary winter night. He sniffed the air, a hint of turf from the hummock of sods tied over with blue plastic sheeting by the wall. He'd footed his own turf these past twenty years. Still a strong man, he was nevertheless finding it harder. Sixty this year, by God. On a whim he went back into the kitchen and lifted the white plastic feed bucket he used to carry the turf indoors. He would have his ease and a fire with a hot whiskey tonight. He went back outside, pulling his heavy coat around him.

Pat plucked aside the tarpaulin and dumped the musty oblongs into the bucket. Straightening, his hand on his back, he was stilled by the strong sense of a presence he felt when the yard light came on. He pushed the kitchen door open with his back and dropped the bucket just inside. He whistled for Kirstie. She bounded past him.

He strode along the wall of the house, following the edge of the light. He wanted to call out, just for the reassurance of sound. The darkness beyond was absolute, no light pollution here on the hillside, his farm the only building for a mile and more around. Kirstie returned to pad by his side. The cow shed was all bovine warmth and hay. The cows shifted, their tails swishing and hooves thumping dully on the muddy concrete.

Back into the drizzle, past the milking shed. The dog whined, pushed ahead then halted, growling. Pat shouted. 'What's your business?'

The night was silent beyond the dog's panting and sniffing. She circled, her nose to the ground. At the light's edge, footprints in the muddy soil. The impressions were smooth; no chunky tread marks from wellies or sneakers here: city shoes. A small foot, almost a woman's size. A light step: Pat's wellies left far deeper dints in the ground, but then he was a big man.

He peered into the darkness, his lined face grim. Shoving his hands deep into his pockets he wheeled and called the dog to him. He fastened all three locks on the door.

Sean Driscoll took a pull of his pint and licked the fine foam off his upper lip. Clean-shaven, a handsome man who knew it; flecks of grey at the temples of his dark head of hair, brown eyes with laughter lines and a strong chin. In his suit he looked every inch the politician he was, rather than the revolutionary he had been. The Brits had wasted no time dubbing him a common terrorist, but everyone was being a great deal more polite about such things these days. A former Freedom Fighter, or perhaps a militant, let's say. The election around the corner, Driscoll was feeling on top of the world as the anticipated victory came closer, the polls putting him way ahead and every new day bringing fresh triumphs in headlines. Sean Driscoll, the man of the hour, by God.

What had that wily old sod Arafat said? 'I bring the gun and the olive branch', that was it. Well, the long, slow road was finally paying off. Driscoll was about to reap the rewards of the olive branch. And it had better, he reflected as he sipped again, be a nice fat juicy olive.

Christ, but Gerry and Martin had done well enough for themselves. It was time for younger guns to have their day at the trough, wasn't it?

He glanced at the door of the pub as it admitted sunshine and the clamour of the street. Brian MacNamara's big frame blocked out the sunlight momentarily. The pub was empty save for the two of them and the young barman, who poured MacNamara's pint unbidden.

'Well, now Sean. How's the man?'

'I'm good, Brian. Looking forward to the win, you know yourself.'

MacNamara eyed the three-quarters full glass resting on the bar, the creamy froth billowing. The barman slid it back under the tap to finish it off. He laid the pint down with a diffident nod and took himself away to the other end of the bar.

'*Slàinte.*' Driscoll raised his glass and drank. 'So what's this great mystery that brings you galloping from campaign headquarters on a Sunday morning right before the election?'

MacNamara brooded over his pint, his keen eye on Driscoll. 'Quinlan is dead.'

Driscoll's beam faded fast. 'Christ, Brian. I thought we'd agreed this stuff? I don't want to know about Quinlan or any of that. We're with Gerry and them, we're clean.'

'He'd lost several teeth.'

'I don't give a shit.' Driscoll's urgent hiss was loud enough to turn the barman's head. 'The election's around the corner, we've a chance of doing something great. We can't afford this sort of stuff to come up now, for God's sake. I thought I made that clear?'

MacNamara's rumbling tone was relentless, his hands gripping his drink. 'He was also missing his fingernails. All his fingers had been broken. They cut his throat, then doused him in petrol and set him on fire.'

'They? How do you know it was a "they"?'

'You know Quinlan, Sean. No one man could have done that to him.'

A Decent Bomber

'Bury it, Brian. We've an election to win.'

'And what if he won't be buried? What if Quinlan gave them the caches? The codes?'

Driscoll's stare was deadpan. 'What caches? I don't know anything about caches, Brian. I'm a feckin' politician. I just understand ballots and polls and kissing babies, me.' Draining his pint, he slid off his barstool, his finger in MacNamara's face. 'I'll hear no more about Quinlan. You hear me? Not a fucking dicky bird.'

Cleaning the farmhouse had taken most of the day and Pat had used up all the bleach, a signal it was time to go into the village for supplies. He drove down to the shop and Mrs Gleeson was full of bustle and gossip. So he was expecting a visitor? Extra bread, please, Mrs Gleeson. Truth be told, he was excited at Orla's visit: he hadn't seen the girl in two months. She'd been holed up in Dublin, studying.

Orla had always been his favourite among Mikey's girls, four of them all fine looking like Anne but with Mikey's humour and that determined streak that often crossed over into stubbornness. His brother was an engineer and the girls had inherited his technician's brain and fine hands. Orla was studying animal husbandry at University and her two week stay at Pat's was part of her course – a chance to learn about farming in action, according to her lecturer. Orla had laughed as she told Pat: she had virtually grown up on his farm, never mind learning about farming in action.

Pat hadn't told her, but his will was made and the farm was to be hers when the time came.

He had also inherited their father's careful technician's hands, although you'd be hard put to tell these days: with them all red and chapped from the cold and working outside. He had put his talents to different uses than Mikey had, perhaps. Back then, when the world was different and he had his Cause to serve.

First thing back from the shop, Pat went into the living room and placed sods of turf on the fire, which had almost gone out. The room was still warm. He flicked in a firelighter, just to get it going again. He went out to the car, his breath steaming, and brought in the shopping. He slid the cardboard apple box onto the kitchen table and unpacked his haul. Chocolate biscuits, Bewley's tea, cheese - Orla loved Brie, which Pat loathed but there was a wedge of it right enough there in the box, wrapped in the waxy paper Mrs Gleeson used for her cut cheeses. There was soda bread, white scones and a piece of lean bacon for Orla's arrival tomorrow by train from Dublin. A savoy cabbage and a packet of parsley sauce. Exotically, packets of Sumatran coffee, ground for filters. Gleeson's stocked it just for Orla's visits. She hadn't sold any of the three packs on the shelf since Orla last been down and, feeling guilty for her trouble, Pat bought them all.

The phone rang. For some reason its peal stilled him. He lifted the handset slowly. The sacred heart lamp was guttering. He'd have to get a new one next time he went down the road.

'Hello?'

The voice on the line had a hint of American. 'This is Patrick O'Carolan?'

'It is, sure.'

'Hello, Mr O'Carolan. Your code word is Dan Breen. Could you confirm you understand me?'

There was something else under the American note in the voice, a hint of something deep and dark. Pat's tongue felt double the size, his voice thick. 'Yes.' Damn his hesitancy, it sounded like he had a stutter. He mustered his wits; his eyes squeezed shut to block out the nightmares of the past. 'Yes, I confirm.' As he spoke, his mind shrieked: *No, tell them no. Tell them you don't know what the fuck they're on about and to leave me and my niece alone.*

'Thank you.' The voice sounded like one of those call centre nuisance calls. There was even that strange flatness to the line, a hint of robot. 'You will receive a visitor. You are to comply with his instructions. He will be from Africa and he will confirm this code word. Is that understood?'

Pat peeled off a scrap from the glued pad he kept by the phone, playing with it distractedly. 'Yes, I understand you.'

'Goodbye, Mr O'Carolan.'

Pat listened to the whoosh and hiss of the empty line. He replaced the handset, his hand shaking. Cupped in his palm was a tiny, beautifully folded paper swan. He hadn't realised he was making it, fiddling with a sheet from the pad. He hadn't made one of those in twenty years and more. He picked it up, took it into the living room and tossed the little bird onto the flames.

'Mikey, it's Pat.'

'Howya, big man?'

'Look, it's about Orla.'

'Ah, Pat if you could have seen her. She was like a six year old when we dropped her to the station. She's on the way down to you right now.'

'Oh, right. Lovely. I was just checking that. Great.'

'Is anything wrong, Pat?'

'No, Mikey, God no. Five fifteen, right?'
'It left on time so it should be there on time.'
'Cheers, Mikey.'
'Cheers then, Pat.'

Chapter Two

Orla pulled her hair back over her shoulder. Its reflection in the train window blended with the russet autumn leaves on the bank flashing by. She squinted, twizzling a glittering red strand around her pale finger and thinking of Róisín.

They had met at Mick McDonnell's party; a real student affair, all warm wine and a bath full of icy beer, loud music and Mick's friends down from Belfast, leery and watchful-eyed. Furtive kids clustered round the back in the courtyard of the terraced house by the old coal shed, the dancing fireflies of reefers glowed in the darkness.

Róisín was there with one of the Belfast lads. Orla admired the poise of her, dark-haired and dangerous-eyed, full lips blush without need of lipstick and her smooth skin tanned; perhaps a hint of the Romany about her. A gypsy from Belfast. Orla lost her in the pack, caught by a bore on her course who wanted to talk about bovine distemper. Distemper. At a party, for Christ's sakes.

She was on the cusp of telling him just how little she wanted to talk to a drunk ugly bloke about animal diseases when the fuss from the living room triggered a wave in the press of people. The pack parted to let the furious-looking gypsy storm through. At the other end of the tunnel two guys were holding back the lad from Belfast, the side of his face red, presumably from a slap. The wall closed like the Red Sea and the tableau of his restrained fury was lost to her. Orla nodded to Distemper Man and followed the gypsy through the kitchen to the biting cold of the courtyard. She found her standing by the coal shed, away from the bunch of plotters, tugging on a reefer.

Orla was a little drunk on warm wine and her escape from the bore had cheered her. 'What, you hit him?'

The gypsy looked as if she was about to tell Orla to fuck off but softened, drawing smoke deep into her lungs. 'He was a wanker.'

'They mostly are.' Orla held out her hand. 'Hi. I'm Orla. Orla O'Carolan.'

'Róisín McManus.'

'You're down from Belfast.'

'Yeah. And clearly not getting a lift back, now.'

'What happened?'

'He seemed to think giving me a lift meant he was going to get a fuck. I put him right.'

Róisín handed the joint to Orla, who shook her head. 'No thanks. Not my thing.' She waved her glass. 'Are you a student too?'

'Sure, I am.'

'What you studying?'

'Terrorists. You?'

Orla searched Róisín's face, but it was without guile. 'Animal husbandry. How do you mean, terrorists?'

'Just that. Terror studies.'

'You're kidding me. That's a *course*?'

Róisín laughed, shaking her head. 'What's so odd about it? You look like someone just slapped your arse.'

'I suppose it seems strange that someone would want to... well, *that*. Oh, I don't know. Don't we see enough about them every day?'

'This nation was founded on terrorism. If it wasn't for Michael Collins, Dan Breen and the likes of them there'd be no Ireland. We'd still be a British colony.'

A Decent Bomber

'Ah, come on. That's ancient history.'

The spark at the end of the reefer stabbed at Orla, the features behind its glow knit in fury. 'The fuck it is. What's a freedom fighter? What's an insurgent? What's a terrorist? That's what I want to know. We let ourselves be governed by old men who tell us what's good for us and what we need and the second we question it we're hauled off to face their idea of justice. You know what democracy is? Say you what you like, do what you're told. And we slap the label of terrorist on anyone who happens not to agree with us and doesn't conform to the restrictions we impose on them.'

'Jesus. You're best off studying anarchy studies, you.'

Róisín's angry expression softened and she flicked the butt of her joint over the fence, a spinning ember flying through the cold darkness. 'Fuck it. Let's get a drink.'

A sharp nasal voice announced the station through the speakers along the carriages. Orla started, shocked out of her reverie. The old lady opposite was wearing a green coat and clutched her handbag on her knee. The bright sunlight accentuated the lines on her face; an ancient monument. She trapped Orla's glance as it careened away from the window, the leaves and the past. Orla returned the woman's smile automatically, a small politeness. Inside, she had never felt so alive, so thrilled by the sheer glory of the world.

Orla was in love with a girl and wondered what the hell she was going to tell her Uncle Pat. She bit her lip and tugged at the rubber bangle on her wrist.

Pat paced the platform of the little Victorian station,

hands dug deep and shoulders hunched against the cold. He'd arrived early and the time weighed heavy. A watched kettle never boils, he thought. His relieved grin when the rails sang drew a smile from the young mother sitting on the bench and rocking her pram.

'You're meeting someone?'

'My niece. She's coming to stay for the week.'

'Ah, that's nice. How old is she?'

'Twenty-one. She's at University in Dublin. Studying farming.'

The train rounded the bend in the blue-grey distance, the yellow oblong on its front shimmering.

'You? Are you meeting someone?'

'Yes, my husband. He's been away.'

Pat knew what that meant. It brought an unpleasant thrill of remembrance. 'Fair play. Good luck to you both.'

She pulled a packet of cigarettes out and waved it but Pat shook his head. She lit up and shrugged. 'Thanks. He'll need it.'

He barely heard her over the train's clatter as it strained to a halt, craning to catch sight of Orla's red hair. Sure enough, a pale hand waved at him from the carriage. The woman with the baby forgotten, he strode up the platform.

Orla dropped her wheelie bag to throw her arms around him, nearly throwing him off balance with her enthusiasm. 'Uncle Pat! Howya?'

She was a fine young woman, red headed with emerald eyes and freckled, milky skin that burned as soon as it was lit by the sun, not that there was much chance of that with the sky like slate and the cold in it. Pat took her bag in his big hand. They passed the woman, who was embracing a man with a crew-cut. She nodded at Pat over her man's shoulder, tears flooding down her cheeks. He gave her a wink and tried to focus on Orla, who was chattering nineteen to the dozen about what a bitch city life was and how she was glad to get away from theory, theory and theory.

A happy man, it wasn't until they'd made the car park he remembered the rich voice on the phone. Orla halted.

'Is there something wrong, Uncle Pat?'

'No, I just forgot something. No great matter. So are you staying off the drink and boys in Dublin? There's fierce temptation in that city. They tell me. I wouldn't know myself.'

She searched his face before answering, shrugging it off. 'Ah, all work makes Orla a dull girl. How's the farm?'

They reached his battered Daihatsu. He unlocked her door and hefted her bag into the litter of rumpled straw-strewn blankets and tools in the back. He bounced into his seat. 'The farm,' he assured her, 'is only lovely.'

Only it wasn't.

The cows' plaintive lowing reached Orla as she banged open the Daihatsu's door and dropped into the muddy yard. Pat had her bag. He opened the farmhouse door and Kirstie leaped out, bounding around Orla and licking her hand. She tickled the collie's ears the way she knew how, but she was distracted. The cows sounded wrong, they were making such a racket. Orla followed her uncle into the farmhouse. He came out of her room slapping his hands.

'Right, your bag's on your bed. Fancy some tea?'

'Uncle Pat, what's wrong with the cows?'

'The cows?'

'Have they been milked today?'

'Milked?'

'Yes, you know. That thing you do when you put teat cups on them and play classical music?'

He swept a hand over his brow. 'Ah, Jesus. I might've forgotten this morning. A lot on my mind, cleaning up and all. I'll see to them now. Put the kettle on and have a cup and I'll be back in a jiffy.'

'How could you forget them, Uncle Pat? The herd?' She took in the look of helpless misery on his face. 'Come on, so. I'll lend you a hand.'

She pulled on her wellies from behind the door, unsure of what they were going to find when they brought the cows into the milking parlour. Just a few hours could mean real problems with a dairy herd, mastitis or even drying up. Uncle Pat's herd could be ruined. It was unconscionable he could have forgotten to milk them, not these cows. They were prime Friesians and he had always got great yields for a small herd. The farm was hilly, boggy land, hardly rich. He'd worked like a Trojan to make this farm pay and she had long admired his conscientiousness and love for the animals that were his livelihood.

What would make Uncle Pat neglect his cows?

As she shoved the cups up onto the first set of distended udders, Orla shot a glance across to him, working alongside her. The cow shuffled, bellowing and twitching her hooves. Orla was cautious: she didn't fancy getting kicked. Uncle Pat was sweating, despite the cold. His good humour had seemed brittle to her, his manner distracted. They worked together on the small herd, but Orla knew it was too late. These cows had missed at least two milkings and some were already showing signs of soreness. She worked as quickly and deftly as she knew, her childhood on this very farm combined with her

A Decent Bomber

school learning from Dublin. She noted down the numbers of the cows showing possible early symptoms of mastitis.

Kirstie lay inside the door on a patch of dry hay, her eyes flickering. Orla clicked her tongue and smiled at the collie, rewarded with a responsive twitch of tail. She wondered if Róisín was a dog person and decided, on balance, yes. Best yes, anyway.

Orla heard the car first. Pat stiffened at the sound of the big engine and she felt he'd been anticipating its arrival, perhaps even dreading it. He darted a glance at her and then away when she caught his eye. The car door's slam, then the doorbell.

'I'll get it. Back in a second,' he called out. He was trying to be reassuring and bluff and she hated it because he just looked and sounded like a liar and he wasn't a liar he was her Uncle Pat, the rock in her newly turbulent life. She felt she doubted him, the first time he had represented anything for her other than absolute certainty.

He stumbled out of the milking parlour. She pulled the cups off the cow at her side and slapped its arse to move it on, the next one lumbering to take its place.

The black Range Rover was mud-spattered around the wheel-arches but otherwise shone as if it had just come out of a showroom. Its owner was black. Not something you found around Kilcommon, Pat thought as he wiped his hand on his trousers and offered it.

It was taken fastidiously, but the grip was strong, despite the man's slight build. He wore a grey suit. His white shirt framed a blue striped tie. Shiny black city shoes, Pat noted. A goatee beard, precisely clipped, framed the flash of white teeth.

'A Mister Dan Breen sent me.'

Pat pushed open the farmhouse door and gestured his guest to enter. 'I'm sure he did,' he murmured, closing the door on Kirstie's curiosity. Following him into the kitchen, he was bluff. 'Will you have a cup of tea?'

'Yes, please. That would be most welcome after the journey. Four sugars, please.'

'Four? Jesus, that's some sweet tooth you have.'

Pat filled the kettle and rooted in the cupboard for cups. His hands were shaking. He wished he'd told Orla not to come into the house until the guy had gone, but then she'd just have been curious and come anyway if he knew her. Cloaking the visit in normalcy was all he could think to do, but this was clearly nothing normal. And why had they sent, of all things, a bloody African?

He gestured to the chairs around the kitchen table. 'Here, take your weight off the floor.'

The man sat, his hands knotted in front of him on the weathered wood. He shone, Pat thought, in the pale sunlight that had somehow escaped the clouds' embrace. He slipped teabags into the cups and filled them from the kettle. He added four spoons of sugar and milk for his guest, a single Hermesetas for himself.

'Here we go.' Pat delivered the mug then leaned against the sink by the window so he could see if Orla came out of the milking parlour. He raised his cup. '*Sláinte*.'

The African smiled, an inwardly focused gesture. He reached for the cup and sipped his tea, bestowing it an appreciative nod. He wore a signet ring with a red stone in it.

Pat crossed his arms. 'So what do you want from me, Dan Breen's friend?'

'We require you to return to your old profession briefly, Mr O'Carolan. We have need of some devices to be manufactured.'

Which were, more or less, precisely the words Pat feared so very much hearing. He put his tea down on the worktop with care and drove his trembling hands into his trouser pockets. Kirstie was barking outside.

'How many?'

'Six.'

'How big?'

'Five Suitcase devices. About five kilos each. Timed, not wireless. And one bigger.' The African smiled condescendingly at Pat.

Pat glowered. 'What do you mean bigger?'

'Like your last bomb, Mr O'Carolan. This big.'

The horror hit Pat, the world stopping for an instant as the past reached out its skeletal hand and squeezed his heart until he felt the life draining out of him. *Christ, not that. Not again. Ever.*

'I'm not doing it. Make 'em yourself.'

'You're the best. We don't have your expertise. You have forgotten more than we hope to learn of these things.'

'I won't do it. That's behind me. You have the wrong man, Mr…'

'You knew you were making a commitment for life, you know refusal is not an option.'

'It fucking well is.'

'Those who serve The Cause never forget.'

'Don't preach at me. There is no cause any more, there's Stormont and politics. That's all there is now. We're not at war. Not with the Brits, not the UVF or anyone else. Let alone any fucking Africans.'

The silky skin tautened. 'There is a wider geo-political

picture you are not required to understand. Your job is to make the devices. Ours is to deploy them as we see fit.'

'What am I supposed to make them out of? Play dough? You can't have enough explosive.'

'We do, I assure you. You will be amply supplied with materials.'

'Is that right? Sail in on the banana boat, did they?'

The African stood. 'I could have your throat slit, my insolent Irish friend.' He tossed a card onto the table. 'You will meet my colleague at this location tomorrow at ten o'clock and he will arrange for your materials.'

'And what if I refuse to meet anyone anywhere,' Pat squinted at the card, 'let alone in bloody Newry? What then?'

'Oh, you will meet him. And you will co-operate. You have far too much to lose, Mr O'Carolan. Thank you for the tea. I shall see myself out.'

Pat followed the man out of the kitchen into the yard, the *chirp chirp* of the Range Rover's remote locking system breaking the silence. He glared at the African clambering up into the big car and was still standing in the doorway as it reversed and drove away down the track to the main road. He briefly patted his pockets for the stub of pencil he habitually carried and noted down the car's registration on the card with the Newry address.

Distracted as he was, Pat didn't notice the silence until it was broken by a tatty-tailed crow flapping into the air and crying out, over in the field. He pushed away from the doorway, his heart pounding as he raced across the yard to the milking parlour. Kirstie was lying on her side on the concrete, blood matting the fur behind her ear.

'Orla? Orla!'

He tore up the length of the shed, bursting out into the grey light, crying out: 'Orla!' His voice was deadened by the grey mist slithering down off the bog. He returned to the milking parlour and checked the dog's pulse. She was alive. He picked her up gently, her fur sodden with blood and muck from the wet floor. On the way over to the house, she licked his arm and whined.

After washing and dressing the collie's wound and giving her a painkiller pushed into a purple Quality Street, Pat searched every building and outhouse on the farm, although he knew well he wasn't going to find Orla there. Back in the house, flicking the Newry address over and over in his hand, he started at the phone's ring.

'O'Carolan.'

'Uncle Pat? I'm okay. I…'

'Newry tomorrow, Mr O'Carolan. Don't miss the appointment.'

'If you harm her, I'll…'

'You had best perform your assigned task. Then your niece will come to no harm. If you fail me or in any way try to betray our cause, it will go badly for her. I hardly need spell this out to a man of your intelligence.'

In the background, Orla screamed.

'Do we understand each other, Mr O'Carolan?'

Pat put his hand over the mouthpiece to mask the sound of his breathing as he brought himself under control. 'We do.'

'Tomorrow then.'

Click.

Oh, God. Dear, sweet Jesus.

Chapter Three

The fire engines had churned up the garden of Cathal Burke's house; the heavy wheels furrowed the soggy grass like a ploughed field. Brian MacNamara parked on the pavement and locked his Mercedes with the remote. Crime scene tape flapped around the bungalow. The Police Service Northern Ireland copper on duty at the gate stepped forward to block MacNamara's way.

A white-haired PSNI officer at the front door called out: 'Leave him through.'

Surveying the roofless house, smoke still spiralling lazily from the blackened ruin, MacNamara strode up the driveway and shook hands with Inspector William Taggart.

'How are you keeping, Billy?'

'Good, Brian. It's been a while. You here official, like?'

'Not as such. A friend of the family.'

Taggart nodded sagely. 'Sure. Well, it's a mess. We've just cleared the major roof debris away from the trapdoor into the cellar.

'Cellar?'

'Sure, a lot of these older houses had cellars, especially the more remote ones. Farms and that. You'd be surprised at how many, in fact. Some of them could be very dangerous, with fires like this breaking out. People store all sorts of things in them.'

Taggart was going heavy on the sarcasm. MacNamara assumed his blandest expression. 'Is that a fact, Billy? Must be all these fireworks they're selling to folk coming up from the South.'

'Fireworks and all sorts. All sorts. You wouldn't

believe it. Come on in. I wouldn't worry about wiping your shoes.'

The wooden front door seemed undamaged from the outside, but the inside surface was charred. The stench of burning was cloying. Men in Tyvek boiler suits were working in the wreckage. A group struggled to shove a still-smouldering beam.

'Cathal Burke was tied up with nylon cable ties and left in the kitchen. He was missing six teeth his dentist's records said he should still have. We found four of them in the wreckage so far. The house appears to have been very liberally doused with diesel. It went up like a dog. Woof. The remains of a gas cylinder in the kitchen suggest it was pitched in from outside once the fire had started. It tore out the back of the house and meant there was very little of Mr Burke indeed remaining. The MO is surprisingly similar to the recent death of a Mr Desmond Quinlan. Who is another friend of the family, if I'm not much mistaken.'

'It's a big family.'

'God, yes. But recently surprisingly prone to tragedy.'

'Ah, now, Billy. We've seen worse.'

One of the white boiler suits gave the thumbs up. 'The cellar door's clear.'

Taggart raised his voice. 'Go ahead, lads.'

They lifted the trap door carefully, three men bearing its weight as it slammed back. A man lugging a big LED light was first down, a second boiler suit carrying an equipment case fast on his heels. Taggart turned to MacNamara. 'Come on down. Obviously don't touch nothing.'

The cellar was cool, the big space starkly lit by the lamp. The second man knelt to pop his case, pulling out swabs and sliding them over the floor and walls.

'It's empty.' MacNamara stared around him.

Taggart rounded on him. 'Well, Brian, that's great detective work. Jesus, but you should have been in the force instead of the other side.'

'Your arse.'

'So what were you expecting to find in here?'

MacNamara hoped his turmoil wasn't showing. He shrugged and lied. 'I don't know. Doll's houses. Exercise bikes. Boxes of shite for the car boot.'

The machine in the case beeped, its operator called to Taggart. 'Sir.'

'Well that's funny, Brian. Because Barton's machine there is telling us it was used to store explosives. I don't think either of us thinks we're talking display fireworks for little Gráinne's confirmation over in Kildare, do we?'

'You know I wouldn't have a clue about that sort of thing these days.' MacNamara's heart was thrashing in his chest and he felt the sweat break out on his forehead.

'Right. Maybe you'd want to ask around in that extended family of yours. Like quite how much of this stuff we could be looking for. Because we appear to have, and I do find this amusing in my own gallows humour sort of way, a shared problem.'

'I don't know what you're talking about, Billy. I have not the faintest clue.'

MacNamara headed for the stairway, Taggart's contempt burning two holes in his back.

Life was normal enough at Banbridge Police Station, with its red brick walls topped with cameras and razor wire. The year hadn't rolled around yet to marching season and it wasn't Friday night, so there was little going on in the reception area.

Upstairs, paused at the end of the cramped meeting room with his knuckles reflecting on the veneered wooden table, McLoughlin's shoulders were stooped. His features, when he raised his face, were taut. The scrawny young plain clothes copper who'd come in with him and sat smugly throughout the meeting was now grinning openly.

His own lips set in a hard line, Brian MacNamara wasn't a happy man. It had been a long time since anyone had talked to him like this. Probably back at school, that old bastard McArdle and his geometry. MacNamara's natural inclination was to tell Detective Superintendent Wayne McLoughlin to go to hell.

Sean Driscoll's face looked like undercooked pastry, MacNamara reckoned. The sort of stuff you found under the lid of his missus' short crust steak pies; grey and sweaty. He wondered if Sean wasn't losing it, what with the election and all. The guy had been one of the coolest and now he'd flung his hat into the ring of Stormont politics, he seemed more afraid than MacNamara ever remembered from the days of internment and criminality. Sean had been hunted around Europe by those SAS wankers and come out of the whole thing grinning triumph like it had been a country hike. Yet now he was paddling his hand ineffectually in the air as he prevaricated and postured. He was getting fat. Mind, MacNamara's own weight was on the up and his gut was slowly eating his belt buckle.

Driscoll stuttered. 'I have said this clearly and won't be tasked again. The party has no knowledge whatsoever of any materiel stored in Mr Burke's farm. He is not an active associate or even an affiliate. You know I would extend my utmost efforts to assist you, Wayne. But this is not our doing.'

McLoughlin, raking the room with his puce furiousness, jerked to a halt. 'Your *doing*?'

Driscoll's lips pursed. MacNamara scowled at the grinning plain clothes man. He tried a reasonable tone. 'He means they're not our explosives.'

'Of course they're yours.' McLoughlin nodded at his colleague, who pulled a tablet from the pocket of his tatty bomber jacket. 'Tell them, Boyle.'

Boyle stared back at MacNamara, his eyes disconcertingly dark like little black pools in the pale skin, a vein pulsing on his temple. He wasn't grinning anymore. His voice rasped. 'Cathal Burke has been known personally to Mister Driscoll here for at least thirty years. We have him photographed with Driscoll and you,' he flipped a long finger at MacNamara, 'in parades, in clandestine meetings and we have voice recordings of conversations between you on a number of separate occasions between '78 going right up until we all decided to play nicely together, only you clearly haven't been quite playing by the rules we all agreed. Burke did six years for aggravated GBH, after he'd turned over a mechanic who'd refused to 'co-operate' with your lot back in '82. He was met from nick by none other than one Brian MacNamara and bought himself a nice house soon after. His reward for keeping quiet all that time in Long Kesh, we always thought. We didn't think to check if that nice new bungalow had a cellar, or we'd have maybe popped by for a nosy before it was too late, when we'd all signed up to our Easter love-in and you lot were out of bounds.' Boyle placed the tablet he hadn't bothered consulting down on the meeting table surface. 'Burke's tied to you two like a fucking albatross and you can jump around shouting about how you don't have anything to do with him 'till you go blue in the face but the fact is he's your doggie and that means you know precisely what he was sitting on when you commanded him sit. And forensics tells us that cellar was packed with Semtex and ammonium nitrate.'

McLoughlin cut in, his finger in Driscoll's face. 'You're only making it worse by pretending this is going to go away, because it's not.'

'It's not about—' Driscoll started before McLoughlin's big hand slammed down on the table top.

'Stop pissing about with us. What was cached at Burke's? It was in direct contravention of every fucking peace agreement you ever signed, whatever it was. But it's not there anymore and now we have to find it. So what are we looking for?' McLoughlin stared Driscoll down. He switched his furious glare to MacNamara. 'Are there more? More caches?'

'I want immunity before I answer anything more.'

'For fuck's sake!' MacNamara recoiled from Boyle's fury. The skinny copper stood over him. Sprawling and trapped, MacNamara felt fat and middle aged. Twenty years ago he would have killed this wee bastard. Now he was aghast to find himself cowering.

Boyle was screaming into his face. 'People are going to die you fucking idiot! Two of your people are dead already. The next man's likely trussed up having his nails pulled and singing like a mad fucking canary.'

MacNamara nodded, sweat pouring down his forehead and cheek. He glimpsed Driscoll pale and holding himself upright against the table, McLoughlin with his head in his hands. Boyle's black eyes glittered and his smoker's breath was hot. 'I suggest you consult with your colleague here and ensure your faulty memories are somehow miraculously patched up because this is serious. People could die because you pricks are holding out on us. You understand me?'

'I think it's time you let us go or we got a lawyer,' Driscoll's voice was shaky. 'I don't appreciate this level of violence from PSNI and intend to raise a formal complaint.'

McLoughlin strode out of the room, shouldering the door open. He turned. 'Release them, Boyle. Have communications issue an apology for our over-zealous pursuit of this important investigation in the face of the unwillingness of Mr Driscoll to help us with our enquiries into the theft of illegal caches of arms being maintained by his associates in contravention of the Good Friday Agreement.'

Driscoll gabbled. 'We'll drop the complaint.'

Contempt was written on McLoughlin's face as he wheeled away. 'See them off the property and make sure they don't steal the fucking silver.'

The Monday after she met Róisín at the party, Orla sat dreaming by the window, her finger against the cold glass and old O'Mara's voice reduced to a drone in the background as he embarked on a monotonous exploration of the finer points of effective animal husbandry on an austerity budget.

She jumped as her mobile went off. She lunged for her backpack as O'Mara halted to glare at her. Curious faces turned towards the source of his displeasure. 'Sorry,' she mumbled, lifting the mobile to her ear and ducking out of the room.

'Orla. It's me.'

'I know. What is it? I was in class and now O'Mara's going to kill me.'

'I'm here.'

A Decent Bomber

'Here? Where?'

'In Dublin, eejit. Coffee?'

She'd have to skip the afternoon lecture. She shrugged. She was already in the shit. 'Sure. Where?'

'Grafton Street, Bewley's. Where else? In twenty?'

'Done.' Bustling back into the classroom and lapped by O'Mara's displeasure, Orla was awed at what an elemental force Róisín was. It hadn't even been an option to say no to her.

O'Mara crossed his arms. Balding and pale, thick pebble glasses wobbled on his fleshy nose. Orla held up her hand to fend him off. 'I'm sorry. Family emergency.' She grabbed her bag, spun around and was out of the classroom before he could muster a reaction.

It was deadly cold and the DART was packed with ruddy-cheeked, miserable looking people. Orla snapped a smile at a greying woman, rewarded with a droopy stare. She jumped off the train and strode up the street towards the canopied sign proclaiming 'Bewley's Oriental Cafés Ltd', pushing through the door to the fuggy interior and its reek of brewing coffee and sweet cake. Róisín waved from way over and they came together, Róisín's hand rubbing Orla's back, her woody heat pressed against Orla's cheek.

The embrace went on too long. Orla broke away first, her heart hammering.

'Something up?'

Orla flicked her hair away from her eye. 'No, no, nothing.'

'Coffee?' Róisín lifted her purse from the table.

Orla nodded, bit her lip.

'Latte?'

'Please.'

Róisín brushed past her. Their breasts rubbed. Orla's

mouth was parched, her mind ablaze and her whole body tingling. She grabbed at the chair, dropping down to muster her wits.

Memories. Dreams. Orla woke not to the smell of coffee shops but the lingering hint of the jute sack they'd pulled over her head and the stench of onions soaked into its rough fibres. Her head was pounding. She blinked, her eyelids swollen and crusted. The light in the room faint, the heavy drapes drawn against the sly intrusion of sunlight. Trying to rub her eyes, she found herself tied. A blanket had been thrown over her. She wriggled free of it, pulling her hands up to her streaming eyes and wiping them with her wrists. The nylon ties bit into her freckled skin. *Róisín? Please God, where am I?*

The saggy mattress creaked with her movements. She tried to bring her breathing under control, to halt her contorting. The room resolved itself, semi-dark and bare of furniture. The floorboards were worn, the walls panelled in dark oak. A slip of light shone through the curtains, a stone window frame. Some sort of old manor house.

Footsteps outside stilled her. She relaxed and closed her eyes, feigning unconsciousness as the door was opened.

'You are awake. You are like elephant. We are hear you from down.'

He was pale-skinned, a heavy-set man, crew-cut and hard jawed. Orla gasped at the sight of the pistol in his hand, a brutish thing that glinted in the light seeping through the curtains. He wore jeans and a dark heavy jumper. A second man came in, smaller and dark-skinned. He carried a tray which he set down on the bed.

A Decent Bomber

The bigger man leaned in to her and she shrank away.

'Not to worry. Eat food.'

He pulled her up into a sitting position. The tray had a triangle of service station sandwich and a bottle of water on it.

'My hands are tied.'

'You can eat.'

'Who are you?'

'Eat. No question. Eat.'

The anger rose in her and she tossed her head only to be assaulted by a tide of nausea and pain. She wavered on the edge of the bed, in danger of pitching forward to the floor. He steadied her shoulder and stepped back.

'Eat.'

She wanted to scream at him, to spit defiance but she was too weak. The door slammed behind them and she whispered to herself, 'Eat them yeself, yer bollix.'

For a long while she stayed on the bed, foetal and miserable, wondering where she was and why. She felt bruised all over, but it was her head hurt her worst of all. The throbbing receded slightly. She uncurled herself and reached out for the water, spilling it as she unscrewed the plastic cap with her hobbled hands. She scrabbled at the plastic sleeve on the sandwich. It was taped shut and she dropped the box twice trying to wrangle the sandwich out of it. Eventually she popped the thing open and drew out the dry white bread encasing the little pink line of ham.

It stuck in her throat. Gagging, she reached for the water and knocked the bottle over, spilling it on the coverlet. She grabbed at it, pulling it up and saving about half of it.

She drank and lay back on the bad exhausted by the effort.

Chapter Four

Pat reached up to the little brown whiskey jug on the dresser in his kitchen and pulled an old-fashioned brass key out from under it. He pocketed the cold metal and pulled his coat down from behind the door. Kirstie struggled to rise. He motioned her down.

'No, girl. Not this time. Stay.'

He pulled the door shut behind him, hunched against the impact of the cold after the kitchen's warmth. The morning air was heavy with what could have been a fine drizzle or perhaps a heavy mist. *Mizzle*, he thought up as he strode out of the muddy yard and struck out left down the lane. The trees dripped and the rich smell of soil was earthy and clean. The tang of peat smoke from his chimney reached him.

Pat's boots on the grainy margin of the road punctuated the silence. He'd have felt contentment taking a walk like this at any other time, soaking up the peace and the smells of the hillside. But his chest was tight with apprehension. A crow's rasp turned his head and brought the fleeting urge to shoot the bloody thing.

He slipped off the road down into the grotto. It was noticeably cooler in the bosky hollow. The Virgin's painted blue vestments were peeling. Her mildewed face seemed quizzical. Pat fished out the key and, from his other pocket, his torch. He squeezed behind the statue and unlocked the little door concealed in the shadows. It creaked as he pushed in.

He hadn't been here for years. Cobwebs festooned the ceiling, dropping down to caress the lumpen, dusty oil-cloth covering. He pulled it away. The layered stacks of boxes lay undisturbed and timeless. He counted off, three from the front. He pulled the box open and it was if he had never left the place. The tidy row of handled plastic cases shone dully in the torchlight. Pat lifted one of them out, snapped the catches and let his eyes run over the brutal, blunt lines of the compact Glock 26 pistol bedded in its grey foam. They had been one of the last acquisitions, these pistols. They'd never been used in anger: ten of the black plastic cases lay in the damp cardboard box, as pristine as the day they were delivered by the nervous Czech they were bought from.

He delved deeper into the box and pulled out a carton of ammunition, which he slipped into his greatcoat pocket. He replaced the flaps and pulled back the tarpaulin.

Back in the kitchen, with the help of a tin of WD40 from the outhouse, Pat sat at the table and cleaned the gun. He was surprised at how familiar the routine was, but when it came to finally holding the thing and pulling the trigger to check the mechanism, a rush hit him; a tumble of conflicting emotions, uncertainty and fear conquered by cold anger and, yes, excitement. He practised sliding the gun out of the his greatcoat pocket, thumbing the safety and firing double taps with his forefinger on the barrel and his middle finger pulling on the sensitive trigger. Satisfied and a little surprised at how easily the routine came back to him, he loaded the gun's magazine and pushed it to click into place.

Pat was ready to hit the road.

It was outright raining in Newry by the time Pat reached Lusitania Gardens. It pattered on the glittering pavement as he rang the bell of number 24, glancing around at the grey line of houses and the parked cars along the quiet street. It had been a long drive up, he'd only stopped for fuel and a breakfast roll that, with hindsight, he regretted. His stomach was churning, whether from the greasy snack or the return of fear to his life, he wasn't quite sure.

The door opened. A man, burly and sallow: bushy eyebrows and a goatee beard. A Turk, no, an Arab. His nose curved like an Arab's. A grubby-looking blue quilted jacket over the open-necked shirt, jeans down below. He was wearing boots and the incongruous thought occurred to Pat that the fellow's missus would give him hell about the carpets later.

'Well, hello. I am,' Pat was facetious, 'Dan Breen.'

'Follow me,' the Arab growled, pulling the door shut behind him as he pushed past into the street. He folded himself into a battered silver Corolla, waving Pat into his own car.

Pat pulled out behind the Corolla. One of its rear brake lights wasn't working. *So it's amateur hour*, he thought savagely. Give the cops a reason to pull you over in a random check and find your car full of stuff, why don't you? He checked his mirrors, but there was no tail.

Pulling on to New Street, Pat caught a shadow in the mirror. He'd underestimated them. A scooter, darting between the lunchtime office workers and delivery lorries. They left the town behind, driving into a long lane of industrial units and warehouses. The scooter hung way back now there was little cover. The Corolla pulled up outside a row of three small roller-doored warehouses. There were no signs up on them. The rain abated, the windscreen wipers squeaking on streaked glass. Pat killed the engine.

The scooter pulled up. The rider slid off and pulled a

A Decent Bomber

pistol out of his black Belstaff. He kept the mirrored skid-lid on. Pat waited. The Arab got out of his car and walked around the side of the warehouse. The pistol was waved at Pat, who took his sweet time getting out. He locked the car and sauntered in the direction the Arab had taken, Scooter Man behind him.

The high lights flickered on and settled to a purple neon hum. Their footsteps echoed in the space, steel roofing spars and suspending tubing criss-crossed high over their heads. All around were square heaps covered in blue plastic sheeting. A scruffy white HiAce van was parked by the roller door and a yellow forklift in the corner.

'So what you want, Paddy?' The Arab barked, flicking a cover back. 'You want some of this?'

Crates, boxes. There were no stencils or other markings. Pat walked over and carved a taped seam with his car key. He pulled open the flaps. Detonators shone dully in the baleful light, laid out in neat foam-cushioned rows. The lid of the top packing crate on the stack behind them was loose. Pat shoved it aside. Squares of plastic. He tore the wrapping off one, squeezed it. Pallets were piled with white plastic sacking carrying cheerful triangular yellow hazmat labels. Pissy-smelling ammonium nitrate. He felt a wash of heat, the itch of sweat. For an instant, he went back in time and the stench of cigarettes in his memory was so strong he could have sworn someone was smoking nearby. Pat took his time prowling around and making a methodical mental inventory. Even the pipe was there, lengths of white plastic two inch tubing.

'Where did you get this?'

'Not your business. Load what you need in the van.'

Pat straightened and glared at the Arab but Scooter Man was getting nervous with the pistol. He nodded and ambled over to the corner by the partitioned-off office cubicle and climbed up into the forklift. Its steering and throttle were unfamiliar and he struggled to keep it in line. Jerking and jamming, he managed to guide the forks into the first strapped pallet of white sacks. The Arab unlocked the rear doors of the HiAce and Pat slid the pallet in, the van's suspension dropping with the load. A second followed. He hefted boxes of plastic, detonators and a reel of wire. He picked at other boxes, adding to the pile in the back of the van. As he worked, he hummed to himself. The Arab shifted. Pat glanced over to him. 'So where are they holding Orla?'

'I don't know what you are talk about. Be quick to take your need.'

'Orla, my niece. Your friends have kidnapped her.'

The Arab was properly nervous. 'I know nothing of this. Just to give you access to this. Finish, now. It is time to leave.'

'I'll be the judge of that, Abdul.'

'That is not my name.'

Pat smiled pleasantly. 'And Paddy's not mine, you little fecker.'

The Arab scowled. 'Give him your car keys. You drive this.'

Pat thought better of making a stand. 'Here, then Stig. Catch.' He threw the keys. Scooter man made the one-handed catch without letting the pistol waver, but for which Pat would have rushed him.

Round one to them, then.

The Arab hit the switch and the roller door rattled open. The rain was milling down again and water spattered from the guttering.

'Thanks for the help, lads. Lovely to meet you both. See you in Tipperary.'

Sliding into the HiAce, he twisted the key in the ignition, watched by the silent pair. He wrenched the wheel savagely and left them behind, two sodden figures standing in the increasing downpour.

He was followed all the way back to Tipperary, at least five cars in the operation. Which made it all quite a big deal as things went. Back in Pat's day, a black cab would be all they'd have to spare. The followers peeled off one by one as they reached Thurles. Two stayed with him right through to the farm. A black Range Rover and, close behind it, his own Daihatsu.

Pat pulled up in the yard, the Range Rover directly behind him. His kitchen door was open, the grinning Somali stood in the doorway. Pat checked the driver of the Range in his mirror; a slim youth, bearded and quick-eyed. He couldn't quite catch a glance at the fellow who'd driven his Daihatsu, but assumed it was Scooter Man.

Pat ignored the Somali's hand. 'Where is she?'

'Your brother daughter? She is safe, Mr O'Carolan. You can trust me in that.'

'I'll need help.'

'Ahmad will help you. It is my sincere hope he can learn from you. The suitcases are in the kitchen. Now, are you certain you have all you need?'

'My car keys.'

'Will stay with us for now.'

Pat pushed past the Somali into his kitchen. 'Where's my fucking dog?'

'She is sleeping, Mr O'Carolan. She has not been harmed.'

Kirstie was by the range on her rug. Pat knelt and checked her breathing. 'You drugged her.'

'She will awaken in time.'

'Who are you?'

'I have many names.'

Pat straightened up. 'What are you getting out of this?'

'I have told you, we simply wish for you to assemble some devices for us. If you intend the question more widely, I serve a cause that you would recognise as familiar. Sadly I do not have the time to discuss this philosophy with you.'

'And if I refuse you?'

'I am sure you do not require me to spell this out.'

'But why me? I'm twenty years and more out of date. Surely you people can make your own bloody bombs.'

'You are the best. Still they talk of you. You can make the big bomb. We wish this from you.'

Pat reached into his coat pocket for his little Glock, but the Somali had gone in the door by the time his hand found the grip. The Range Rover's engine rumbled into life outside as the sallow youth came into the kitchen lugging a box of Semtex.

'You're Ahmad, are you?' Pat was rewarded with a nod. 'Well I don't want that in here. Put it in the shed by the haggart,' he growled. Ahmad paused, incomprehension plastered on his face. 'Jesus. Like a lighthouse in a bog. This way.'

He grabbed the key from the back of the door and strode to the rickety row of corrugated tin-roofed outhouses behind the yard. He kicked the door open and waved the man in. Ahmad hesitated.

'I'm not going to lock you in, you idiot. Just put the box down on the workbench.'

Pat managed not to flinch at the voice in his ear. 'He was waiting for me, Mr O'Carolan. It is nice to meet you. I am called Yousuf. I am here to help you work on our project.'

The melodious tone sounded like it belonged to a big man. Pat turned slowly and wasn't disappointed. The ugly little revolver in Yousuf's huge hand looked like a Monopoly game piece as the giant straightened up, smiling down at Pat. He shrugged comically. 'I am sorry we are meet in such circumstance, but you understand we have great,' Yousuf paused, 'respect for your abilities. Your story is big inspiration for us.'

'My story?'

'As the freedom fighter.'

Pat grimaced. 'Drop it. I retired.'

'You have come back to aid us. We are grateful to you.' Yousuf threw his arms open.

Pat turned away from the haggart, striding around the giant, 'Are you out of your tiny fucking mind? Shove your gratitude. Tell him to shut the door behind him when he's put all the stuff away. I need to wash the smell of you people off my hands.'

Yousuf's boots thumped the ground, following him. Banging his way into the kitchen, Pat turned as the giant folded his frame to fit through the door. The gun was held steady pointing at Pat's gut and the tension in Pat's leg, readying for a kick, relaxed. He slid his hand out of his pocket, but Yousuf waggled his pistol and Pat nodded, extricating his Glock with elaborate care. Following Yousuf's gestures, he placed the gun on the table and stepped back. They smiled mutual acknowledgement. Pat turned away to the sink and scrubbed his hands. Yousuf pocketed the Glock.

'So he's Ahmad, you're Yousuf. Who's the African guy?'

'You can call him The Accountant. We will know who you mean.'

'He have a name?'

'The Accountant.'

'You African too, then?'

'No.'

'And beardy boy out there? Pakistani?'

'Is nationality so important to you, Mr Pat O'Carolan?'

His deep tones and accent made Pat's name sound exotic, *Parto Caro Larne*. Pat turned from his gazing into the yard, his wet hands dripping onto the flagstone floor. 'Nationality? Sure, it used to be everything to me. Now it doesn't seem terribly important, tell the truth. Where are you holding my niece?'

'I am not holding her. She is safe.' Yousuf gestured at the stack of black briefcases in their plastic wrappers stacked along the kitchen wall. 'You wish for to begin? The more quick you finish these, you see your brother daughter.'

Pat opened the cupboard under the sink and dried his hands on the hooked towel. 'Sure, I'll take me sweet time if it's all the same to you.'

'They will hurt her.'

'You said she was safe.'

'This is in your hands.'

Pat nodded. 'So we'd best get started, hadn't we?'

'I am happy you have resolve to co-operate.'

'I am most resolved, Yousuf. Most resolved.' Pat pulled a suitcase onto the kitchen table, ripping open the plastic wrapping. He thumbed the double locks. They clicked open, the case opening with a waft of leather. He ran a finger along a stitched seam. 'Your friend has expensive tastes.'

'He is a man of great resource.'

Pat pulled on his coat and led the way out to the yard, Yousuf quietly padding at his side. There was no sign of Ahmad. He opened the rickety outhouse door, the corrugated iron screeching against the concrete. He flicked on the light, the bare bulb hanging from the roof giving off a sulky orange glow. The boxes from Newry were on the battered workbench, tools hung from nails stuck between the rough bricks on the wall and strings hung from the gnarled rafters. Old stuff was stacked against the walls, bits and pieces of agricultural junk rusting everywhere.

Delving into one of the boxes, he pulled out five slabs of plastic and two smaller cartons. He reached up to the dangling collection on the wall and selected pliers, a knife and a reel of lightweight wire. Without a glance at Yousuf he wandered back outside. It was raining again, a light drizzle. His breath made little puffs.

Kirstie was awake when he came back into the kitchen. He laid the collection of tools and explosive on the kitchen table and went to her, careful to avoid the dressing on her head when he stroked her. She whined, licking her chops. He brought her water bowl over to her and she drank greedily. Yousuf came into the kitchen and she growled. 'There, there girl. *Fág agamsa*,' Pat whispered to her.

He pushed himself up, raising his voice. 'If you're going to hang around, why not make yourself useful and make a pot of tea?'

Yousuf's glance found the kettle. Pat taped up the slabs of plastic. Picking up one of the boxes he'd brought in, he pulled the end flap open and slid out a set of five silver tubes dangling from the end of yellow cables tied into a circle. Snipping the cable tie, he glanced up at Yousuf. The black face was impassive but his eyes were wide and his tongue flicked nervously over his lips.

'Blow us to kingdom come, this stuff. They'd find nothing. You'd better hurry with that tea, son. I get awful nervous without a cuppa.' Pat opened the other box he'd brought from the outhouse and slipped out a digital timer. 'You know how to use one of these?'

Yousuf nodded.

'I assume you want a timed delay, because if you want remote detonation you'll have to find me five radios. It's remarkable, really, how simple these things are when you have the right gear. Two sugars, if you don't mind. Milk's in the fridge.'

The kettle clicked off and Yousuf turned to pour water into the teapot. Pat worked away at his case, packing the plastic away carefully, securing it with Velcro bands. Yousuf brought a steaming mug over to the kitchen table. 'Steady there, boyo.'

The kitchen door opened. The rain had intensified and the air behind Ahmad's figure silhouetted in the doorway was grey with the downpour. Ahmad ran his hands through his sodden hair as he kicked the door shut behind him.

'Wipe your feet,' Pat growled. Yousuf waved Ahmad quiet. Pat sipped his tea. 'Nice cup there, Yousuf. Good man.'

Ahmad sat by the door. Yousuf pushed a mug towards him and he got up to sugar the tea. Pat watched the young man dip the teaspoon into the bag seven times.

'Jesus, but you'll get worms. Do all you boys have

sweet teeth?'

He returned to his attaché case. Silence reigned apart from the occasional snip of the wire cutters as Pat worked. He straightened up, his hand on the small of his back. 'Ahmad, you want to make yourself useful, son? Go on into the shed by the haggart and bring me five packs of plastic and two boxes like these.'

Ahmad glanced at Yousuf, who nodded. The little pistol was lying on the sideboard. As the young man left the kitchen, Yousuf smiled at Pat and picked it up.

Pat relaxed and turned back to his work.

'So where are you from, Yousuf?'

'I can not tell.'

Pat curled the lead around the digital timer and placed it gently into its cushion of plastic. He patted it. 'I'm hardly going to be dashing off to sell me story to the papers, now. I'd guess you're a Saudi. Slave stock, are you?'

Yousuf's frown was reward in itself. 'How you know this?'

Pat beamed at him and downed the last of his fourth cup of tea. 'Call it an educated guess. I worked with a couple of your boys a long time ago. They had some new fancy American detonators they'd been given by the CIA over in Afghanistan. They were meant to blow up Russian convoys. You ever been in Afghanistan, Yousuf?'

'This is classified.'

'Ah, come on. That's just being coy, so it is. You were, weren't you? With Osama or one of the other bandits up there in the mountains? Jesus you were lucky to get away out of that.'

The big man shifted in his discomfort. Pat couldn't

help but glance at the little gun as it dropped, Yousuf's confusion relaxing his grip. It was a mistake. The little black eye stared back at Pat, its gunmetal rim glinting. Yousuf's brown finger tautened on the trigger.

'Stop talking. Make bombs. *Halas*.'

Pat put his arms up. 'Okay, okay, *habibi*. I get the message.'

'How you know Arabic?'

'How do I know Arabic? Sure, didn't we work with the PLO? Remember them, Yousuf? Real terrorists. Men fighting for a cause, for freedom. Not some ragged bunch of fanatics hiding in rabbit holes in Tora Bora while Uncle Sam bombs them to ratshit.'

For a second Pat thought he'd gone too far. Yousuf's knuckle on the trigger was pale and Pat fought to keep his face and shoulders relaxed. His arse was tense enough. The snarl on Yousuf's broad face softened. Pat breathed.

'You are try to make me angry, Mr Pat. No. This will not work for you. I fight in Afghanistan. I fight in Sudan. I am good fighter. I fight with Him, yes. This man he is like giant. He is tool of God. You are small man. You should not to speak of him.'

Pat lowered his hands slowly. 'Whatever you say there, Yousuf. Sure, aren't you holding the talking stick?'

It was dark as Pat placed the last of the five cases on the workbench in the outhouse. The rain had stopped, the cold night air clear and fresh-smelling. He had stopped work to milk the herd, which had gathered noisily by the gate as the light left the day. Some of the cows were in a state, their udders badly swollen. Pat cursed himself for a fool. They needed a vet. Yousuf and Ahmad had stood

A Decent Bomber

by watching him, Yousuf with his little gun constantly at the ready.

Now Pat pulled five lengths of white plastic tubing from the outhouse and started rolling the pliable Semtex into sausages, which he fed into the lengths. Leading the way out to the HiAce, he guided the packed lengths of tubing into the spaces between the piled sacking. He pushed a detonator into the end of each tube. Working methodically, he snipped wire and cut tape, securing everything carefully. He used a hand bander to tie the sacks tightly down onto the pallets, four blue plastic bands to each, secured with little metal lugs.

Sweat dripped down his nose as he connected the cables together and ran a connection from the cable block to the digital timer. As with all of the smaller devices he had made bar one, he ensured the plastic insulation shielded the cable from the connector. The timer would go off, but the bomb wouldn't.

He clambered off the back of the Hi-Ace and straightened up, massaging his back. He closed the doors and without a word to his two silent helpers, walked into the farmhouse. He was feeling every one of his years, the fatigue deep in his bones. Ahmad followed him back into the kitchen. Yousuf was murmuring into his mobile. Pat sat at the table, his hands on his lap. Yousuf ended the call.

'Your niece she is safe and well. The van and cases will be pick up now and soon you can see her.'

Pat nodded. 'Fair play. I'll be pleased to see the last of the lot of ye.'

'I am sure. But you have done a great service, Mister O'Carolan. A great service. We are grateful.'

Pat massaged his temples. 'Whatever. Just give me Orla back and get out. It's done now. You have your bombs.'

Yousuf nodded sympathetically. 'Our cause is great. As great as yours, a fight for freedom and justice.'

'Look, son, I don't give a monkey's, honestly.'

Yousuf stilled. Pat heard the car engine moments later. The headlights flashed in the kitchen window. Ahmad slipped out of the kitchen into the yard. Yousuf stood watchful in the doorway, covering Pat with the little revolver as Ahmad loaded the suitcases into the back of the black Range Rover.

The Somali came into the kitchen. 'I am sorry we inconvenienced you, Mr O'Carolan. But as you will understand, when we serve a cause we have to do the things required in order to enable such service.'

'My niece.'

'In time. Not yet. We may have further need of your services.'

Pat's instinctive lurch was halted by Yousuf's little gun, lifted to eye level. It was steady. His heart was racing in his chest, tightened by fury. 'You bastard.'

'I shall return.' The Somali was impassive. 'Yousuf will stay with you until I do.'

He turned, beckoning to Ahmad to follow. The headlights swooped around the yard, the roar of the big car and heavily laden HiAce's engines swallowed by the cold night. Yousuf closed the door carefully, covering Pat with the gun and waving him away from the kid's radio transmitter he was grasping for.

'What is that?'

'It's nothing. I was just tidying.'

'A transmitter? Did you build a gift for us into your bombs, Mr Pat?'

Pat grinned weakly. He backed away from the handset and towards the kitchen table.

'Can I clear this stuff up, at least?'

'Slow.'

Sweat dampened his armpits and his heart pounded. Pat shuffled the snipped cable ends and packaging around the table, trying desperately to appear nonchalant, waiting for Yousuf to relax and the angle of the gun to soften, acutely aware of how little time he had. 'So what about another cup of tea?'

'You make it,' said Yousuf.

'Fine by me. Here,' Pat said. 'Catch.'

He flung the box underarm at Yousuf, who instinctively put out both hands to field it. His shriek mingled with the crump of the explosion. The billowing force tore the gun out of the remnants of his tattered hands, a fine mist of blood mingling with the flash and smoke from the blast. Pat had twisted away and covered his head in his arms, now he uncurled and launched himself across the kitchen to slam his fist into the tottering man's astonished face. Blood gushed from the big, ruined hands. Kirstie was barking, darting forward to snap at the flailing man as he crashed to the floor, dragging dishes from the sideboard. Blood sprayed across the cupboard doors.

Pat lunged for the little pink radio handset and hit the 'message' button. It didn't have the range of a proper radio, but he hadn't had a proper radio to play with. Sometimes a man has just to do with what God gives him. He wrenched open the front door and dashed into the yard, thumbing the send button, but he was too late. There was no answering orange flare and explosion. They'd got out of range.

Pat slipped back into the kitchen. He worked quickly. He put the dog in the living room and pulled the first aid kit from under the sink. Striding to the outhouse he pulled a length of plastic rope down from the rafters. He bound the big figure to one of the kitchen chairs, dressing the butchered hands, padding and binding them as best he could and wrapping a tourniquet under the bunched muscles of the huge man's left shoulder. Yousuf had lost six fingers for sure: the gun had protected his right hand to a degree, but the left was a meaty mess, bone shards chalky in the blackened wounds. The gun itself was undamaged. Pat wiped it clean of gore with a rag. He found his Glock in Yousuf's pocket. He checked the safety and slid the gun into his coat pocket.

The huge man moaned as he came to, his face distorted.

Pat bent down to murmur into Yousuf's ear. 'Now, my friend. It's time we had a chat, you and me. Am I getting through to you there?'

Yousuf writhed, the twisting of his big frame threatening to topple the chair. Pat slapped the man's sweat-slicked cheek to calm him. He raised his voice to a conversational tone. 'A small shaped charge with a micro fuse. It's based on a trembler. You'd sort of need to know what you were doing otherwise you'd take your own hands off. Sure, it's lucky you're a good catch now, isn't it?' Pat kept up the banter as Yousuf's eyes focused and the madness left them, the big chest heaving with great shuddering breaths. 'Look, here's the way of it. If you don't get medical help in the next couple of hours, you're a dead man. So why don't you tell me where they're keeping Orla and then I can call you a nice, Irish ambulance?'

Yousuf shook his head, sweat flying. Pat dropped down, grabbed the man's bandaged right hand and squeezed. Yousuf shrieked; his body in spasm. The chair jerked back against the worktop. To Pat's horror, Yousuf tried to dash his own brains out against the kitchen surface, the muscles on the thick neck corded as he head-butted the hard wood edge. Pat dragged him away after the first massive blow

'No way, *mo chara*. You're not escaping me. Where is she?' He squeezed again, drawing another cry of agony from the hulking figure. He kept the pressure on the hand until blood seeped through the dressing. The aubergine skin was grey, sheened with sweat and the big head lolled.

'Cashel,' Yousuf whispered. 'Farm. Paddock.'

'The Paddocks? Big place? Stud farm? That the one? On the Thurles Road?'

'Yes.'

'How many men there?'

'Two, maybe three.'

'The Somali? The Accountant?'

Yousuf didn't respond, his breathing a series of ragged gasps. Pat slapped him again, but his head stayed down.

Pat picked up Yousuf's gun and clicked off the safety. The crack of the shot was surprisingly loud in the small room. But then, as Pat reflected, it had been a very long time indeed since he had heard a shot fired.

Pat drove down the lane to the grotto. He parked his battered Daihatsu by the little hollow with its stone-lined cave. The statue shone pale in the light from his torch. He squeezed into the little space behind. The door creaked open, the reek of leaf mould making Pat's nose wrinkle.

Pat pulled off the tarpaulins and delved into the boxes and cases underneath. He pulled out bundles and cartons, methodically packing his holdall with what he needed. He remembered each case as if it had been yesterday. This one rifles, this one pistols, here ammunition and at the back a lone, long case. Pat lifted the lid just to look at them; he had no conceivable use for these. The rows of big, cone-nosed RPG 7s lay evilly shadowed. Impressive though they looked, the things were next to useless. He remembered their excitement when the shipment had first arrived and their first test firing in a remote Donegal field. Four of them had misfired, one had launched its shell which was a dud. The cow, in short, had survived. They'd been in this box ever since, shipped down from the North by Pat and a girl called Marie, who wore a scandalously short orange dress to give any curious Gards something to look at. Truth be told, he'd found her a distraction himself.

Pat pulled the bulky holdall through the gap, slinging it into the back of the little four wheel drive. He returned to lock the door, patting the statue on the way out.

He drove back to the farm. It was past midnight. He had cleaned the kitchen as best he could, swabbing down the bloodstains and binning all the smashed crockery. Yousuf's mortal remains were up on the bog, together with his gun, dropped into a hollow and covered over hurriedly but well enough for now. Pat had recovered his car keys from the dead man's pocket.

Pat opened the holdall on the kitchen table and examined its contents carefully. One by one, he wiped the guns clean of grease using a cloth dipped in Trike from the tin in the shed by the haggart and then oiled and re-assembled them. He repacked them carefully, keeping an AK-47 out. He loaded two magazines and packed a box of ammunition into the Daihatsu's glove box. He rolled the holdall under his bed before he let Kirstie out of the living room and watched her pad,

A Decent Bomber

sniffing around the kitchen. He fed her then let her out of the kitchen door. Leaving the kitchen light on, he locked the door and climbed up into the Daihatsu. He draped a blanket over the AK-47 on the passenger seat, the compact Glock 26 weighing down his pocket.

Pat parked the Daihatsu a little down the main road from the gateway to The Paddocks, tucked into a field entrance. The cloud had parted to let the moonlight through and the land was a ghostly grey peppered with dark clumps of trees. He unwrapped the AK-47 from its blanket. He locked the car and slipped into the field adjoining the big house, following the ditch along until he was parallel with the building. He felt a strong sense of unreality. Kneeling, he pulled a balaclava over his head and pushed his hands into black leather gloves. The familiarity of the gestures calmed him. Flexing his fingers, he felt the old familiar thrill of adrenaline.

Slipping through the bush he paused to listen for dogs but the night was silent. There was a light on downstairs. It was a big house, pebble dashed with stone edging and big mullioned windows. *Big budget, this accountant,* Pat thought grimly as he slipped along the hedge to get a look into the kitchen.

Two men sat together, a bottle between them. One was clearly African, the other was a crew cut Slav. Pat slipped the AK-47 back over his shoulder and took out the Glock. The gesture felt as familiar to him as putting on his coat. He settled his legs wider and sighted the gun, his index finger along the stubby little barrel and his middle finger poised to double tap the trigger.

It felt good. It felt *right*.

The gun kicked twice, two flat cracks sounding in the

cold, still morning. The kitchen window starred, the Arab thrown back by the impact. The Slav jumped to his feet too late. A third shot took him in the chest and he dropped. Pat raced across the patio to the kitchen door, the AK-47 banging against his back. He was about to shoot out the lock when something made him try the handle. It was open. *Jesus. Amateurs.*

The kitchen was warm, two bodies lying on the floor and remarkably little blood. Clean shots, albeit one too many. Pat stilled, listening for any reaction to the shots and commotion of smashed windows but the house was silent. Pat slipped his AK-47 behind the door and crept into the hallway with the Glock held out ahead of him. He stole up the stairs, testing each step in case it creaked. One of the bedroom doors was locked, the key sticking out. On the off chance, Pat tried it. He switched on his torch. Orla's wide-open, scared eyes screwed shut as the beam flashed across her face.

'Orla. It's me.'

'Uncle Pat? What are you doing here?'

'How many men are there here?'

'Two. Who are they?'

'Are you okay?'

'Yes, I'm fine.'

'Come on. We'd best get moving.' Pat switched on the light. 'Are you dressed?'

'Yes. My hands are tied.'

Pat helped her off the bed. 'Come on. Hurry.'

Pat padded through the silence of the house, Orla behind him.

Reaching the kitchen, he retrieved the AK-47 from behind the door. Orla froze, staring at the two bloody corpses.

He pulled open a kitchen drawer and selected a knife.

He sawed at the tie on her hands, two quick rasps and the nylon gave. Orla rubbed at the red welts on her wrists.

'Come on.'

'Did… did you...'

'Yes. Come on, Orla. We need out of here, now.' He took her arm and pulled her, unresisting, out of the kitchen door into the garden.

'Jesus, Uncle Pat. You killed them.'

'Forget what you saw, Orla. You have to go home now. We'll pick up your things from my place then I'll take you down to the station.' Pat pulled off the balaclava and gloves as he walked a path through the dewy grass.

They reached the car together, Orla breathless and uncertain as he pushed open her door. Pat twisted the key in the ignition and the engine barked. As they pulled away, she turned to him. 'Who were they, Uncle Pat? What's going on?'

'I have very little idea myself. And the less you know the better. We just need to get you out of here for now.'

'Are you in some kind of trouble?'

'You could say that. And no, I have no clue whatsoever who they are or what they're up to.'

They drove silently through the night. Orla gazed out of the passenger window at the hedgerow flashing by and the dark countryside beyond. She turned as if to speak to him twice before finally asking, 'Who are you, Uncle Pat?'

'And what precisely do you mean by that?'

'There are two men dead back in that house. You were wearing a balaclava and gloves. You have guns.'

'I reckon this is where I'd say something like "I can explain", isn't it?'

He got a tremulous smile from her. 'Just about here,

yes.'

'I can't. I have a past. For some reason it's come up to date in some way I don't quite understand. But I'm going to find out. And I need to be sure you're safe so I can do just that.'

'You mean I'd get in the way.'

'That's right on the money.' Pat steered the car into his yard. 'Come on. Let's get you packed.'

Orla followed him into the kitchen, stooping to wipe Kirstie's paws. 'They hit her. I thought they'd killed her.'

'She's hardier than that.'

'That's for sure.' Orla sniffed the air. 'There's been a fight in here.'

She never failed to impress him. 'How do you know that, clever clogs?'

'Scuff marks on that cupboard, that chair's cracked and there's blood on the floor over. It stinks of blood in here. Where is he?'

Pat met her level gaze for fully ten seconds. His voice croaked when he managed to speak. 'In the bog.'

'Jesus, Uncle Pat.'

Pat nodded. There had never been any flies on Orla and right now he was feeling like a naughty schoolboy. A particularly exhausted one, at that.

'Has the herd been milked?'

'Yes, this...' Pat checked his watch. 'Last night.'

'So how about this. You look totally in. So how about I milk the herd while you get two hours' sleep and then we can work out what we do next?'

'There's no "we next", Orla. This is a dangerous situation. You have to get away and leave me to deal with it.' He shook his head to clear it.

'You're not a young man any more, Uncle Pat. You've been up all night. You know I'm right.'

'Two hours. Then you're off to the station.'

Pat woke to the smell of frying bacon. It was midday. He flung the coverlet aside and slid out of bed. His shoulders and back ached, likely from the effort of dragging the big corpse from the back of the Daihatsu up to the bog. He kept in shape, had done so ever since starting daily exercise to pass the time back in Long Kesh, but dragging giants around bogs wasn't quite part of his daily routine.

He pulled his clothes on without bothering to shave and stumbled into the kitchen. Orla tipped the contents of the pan onto a plate and slid it onto the table. 'Just in time. Here. The kettle's boiled, hang on.'

She turned and poured hot water into the pot and Pat sat to eat, mopping up egg and tomato sauce with his buttered bread. She had washed and changed, her fiery hair tied up behind. 'So tell me, first things first. What's this past of yours?'

He glanced up at her, but she was pressing the teabags in the pot. His first instinct was to lie, but no lie came to him. He cleared his throat. 'I was in an IRA active service unit back in the eighties.'

'Which means you killed people?'

He held her gaze. 'It does.'

Orla pulled out a chair and sat, her troubled eyes searching his face. She glanced away from him, around the kitchen. He watched her warily as she seemed to take an inventory of the familiar objects around her. The clock's soft beat punctuated the gentle hiss of the range.

Her gaze found him again, her eyes bright. 'How many?'

'How many what?'

'People did you kill?'

'Christ, I don't know Orla. I never counted. I wasn't exactly proud of it.'

'Pull the other one. I bet you were completely full of yourself. One of the boyos with the balaclavas and the guns. You were *good* at it, remember?'

'It wasn't like that. It was a war.'

'Against women and children, right.'

'No, against the Brits. Against an occupying power in the land of our fathers.'

'Listen to you. You don't even believe it yourself.'

He regarded his hands, clasped together on his lap. 'Well, maybe I believed it back then.'

'It just sounds hollow now. Empty. You were always so gentle. You were the one I admired, the man who loved animals and simply farmed the land. You were so kind, so, humble. I thought of you as a gentle giant. Christ. How wrong can you be?'

'Look, Orla.'

'No. I don't want to hear any more about it.' She put her hands over her ears. 'You've taken away my Uncle Pat. I don't want to know who you are any more. I don't know. There's nothing left to believe in.'

'Well, don't I know how that feels myself? Do you think I didn't feel it had all been futile myself? All that running, the violence and murder so we could just give up the whole cause? All the dead hunger strikers, the time we spent in filthy cells to protest the way they treated us like common criminals?'

'You went to *jail*?'

He felt poised at the top of a roller coaster. He could stop it here, just avoid it. He took the drop. 'I was in Long Kesh for eleven years.'

She threw her hands up and kicked her chair back,

twisting to stand looking out over the yard. 'For the love of God, why didn't anyone see fit to tell me my Uncle was a convicted IRA murderer? Why didn't mum or dad say anything?'

'Orla, I wasn't a murderer. We were fighting a war.'

'Wars are fought between nations. You weren't a nation, you were the IRA. You were a terrorist. A stinking fucking terrorist.'

She strode to the front door and wrenched it open. She turned and flung 'A coward!' at him before slamming the door behind her.

Pat sat back and wondered if she wasn't perhaps right. Kirstie, lying by the range with her bandaged head laid on her paws, whined.

Orla splashed through the muddy yard, angry tears coursing down her cold cheeks. She pushed her hands into her pockets and strode past the barns, the mixture of mud and slurry splashing under her boots. She reached the road and stood, unsure which way to go.

How could this have happened? Her Uncle Pat. The kind, gentle man who had given her so much affection and been with her during some of the happiest days of her life. A killer.

She decided to turn right and walk up towards the bog. It was drizzling, the misty droplets against her face washing away the tears. What had Róisín said? 'Terror organisations recruit psychopaths to their causes. They prefer people who like to kill.'

Those earnest eyes and carmine lips. The cool hand that had held her cheek cupped in its palm as their lips met. Orla melting and then breaking away in confusion. Róisín's hurt look.

They went out for drinks two nights before Orla was to travel to Tipperary to be with her uncle Pat, the long anticipated two weeks on the farm sanctioned by her college as a study break. Two weeks without Róisín? What was she going to do? She went up to Belfast and they hit the town something fierce. They'd talked and laughed and drunk wine, flipped off two bucks up from Mallow and got in with a crowd from Newry who'd been good craic, but the two of them had waved their goodbyes and walked back to the station together.

Orla didn't hear the strain in Róisín's voice, the attempt to make the question sound light until later when she played back the conversation in her mind over and over. 'Why go back? Come stay at mine. I'm sure Rory won't mind.'

'I can't, I have to get back. I haven't anything with me and I'm behind with things before I go to Uncle Pat's. But thanks all the same.'

'No biggie.'

Which of course, again with hindsight, meant the opposite. Goodbyes. Held hands. Laughter. And then the kiss, Orla breaking away first, bruised-looking eyes. Sitting on the train, her mind in freefall, her breathing all over the place. Wiping her lip with her trembling fingertip and pulling it away streaked crimson.

Christ, as if she weren't confused enough. How many people fall in love and get kidnapped in the same week? Let alone find out their sweet old Uncle is a cold blooded IRA killer.

She didn't know what to do. The rain was getting heavier and Orla was drenched, but she stood gazing out sightlessly across the misty bog.

A Decent Bomber

She came back into the kitchen half an hour later. Pat had made more tea and was sitting with his hands wrapped around the mug to banish the cold coming from inside him. He couldn't read the look on her face. She sat at the table opposite him.

'Jesus, you're soaked. Get some warm clothes on, then I'd better take you down to the station.'

She snorted. 'You're kidding me. Like things were normal around here? You think I can face my parents after this?'

'Just say you decided to come home. You need away from here, Orla.'

'And what if that's just not going to happen? I mean, I can hardly pretend this has been a normal day.'

'Just forget it.'

'You're not real. How will I forget this? Can you forget so easily, then, Pat?'

He pressed his hands together, felt their dryness as the chapped skin scraped. 'I've spent a long time forgetting.'

'Well remember this: forgetting to tell the truth is no different to lying. If this all hadn't happened, when were you going to tell me about who you were?'

'Never. It was in the past. It wasn't a part of your life and I didn't ever think it needed to be. You weren't even born. It's not that I purposefully didn't tell you. It just wasn't part of... my future. Our future.'

She nodded slowly. 'That's actually nice. I think.'

'Come on. Let's get you to the station.'

'I want to tell you something.'

There was something in her tone that stilled Pat as he rose. He lowered himself back down on his chair. 'What?'

Her green eyes met his and slid away. She bit her lip and glanced at the sleeve of her green cable sweater, dark with the rain. 'Ah, Jesus, look at the state of me. I'll get changed. Forget it, I'll tell you later.'

Kirstie's gaze followed Orla out of the kitchen, the collie's snout on her paws. Pat got up and stood at the window, staring at the rain outside and sipping at his English Breakfast.

Chapter Five

Brian MacNamara waited patiently in the meeting room at PSNI's Brooklyn House headquarters for Wayne McLoughlin to show up. The Detective Superintendent had asked to see him as a matter of urgency. He grimaced as he drained the paper cup of stewed coffee. Sure enough, the sugar was all there, stuck to the bottom.

There was a hubbub outside the meeting room. The door burst open to admit McLoughlin, Boyle and two men in suits. MacNamara stood and offered his hand. 'Wayne.'

'Brian. Thanks for coming. I thought it would be easier if we talked and you could perhaps brief Mr Driscoll later. To be honest, I find his style of politics tiresome when we're discussing matters that could carry a cost in human life.'

MacNamara nodded carefully. He avoided Boyle's furious glare and glanced across at the two suits.

'Sorry, introductions. This is Tony McKee, he's our primary legal counsel. Colin here is his assistant. You've met Boyle.'

'We weren't actually introduced, as I recall.' MacNamara's jaw jutted.

'Is that right?' McLoughlin frowned. 'Boyle heads the Region Intelligence Unit of C3. Boyle, this is Brian MacNamara. Are we all good now?' He gazed around at them. 'Right. Well, we seem to have a problem.'

'Anything we can do to help, we will.' MacNamara blurted.

McLoughlin stared at him. 'Help? We'll see. A bomb was planted in the Forestside Square Shopping Centre this morning. Five kilos of Semtex packed in an unusually expensive leather attaché case. We received a call using a valid IRA code twenty minutes after the bomb was timed to detonate. We know that because it didn't go off. The Army disposal guy was particularly puzzled because the bomb was viable; just one wire was twisted out of place. You'd not spot it if you weren't looking very closely.'

MacNamara sat back, gripping the arms of his chair. 'It wasn't us. We've gone way beyond that.'

'I appreciate that. But I think we both know where the materiel that was used to create this device came from, don't we?' McLoughlin placed a little origami swan on the meeting table. He pushed it towards MacNamara with a finger. 'Does this mean anything to you?'

MacNamara's mind reeled, sweat pricked his armpits. Thank fuck for those nights playing poker with the lads. He pretended to scrutinise the little model. 'No, not specifically. Why do you ask?'

'They found it in the bomb. They reckon it's what they call the bomber's signature, but it seems an odd thing to put in a bomb that will just tear it apart. You sure?'

'Sure.'

'I'm having an officer look back over the archives to see if there's anything out of the past. You'd maybe save us a lot of time if your memory improved.'

MacNamara finally summoned the nerve to meet McLoughlin's eye. 'It's not a memory problem, Wayne, I genuinely have never seen one of these before.'

McLoughlin consulted the tablet in his hands. 'You are perhaps inclined not to take the threat of this seriously enough. Play it to them, Boyle.'

The plain clothes man tapped on his mobile and a rich, African-accented voice rang out, flattened by audio

A Decent Bomber

compression. 'This is the Al Shabab Liberation Army. By now you will have appreciated we command a force of considerable capability and scope which is operationally effective. This is just the beginning. We are prepared not to pursue this campaign with the inevitable loss of property and life it will entail provided you confirm you will pay a sum of not less than one hundred million pounds in used notes to us in a manner we shall communicate once you have acceded to our reasonable request. A further device will explode tomorrow if you do not confirm acceptance by placing an item on the BBC World News six o'clock news bulletin that specifically discusses the prospects for peace between Somalia and Kenya thanks to the mediation of the wise leaders of Al Shabab.'

The room was silent. McLoughlin's voice was a croak. 'That was called in using the same code. In the circumstances, my Chief Constable and the Minister of Justice have decided to notify the Home Secretary. This is clearly highly classified.'

'Look, I'm playing straight.' MacNamara spread his hands. 'We don't even *know* any Africans.'

McLoughlin held MacNamara's gaze for a subjective eternity. 'Sure, Brian. Sure. Well, thanks for all your help.'

Sean Driscoll was giving the faithful a pep talk when MacNamara turned up at the Party's Belfast Headquarters. The meeting hall had been transformed into a campaign room, the social media team pecking away stalk-like at their laptops and a noisy group in a makeshift call centre putting the word out to drum up support for the Man Of The Future.

MacNamara waited in the background, listening idly to Sean's campaign team Q&A. This issue didn't matter, that issue was to be handled. He wondered what a wedge issue was. Sean was particularly excited about wedge issues but MacNamara could only think of pulling up someone's belt so their trousers went up their cracks. He was not, he would be the first man to admit it, a politician. He was a more practical man altogether. He got stuff done. It was Sean did the talking.

A pretty girl wearing a blouse two sizes too small for her had her hand up and MacNamara caught a flash of full, pale breast and red lace. Driscoll nodded to her. 'Annette.'

'What's our position on the war against terror?'

There was some general shuffling and giggling, but Driscoll signalled for quiet. 'It's a valid question and one I know concerns the electorate. And their concerns should be shared by us in all sincerity. Nobody knows the cost of terrorism more than we do, we have sat on both sides of this particular fence and there's no point denying it, we spent decades fighting for this country's freedom from an occupying foreign power. But to paraphrase Yasser Arafat, we came to the table with a gun and an olive branch and the struggle built a platform for us to become partners for peace from a standpoint of strength and with a clear mandate from our people. Today, I think we acknowledge the way forward is through dialogue and the political process, but that process has only been made possible by the sacrifice and enormous dedication of a huge number of young people across Ireland who literally struggled and fought for peace. We totally condemn terrorism, we seek peaceful conciliation and dialogue and I am absolutely unequivocal in that. Thank you, ladies and gentlemen; let us go on to win this victory in the name of peace!'

The line between genius and wank was about the same thickness as the one between love and hate, MacNamara reflected as Driscoll beckoned him to follow into his office. Driscoll was bluff with the excitement of his talk as he cast off his jacket and rounded his desk to plump down on the big leather chair.

'So, Brian, what was McLoughlin after? Another finger wagging, was it?'

'Not precisely. There was a bomb at Forestside this morning. It didn't go off.'

'Christ almighty, man. Why does he think it concerns us?'

'They called it in with one of our codes.'

'He's perfectly well aware Quinlan was compromised.'

'They called it in twenty minutes after it would have gone off. The bomb was a viable device, except there was one wire disconnected. Five kilos of Semtex and a white paper swan.'

Driscoll blanched and swiped a finger against the corner of his leaky eye. 'A swan, you say?'

'Pat O'Carolan's trademark, yes. And we know where the Semtex came from, too.'

'I see.' Driscoll steepled his fingers. 'Shit. Shit. Shit.'

'You should have copped McLoughlin's face when he dropped that wee swan on the table. He was like a starved cat in a creamery.'

'Did you tell him it was O'Carolan's? Did you recognise it?'

'I recognised it, sure. I told him nothing. But they'll find out in time. I really think we're best to tell them before they figure it out for themselves. The bombers have been in touch, they've made a ransom demand, a hundred million quid. PSNI have briefed the Home Secretary. This is going to go really big.'

'No. Absolutely not. It won't do, Brian. I won't have it. This has nothing to do with us. This is all in the past. Christ, we're about the fucking future, man!'

'What if the future is us facing a series of bombs planted by unknown terrorists holding the whole country to ransom, using our codes and our materials? Made by our best ever bomb-maker? The man who made the biggest bombs ever to go off on the British mainland? We'd be toast, Sean. Surely you see that?'

Driscoll gripped his chair arms, his furious glare focused on his desktop. MacNamara willed the man to look up and face him, but Driscoll ground out his words at the blotter. 'O'Carolan's not ours. We disown him. He's a maverick. We have an election to contest and I won't have it dominated by this mad sideshow. Get rid of him, Brian. Get rid.'

'It's not his fault. And it won't end with him. Someone is using us, our stuff and our old operational methods. And it won't end with O'Carolan—'

'Make it go away, Brian. Fast. We can't let this dominate the election.' Driscoll finally glanced up and MacNamara was shocked to see tears in the hard eyes. And lines, black smudges. The man was exhausted and, in that moment, MacNamara understood quite how scared and weak Driscoll was. He nodded.

'Don't worry. I'll deal with it.'

His leader's tremulous, grateful smile was heart-breaking.

Boyle stood smoking outside PSNI headquarters at Brooklyn House. The rain had let up and his feet

A Decent Bomber

scrunched on the loose stones scattered on the puddled tarmac as he paced, waiting for his mobile to be answered. He was about to hang up when the ring tone finally gave way to a click and a querulous voice.

'Yes?'

'Martin Cavanagh?'

'This is he.'

'Hello, sir. This is Detective Sergeant Boyle from Police Service Northern Ireland. I wonder if you might have two minutes to talk to me about an investigation we're working on. Nothing formal, you understand, I was hoping you could help us with a little background.'

'I've retired.'

'I'm aware of that, sir. It's your memory I'm after, really.'

'How do I know you're not a journalist?'

'You can call me back right here at PSNI headquarters.'

Cavanagh sighed. 'No. Go on ahead. What do you want to know?'

'It's about your time as a prison officer in the Maze—'

The laugh was more a bark. 'Well, I didn't think it was going to be about my time as an ice cream man, now.'

Boyle forced a smile so Cavanagh would hear it. 'Right enough. Fair play. I'm interested in a prisoner, name of O'Carolan. With you between seventy-eight and eighty-nine.'

'Swan? I remember him right enough. Big man. Provo.'

'That'll be the one.'

'Bomber, he was. By trade.'

'You called him Swan?'

'We did. He used to fold little origami swans. We'd

clear them away from his cell every day and give him new paper. We withdrew the privilege when he joined the dirty protest.'

'How did he react to that?'

'Nothing. Not a thing. Never said a word about it. He was a strong man, quiet, like.'

'Any known associates?'

'You mean was he thick with anyone? They all were. They kept to themselves, right enough. I suppose Cathal Burke, if anyone. Brian MacNamara, for the brief time he was in. They came in together. I'd see them chat a lot on exercise, when that was allowed. It was stopped on account of the protests.'

'He got full parole, didn't he? Despite joining the dirty protest?'

'We recommended that after he came off the protest. He never gave us a moment's bother, did Swan. Always quiet, always polite. You'd not have him down as a common criminal, a murderer, at all, except that's just what he was, wasn't he?'

'The dirty protest was about changing that status.'

'You can put any label you like on murder. But he was a killer, right enough.'

'Thank you Mr Cavanagh.'

'Any time, Inspector.'

The knock on his office door spun Wayne McLoughlin away from his reverie at the window, his thoughts on the operation underway to secure public places across Belfast and the consequent strain on his already insufficient budget. 'Come'

Boyle was his usual shabby self, bomber jacket, jeans and a t-shirt that proclaimed him a savage for bacon and cabbage. McLoughlin suppressed a twinge of irritation at the cut of the man. Boyle might be a pain to work with but he was an effective intelligence officer who got the job done. Sometimes McLoughlin wondered at the price he paid for the man's capability. For instance, now, grinning, he was at his most irritating.

'We've got it. Mary came up trumps with Niche again. By God that girl can work that database like a master. It's Pat O'Carolan for sure. He went down for a twenty year stretch after his fingerprints linked him to a device that didn't go off. It had an origami swan in it.'

'It's a funny thing to leave in a bomb.'

'He was folding them obsessively throughout the interviews. He lost his appetite for murder, they reckoned, from the notes of the time. He wouldn't say a single word throughout the whole investigation and trial, just sat folding paper swans. They gave him full parole, despite he was a protestor. I spoke to one of the screws, apparently he was a model prisoner, apart from the usual uniform and slopping out protest stuff. And he spent his time there folding paper swans 'till they took away his paper privileges.'

'The Maze?'

'Yup. Eleven years, he served in the end. A known associate of Cathal Burke. And Brian bloody MacNamara.'

'So all roads lead to O'Carolan. Where is he?'

'South Tipperary. On a farm in a bog. We've been on to the *Gardaí*. They'll go in this afternoon.'

'Go in with them. Let me know if they require a formal request for you to be seconded to their operation and I'll arrange it'

'It'll be fine. It's the lads from Thurles are handling it and I go back with Eamonn Dunphy. We worked the border together back in the nineties.'

'Keep me in the loop, then.'

Boyle had the door open when McLoughlin called him back. 'Hang on, Boyle. Take MacNamara with you. I have a strong feeling he knows a great deal more than he's letting on. Tell him he's needed for identification purposes.'

'Sir, he's a—'

'I know what he is, Boyle. Be civil to him, I'll have no complaints about our behaviour towards a citizen and councillor, whether or not he's a Shinner.'

'What if he won't come?'

'I have the feeling he will. If he refuses, tell him we may want to interview him formally in connection with the arms cache at Burke's farm.'

Boyle's pinched features were taut. He glared at McLoughlin, his mouth working. Finally he nodded. 'Okay. I'll need his mobile.'

'Sheila will give it you. He's a high profile public figure and he's co-operating with us, Boyle. We need him to co-operate more. No more heavy stuff, you hear?'

'I hear, you, right enough.'

MacNamara was waiting outside the school when his mobile rang. The raindrops pooled on the windscreen, blotting the shadowy figures of hurrying parents flitting around the gates in the rain. Jean hadn't been able to make the school run, something about an emergency in the office. Brian and Jean MacNamara cared for their granddaughter Riley until their daughter Simone finished work of a day. The MacNamara's were both proud their wayward daughter had not only settled, but had studied with a ferocity that eclipsed her teenage rebellion and had seen her mature into a successful lawyer, a partner in the practice before she turned thirty. It was often past seven when Simone would arrive to pick Riley up. Simone worked too hard, they told each other pretty much daily as they stood on the doorstep in the dark waving the two of them off home.

Riley's puffy purple raincoat bobbed towards the car. She pulled the passenger door open, laughing as she bundled into the warmth. He put his finger to his lips as he answered the mobile and heard Boyle's rasp. 'It's Boyle. Listen, the Gards are going into Pat O'Carolan's this afternoon. Don't pretend you don't know he was the man made the Forestside Shopping Centre bomb, we know about his swan habit. You're to come with me.'

'I can't.'

'You have no choice. Don't make me play hardball. You're needed for identification.'

'For God's sake, man, I've just picked up my granddaughter from school.'

'Drop her. Where will I pick you up from? Your house?'

'There's nobody to look after her.'

'Seriously, in the scheme of things, I couldn't give a fuck. You're in this up to your neck and the Gards aren't going to wait up for us. If the shit hits the fan you're the only man O'Carolan will listen to and you know it. And the shit is most certainly going to hit the fan. Yours, then. I'll see you in twenty.'

'You know where I live?'

'I know where you *crap*, MacNamara.'

MacNamara tossed the mobile into the cubby set into the dash, his face grim.

'Granpa?' Riley's face was a mixture of puzzlement and concern.

He forced a smile. 'Heya, sweetpea. Sorry, I just have something urgent to do. I'm going to have to leave you at home to look after yourself a little while until Nana comes home. Is that okay?'

She pulled her seatbelt around. 'I guess so.' Her pensive face brightened. 'Can I have cookies?'

MacNamara pulled out into the press of school traffic, the wiper clearing the opaque windscreen. 'You can have all the cookies a princess can eat.' He shot a wry glance at her. 'Without making herself sick.'

'That's a whole packet. I can eat a whole packet, so.'

The passenger seat of Boyle's battered BMW was strewn with paperwork, sweet wrappers and empty cigarette packets. He caught MacNamara's look of disgust and leant over to sweep it all into the footwell. 'My, we're fastidious these days.'

'I'm keeping stranger company now than ever I did.'

'Aye, so you are. We've got three hours so belt up, we'll be shifting. The Gards have the area staked out; nothing's moved since they got in place this morning. It's simple enough to keep an eye on O'Carolan's, there's a lane in and a lane out and nothing but bog above. And as you well know, we put our faith in bog above.'

They drove through the suburbs of Belfast onto the A1, the rain spattering the windscreen, the tatty wipers leaving streaks behind them. Boyle drove skilfully and with little regard for the speed limit. At times the traffic slowed and he jinked wildly to carve a way through, drawing outraged beeps.

'Can we not slow it down a bit?'

'Actually, no. It's an easy four hour drive and we haven't got four hours. So sit back and enjoy the ride.

Christ, for once you've actually got the law on your side.'

'I'd have thought it would feel more comfortable than this.'

'Fat chance.' Boyle sent the car scooting between a container lorry and a dumper truck, sliding between the lanes. The big wheels looming above them sent gouts of spray slamming into the screen. 'So tell me about Pat O'Carolan.'

'He's a good man.'

'We have different definitions of what *good* is, clearly.'

'You can depend on him. He's a solid man to have with you in a scrape. Whatever you think of his politics, he was a man of conviction.'

'Was. You said was.'

'A slip.'

'No, it wasn't a slip. You know as well as I do he threw in the towel. He deliberately screwed up the last bomb you bastards had him make before he was arrested. Like he screwed up the Forestside Shopping Centre one. And he left his trademark there in that suitcase so's we'd find him again. Why?'

'What the Christ do I know?'

'And why didn't you kick the shit out of him in Long Kesh? He'd broke ranks, so he had. He capitulated. Quit. And you didn't punish him. What was so special about O'Carolan, then?'

'Nothing. He was a good man who served the Cause well.'

'Did he fuck. He surrendered and you condoned it. Was it all going tits up for ye, then? Did you have to go soft on the old soldier because he wasn't the only one to lose his taste for blood?'

MacNamara tried not to let the memories overwhelm him. He pressed his fingers together and brooded over his bitten nails. When did he start doing that again? The slap of wet mop on granite, the clang of doors echoing through the corridors. MacNamara could almost smell the disinfectant and sour stink of boiled vegetables. He fought the urge to confess, to tell Boyle that Pat hadn't stopped making bombs when he came out of jail. That he'd ended up going to London and made bigger and bigger bombs. He glanced at Boyle, the man's anger focused on the road, his tight-set lips. MacNamara kept his counsel.

Boyle jerked the wheel to avoid a sluggish Punto. A sign for Newry flashed past. 'Come on, MacNamara. You people kept arms caches in contravention of the Good Friday Agreement. You pulled the wool over the eyes of the disarmament people, that stupid Canuck. Was O'Carolan valuable because he was hiding a cache like Burke's? Did he go on bombing after he got out?'

MacNamara stayed silent. Boyle's quiet fury was claustrophobic. He gazed out of the window at the grey day and looming shapes of lorries, white spray and glittering drops. A tear in the leather trim by the BMW's electric window. Condensation. Sending Pat over to join the London active service unit, seeing the broken man sweating with the Fear, the dread that claimed them all sooner or later. Smoking fags and drinking too much. Pat had pleaded with him. He'd spent eleven years of his life in jail, he didn't want to go back. He'd done enough, more than any man. MacNamara pushed his man hard to get him back into action. And Pat had gone, eventually. Over to the mainland not only to make the biggest bomb ever but then to do it again before his nerve had finally broken. This time there was no talking Pat around. But by then they were talking about peace, even if few were convinced there'd ever be peace in the North.

Boyle was relentless. 'Say it. Just say it. Yes we did keep caches. Yes we were actually scared and wanted something in reserve in case it all went to shit and we were left defenceless with the UVF and all them other Unionist bastards out there armed to the teeth because they were up the Brit's arses and we were out in the cold. Say it.'

'Fuck off, Boyle. I'll say nothing to suit you or anyone else.'

'Oh Jesus, you're *proud*. A proud Shinner politician. Now that's a new one, isn't it?'

'Why bother, Boyle? Needling me? I couldn't care what you say. You're a kid. You'd have been in short trousers.'

Boyle drove in the fast lane. A Mercedes flashed him from behind, his right indicator on as he tried to bully Boyle into the middle lane. 'Christ, I should nick the bastard.'

'We're in the South. You can't.'

Boyle pulled over, flipping a V at the Merc. 'I bow to your refined political instinct, Mr MacNamara. You have great respect for borders these days.'

'Jesus, give your arse a chance.'

Boyle drove on, the wipers sweeping, the steady engine tone of the open road lulling MacNamara.

'You mind if I smoke?'

'Go ahead, kill yourself.'

Boyle lit up, slipping the window open a shard and puffing out of it. 'Kill yourself. Ha, that's good. Your people killed my Da. You know that, big man?'

MacNamara shook his head and stared out of the windscreen.

'They came to our house and dragged him out into the garden and made him kneel down. And then they put a gun to his neck.' Boyle flicked ash through the slit. 'This uncomfortable for you? To have to listen to this sort of thing?'

MacNamara closed his eyes. 'We all lost people.'

'The guy pulled the trigger while we stood in the doorway of our house looking on. Our Ma tried to stop us seeing, but we wriggled too much and she was too busy crying and pleading with them. Three of them. All wearing balaclavas, they were. One was a big lad, a bit daft if you ask me. You remember any big daft lads?' Boyle twisted the wheel savagely and shot between two cars back into the clear fast lane. They passed the Dundalk exit.

MacNamara pressed his hands together between his legs. 'There were plenty big daft lads. On both sides. We depended on them.'

'Well this one shot my Da. Dropped him there in the garden. Bang. Not even bang bang. Just bang.'

'I'm sorry.' MacNamara struggled to still his twisting hands, to lay them on his knees. He caught Boyle's sideways glower.

Boyle focused back on the road. 'Sure you are.'

The windscreen was fogging. MacNamara opened his window. The spray cooled his face. He breathed in the fresh air, clearing his mind and escaping Boyle's smoke and fury. He felt the past pressing down on him. On them both. He hooked the switch to close the window.

'Look, the caches weren't supposed to be there, right? They were an embarrassment we didn't know what to do with and that's the truth. The deadline came and went and suddenly we had something on our hands we realised we didn't want but couldn't get shot of. We couldn't give them up a week late. You wouldn't believe how long a week late can be. So we just let them, you know, *be*. We had good men sitting on them and soon enough they weren't a priority anymore. Not until Quinlan. He had the codes.'

'So whoever killed him got access to your codes. And the contacts for your caretakers.'

MacNamara breathed in deeply. 'Yes.'

'Including the code for Burke's place.'

'Yes.'

'And for O'Carolan.'

'Yes.'

'And the code for calling in a bombing to PSNI.'

'The RUC. But yes.'

'You stupid, stupid fuckers.'

MacNamara let that ride for a while as they coasted through the bleak countryside, the rain sheeting and the grim sky pressing down. Boyle was easily pushing 120 but the road had cleared up, the traffic beyond Drogheda was sparse and even the downpour let up a little as they passed Swords. He cleared his throat, marshalled his thoughts.

'Look, the caches weren't something we were proud of or even thought of as an asset anymore. They were an embarrassment we got caught in. Sometimes you just want to put the past behind you, you're moving ahead so fast you end up having more to lose by going back than you do by actually, you know, aiming for progress. The second I heard about Quinlan, I knew we'd have no good of it. Not just us, not just Sean Driscoll and me and the Party, but all of us. I am truly sorry about your father. I lost people myself, saw the cost of it all, the human cost. Which is why I don't think we want to go back there. Any of us. And yet something has happened that, well, threatens to drag us back.' MacNamara studied Boyle's reaction. The grim face was focused on the road ahead.

'It's why I'm here, Boyle. I didn't have to come, for all your threats. I didn't have to leave my wee granddaughter home alone. I think we need to deal with whatever's happened together. As partners. I'm serious.'

The rain abated, the car's wheels skimming wet tarmac. The traffic thinned and Boyle turned the wipers off. They drove on in silence and were past Dublin when Boyle spoke.

'You ever kill a man?'

'Jesus. No. I haven't.'

'Ordered one killed?'

MacNamara stared at Boyle's knuckles on the steering wheel. His pale hands were darkly hairy and sported a black plastic digital watch. MacNamara sighed. 'Yes.'

'Feel good?'

MacNamara considered the question. 'You know what? In all truth? Because almost whatever I say you'll think I'm shitting you? Yes, I remember times when it felt good. When I was happy to lash out and order reprisals. When I lost the head. Does that help you?'

Boyle glanced at him. 'That was pretty straight for a politician.'

'You know, I'm not the politician. That's Sean. I just get stuff done. I'm truly sorry about your Da. I'm sorry about my sister, too. I'm not saying they cancel each other out, just that… Shit. Just that we need to move on. Not just us two, all of us. And I know it can be hard, when the drink's on you and you think the world's a piece of shit that needs put to rights. When you stand on a familiar street corner and the past comes flooding back to you and you remember the fire and anger, the running and bricks flying. Or the smells. I've never forgotten the stink of burning tyres, you know? For what it's worth I never heard of any Boyle. It wasn't on my say-so or my watch. And I know that's not worth much.'

'No. No, it's not. But it's better than nothing. So I'll take it.'

'Grand.'

They passed a sign to Portlaoise.

'Nearly there,' said Boyle.

MacNamara's mobile rang. It was Simone. 'Dad. What the fuck?'

'Simone, don't swear.'

'Riley's home alone here and you're telling me not to swear? You left my daughter alone in an empty house for three hours? She's in fucking pieces, so she is.'

'I had no choice. Riley was fine, she was happy enough and safe. I just had to leave quickly.'

'Crap. That's just crap. What was it, a Party meeting or something? Christ, I grew up with thugs calling at all hours and men smoking in the kitchen all day. I thought I could give my own daughter something better and you went and locked her in a house all by herself and every single ghost is in here with me right now and I just fucking hate you for it.'

MacNamara jerked away from the slam of the phone.

'Problem?' Asked Boyle.

MacNamara stared at the mobile as if it were melting in his hand. He thumbed along the bevelled aluminium edge, tossed it from hand to hand. He clenched it, his hand shaking. 'No. Not really.' He slipped it back into his coat.

'Riley?'

'My granddaughter. It's okay.'

Chapter Six

Pat drove out of the yard. Mud splashed and the suspension creaked as the wheel hit a pothole. He glanced over at Orla, who was holding onto the handle set into the front window sill. Someone had picked at the foam covering, breaking through the plastic. He'd always meant to put tape or something over the scags. They lurched onto the smooth tarmac of the lane. Pat pulled over.

He mumbled, reaching for the door handle. 'Hang on a second. Something I forgot.'

He was out the door before she could ask him anything, shoving it to behind him. He squelched back across the yard and rescued his canvas holdall from the haggart. It felt like deadweight, clinking as he heaved his way to the shed.

He kicked the door shut behind him. The herd was there as he'd left them, tethered to the rust-brown iron rings set into the stone wall. The big, curious brown eyes were on him, tails flicking. They chewed, shifting slightly as they appraised him. He stood for a second, appreciating fuggy hay and animal warmth, the underlying reek of ammonia and shite. He let down the holdall, crouching to unzip it and riddle around for the Glock and two spare clips.

He blinked furiously, wiping at his eyes with his wrist as he regarded the animals he had given the past twenty years to; he had raised them by hand, all of them. Most were the grandchildren of his own grandparents' tiny herd, a few of the Holsteins had been bought in as calves. He soothed the first animal, knotted muscle pulling

A Decent Bomber

against the rope tether as he held the gunmetal against the white patch of coarse hair. He murmured, 'There, there, come on gal, come on,' a series of meaningless endearments as the big head strained at the rope.

He'd never cared to give them names. He was sweating. He opened and closed his fingers on the butt of the Glock, his middle finger slick against the trigger. The wide, fearful eyes bulged.

The gunshot was loud, a flat report amplified by the metal-walled shed. Pat stepped back as the animal went down, hooves skittering on the concrete. It voided itself, a mighty crash as the body hit the ground, the tension ebbing as a gout of blood streamed down over the wet muzzle. It slowed to a trickle, the great heart was still.

Pat stepped over to the second stall. The cows were panicked, making a fearful racket. He moved as fast as he could, the cow straining against its tether, horn on concrete as it struggled to back away from him. He jammed the muzzle against the animal's skull, the recoil impelling him to the next stall without waiting to watch the cow drop and die. Another pair of terrified brown eyes, another shot. The piss and shite were overpowering now, the rusty reek of blood laid over the sharp stench.

There was nowhere to send them, nobody to look after them. Half of them were crippled with mastitis already thanks to his neglect. Now he had to leave, he couldn't let them suffer more. He shook his head against the weak justifications, tried to focus on getting the job done. He wiped his eyes on his wrist and sleeve again, his hand aching from the juddering gun. Again, leaping clear of a big body collapsing. The dull smack of the shots, the thud of bodies, the lowing of the terrified cows and the banging of the big frames against the stalls as they tried to break away. He muffed a shot, the blood-slicked barrel slipped and the shot blew a hole out of the poor animal's right cheek. It screamed pain, blood flying as it lost its footing and crashed to the stinking floor. Slamming its mutilated head against the sodden hay, it bucked and thrashed as Pat tried to get close enough to put an effective shot through the thick skull. Warm blood coursed over his hand as he pushed the gun against the animal's head and fired. The gun clicked and Pat cried out in impotent rage as he scrabbled for the spare magazine. The gun was slick with sweat and blood and he damn near shot himself changing the magazine over, remembering the safety just in time. The magazine clicked into place, the old one discarded in the hay and shit. He snatched the shot and the animal slumped.

Pat paused to clean his hand in the Belfast sink, wiping the gun clean as best he could. The last five cows started to calm in the stillness of the shed. The stench was appalling, worse than anything Pat had ever experienced. Reluctant to plunge back into the madness, he realised his shirt was sweat-sodden. He picked his way back to the stalls and shot his last five cows as clinically and swiftly as he could.

Done, he was left staring at his hand, the rust-smeared gunmetal nestled in the reddened palm, glistening droplets of blood caught in the gingery hairs on the back. There was even blood on his old watch, the leather strap had soaked it up. It had all taken just under ten minutes.

He got back to the car twenty minutes later. He slung the holdall into the back before sliding onto the driver's seat and starting up the engine. She was pale-faced, even for Orla. Tears shone on her cheeks She had pulled up her legs and had her arms around her knees, rocking. 'What kept you?'

'Unfinished business.'

'It's okay, you don't have to lie. I know what you did.'

He pulled away down the lane, leaving a wee cloud of blue smoke as he changed gear. 'What would that be, then?'

'You killed the herd. I heard the shots, Pat. You must think I came down in the last shower.'

He thought the sound would be deadened by the shed. He imagined her flinching at each shot, sitting alone in the car waiting for the next dull percussion to carry through the damp morning air.

'I'm sorry. I had no choice, there's nobody to ask look after them and they were sickening. You know that. I couldn't leave them suffer. I might not be coming back here.'

She laughed. 'Suffer?'

He could smell the soap from his scrubbed-red hands. 'It was best.'

'You could have called Con or the Gleesons.'

'And said what? Here's a nice trail for the Gards or the people who took you to follow? Come on, Orla. It's done.'

'How? How do you shoot a herd of cows, Pat?'

'You just do. Leave it alone.'

'Kirstie?'

He didn't answer her, just concentrated on driving. They reached the main road. 'Put on your seat belt.'

She scowled back at him and he ignored her. He could feel her fury boring holes into his cheek but kept his eye on the road ahead.

Her buckle clicked. 'I think it's time you told me what's going on.'

'I'm driving you to Thurles and putting you on the train home, Orla. That's all is going on.'

'You can't just dump me like that. Maybe you should have shot me when you murdered the herd.'

'Don't be childish. I have to deal with this and you're in danger because of me. I won't have that. The best thing is for you to go home to your mum and dad and forget this.'

Her eyes flashed and, not for the first time, Pat marvelled at the heat of her temper. Orla had always been fiery, but now she was ardent. 'Jesus, you keep telling me to forget. So what am I to forget here? Being kidnapped by armed terrorists or watching you blow them away? Or perhaps the dead man up in the bog? Or a herd of dead fucking cattle? I'll forget that, will I?'

'Yes. Look, Orla, there's no point you staying. It's dangerous and you'll just be in my way. I'm sorry, I can't look after you. These men are for real.'

'Well, right now nothing seems for real, tell the truth. What men? Who are they?'

'It's best you know as little as possible. It's safer for you.'

'Do you have any fucking notion how pompous you sound? Christ almighty, I was *kidnapped,* Pat. Surely you owe me that much, to tell me why?' Orla twisted in her seat, focusing her glare on the road ahead. In the distance, blue lights flashed. Pat took his foot off the accelerator as he watched the Gard peel off the main road to park up in the waste ground opposite the Shevry Garda station. Orla swung back to him. 'They're after you already.'

'They are. That's why it's time for you to leave.'

'Who are the men you killed? Why did they take me?'

'To blackmail me.'

A Decent Bomber

'Why?'

Pat glanced back as they passed out the car with its whirling blue lights, but there was no sign of interest from the two Gards.

'Why did they blackmail you?'

Her green eyes had an unusual luminosity. She had always been a looker, but her feral intensity could be hard to handle when she was roused. Pat sighed. 'As far as I can make out, they're a terrorist group, an offshoot of Al Qaeda or something like that. African lads, Arabs. A real mix. They've got all the old IRA code words. They managed to get access to stuff, explosives and the like. And they wanted me to make them some bombs.'

'But you can't make bombs.'

He murmured, his head bowed with the weight of the past. 'I can. That's what I did. Back then.'

'You were a bomb maker?'

'I was.'

'Which bombs? Enniskillen? Warrenpoint?'

'Just bombs, Orla.'

'How can they be *just* bombs? Like they took away *just* lives? Like that?'

'That's all in the past. Leave it there. Jesus, Orla, you weren't even born back then.'

Orla's fists were balled, the tendons standing out under the freckled skin. 'So they can't make their own bombs, then?'

'Seems not. They don't make terrorists like they used to.' She opened and closed her mouth, gulping. Pat raised his palm. 'I'm sorry. Not funny.'

'So you agreed? To make bombs for them?'

'They'd kidnapped you. I could hardly disagree.'

'How many?'

'Six. Five wee ones, one big one. I made them all

broken, but they'll work that out soon enough. Which is why I have to find them, I have to undo this. I thought I could deal with things before the bombs got taken away, but I'm not as clever as I used be. Old age, see?'

She slumped back into her seat, her wide-eyed regard on the road ahead. A light drizzle fell, Pat eventually switched on the wipers. The windscreen started to fog and he opened his window a little. The cool fresh air on his cheek sharpened him.

'Thank you.'

'It's nothing. What for?'

'For doing that. For coming for me.'

'Sure, what else was I to do? But you were put in danger on my account and I'm not having that happen again.'

'And you think I'm going to let you roam around the country shooting people without me around to clean up after you?'

'That's precisely what I think Orla O'Carolan and what's more that is what is without any shadow of a doubt going to happen.'

They left the rain behind, the sky still brooding but the spray on the road died down as the hills around them reflected brilliant emerald spots of escaping sunlight. The ancient Daihatsu's engine had a nasty mosquito whine Pat hadn't heard before. He flashed a glance at Orla hunkered down in the passenger seat, her green padded jacket folded around her.

They came into Thurles. Pat turned off at the GAA ground towards the station. The station car park was unusually busy, the queue to get in tailing back into The Colmyard. Orla spotted them first, but Pat wasn't far behind. More blue lights. Pat steered away from the press of cars leading into the station.

'I'll drop you off a little down the road, so.'

The wail of a siren was accompanied by the flashing behind them. Pat hit the steering wheel with his palm and shouted 'Shit!' He gunned the Daihatsu's engine and wrenched the wheel around to take them down the one-way system to the high street. As usual, the narrow entrance onto Liberty Square was backed up. Pat took the Daihatsu onto the pavement. Horns sounded as he shoved past, scraping one car with his wing mirror. They broke out onto the square. Pat fought the wheel as he sent them darting through the traffic. Orla twisted to look back. 'There's nobody following. Do you think the siren was for us?'

Pat's forehead was beaded with sweat. He battled to calm himself, took his foot off the throttle and relaxed back into his worn seat. 'I'm too bloody old for this.'

'Where are we going now?'

They left the town and drove through rainy countryside. Pat was silent a long while as he wrestled with the choices open to him. They turned onto the M8, the big motorway quiet and few other cars sloshing through the increasingly heavy downpour.

'Okay, so don't answer me. But you can listen to this,' Orla pulled back her hair. 'I'm coming with you. You were right back there, you're not a young man any more. I can help out, I can be a second set of eyes. I'm not sure about the gun skills, but the way I see it we've been in this together from the start and if you'll stop messing around and let me come with you we've got a better chance of tracking these people and their bombs down than if I'm not with you.'

Pat fixed his gaze on the road ahead and stayed quiet.

*

The service station was warm, desultory groups of people sitting and eating their lunches, the odd truck driver taking his break; messy trays, cups of tea and the smell of frying heavy in the air. Orla felt tired and dispirited. Pat had gone to the toilet, the ruins of their hasty lunch strewn on the table.

She watched a man at the food service counter. He was lanky and bearded, wearing a boiler suit of sorts. He moved oddly, his gestures hesitant and his focus on getting the tray away from the cash till arrested her attention. The women he was walking towards wore similar grey overalls and thick pebble glasses. The dependency and love in her eyes was clear and Orla felt its painful intensity as the man shuffled across the brown-tiled floor towards her, the food-laden tray balanced carefully. He was damaged and Orla wanted to cry at his smile across at the woman. His hands were awkward, misshapen as they gripped the plastic. He placed the tray carefully and then folded himself into the orange chair. Her hand was laid on his, a congratulation. She beamed and it was like the sun had come out. Orla had to look away because it made her feel so happy and so sad. She missed Róisín at that moment, bitterly.

Pat was just coming out of the toilets when Orla spotted the uniformed Gard stroll into the service station and scan the room. Pat slipped back into the toilets as she slid off the chair. Her back turned to the Gard, she struck out for the opposite exit. She reached the Daihatsu after him. He was just moving off as she pulled open the passenger door.

'You'd have left without me?'

'That was the plan. I told you, I don't want you involved in this.'

'You saw the Gard?'

'Yes. No big deal though. It was business as usual, not a manhunt.'

'How do you know that?'

'They'd have staked out the car park, stationed patrols at the exits. It was just one squad car, more likely he was on the lookout for a decent sandwich. We've time yet.'

'I knew you'd come around.'

'I haven't.'

'You said *we've* time.'

'Figure of speech. Here, you want a sucky sweet?'

Orla grinned. 'Don't mind if I do.' She reached into the bag and unwrapped a Murray Mint. Sitting back she popped it into her mouth and gazed out contentedly at the spray from the lorries headed North for Dublin.

Pat switched on the cassette player and settled back. She rolled the sweet around, clicking it against her teeth as guitar chords rang out. She weathered it for a few more seconds. 'Yew. What's this sleazy noise?'

He stared across at her. 'You seriously don't know it?'

'I'd know to avoid it if I did.'

'This is Thin Lizzy. Dancing in the moonlight. This is…' He closed his hand and clasped it to his heart. '*Life*.'

Orla settled down for a long journey.

She must have dozed. It took a few disorientating seconds to realise where she was. She had dreamed about Róisín and loss. Something in her wanted to forget all this, to curl up on a sofa in her friend's calm, worldly-wise gypsy arms. The image of a milking shed full of still, cold humps took Róisín's place in her mind. She shuddered, shifted in her seat and tried to banish it. They were just passing the toll in Dublin. Pat was talking in a low voice on his mobile. He hung up and glanced over at her. 'You okay?'

'Yes, must have dropped off. Dublin?'

'We're going to ditch the car. A friend of mine has arranged a replacement.'

'Do you have a lot of friends from your old days?'

'A few. I haven't really stayed in touch. Like I said, I'd put it all behind me.'

Orla shifted in her seat to get a better view of him. He would have been handsome as a younger man. He had a strong jaw and his bearing was more driven than her father's. Da was a bit chubbier, too, fully four years younger than Pat and somehow softer. Pat was, well, *big*. Not fat, just bulky. He needed a shave now she came to think of it. And he was looking tired, the skin around his eyes bruised. This man who had been more readily accessible as a shoulder and friend than the slightly distant figure of authority her father had been to her, this man she thought she knew and didn't know at all.

'What got you into it in the first place? The IRA?'

'I suppose these days you'd say I was radicalised, right? Singing rebel songs an' all.'

'We all do that.'

'Well, I was a bit wilder than most. My pals were a cut apart from the other kids at school, we were just a bit madder, I suppose. There was a chap called Donnelly used get us to do errands. He was a big fellow, craggy like. He played the fiddle and sang like an angel, but he was a fighter. We idolised him, he was everything the Struggle was about. And the errands became bigger each time. More important.'

They filtered off the motorway and waited at a red light.

'Bigger until?'

Pat tapped on the wheel waiting for the light to change. 'Until I got a job one midnight. Some *ludraman* had to be brought in line. I was the man of the hour.' The light changed and they pulled away, Pat guiding the car to an intersection, indicating right. 'Except I was a boy.'

'And you went too far.'

He grunted. 'Good guess, but not me, no. It was the guy with me did, nearly killed the poor fellow. He only just made it to hospital, critical and all. After that I was trusted.' Pat took the right turn and drove watchfully, peering at the broken roadside fencing. 'I'll tell ye the truth, Orla, and nothing but the truth. I wanted to be trusted more than anything else. I was inside, part of the fight and I had a cause that burned in my heart, maybe even more than love itself. And looking back on myself I think I was young and stupid, but that's what it is to be young and stupid. You're sure of everything, and when you're old you're sure of nothing. They were different times. So what I think I'm saying is I'm not proud of myself or the things I did back in the day, but I'm trying to do the right thing now.'

Orla nodded. 'I understand. I think.'

He'd sworn to tell nothing but the truth, but Lord love him not the whole truth. Watching for his turning, Pat tried not to think about the past any more, but She was in his head now and he couldn't shake the shade of his dead love. Because she was the real reason he had taken up arms against the Brits with a fury that had brought the fear and admiration of his fellows. Revenge had been Pat's cleansing fire until the day he had walked up to Brian MacNamara and simply said 'Enough' before going off to become a farmer.

He pulled off the road through a gateway with rust-streaked blue slab doors, the car jolting on the uneven track. Piles of car parts surrounded them, shells of battered old jalopies were piled up in crazy stacks.

Orla was peering around. 'Where are we?'

'We're getting rid of the car. Come on.'

Orla followed Pat across the yard to a shabby Portakabin. It rocked as he pulled open the door and stepped in. 'Vinny?'

She followed him, her eyes adjusting to the dim light inside. It reeked of cigarette smoke, the walls were yellowed with it. The grey-faced, thin man at the table ground out his cigarette in an over-filled foil ashtray. 'Jesus, if it isn't himself. Pat O'Carolan. It's been a lifetime, man. How'ye?'

'I'm good, Vinny, never finer. This is my niece Orla. Orla, this is Vinny Byrne. We go back.'

'Orla. Welcome.'

Orla took his cold hand. Byrne lit another cigarette and reached behind his chair to pull out a light nylon cagoule. 'Let's take a look at her, then.'

They walked out together. The rain had settled down to a faint drizzle that glittered on the rusty piles of metal, the crazed windscreens and flat tyres overgrown with tufts of glistening grass. Byrne stalked around the Daihatsu, slipped into the driver's side and pulled the bonnet release.

'Well, Pat, but she's had a hard time. She's fair knackered, ha?'

'Farm life, Vinny. She's tough as nails, though.'

Byrne hooked the catch and lifted the bonnet. He checked the oil, then pulled and pushed things around. Orla watched the performance, curled up in her warm jacket. Byrne pulled an oily rag from his pocket and wiped his hands, letting the bonnet fall. Reaching back into the driver's side he turned the key and stood listening to the engine. Even Orla could hear the high whine above the engine's rhythmic cough. Byrne pushed down on the throttle a couple of times. He switched the engine off.

'I've got a Volkswagen Polo. Documents included. I'll sort 'em out now for ye. But I'm hurtin', Pat. This one's ready for the heap.'

'I'll take what you've got, Vinny.'

'You in trouble there, Pat?'

'Nothing I can't handle, but I'm sort of in a hurry.'

Byrne flicked his cigarette butt into a pile of rusty clutches and engine blocks. 'I reckoned you might be. You'll need a couple of new mobiles too, then? Credit card?'

'That would be handy, right enough.'

Byrne ushered them back into the Portakabin. Orla left the door open and stood in the opening, trying to breathe fresh air.

Byrne lit a fresh cigarette. 'I'll have to charge you for the mobiles, Pat. Call it five hundred.'

'Fine. Done.' Pat pulled his wallet out. It was a deal fatter than she'd ever remembered seeing it: Pat had never wanted for money, had always had treats for her when she visited but she had always admired how he was careful. Now he was high rolling.

Byrne held out his hand. 'Mobiles. I'll need your ones so I can run them around Dublin for a couple of days.'

Pat handed his shiny old Alcatel over. Orla fished out her own mobile. Byrne took it from her. 'Here.' He pressed a Nokia 3310 into her hand. 'It's a great phone. Indestructible, these are.'

Orla worked out what was happening. 'You're not

swapping this piece of junk for my Nexus?'

'I am. This is tied into your Google account. This yoke has you stamped all over it. The second you get data or WiFi you're checking in, loving the world to death and locating yourself to every social account and app you're running. Even if you change the SIM it'll check in with your ID. It's traceable and you don't want to be traced.'

'But… Pat...'

'He's right. That's your new mobile from now on.'

Pat took the 3310 Byrne was handing out to him. 'Both of them have the other number programmed in so you can use them straight off.'

'But my mobile's worth—'

Pat was insistent. 'It's worth leaving behind you, Orla.'

Orla realised she was worrying about losing her game scores and felt stupid. She stared down at the antique in her hand.

Byrne slipped the shiny handset into a drawer and took Pat's credit card. 'Anything on this?'

'Yes. There's three grand to spare. Will that cover you?'

'It will.' Byrne put the card in his pocket. He slid an envelope from his desktop to Pat. 'There's a thousand Euro on this one. It's clean.'

'Patrick Shaughnessy?'

'Your new name. You should sign it now, you never know what sorts of hands it could fall into. The PIN is 1234, you might want to change that at the nearest Bank of Ireland ATM, you know? Here's the bank account number. There's another five hundred in that. You need to copy this here signature.'

'Thanks, Vinny.'

'No problem. Here are the keys. It's the VW Polo

parked over there to the side. That'll be three thousand Euro with the car.'

'Put it on my credit card.'

Byrne nodded. 'I will, at that. You see any of the gang these days?'

'I've been on a farm these past twenty years.'

'Funny you should turn up like this. Old Hamid was round here just the other day.'

'The Libyan fellow? He still kickin' around is he?'

'He is, so. Haven't seen him in years, either. He's got three grown up kids. Makes you feel old, people turning up and telling you things like that.'

'Take care, Vinny.'

'Yourself, Pat.'

Orla breathed fresh air as she waited for Pat to come down the steps behind her. He led the way over to the car, parked in front of a wrecked yellow Bedford school bus. They walked around it together. The Polo's battered teal metallic finish was lumpy on the passenger side wing and the rear door didn't fit flush. It smelled of stale cigarette smoke and something sour/sweet Orla guessed was vomit. Getting in, she didn't want to touch the stained seatbelt, pulling it round with thumb and forefinger.

The car's suspension creaked as they scraped through the potholes in the dirt track leading out of the yard. Pat seemed more furtive leaving than he had arriving.

She twisted the 3310 in her hands and wanted to run a wipe over it. 'That was pretty shifty, Pat.'

'That it was. But you have to do these things if you're to stay ahead.'

Orla nodded. She was learning fast. They joined the motorway, the wipers leaving streaks on the screen. The car swerved as Pat leaned over to delve into his coat pocket. He fished out a little plastic cassette and slotted it into the dash.

'Hope this thing works.'

To Orla's quiet despair, it did. She stared out of the window at the rainy streets and rows of red brick houses as Pat joined in singing *Little Darling*.

The rain started again in earnest as they neared Newry, passing a sign advertising fireworks for sale. It was framed by green fields below a roiling, gunmetal sky. Orla had managed to convince Pat to turn off the music as they passed Drogheda.

He broke the companionable silence. 'See that? Great, isn't it? People come North these days to buy explosives.'

'That's not even remotely funny.'

'No, that's where you're wrong. It's funny.' Pat rummaged in the central console. 'What's not funny is I left the sucky sweets in the Daihatsu. And I bet that bastard Byrne eats them on me.'

'Look, this… Oh, never mind.'

'Is no time to be joking? Come on, Orla. We've ourselves a little time, there's no blue lights on our tail and an open road ahead. Being in the shit doesn't have to mean walking around looking like a blasted heath all the time. God knows, I've been in worse trouble than this.'

She shifted to face him. 'Is that right? And where did you end up?'

'Ah, come on now, ye're cheatin'.'

'In the H blocks, then?'

'Look, here's our turning. How handy is that?'

Orla smiled despite herself, but averted her head so he wouldn't see. She focused on the mobile, well, phone. Its blue body and that silver swoosh around the stupid pixelated screen reminded her of school and jeering boys. She twisted the thing in her hand. It rang and she nearly died, close to dropping it.

It was Pat.

'For fuck's sake, Pat!'

He was thumbing the red button on his handset, one hand on the steering, one on the stupid mobile and in silent hegs of laughter. She wanted to lamp him and settled for tossing the handset into the console, but she was laughing with him and something was, well, *right* again.

They pulled up outside the row of warehouses, the tyres scrunching on the pebbles scattered on the damp concrete scree. The rain had stopped, but water was still dripping off the leaves and the leaf-mould was rich in the air.

Shoved, the Polo's door groaned before it clunked shut. Orla waited, her hand on the cold metal of the wet roof. Pat stalked down the side of the wall, paddling his hand at her to stay where she was.

She was happy to comply.

He tried the handle, peered in the window. He was on the way back when the man in the boiler suit rounded the corner of the unit next door and called out to Orla. 'Looking for someone, love?'

She smiled weakly, lacking any coherent idea of how to answer his bluff query. Pat came to her rescue. 'We were supposed to pick up an exercise bike from here. Bought it on eBay. Name of Fordham.'

'Fordham, was it? You've been stitched up. There's nobody of that name around here. This place has been empty a year and more.'

'I'd best double check that address. Still, it's a handsome lockup. To let, is it?'

'Bonners have it up. The estate agents. They had a sign here till a couple weeks ago, vandals knocked it down. Little sods.'

Pat pulled open the driver's side door. 'Thanks. We'd best be on our way and find us that bike bloke.'

Chapter Seven

Boyle and MacNamara pulled up at the half-brick, half-pebbledash 1970s building, the peeling square portico to the street proclaiming *Garda* in old-fashioned lettering pressed deep into the concrete.

'There we go. Three hours on the nail,' Boyle announced, waggling the plastic display on his wrist.

MacNamara heaved himself out of the car. He was back in the 1980s, a time and place he didn't want to be. Thurles in '81 wasn't his happiest memory by a long chalk. The drizzle settled on his coat as he slammed the door and strode around the square bonnet. Boyle massaged the remote, twisting his wrist until finally the *cheep cheep* of the locking system sounded and the lights blinked twice.

'Fecker.' He muttered. They walked into the reception area together. A pair of surly youths perched on the row of plastic chairs, waiting on a friend or a decision. Boyle leaned into the arch cut in the glass barrier. 'Boyle for Carla Keough.'

The blue-shirted cop on duty didn't even look up. 'Sure. We've been waiting for ye. Go on upstairs there.'

Boyle led the way up the stairs. MacNamara tried to keep the past away as he pushed up behind the younger man. But even the smell of the place haunted him and brought back his time on remand before they'd taken him to the stink of Long Kesh.

Chief Superintendent Carla Keough was waiting for them at the head of the stairs. She was slight, brunette and the epaulettes on her blouse seemed too large and stiff. Smiling, she held her hand out. 'Mr Boyle? Welcome to Thurles, John. You've been brightening our boring lives, so you have.'

Boyle took her hand. 'Good to meet you. This is Brian MacNamara.'

She turned to MacNamara. 'You're welcome, Brian.'

'Thanks. I'm delighted…' He took her hand and blinked at her direct, open gaze. 'Actually, I'm not. I'm more puzzled to be here, but I hope we can get to the bottom of this and clear it up as quickly as possible for all concerned.'

Keough let his grip go. 'That's what we all want, I'd say. Come on to the briefing room, we don't have much time.'

She led the way and MacNamara gestured Boyle to go on ahead of him. They rolled into the room with its beech veneer meeting table and four chairs arrayed either side. Two blue-shirted Gards stood as they entered. Keough strode to the head of the table, a projector screen already showing a map of Tipperary split into six districts. She waved everyone to sit. 'Lads, Detective Sergeant Boyle and Mr MacNamara from Belfast. This is Superintendent Eamonn Dunphy and DS Sean Hayes.' She turned to Boyle. 'I understand you and Eamonn know each other already.'

'That we do.'

'Grand. As you're joining us for the operation on the O'Carolan farm,' she turned to the PowerPoint slide. 'I thought it might be useful to show you how we're thinking about this. The farm actually sits bang on the red line between three of our districts, Thurles, Roscrea and Tipperary. The nearest station is in the Thurles district so I've assigned it to Eamonn and his team. Eamonn, would you like to bring us up to speed?'

Dunphy stood, puffing out his chest. He was thinning

on top and had combed his fine hair over. There was a good paunch pressing against the over-tight shirt and MacNamara right away had the man down as an incurable optimist. *Keep these shirts for the while; sure I'll lose the weight* he imagined was the line. Dunphy tapped the screen. 'Our nearest station to O'Carolan's place is Shevry. The Gard there is a strong community man. He tells us O'Carolan has a niece staying with him at present. Apparently the village shop has been busy supplying him cleaning materials because he's spruced up the place for her visit. I must say,' he glanced at Keough then across at Boyle, 'it doesn't strike us as a dangerous suspect profile. He's known in the community, well liked and hasn't done a thing in any way unusual or out of place in the twenty years since he inherited the farm from his gran. Mrs Gleeson at the shop says he bought a lot of coffee, if that counts as suspicious activity.'

Boyle leaned forwards, throwing an evil glance at MacNamara. 'And yet he's sitting on an illegal IRA arms cache.'

Dunphy nodded. 'As you say, John. And we've taken the request from PNSI seriously. I have six cars in the area, two plain cars on surveillance either end of the lane to O'Carolan's, two squad cars on standby in Shevry, one in Roscommon and one in Gurth. That's something like 20% of our total resource. We have a specially trained drugs interdiction unit who are capable with dealing with armed suspects and they are fully armed. I have a marksman, too. He'll be travelling with me. One of the cars from Shevry will make the first approach and we'll be right behind him. And we have a crime scene investigation unit coming with us. We're on top of it, to cut to the chase.' He smiled at Boyle. 'Are we all ready?'

Boyle tapped on the table. 'As I'll ever be. At least it's stopped raining.'

'Come on, so. Let's see what's going on up there on Cummermore.'

Boyle had been issued with a Garda Tetra radio handset tuned into the operation's agreed channel. It was quiet as they left the main road and drove up the overgrown lane following Dunphy's Ford Focus. The crime scene van brought up their rear. A Land Rover Defender with two officers in it headed up the little convoy and led the way. It turned right into the farm. The lead car came on the radio. 'O'Brien here. Okay we're in the yard. It's quiet. We've stopped. Ringing the door now.'

Dunphy's brake lights flickered ahead up the lane and they all slowed to a stop.

O'Brien came on the radio again. 'No answer. It feels empty. O'Donnell's taking a look in the barn. I'm going to check the windows around the house.'

A new voice came on the radio. 'O'Donnell. Just going into the milking shed. There's a funny sm… oh Jesus. Fucking hell.' The airwaves filled with the sound of retching. 'It's the cows. The herd. They're here.'

O'Brien cut in. 'Tom? Tom? You okay?'

Dunphy's voice on the radio was tight. 'We're coming in. All units block access roads.'

Blue lights flashing, Dunphy's car jerked forwards and right, sliding into the yard.

O'Donnell sounded shaky. 'Dead. They're all dead. Must be twenty head. It's like Beirut in here.'

They followed the Garda car into the yard. Boyle jumped out and joined Dunphy at the door of the barn. The tang of slurry was in the air but there was an iron stench mixed in with it. They pushed in, O'Donnell was standing propped against the corrugated wall, wide-eyed, pale and wiping his mouth against the back of his hand.

Each cow had been shot precisely in the centre of the head. MacNamara walked the row. The flies had already found the place and clouds of them rose as MacNamara approached. He found Boyle at his elbow. The blood on the floor had pooled with the other liquids, its surface dull.

'This is mad.'

'You okay?'

'Yes. I think. I dread to think of what we'll find in the house.'

Boyle put a hand on MacNamara's shoulder. 'Come on, let's take a gander.'

The crime scene investigation team was already spreading out. Boyle and MacNamara joined Dunphy.

Boyle asked, 'The house?'

Dunphy nodded. Two of his men were already swinging a battering ram at the door. The lock gave after two blows. MacNamara and Boyle took the shoe covers offered them at the door, leaning against the wall to put them on before they followed the men in and stood, unsure of themselves, in the empty kitchen. There was a bowl of fruit on the table.

MacNamara wondered. 'It's like the Marie bloody Celeste.'

'Except with a lot of dead cows.' Added Boyle.

Boyle and MacNamara were preparing to leave when one of the crime scene team burst into the kitchen. MacNamara didn't think he could deal with any more drama, jumping at the slam of the door against the wall and the spectacle of the man in his black uniform hung with lights and radios, walkie talkies and CS gas canisters and all.

The man was excited, right enough. 'There's a dead dog in the garden. It was in a freshly dug grave. It was shot through the head. Single slug, close range.'

Another clamoured in after him, a silver-haired man in Gardaí uniform, flushed and wild-eyed. 'Kirstie. His collie. Lovely dog. Jesus.'

Eamonn Dunphy was sat at the kitchen table playing with an apple. He raised a finger at the older man and glanced across at Boyle. 'This is Conor, he's the Gard at Shevry. Conor, Boyle and MacNamara from PSNI.'

Boyle tipped his forehead. 'Nice to meet ye.'

Dunphy sat back. 'Keep looking around, lads. There's more here, I can smell it. Go away with you.' He waited until they clattered out, examining the apple closely. It had been dusted and he wiped the white powder off with his sleeve. 'What's been going on here, John?'

Boyle shrugged. 'Search me. Burke and Quinlan were tortured and their places were torched. This is a totally different MO. It makes no sense. Why would you shoot a man's cows and his dog?'

'To get him to talk?' MacNamara ventured.

Boyle laughed. 'That's a bit subtle for those boys. They'd pull out your nails first. They're not big into asking nicely.'

'So it's not them. It's O'Carolan. He's gone on the run. He couldn't take care of his animals and killed them as humanely as he could,' MacNamara mused.

Boyle stared at MacNamara, nodding slowly. 'You could just have the hammer nail occlusion thing sorted out there.'

The kitchen door burst open again, a different face: blue eyes and a spotty forehead under a shock of blond hair. 'Super. It's the bog. We followed a set of tyre tracks up there. Another fresh grave. Looks man-sized.'

'Christ,' Dunphy tossed the apple back in the bowl and kicked his chair back. 'Show me.'

The door slammed. MacNamara and Boyle were left together at the kitchen table. MacNamara was wondering what Sean Driscoll would make of all this – shit himself more than likely - when Boyle broke the silence.

'So where's the cache?'

MacNamara glanced up at him. 'What good's that to anyone?'

'You know, don't you? You know where it is. You could have told us to begin with but you were hoping it would all go away. It's all you and Driscoll have been doing since this first started. It's not going away, MacNamara. You'd be best just telling me and we can all get on. Seriously.'

'Look, Boyle. John. The political implications alone make me sick just to think of them. I'd love to help you, but I don't see how I can.'

Boyle's suppressed fury was intimidating. 'Just tell the fucking truth, man.'

'I don't have the authority.'

'Any man has the authority to dictate what he considers to be right and wrong. And you know whatever has happened here is wrong. Where's the bloody cache?'

MacNamara stared up at the ceiling, his fists clenched. He sighed and focused on Boyle. 'You empty it; dispose of the contents and not one official or even unofficial word about its existence. Or it stays right where it is.'

Boyle glared at MacNamara, poised and furious. He raised his finger, his mouth set. He dropped his hand. 'Okay. Deal.'

MacNamara sighed and stood. 'Which I am quite sure you don't have the authority to make. Come with me.'

He reached for the whiskey jar on the dresser and found the brass key. It had a knot of string tied through its eye and MacNamara looped this around his finger. He led the way out into the yard. They wandered down the lane to the grotto. Boyle's hands were thrust in his pockets, his shoulders hunched against the cold. They turned down into the stone-lined hollow with its Virgin Mary, her face florid in the late afternoon sun breaking through the cloud.

'You trying to convert me, so?'

'Come on. Down here.' MacNamara slipped behind the statue. He slipped the key into the door and led the way into the dark little space. He used his mobile to illuminate the store. A few feet across, brick lined and perhaps fourteen feet long, it was piled with crates.

'Jesus. And you even knew where the key was.'

'Pat told me where to find it twenty years ago. I was surprised to find it still there, to be honest.'

'And Burke's?'

'No. I didn't have a key to Burke's. Pat and I go back; it was something he asked me to do.'

'So what's in here?'

'Mostly firearms and ammunition. Some of the guns are ancient. We even had a couple of Brens. And I would dearly like this to all go away.'

Boyle was scanning the dark boxes with his mobile light. 'Burke's place burning down was a Godsend for you in its way, wasn't it?'

'I hadn't thought of it like that.'

'No, perhaps not. We can turn this over to the Gards. There's nothing to connect it to you.'

'Except you.'

'Ah, and so you'd have to kill me. No, I have no interest in this. This is the past and perhaps you had a point back there. When we were driving down.'

'Let's get back. Here, the key.'

'You're putting a lot of faith in me.'

'You're very young, you know that? I understand your anger, I really do. But I've lived through too much of what happened to your Da. Maybe your generation can be better than we were. But when it comes down to brass tacks you're the law, Boyle and I'm putting my faith in you as the law, not as a person.'

'In that case I arrest you in the name of—' Boyle broke off laughing. 'Christ man, you should see your face!'

'I should beat the shit out of you, you whelp.'

'Bring your army, so. Come on. Let's find Dunphy.'

They walked together up the lane in the fading light. They turned into the farmyard and Boyle fished his Tetra handset out of the BMW. They had deployed lamps up on the bog, white sheeting around the crime scene. MacNamara shivered. Boyle muttered into his handset.

The light was leaving the land fast, the lights up on the bog seeming brighter by the minute. The yard was packed with cars, flapping lines of tape defining walkways and men in white Tyvek picking their way around.

'Dunphy's sending the Land Rover down from the bog for us. Apparently it's four wheel drive country up there. They got the crime scene van so stuck they had to call a rescue vehicle in from Thurles. Some red faces over that it seems. I'd say we're here overnight if you want to call anyone.'

'No,' MacNamara thought it over. 'Yes. Where will we stay?'

'Dunno. Sure, Thurles will find us a B&B or something.'

He called Jean, wandering away from Boyle. She picked up on the second ring.

'Brian?'

'Hi, love. It's been a strange day.'

'What the hell's going on? Simone's beside herself. She says you abandoned Riley in the house all alone for the afternoon.'

'She was safe enough. I had to go away. I had no choice.'

'You could have called me or something.'

'There was no time. It's a long story. I'm in South Tipp, I'll have to stay here overnight. Something's cropped up from the past and it has to be dealt with. I'm truly sorry.'

'Are you in some sort of trouble Brian?'

'No, nothing like that. But there's trouble enough over all this. Say sorry to Simone for me and I'll see you tomorrow.'

'When tomorrow?'

'I haven't got a clue. I'll ring in the morning.'

'Before nine then, I'll be at work after that.'

'Sure.'

He cut the line. Jean would never have thought to compromise on her being at work and of course was unable to take a call from him, even when he was managing a problem that had clearly taken him halfway across the country. He banished the self-pitying thought. He caught up with Boyle just as the Land Rover arrived.

A Decent Bomber

'We're booked into Hayes Hotel in Thurles.'

MacNamara clambered into the Land Rover and they bounced up the rutted track towards whatever had been buried up on the bleak blanket of the Cummermore bog. MacNamara felt a deep foreboding.

The lights were dazzling, little clouds of moths circling and battering the lenses. A tent had been erected over the burial site. A cold drizzle fell.

Dunphy came out of the tent grim-faced. 'If I were you gents I'd head back to Thurles and get a warm meal and some sleep. That's my plan in any case. These boys are going to be out here all night. It's a body alright, more than that we don't know right now. It's a muddy lump. Unusually tall from the look of it. A black fellow. We won't have a full picture 'till morning.

MacNamara held his hand up. 'Sorry. You said black?'

'The body. He was black. A black man.'

What the hell has Pat done? His relief at having solved the longstanding problem of the Tipperary cache gave way to a sense of helplessness and frustration. MacNamara wanted a drink. Badly.

The tatty Cusack Bar at Hayes Hotel was busy. Brian MacNamara took the one free barstool and waved at the freckled girl pulling pints. 'A pint and Powers. On ice.'

'Sure.'

He sipped the whiskey as he waited for the brown cloud to swirl up the pint leaving behind the clear darkness. There was too much, he reflected, darkness around these days. He let the empty whiskey glass go onto the bar just as she placed the Guinness in front of him.

'Cheers.' He lifted his pint.

She smiled a dutiful smile and went off to serve a loud young fellow down along the bar. MacNamara pulled on the pint, enjoying the bitterness. Christ what a day. What a week.

She had a nice arse in that tight black dress. The white frilly blouse was too tight and let flashes show. She turned the wrong way and caught his gaze as it sought to leave her tits and simultaneously avoid her eyes. Her mouth tightened and MacNamara felt old.

Fuck it. 'A pint and a Powers.'

Boyle appeared from nowhere. 'How's things?'

'Shit, actually. I'm supposed to be at home with my wife and I'm in this cowp with you. No offense, but I suspect ye're not my kind of girl.'

'Guinness, please love.' Boyle winked at her and she smiled at him. MacNamara cast his eyes to heaven. 'Dunphy's on the way over. They found two more shot, in a house near Cashel.'

'Thought he was off duty.'

'He is now. I think he fancied a drink and we're free spirits for the night.'

'Oh, aye, free as a bird, me. Now let me see where I'd want to be on a night with the world at my feet and an out pass signed by the wife. New York? London? Dubai maybe? Ah, no, give me Thurles every time. Blinder.'

'Could be worse, Brian. The barmaid's a feckin' peach.'

She slammed down MacNamara's pint and he picked it up to clink against Boyle's Guinness. 'If under-ripe and bitter. Cheers.'

MacNamara drained his whiskey and watched

A Decent Bomber

Dunphy's shiny pate bobbing through the growing crowd. 'Here's yer man.'

'Lads.' Dunphy was already sweaty, despite the Baltic weather outside.

MacNamara twisted to make room. 'What ye fancy?'

'Pint.'

'Hi, love? Another pint here please.' MacNamara sipped the foam on his own drink, which the barmaid had spilled banging it down. He cleaned the bottom of the glass with the edge of his finger. 'She's not a happy girl, that one.'

Dunphy massaged Boyle's shoulder. 'Jesus, that was a fuckin' mess at O'Carolan's. fifteen dead cows, a Collie dog and a black man. That's the biggest crime scene I've ever seen, I swear.'

MacNamara reached Dunphy's pint across to him. 'Cheers. What's this Boyle was saying about another shooting?'

'Another two dead, sure enough.' Dunphy drew gratefully on his pint, a tide-mark of foam on his upper lip. 'Cashel. A stud farm north of the town called The Paddocks. Some strain of an old Arab and a Georgian. Not, you understand, an Englishman from two hundred years ago.'

MacNamara glanced around the busy bar, the young crowd chattering, jackets and scarves shucked off, groups of lads feral as they clustered around their pints and cast around for talent. He turned back to Dunphy. 'What the fuck's a Georgian want in Cashel?'

'We're looking into it. There's a team working overnight on the place, finding out who bought it, lived in it. The crime scene and forensics teams have gone in. Tell the truth we're stretched, we've not seen two major crime scenes in one night in a long time. We spend most of our time on petty stuff and domestic violence. There are shocking few murders on the average night in Tipp. We won't see any results until the morning.'

'Fair enough,' said MacNamara as he turned to the barmaid. 'Three pints and a Powers. Please.' He beamed. 'Love.'

It was a soft day and although the sky was mottled grey the pavements were dry. MacNamara had a head on him, no doubt about it. He sat in the meeting room at Thurles' Garda Station and cradled his black coffee as if his life depended on it. His teeth felt furry and he wanted a bacon sandwich more than anything else in the world. Clearly Eamonn Dunphy was a mind reader. His portly figure reversed through the meeting room door, a coffee in one hand and two brown paper bags in the other. Boyle followed him in with his own paper bag and two cups. Dunphy slid one of the bags in front of MacNamara, who reached out a doorstop of white bread and bit down gratefully. Bacon, tomato sauce, black pepper. Heaven.

Dunphy surfaced from his own sandwich, his cheeks distended. 'Jesus, Brian, you can drink I'll say that for ye.'

'I blame Boyle. He's trouble.'

'I am an innocent man.' Boyle waved his sandwich. 'Jesus, I needed this though.'

The door opened again and Chief Superintendent Carla Keough slipped into the room with a takeaway cup in her hand, a sheaf of papers in the other and a laptop clutched under her arm. 'Good morning gentlemen. It smells like a greasy spoon in here. I take it you were hard at it last night.'

MacNamara felt like a schoolboy and noted the other

two looking sheepish too. She was smiling a 'boys will be boys' smile and MacNamara somehow felt his mother's presence in the room.

'Well, as you were comparing notes and familiarising yourselves with each other's procedures, the crime scene units were busy all night. It's a mess. Shall I bring you up to speed?'

MacNamara cleared his throat. 'That would be appreciated, ma'am.'

She smiled drily. His mother left the room to be replaced by his headmistress. He wondered if she used a whip. Soft bread, salty bacon. A semi. Christ.

'First the O'Carolan farm. Fifteen head of dead milch cows, executed with surgical precision using a nine millimetre calibre pistol, a powerful one: cows have thick skulls even at point blank range. The same weapon was used to kill a collie, believed to be Patrick O'Carolan's dog, Kirstie. Time of death of all the animals reasonably consistent at around yesterday lunchtime. The man in the bog is African in origin, bearded and six foot six in height. Excellent dental health, manicured and pedicured. Six of his fingers had been blown off, 90% burns to the skin on his palms and wrists, some burning to the face, stomach and chest. The pathologist said it looked as if he had been holding a very big firework.'

'Killed by a firework?' Boyle's expression was somewhere between amusement and incredulity. His grin faded under the lighthouse beam of Keough's dry ice smile.

'No. He was killed by a rimless nine millimetre round, likely fired from a different gun to the one that killed the animals. The shot was to the forehead at close range. It was angled, if you choose to believe the cynics in forensics, to avoid too much exit spatter. It was fired down towards the body, which would make the executioner worryingly practised and thoughtful.' She turned to MacNamara. 'Was Mr O'Carolan what you would describe as a practised and thoughtful killer, Mr MacNamara? In his time? Your time?'

MacNamara couldn't help shifting uncomfortably in his chair. He realised there was tomato sauce on his finger, went to lick it off and thought better of the gesture. 'Pat was always a methodical operator, yes, ma'am.'

'Methodical.'

'Time of death?' Boyle spoke with his mouth full. Dunphy shoved the last of his bacon sandwich in with evident relish. MacNamara had paused eating his own. He put it down on the brown paper and wiped the sauce from his finger on the spongy bread. He glanced up to see her cool regard on his hands.

'Approximately 72 hours. Dublin has circulated his image to Interpol. No ID back so far. Now we progress to the stud farm.' She plugged the laptop into the cable snaking from the conference system console at the centre of the meeting room table. 'This is a picture of the front of The Paddocks. It is a smaller stud farm, some 50 acres, owned by an American gentleman who has let it for the past two years to a company in Belfast who use it for corporate hospitality, apparently. We are clearly looking into the ownership of that company as a matter of some urgency.'

'What's it called?' Boyle's mouth was still full. 'The company?'

Keough flicked through her papers. 'Ballymany Holdings.'

MacNamara turned to meet Boyle's savage glare. All the bonhomie of the night before was gone, Boyle was once again clearly in a state of fury. MacNamara dropped his gaze to his cold sandwich.

Dunphy threw his hands out. 'What kind of name is that?'

'It's the name of the stud,' Keough paused for effect and MacNamara hated her for it, 'that raised Shergar. The horse the Provisionals abducted in the eighties.'

MacNamara raised his head to deny it but caught Boyle's white knuckles on the way up. Fuck it, he thought. Too much history. Way too much. He returned his attention to tracing the veins of the beech that had died to give them a meeting table.

'The two men were both found dead in the kitchen. Time of death late last night, probably around the turn of midnight. Both shot from a position in the garden with a nine by nineteen millimetre parabellum round. The shots shattered the kitchen window. Could have been any pistol you like, but there were three shots fired and they were excellent. The three cartridge cases forensics found in the garden tell us the killer stood off by about fifty feet to fire them. Chances are he'd fired sixteen previous shots with the same gun.' She smiled coldly at MacNamara. 'Methodical.'

'If you seek peace, prepare for war.' Boyle rocked back, wiping his hands and frowning at MacNamara.

Keough paused in her presentation. 'Sorry?'

'Parabellum. It's where the word comes from, the Latin saying.'

'Thank you. We found evidence of a third person in the house. We found long hairs in the upstairs bed, consistent with a young woman. A redhead. There was no other sign of female occupation or toiletries in the bathrooms. Pat O'Carolan's niece, Orla was staying with him. And she was a redhead.'

'Great.' Boyle twisted off his chair and stood clutching the back of it. 'So we've got a heavily armed IRA vigilante on our hands. Nice one.' He flicked a finger at MacNamara. 'Thought you lot had more discipline than that. How much would he have taken from the cache with no name?'

MacNamara wiped his hands over his face. They niffed of fried bacon, butter and tomato. 'Whatever he may've wanted. I don't have an inventory of what was there, if that's what you're asking.'

'And now he's gone rogue.' Dunphy licked wet lips. 'He could be anywhere. Armed and dangerous.'

'We can assume he has his niece with him. He's hardly a threat.'

Boyle smacked the back of the chair. 'Jesus, MacNamara, you're rakin' us. A known paramilitary killer and bomb maker packing an unknown amount of firepower, linked to a viable explosive device dumped in a busy shopping centre with an IRA code given too late. And now he's on the lam with three men dead from his hand. Hardly a threat? You're fucking nuts.'

'He was protecting his niece from whoever it was turned over Burke and Quinlan. Surely you can see that,' MacNamara urged. 'There's been some sort of breach here and O'Carolan was caught up in it same as the others, but he was better and got away. You can't surely condemn him for that.'

Dunphy broke in, his ponderous voice punctuated by nervous swallows. 'We're concerned about three men dead in the Republic of Ireland. The courts can decide whether their murder was somehow justifiable. O'Carolan is the most wanted man in this country right now.'

'He's right.' Keough pressed. 'And Dublin agrees.

Which is why we're closing the border and have a warrant out for his urgent arrest as an armed and dangerous suspect. We're going on the news with a manhunt story at six tonight.'

'Excuse me,' Boyle nodded at Keough and left the room, his mobile lifted to his ear. MacNamara sat and gazed at his hands on the wooden surface. His skin was wrinkled, inelastic. He was getting old. And Jesus, but he was tired.

'What would you do, Mr MacNamara, if you were Pat O'Carolan? Would you shoot your herd and dog?' Keough pulled up a seat. 'Forget the men. Why the animals?'

'Because he was leaving. Something had threatened him. This dead African is presumably linked to the men who were holding his niece. So let's say he got the location where they were holding her out of the African and killed him, then took off after Orla. A dairy herd can't last long without being milked. The cows get sick. They can die. It was maybe the kindest thing to do.'

'And he's a man motivated by kindness?'

'He was a farmer. He loved animals. He was retired, Chief Superintendent. He'd had nothing to do with active service for over twenty years. All that was long in his past.'

'Something's brought it all back home, though, hasn't it?'

'I couldn't disagree. The question is who, and why. As I have explained to our friends in the PSNI, this particular aspect of the past is embarrassing to us. But we have no more idea of what the hell is going on around here than you or they do. And we'd rather, believe me with an election hanging over our heads, it all wasn't happening. So we're more than pleased to help in any small way we can.'

The sound of slow clapping came from Boyle, who'd re-entered the room. 'Oh, bravo, MacNamara. You're the man, sure you are. Politician 'till yer dying breath.' He slid his mobile onto the table.

It was Keough's turn to take a call. She listened and thanked her caller. 'That was Dublin. O'Carolan passed through the city an hour ago. The eFlow picked his number plate up. We've missed him.' She nodded to Boyle. 'You might catch up with him on the M1? Sorry about the late notice. He's driving a silver 2001 model Daihatsu Rocky and has a red-headed girl in the passenger seat. It's an old Tipperary South number plate, 52424.'

'Right, thanks.' Boyle scooped up his mobile. 'Ball's back in our court. Thank you, Ms Keough, Eamonn, for your hospitality. I'm afraid we have to leave you to clean up the mess here. We've ourselves a messer to catch.'

Chapter Eight

They stood in the reception of the Premier Inn, waiting for the girl to finish tapping on her screen. She smiled and handed Pat his credit card back. 'Thank you Mr Shaughnessy. Adjacent rooms as you requested. Breakfast is from 7am. We hope you enjoy your stay. Here are your keys.'

Pat took his card key, handed Orla hers. 'Thanks. The lifts?'

'Just over to your right.'

'Grand. Thank you.'

Pat and Orla bustled off to the lifts, Pat hefting the bulky holdall as well as his overnight bag. The lift came and they got in.

'Why not leave that stupid thing in the car?' Orla hissed, hitching her backpack.

'Because,' Pat selected the fifth floor. 'I feel more secure with it near me and not in a public car park.'

'I never thought I'd see the day—'

'Stop, now, Orla.'

They got out at the third floor and followed the signs. Pat slid his key into the door. 'I'll call you in half an hour? I need to freshen up.'

'Sure. Me too.'

The rooms were blue themed, functional and looked out over Belfast's Cathedral Quarter. Pat let the holdall clank to the floor on the other side of the bed to the door and tossed his own bag onto the blue coverlet. He held his hand out and spread his fingers, watching for shaking. He must be getting used to all this stuff again, he supposed as he ducked into the small white bathroom and twisted the shower on. He stepped out of his clothes, adjusted the water temperature and slipped into the water's welcome sting and steam.

Fifteen minutes later, shower, shit and shave respectively behind him, Pat sat on the bed with the little Glock pistol he'd pulled from the holdall. He had meticulously stripped it down, cleaned it and reassembled its dully gleaming body, packing the little stack of magazines carefully, each carrying ten rounds. The gun had killed his herd of cows and yet he didn't blame it, it was just a tool, bucking in his sweating hand as he had pushed the square barrel against those rough curls of hair and fired. Now the Baby Glock was free of dried blood from the spray, ready to do its work again. Pat pocketed the magazines and slipped the gun into his greatcoat. He peered at himself for a second in the mirror before wheeling and snatching his wallet from the table. He knocked on Orla's door.

'I have to go out, do some stuff. Please don't go anywhere or do anything, just get some dinner on room service and wait to hear from me. Only answer your mobile to me, only answer the door if you've called room service or I've rung you to say I'm coming. Do you understand?'

'But—'

'No buts. This is dangerous. Okay, we're a team but for this one bit of a thing I need to be by myself and to know you're safe. You understand me?'

'Take care.'

He reached out to her cheek. 'I will, sure. Now go in and do as I said.'

The last worshipper had left, stepping out into the rainy

A Decent Bomber

evening darkness. Pat waited in the little office behind the large open room in the big townhouse that had been converted into a mosque. He sat in one of the battered office chairs. Someone had been picking at the foam armrest.

The door opened and the white-haired Imam stepped in, his robes rucked in one hand, a gnarled walking stick in the other. He turned and closed the door carefully behind him. 'I thought perhaps someone was waiting for me. Welcome. I am Abdelkader Ul-Haq.'

'Hello Father. My name's Pat.'

Abdelkader hobbled to behind the desk and lowered himself into the wooden armchair. 'I am not your father. May I sit?'

'Of course. I'm not holding you up. And father is what we call our priests.'

'I know. I was joking with you. It is always best to joke with men who have guns, I am finding.'

'What gun?'

'I know the shapes guns make in clothes, Mister Pat. I come from a troubled place.'

'Well you've certainly hopped out of the frying pan into the fire.'

'Belfast? It is peaceful now. Before, there were troubles. No more. How may I be of assistance to you?'

'I'm looking for a man. Somali or perhaps Ethiopian. He'd perhaps be known to your community.'

Abdelkader's white eyebrow lifted. 'What is his name?

'I don't know. They call him The Accountant. He wears a suit, has expensive tastes. His associates would be known in places like Kabul and Khartoum.'

Abdelkader smiled ruefully, scrutinising the cloth in his hand as it rested on his knee. 'Most accountants are having expensive tastes.'

'You know the man.'

'I have not met him. He is indeed Somali.'

Pat glanced around at the stacks of books pressed in the shelves lining the walls, chipped cream paint shining in the baleful light from the naked bulb above. 'It's funny, these days nobody's ever met anybody.' He waved away the quizzical expression on Abdelkader's face. 'Forget it, it's nothing. What's his real name, this accountant?'

'Hassan Ali Jaffar. May I ask why you seek him?'

'He is a terrorist.'

'And so you come to me? The Muslim?'

Pat nodded. 'I do.'

Abdelkader sighed and shook his head. He pulled at his wispy goatee. 'Most men flee terror, Mister Pat. They do not seek it. Why are you different?'

'He has taken something from me he had no right to.'

'What kind of thing?'

'I can't say.'

'Then where is the trust between us? You ask for information but do not give information. That is a one sided transaction, is it not?'

'As you say, I have a gun.'

'And it is clear you are not minded to simpler methods of negotiation. So. A violent man seeks a violent man. Why am I to be involved?'

'I was man of violence in the past. I retired. If you know where I can find him, tell me and I can leave you in peace.'

'I do not know *him*. Only I know *of* him. He is in Africa, no?'

'No. He is here.'

Abdelkader's shoulder's sagged. 'I am not glad to

hear this. Should you not take this information to the authorities? They would wish to detain him, I think.'

'Perhaps. I thought I might find him first.'

'And what would you do with him, Mister Pat?' Abdelkader pushed himself up using his stick and a hand on the table. His brown eyes were steady under his bushy brows. Pat waited, passive as the old man searched his face. Abdelkader nodded. 'I see. Come back later, perhaps near to eleven o'clock, after the *'Isha* prayer. The door will be open.

'Thank you, father.'

'Go in peace, Mister Pat. *Salaam*.'

The pub was busy, the bar heaving with the football crowd. It was getting loud, even this early, barely past nine. The air was thick with hoppy tang. Pat emerged from the scrum with his glass held high. The match was over and they were getting lary. The landlord of The Boston had a burly security man on the stairs who nodded Pat up. The tiredness weighed heavy on him as he dragged himself up the steps, stopping to pull on his pint so it didn't spill. When he got to the top, he didn't bother knocking. MacNamara sat at the desk, as Pat remembered him some twenty years ago, only there was no smoke in the air or huddle of lads shadowed in the mean light from the yellowed lamp. And MacNamara was older and fatter, of course. A lot fatter.

'We haven't met.'

'Jesus, Brian. How much isn't happening these days? Are ye some sort of ghost?'

'You left an awful mess at the farm.'

'I was in a hurry to get gone.'

'You've been killing people.'

'Never bothered you in the past.'

'Stop. The African boyo. And the two men at the stud farm.'

'You sent him and his friends to me, Brian. And they took my niece.'

'I sent no man.'

'They had the code. They had our stuff. I know it. I helped Cathal stack that gear in his cellar over twenty year ago. Semtex, the lot. I made them boys five briefcase bombs and a bloody big car bomb and it was you told me to do it.'

'I did no such thing. Cathal's dead by their hands.'

'Well now, is that right? I wondered why you were playing around with a load of African boys. You always preferred the Arab boys, didn't you?'

MacNamara raised his finger but shook his head and laid it back down on the desk. 'You're a cheeky fucker, Pat.'

'Did your friends trace the plate I text you?'

'They did. It was a Range Rover, found burned out in a ditch south of Newry. PSNI forensics are all over it and my contact's having to fend off questions about why he was interested in the vehicle. You know one bomb was placed already?'

'No. I've been busy. It didn't go off, then.'

'It didn't, no. They used one of our codes to get through to PSNI. The call came twenty minutes after the device was timed to go. If it had gone off, a lot of people would have been hurt.'

'But it didn't. I made them all broken, but they'll have worked that out by now. The second one will go off, Brian. The others will, too. The big one's 25 kilos of Semtex and about eight hundred kilos of ammonium nitrate packed in a HiAce van. That's going to make a big

A Decent Bomber

hole in somewhere and I'd rather it didn't get that far.'

'They've made a ransom demand. A hundred million quid. The polis found your little piece of origami and they've put two and two together. That and the mess at the farm, you're a very wanted man. I'm probably certifiable for meeting you. Even here.'

'The bombs, Brian. They need to know about the other ones. I tried to stop them, but…'

'They need to know nothing. Christ, there's an election. What the hell did we think all that stuff was for, if not this? We've a chance of changing things now and the last thing we need is being tainted by the past.'

'Tainted? Jesus, Brian, it was the past got you here. You and Sean. I've been watching you both in the papers. Was that what it was all about, the struggle? Getting you two to the trough?'

'We've got peace, Pat. We've got a political process because of that struggle and few men were more important to that fight for our freedom and representation than you were. But this unearthing of the past will drag us down a fucking pit if we're not careful. This whole thing is toxic. We don't need to be caught in between PSNI and these people.'

'What people, though, Brian? The top man's an African, The others are mongrels, all Arabs, Pakis and Chechens. The guy in the bog was Saudi, I'll swear. He spoke Arabic. It's like an Al Qaeda nightmare, isn't it? And they're useless except they got hold of our codes, our explosives and now they've got a load of viable bombs. The whole world has been dancing around with increased security and no liquids and all that stuff, but since 9/11 they haven't managed to do shit. Not really. They're bogeymen, mountain fighters, not urban terrorists. So they crashed into us and you let them use me because you an' Sean are so focused on your *political process,* you're desperate to hide the past.' Pat gulped his pint. 'Ah, shit.'

'Look, it's not like that. We…'

'Trouble is, Brian, you're embarrassed by the likes of me. I'm an *anachronism*. I'm the inconvenient truth, me. Me an' Burke alike. Except these African boys have somehow made their way into our past, burrowing into us like some tropical maggot. Jesus, I was happy left on my farm, I was content enough for over twenty years up on the empty bog with me cattle, except you sold me out to them. Worse, you sold Orla to them. She didn't deserve that. So I reckon I don't owe you anything anymore. And I owe Sean less. Fuck him, to be honest. And fuck the *cause*, whatever the *cause* is these days.'

'You don't want to cross us, Pat.'

A red mist came to him then. His movement was an instinctive blur. MacNamara had no time even to recoil as Pat whipped the pistol out. He squinted down the sheen of the barrel, MacNamara's wide open eyes framed either side of its steel hump. Pat's middle finger curled white around the trigger. His body shook with rage, but his hand was steady. 'Cross *you*? Are you fucking joking me?'

The gun sight glinted with reflected light from the bare bulb above them. MacNamara put his hands up slowly. 'Now then, Pat, let's not be hasty.'

Pat enjoyed MacNamara's pasty-looking face for a few more seconds before raising the gun.

'That bomb. The dud. Where was it?'

'Forestside Shopping Centre.'

'We'll have to find the others before there's a disaster.'

'We, Pat? Who's this 'we'? The police are doing all they can and we support them, clearly. But I'm not about to sanction some vigilante operation.'

Pat slid the gun back into his pocket. 'Will you listen to yourself, man? I've thought many things over the years, but I'd never thought you a coward. There are five viable bombs out there. One of them will blow out a town centre. Remember Manchester?'

MacNamara's head was lowered to his hands. Pat swung around and strode out of the room, the door's slam cutting out MacNamara's voice calling out to him.

Pat parked up a way down the road from the Islamic Centre, preferring to take a soaking and yet choose his own route in to the old Imam. He slipped into the car park, empty now the last prayer of the day was over. The rain glittered in the sodium streetlight. Pat hugged the shadows, taking his time and moving casually, without hesitation but with infinite care. His hand in his greatcoat pocket gripped his Glock. It was quiet, the rain and the hour combining to keep the streets empty. Pat didn't mind rain.

The fish supper he'd had was sitting heavily on him now. He still had salt on his lips, the hint of taste brought by the rainwater running down his face was a remembrance. The back of the building was dark, the front entrance as he had passed it was lit.

Pat tried the back door. The round handle was cold and wet and it turned quietly in his whitened fingers. He pushed against it, letting the door open gently, pausing in the opening of it so the frame wouldn't brush the carpet. The warmth from the building rushed at him. He twisted around and pressed the door closed, quiet as the grave.

Somewhere a clock ticked. Pat stalked down the

carpet-tiled rear hallway, running his hand along the wall. The faint light from the front hallway helped him find the room he'd met the Imam in earlier. He pressed gently on the handle of the office door, the air still and quiet. He could almost hear the building breathing.

The door gave the faintest squeak. He felt the handle buck gently as the ill-fitting lock freed the door. He paused for a heartbeat, listening.

Nothing.

Pat relaxed, pushing the door open. He straightened, taking a breath to greet the old man. He was stilled by the rusty stench of blood in the air. He pulled his hand with the Glock free from his pocket, but it was grabbed from behind as a strong forearm slid around and jerked back against his neck. He felt beard against his cheek as he strained against the force driving his gun hand at the wall. Two massive blows against the plaster numbed his fingers and he dropped the gun, gasping as his neck was freed. He tried to turn and slam his elbow into his assailant, but a heavy metal bar smashed across his back with a force that propelled him into the room. He stumbled, grabbed at the Imam's desk as he tried to arrest his fall, caroming into the body of the Imam in his chair. The slashed throat leered wetly at him, the rubberised hilt of an army knife protruded from the stained chest.

Pat recovered his balance, taking in the big man in the doorway; it had been an AK-47 against his back, not an iron bar. The gun was slung over the man's shoulder, pointed at him. He was wearing fatigues, pale-faced and brown-eyed, straddling the door frame with a sneer on his whiskered face. Behind the door, sitting in the Imam's guest chair with its picked-at foam covering was The Accountant. The African was examining his fingers in the mean light.

'Good evening, Mister Pat. You have come back to me. It is most pleasant to make your acquaintance a further time.'

He was wearing a brown suit and an open-collared white shirt. His cufflinks glinted as he twisted his wrist, holding his hand out to admire it. He grinned at Pat, the light reflecting on his high forehead.

Pat regained his breath, glancing across at the gunman standing in the doorway with his finger on the trigger of the AK-47. He held Pat's Glock loosely in his left hand. The gunman smiled, acknowledging Pat's interest and assuring him he was anticipating a move. Pat relaxed, turning back to the African, who had folded his hands on his lap.

'When I was a child in Mogadishu, I watched a cat have its kittens. A dustbin cat, one of the ones that are thin. You have fat cats here, Mister Pat. In Somalia they are thin. Our dustbins are not so rich. I became interested in the cat and her family, I used to follow their progress, those little kittens playing in the trash of my neighbourhood. I saw myself in them. How slender life can be, how chance it is! These tiny animals, charting their hazardous course through the pickings of a starving nation.' He sighed, shaking his head. 'I befriended one, fed it scraps. I fancied I had saved it from death because its brothers and sisters, they did not make it. Only my cat. He grew bolder and stronger with every day.'

The raised pink palm stilled Pat's urge to tell the man to go to hell and take his cats with him. 'When it was old enough, I shot it. It came to me, even though I held my brother's gun, so I took its life. In coming to me it had given me back the life I had given to it and I took the gift, even as Allah takes us into himself because we took his gift of life. I owned that cat and I took it back.

'Jesus. You're nuts.' Pat recoiled, taking a step back from the seated man and closer to the Imam's corpse in its chair.

'Your leaders rave about poisoned ideologies, about how hopelessness spawns radicalisation, but they're just parroting words. It's about opportunity. If I can serve Allah by cutting down *Kaffirs* and make money from their weakness and idolatry, why wouldn't I choose to take God's work into my hands like I took that cat's life into my hands? I serve God and myself, Mister Pat. We are one. So you see why I am so happy to see you come back to me? I thank you for your gift.'

The gunman shifted and Pat made his move. He hadn't thrown a knife in decades and prayed to God the skill hadn't left him. He reached back and gripped the rubber handle, pulling it from the Imam's chest and firing it at the gunman's throat in a single fluid movement. The throw hit home, burying the knife in the man's neck. The muzzle of the AK-47 blazed. Pat dropped, letting momentum carry him forward to spring at the gunman. The man fell backwards. The deafening automatic fire tore through the ceiling, showering shards of plaster. The magazine empty, the gun clattered against the wall. Pat hit the falling man with his shoulder, punching downwards and desperately reaching out to grab for his Glock as the lifeless hand opened.

They crashed to the floor together, entwined. A single shot rang out from behind and the gunman's body jerked. Pat fired back sightlessly, scrambling to his feet. Snapping off shots behind him, he raced down the darkened corridor. He bounced painfully off the wall as he made the turn. The glow of orange streetlight from the back door snuffed out and Pat fired twice in panic,

A Decent Bomber

snatching at the trigger. The first shot went wide, the second dropped the man. Pat hit the door side on and hard as he twisted to fire behind him. The African ducked back behind the corner, Pat's wild shot tearing into the plaster wall.

Fresh air and a fall onto the tarmac of the car park, the outline of a disabled man painted on the ground rushing up to meet Pat as he tumbled. The door swung back behind him. Pat tried to roll with the fall, almost pulled it off but caught his knee going down. The glass in the door shattered and the wood panel was torn open by a fusillade from inside. Pat barked with the pain in his knee, dragging himself to his feet to run for the shadowed wall.

He sprinted, limping, down the street as sirens sounded. He made it to the car, sobbing for breath. He fumbled with the keys, peering behind him down the street but it stayed empty. He wrenched open the door and flung the Glock into the glove box. He drove off as slowly and calmly as he could, turning left and then right onto the Lisburn Road. Blue lights flickered in the darkness, briefly reflected in his rear view mirror as he turned. Driving along the empty carriageway, he glanced back constantly, but the lights didn't reappear.

Pat woke, disoriented, a confusion of dreams fresh in his head. Turning in the bed, his knee shrieked pain. It was still dark. He calmed himself, glancing around until he got his bearings. *Premier Inn, Belfast*. He groped for the bedside light and winced at its brightness. Blinking and shielding his eyes with a cupped hand, he flicked the hotel duvet back to examine his leg. Christ, but it was a mess. The contusion was ugly, blues and purples; an old man's thin skin torn by the rough tarmac, the bruising livid against his paleness.

He pivoted out of the bed, his bladder was full. He stood, gingerly testing his weight against his wrecked leg. It wasn't so bad. He lurched towards the bathroom, hands reaching for reassuring surfaces.

The bathroom light snapped on, another painful flood of brightness. Pat stumbled, blinking, for the toilet. He leaned against the wall and let the warm stream leave him.

He avoided looking into the bathroom mirror afterwards, knowing he'd just find a pale, tired looking old man staring back at him. He lay back on the bed and stared at the ceiling, resenting the way his quiet life had been torn apart. Sleep finally overcame him.

Orla's call woke him at eight. They met downstairs for breakfast and together they shuffled around, picking at the buffet. Pat tried not to limp, but it was hard. The coffee was good and Pat was on his second cup. Other guests were starting to trickle in as they finished eating. He breathed the rich air, fried food, blasts of cold air now and then as the street door was opened. Coffee.

'What did you do to your leg?'

'Nothing. Fetched it a bump. Getting old and careless, so I am.'

'Where did you go last night?'

'See some people. Got to go and see more now. I'm sorry, it must be boring, but you'll have to hang around here a while longer.'

'I feel like I'm in purdah.'

'It's only for a couple of hours. I reckon we'll be on the move again pretty soon. I'll need to leave the holdall with you in case they make up my room. You can put it back when they're done.'

'Fine. So now I get to look after bags full of—'

'Shhh. Right, I'd best get going. Here's my key. I'll call you in a while.'

Pat wished the receptionist a good morning back as he glanced out of the rain-spattered window on the way to the front door. He pulled his old Crombie around him and braced to meet the weather; the rain hurled at him by the cold wind. He hugged the wall down the road to the car park, thankful to reach the building's cover.

The streets were quiet until the A12, which was heavy with rush hour traffic ploughing through the sheeting rain. Pat had the radio on but switched off in irritation at a particularly bad ad for a bedding shop.

He pulled off the main road into Broadway, terraced houses grim in the grey weather. He parked up outside the tatty little bar to the left, the yellow sign proclaiming it to be *An Bhonnán Bhuí,* The Yellow Bittern. He locked the car and, hunched against the rain, went in.

The bar was fuggy, too early to be busy but a handful of old soaks were propping up the counter already. Conversation lulled as they peered at the newcomer in the door but Pat wasn't bothering with them. He headed for the slot machine where, sure enough, Jackie O'Brien was holding on to the sides of the thing for dear life, an unlit roll-up hanging from his blue-tinged lips. Lank-haired and thin as a rake, O'Brien's pallid skin was bagged up under his lidded eyes.

Jackie's eyes didn't leave the spinning display. 'Now, Pat. How's the craic?'

'Been a while, Jackie.'

Jackie glanced up. He blinked and studied Pat's face for a second, then nodded. 'It has, right enough.'

Pat hadn't seen the man in over twenty years. Jackie returned his attention to the slot machine.

'Bunch of Somali lads in town. Hear anything of them?'

'Them the ones jumped Quinlan and Burke?'

MacNamara hadn't mentioned Quinlan, but it made sense now Jackie mentioned the man.

'That'd be them.'

'Don't know anything about 'em. Just heard they were a nasty shower. Made a mess of Quinlan, right enough.'

'Pint?'

'Go on, so.'

The blonde girl behind the bar was sullen, a spotty rash on the pale breasts pushing at her blouse. Pat paid her and took the two glasses back to the fruit machine.

'See any of the old gang these days?'

'There are a few knocking around here and there. Sean Driscoll's going to be president of the world, apparently. He's been kissing every fucking baby in Belfast. MacNamara holds 'em, Driscoll kisses 'em.'

The machine whooped, lights flashing a celebration that lit O'Brien's chalky skin and bathed it orange and yellow. The pale eyes glistened and a tongue darted out to lick the thin lips as the machine started to pulse, jamming out coins into the tray below. He bent down to scoop them out. He hoisted his catch to the nearest table, piling them in the centre. He sat, placing his pint to one side and started to slide coins away from the pile into his palm, cupped around each little stack of ten he made. Pat joined him at the table. He sipped at his pint and watched the trembling hands and lifeless eyes as they counted up the win. O'Brien eventually sat back with a sigh. 'Eighty eight quid. Fuck me.'

'Quit while you're ahead, Jacks.'

'You're thirty year too late with that advice, Pat.'

'So Driscoll's a politician these days?'

'Fuck, aye. He's the next Gerry, so he is. Only without the beard. Or the personality. Or intelligence. But he kisses babies beautifully, they say.'

Orla was going stir crazy in the airless room at the Premier Inn. She had moved Pat's clunky holdall and asked his room be turned over then dragged it back and slung the 'Do Not Disturb' sign on the door. She didn't look in the bag. She didn't fancy what she'd find in there. Guns had always repelled her, even back at school when the boys had pulled out plastic pistols in the playground and pushed them into her face screaming 'Bang Bang.' The teacher had banned the guns so the boys used the plastic bananas from the toy tray instead.

Beyond the holdall, the morning had brought little excitement. There was TV, but she was never much of a one for gazing vacantly at game shows and that's pretty much all there seemed to be on. That and a programme about Ancient Rome on the History Channel which seemed to consist mostly of fillers promoting the History Channel. She switched off in exasperation.

She had been trying not to think of Róisín and failing. Earlier, waking, she had touched herself, imagining it was Róisín's finger running down from her shoulder. Lying afterwards, cooling and dreamy, she reached for the mobile. Her fingers found the little blue Nokia with the silver swoosh on her bedside table where they'd expected the smooth glass of her Nexus.

It hit her hard, then. She didn't know Róisín's

number. She was cut off. She didn't know anyone's number. The profiles she used to tap were locked away from her.

She called directory enquiries for the number of Queen's College and set about the long task of negotiating the tortuous corridors of the University's Byzantine telephone system. She paced the room, pulled back constantly to the hotel phone handset by the tangled twist of cord. She forced her voice to measured, reasonable tones as she answered the same question ten times over. *What do you mean, how are you spelling Róisín? Christ, you're Irish, you should know what a fucking fáda is.*

She was almost ready to go back to the History Channel when her heart jumped at the rich voice on the line. 'Hello? This is Róisín McManus.'

'Róisín? It's me. Orla.'

'Orla? Why didn't you call my mobile? I've been calling you.'

'Long story. I'm here. Belfast. Can we meet?'

'I have a class coming up. How about later?'

'No. Now. It's important.'

'Why? What is? You went dead on me. Is everything okay? What gives?'

'I'm in trouble and I need help. I shouldn't even be calling you. I can't talk about it. Christ, I'm in the shit, Róisín. Meet me now.'

'Okay, okay. There's a posh restaurant at House of Fraser over at the Victoria does a mean scone, how about there?'

'Done. See you in twenty minutes flat.'

In the end it took her twenty two.

The Ivory was a funky eatery, all slate plates and

leather-cushioned dark wood seats, a curved bar was marble topped and mosaic tiles added to the *beigeness* of it all. Róisín was wearing a leather jacket, drainpipes and a Therapy? t-shirt, a black leather shoulder bag completing the rock chick look, tumbles of black hair, latte skin and black mascara. Orla felt short of breath, her stomach was on a roller coaster somewhere. Róisín stood, smiling her lopsided grin and they hugged. Orla wanted to cry. Róisín kissed Orla's cheeks, inhaling deeply in Orla's ear and the kisses lingering longer than social pecks. Her lips were warm and soft. Their lips met and parted. Their tongues touched and Orla felt herself melting down below, a combination of alarm and euphoria coursing through her like electricity. She broke the embrace, her mind reeling. She grabbed the back of a chair for balance.

'You been ignoring my missed calls?'

'Things have been a bit mad. It's not what you think.'

Róisín tilted her head. 'What I think?'

'Us. That. This. Us.'

'What, then?'

'I don't even know where to begin. My Uncle Pat was in the IRA.'

Róisín snorted. 'Hardly marks him out in South Tipp, does it?'

'No, properly. Not collecting for the boys and wearing Easter Lilies. He made bombs. He went to prison. He was a killer. My Uncle Pat.'

'Orla, a lot of men did all that.'

'That's not it. I mean, that's bad enough, but… Look, I was kidnapped. They took me from the farm to blackmail him into making more bombs for them. He did it and then shot the guy they left to guard him and tracked me down. They had me in a big house somewhere north of

Cashel and he shot them, two men. He killed them both. Now he's looking for his bombs. We're on the run.'

'You're fucking me.'

'*Róisín!*'

Róisín laughed, tossing her jet hair. 'Orla? Do you have any idea of how mad you sound?'

'Yes. Listen. We're on the road together. I'm serious. He's killed three men and he's shot his herd. All of them. He's armed and chasing the terrorists. And I'm with him.'

'Who are "they", anyway?'

'Terrorists. I don't know. They're a mix, Africans, Arabs and the like. The man at the top is called The Accountant. I thought you might know something about him, you know with the terrorism course and everything.'

Róisín's smile faded. 'Jesus. You're not kidding, are you?'

'No, no I'm not. Look.' She held her wrists up to be examined. The bruising from the cable ties they'd used on her was yellowing. 'You know who he is, don't you?'

'Hassan Ali Jaffar. He was Somali. The worst of them. He was too crazy for Al Qaeda. They threw him out. He headed up an African group called Al Shabab, terrorised half of East Africa and then went quiet, presumed dead. But then it can be hard working out who's who. It's like trying to herd cats. Just when you think you've understood the links between one group and another, something else complicates things. It's one of the things that attracted me to the whole idea of taking the course, the complexity and scope of it all.'

'This isn't academic. He's not dead, he's here in Ireland and his people kidnapped me.'

Róisín's features were pinched in recollection. 'Al

Shabab were the people behind the Westgate Shopping Centre attack in Nairobi.'

'The White Widow one?'

'Samantha Lewthwaite. The Kenyan government's been fighting a war against the group, but they're well organised and smart. And they're the most complex of all. They pop up being all Islamic and the next thing you find their hands are in the till. They're commercialising terror. They're behind all sorts of piracy and extortion, like a sort of Muslim Mafia. Basically, any *kaffir* is fair game.'

'*Kaffir*?'

'Unbeliever. You and me, dear.'

'So why can't they make bombs? Why did they need my Uncle?'

Róisín fiddled with the empty espresso cup on the table in front of her. 'At home they're guerrillas, bandits. They're on their own territory, exploiting local networks and all that. Exporting terror's not quite as easy as running amok in a failed state in Africa or the Middle East. They probably don't have the resources or expertise for this. So they found it in Ireland's past. Interesting, actually.'

'I'm glad it's giving you an intellectual challenge.'

'Oh, Christ, I'm sorry. Look, I'm not sure how I can help. The best thing would be to go to the police or the intelligence people. I think one of my lecturers is connected with them, if you want me to have a word.'

Orla didn't know what to do or say. The incongruity of it all hit her hard, here in a café in a shopping mall, with ordinary sounds and people all around her. With this extraordinary girl who had woken something in Orla she had never truly known was there. Orla opened her mouth to speak and realised she didn't know what to say. Tears stung her eyes.

Róisín reached out to her. The restaurant's front door was pushed open by a couple with a small boy toddling suspended between them. Somewhere out in the mall a woman cried out, 'Riley!'

The glass wall of the restaurant turned opaque as it shattered, the table turned to jelly. The glass billowed inwards and blew out, a tide of tiny shards dancing and careening across the wooden floor. A giant warm hand pushed them both with a force that lifted their feet from the floor. Orla fell sideways, glimpsing Róisín hitting the table, upending it as she fell. The concussion wave sent crockery flying.

Orla had never heard anything like the sound of the explosion. The world was silent for a second before it all rushed back in, a clap of thunder that echoed in the mall's high spaces, followed by screams. She curled up foetally, her eyes squeezed shut. There was warmth on her hand, something liquid. She didn't want to see if it was blood but it started to trickle. She opened one eye. It was coffee but her face stung and when she put her fingers up to her cheek they came back red. She managed to still the urge to be sick and pushed herself upright against a table that had fallen on its side. Róisín was spread out on the floor, lying on her back and her leg was at an odd angle. There were other people starting to move in the wreckage of the restaurant, coughing and a man groaning. Something was dripping behind the bar. Wailing alarms echoed alongside screaming from outside in the shopping centre. A man's voice shouted 'Get down!'

Orla crawled over to Róisín. There was blood coming out of her friend's ear. Her eyelids were fluttering and the side of her face was livid and cut, already starting to swell. 'Róisín? It's me, Orla. Can you hear me?'

Róisín tried to nod but winced. She opened dry lips. 'Yes.'

Orla patted herself down to check for damage, then struggled to her feet. She reached behind the bar and lifted a plastic bottle of water. She twisted off the cap and put the bottle to the girl's pale lips, tipping it gently as she drank. Róisín turned her head away from the water. She swallowed, a series of little dry convulsions. She struggled to speak.

'Hush. Leave it. Keep your energy.' Orla turned and shouted 'Help! Help!'

'Orla. Orla. Listen. He's the worst.'

'I know, but stop talking now. Save it for later.'

Róisín's smile was a tired grimace, her eyes closed. She shook her head. 'Too weak. Oh, God.'

Orla picked up her friend's hand and rubbed it. 'It'll be fine. Help's on the way.'

'Orla, I… I want to…'

'Hush, please, for the love of God, Róisín.'

Chapter Nine

Boyle met Detective Superintendent Wayne McLoughlin outside the mall, just beyond the flapping tape cordon, the crowd behind them. Sirens were still sounding, an ambulance pulling away as another took its place, paramedics wheeling gurneys out to meet it. As always, McLoughlin's uniform was impeccable, the chrome buttons and rosettes gleaming. They paused a few hundred feet from the front entrance and stood together surveying the great glass dome, now a misshapen empty frame with a few shards still clinging to the lower corners. The grey sky roiled behind it. The rain had stopped at last.

'Who did this?'

'Same group as last time only this one went off. Same MO, a call using a Provo code placed just as the device detonated. That's all we know for now.'

'It's a mess.'

They strode into the mall together. Glass crunched underfoot. Boyle marvelled at the carpet of the stuff strewn across the shining marble floor. A young officer walked over to join them. He had a crew-cut and wore a flak jacket, his G17 pistol handle gleaming dully in its black holster. 'Good morning sir.'

'Nothing good about it, Bates.' McLoughlin was gruff.

Boyle's deputy, Ewan Bates was well known for his detachment and professionalism in extreme situations. The grip in response to Boyle's handshake was cool and firm.

McLoughlin kicked at glass on the floor as they walked. 'What's the situation?'

'We've four dead and about eighty injured, twelve serious and two critical. Most of the injuries are glass cuts or flesh wounds from shrapnel. It was a single device, likely five kilos or so of plastic explosive, packed into a briefcase. This one contained nails and ball bearings. Dirty bastards, sir.'

Bates halted. Boyle peered up at the concentric circles of shattered shop windows arcing up to the ruined dome above. Bates gestured towards a taped-off area, a white tent already erected. 'The epicentre of the blast. It's pretty much the perfect place for maximum damage and impact. If I had to guess, I'd say it would be a copycat of the device that didn't go off at Forestside, except for the additional hardware. Looks like they've properly got the hang of it now.'

McLoughlin took his hat off and stood in silence, his head down and his hat clutched in both hands. He turned to Boyle, who fancied he saw moisture in those hard eyes. 'Have MacNamara and Driscoll brought in to Brooklyn House. Don't feel you have to be particularly subtle or gentle about it. Let Driscoll know they're being detained under prevention of terror and I'd be just as happy see them held in cells but I'm feeling generous. Ring me when they're both there.'

Boyle tipped an imaginary forelock. 'Righty-ho, chief.'

The press had already formed a scrum outside the shopping centre when Boyle had left and he had to admit to being pretty impressed at the speed another pack had assembled to camp out along the street outside the entrance to Brooklyn House. Boyle had never liked journalists much and he liked them even less right now. The apocalyptic scene at the Victoria Square Shopping

Centre was still fresh in his memory as the pack clambered on wheelie bins to try and poke cameras thorough the razor wire topping the boundary wall of the PSNI compound.

He flipped his ID at the gate as he drove through after the squad car containing a furious Sean Driscoll. Following McLoughlin's instructions to the letter, Boyle had made a big scene dragging Driscoll out of a women's group meeting, ably supported by four well-briefed PSNI uniforms who had called Driscoll 'Sir' in loud and hectoring tones. The sort of 'Sir', Boyle reflected happily, you use when a dog's not sitting down properly.

Boyle strode up to the meeting room, Driscoll buffaloed along behind him by the uniforms. He kicked the door open. 'Mister MacNamara. Nice to see you again.'

Brian MacNamara was halfway to his feet. 'Boyle. What the hell's going on?'

'The fruits of your careful hoarding are being enjoyed by the people of Belfast. Or are you deaf?'

'So it was a bomb.'

'Aye, a big, dirty one full of IRA Semtex along with a load of nails and ball bearings. Four dead.' Driscoll was barged into the room. 'So the two of youse are properly in the shite.'

Boyle hit the screen of his mobile and lifted it to his ear as he left the room.

'McLoughlin.'

'Boyle. Got 'em both.'

'Be there in ten. No refreshments.'

'Got it.'

Boyle sauntered back into the meeting room, standing at the picture window and gazing out at the flat sky.

Driscoll rearranged his clothing dramatically, a man

roughed up by brutal police. 'Look here, I don't know what you lot think you're doing, but you've gone too far. I demand you press charges immediately or let us go.'

Boyle pulled up a seat at the meeting table and keyed up Angry Birds on his mobile. He rocked back on the hind legs of his chair, playing with the sound turned up. He glanced up, raising an eyebrow at MacNamara's low laughter.

'Jesus, Boyle, but you are some bollix, you know that?'

Boyle returned to the serious business of smashing piggies and had just demolished a particularly difficult bunch when McLoughlin burst in, all skinny six foot two of him exuding angry energy. Boyle killed the game, slowly letting his chair tip forward.

'I'll charge you in an instant, so don't waste my time with bluster, Driscoll. There has been a deadly bombing and I'm holding you two responsible. I want all your cards on the table where I can see them or I'm throwing every charge in the book at you, including bringing in MI5 to test the legal implications of turning you over to the Americans for some mid-Atlantic in-air waterboarding. Four people are dead and over eighty injured, a major shopping centre is in tatters and you supplied the fucking explosives that did it.'

'I want a lawyer.'

'Driscoll, you're not listening to me. I have men and warrants ready to raid every single member of your party at home, turn over your headquarters and freeze the last penny you own jointly and severally. I'm done fucking around with you. You haven't pissed straight with me since this all started and you're going to piss straight now or I'll roast you.'

Boyle was impressed. For the first time ever he saw real emotion on Sean Driscoll's features and it was a fascinating spectacle. Driscoll rose to his feet, puce and trembling and the cloth of his tan jacket tight over his shoulders. 'You want to reverse the whole fucking peace process in one meeting McLoughlin? You got it. We'll go back to the way it was and fine by me.'

'Ten years ago, you'd have scared me. Right now I don't buy it. Your caches are blown and the men who'd bear arms for you have learned that gardening is altogether more pleasurable than bombing. You're a spent force and you just won't face the truth of that. But then the truth is something you simply can't deal with anyway.'

'Enough.' MacNamara was on his feet too. 'Jesus, you both sound like school kids. We'll tell you everything we know, but we need immunity from prosecution in return.'

'No deals. Just the truth.'

'You'll have the truth and all of it, but with immunity.'

McLoughlin banged the table. 'Four innocent people dead? All those injured? A shopping mall in ruins? And you're still worrying about your own skin?'

A female officer put her head around the door and caught Boyle's eye. She beckoned urgently to him. He slipped away from the table, joining her out in the corridor. 'What is it, Mary?'

Her voice was low. 'We've got the final list of dead and wounded. One of the dead is a six year old girl, Riley Burnock. Her mother, Simone, is in a critical condition.'

An unusual name, Riley. Mary was waiting for his reaction, an expectant look in those clear blue eyes. Boyle was bewildered for a second and then light dawned and his jaw dropped. 'Oh, fuck, no.'

'Yes. She's Brian MacNamara's granddaughter.'

A Decent Bomber

'Right. Get me a meeting room arranged, a small one and fast. And get me some brandy in there.'

Boyle kicked back into the meeting room. 'Mister MacNamara, can I ask you to come with me, please?'

'He's going nowhere,' McLoughlin thundered.

'Brian.'

MacNamara's face clouded and he stood, uncertain. He stepped towards Boyle.

'I'm telling you, Boyle. He's going nowhere.'

'Just one second. Sir.'

It was the 'Sir' did it. Boyle hadn't called McLoughlin that in the ten years he'd been in C3. McLoughlin was stunned into silence and MacNamara stepped towards Boyle enough that he could take the man's arm and shepherd him out of that poisonous room and follow Mary Dwyer down the corridor to a smaller meeting room where, miraculously, she had managed to place two glasses and a half-empty bottle of Tyrconnell.

Boyle poured. 'Sit down, Brian. Here.'

MacNamara's face was ashen. 'What is it?'

'It's Riley. Your wee granddaughter. She was at the shopping centre. She's one of the four dead. Simone's hurt bad. I'm getting more information for you right now but I wanted you to know as soon as we heard. I'm sorry, I'm truly sorry.'

MacNamara's craggy features crumpled. Boyle took a gulp of whiskey and wished he'd asked Mary for tissues as well. He turned away as tears splashed down the big man's cheeks, dropping to the blue Formica surface of the meeting room table, where they glittered in the neon light.

'Please God, no. No, no.'

Boyle fidgeted, everything he thought of saying dismissed before his lips could form the words.

MacNamara lifted his head to face Boyle. 'How? How did she die?'

His dry throat turned Boyle's answer into a croak. 'It was instant. She had run away from her mum, an eyewitness heard her name called. She wouldn't have known a thing about it.'

'Simone?'

'She's critical but stable. I don't have more details yet but I've asked for them.'

'What am I going to do? Who's going to tell Jean? Christ, this'll kill her. She lived for that child. That beautiful, baby child.'

Boyle put a hand out to touch MacNamara's shoulder only to have it batted away savagely. MacNamara twisted to face him, his tear-streaked face red and furious. The anger drained away in an instant. 'I'm sorry. Sorry. You've been good. I don't… I can't…'

'It's okay, Brian. Nobody should be given news like this. Look, stay here a while and I'll try and find out more about Simone. I'll send Mary in and she'll keep McLoughlin at bay while you gather yourself together.'

He found Mary down the corridor chatting to a colleague. She turned to him, tucking a strand of hair behind her ear. 'He's in a bad way. Could you go in and hold his hand for me while I deal with McLoughlin?

'Of course. Leave it with me.'

His hand on the meeting room door handle, Boyle turned to watch her walking down the corridor. Boyle and Mary Dwyer had history and she had a fine arse, even in PSNI issue trousers. He sighed and pushed the door open.

MacNamara was hunched in on himself when Boyle

crept back into the meeting room and pulled up a chair. He was careful to keep his tone gentle. 'Will I take you home to her?'

'No. I'll drive.'

'I don't think so, you've drink taken. I'll drop you off and we can bring the car later.'

MacNamara gaped up, blinking at the empty bottle. 'Fair play.'

'Simone is hurt badly. She got hit by two nails, one severed an artery but they got to her in time and stopped the bleed. She's lost a lot of blood, but she's alive.'

'Thank God for small mercies,' MacNamara whispered. 'But Riley…'

MacNamara reached out for a clutch of paper tissues. He blew his nose and folded the hankies over and over in his big hands.

MacNamara's shoulders started to heave again and Boyle sat in silence until he had stilled. 'Tell me about Pat O'Carolan.'

'What is there to tell? You know it all. He made bombs, got caught, served his time and retired. That's all there is. We lost touch, went our ways. Until these crazies showed up.'

Boyle curbed his instinctive snort of derision.

'I'm telling you all I can, Boyle, the best way I know. I'm not at my cleverest right now. Cathal Burke was storing about fifty kilos of Semtex. There were detonators, tremblers and ammonium nitrate. The Africans forced O'Carolan to make five suitcase bombs, each one is packed with about five kilos of Semtex. And they had him make a car bomb. There's about eight hundred pounds of ammonium nitrate and Semtex packed into a white Toyota HiAce van. He says they're all timer based but he fixed one with a wireless detonator as well. He'd planned to trigger it when they left with the bombs, but it didn't work out that way. He'd never meant to let those bombs into the wild.'

'You've been in touch with him?'

'Aye.'

'So he took a big gamble, tried to take things into his own hands. And he lost. They packed the second suitcase with nails and ball bearings before they planted it. That's what hit your daughter and her kid.'

'He tried to stop them getting away with it, sure.' MacNamara fumbled with the wad of tissues. 'Pat's going after them. He was an operator in his day, a dangerous man. You're best working with him rather than trying to pull him in.'

'That's not how we work. There's a law to be upheld here and we won't allow vigilantism. His best bet is to give himself up and I'll see to it he has a fair trial.'

MacNamara chuckled, a grim little detonation. 'You have very little chance of that happening.' He straightened and Boyle caught the hard gleam in MacNamara's eye, the man was tight-lipped and trembling. 'A snowball's chance in hell, in fact.'

'Come on. Let's get you home.'

Boyle went to sleep that night with Jean MacNamara's look of dawning comprehension etched in his mind. She had opened the door to them, the light fading and a cold, lazy wind blowing. She was curly-haired and going grey; her face was lined, smoker's skin. She had stared at MacNamara, her eyes flickering between his and her hand flying to her mouth. 'Oh God, no. Not the Victoria. Don't say they were at the Victoria.'

'Simone's okay, love. I've just been at the hospital.

They say she's going to be fine.'
 It was a whisper. 'Riley.'
 Boyle had to look away.

Chapter Ten

Orla woke in pain. The room swam, came slowly into focus and then wasn't a room, but a curtain drawn around her. The back of her hand felt strange, she glanced down and saw the little blue plastic cannula taped there, the gleaming tube leading away up to the drip above her.

It was noisy beyond the curtain, the sound of doors smashed open and then flapping as a gurney was pushed through, urgent voices. Orla prised her dry lips apart and tried to reach for the water on the bedside cabinet but she was too weak and scared she'd upset the drip somehow.

'Hello?' She croaked. She tried again, louder. 'Hello?'

The curtain twitched open and a face appeared. She was Asian: almond-eyed with bad acne and full lips. 'Hello back. You're awake, then.' The nurse rustled in her crisp cotton uniform as she slipped through the curtain, pulling it shut behind her. She smiled down at Orla. 'You're probably feeling a bit rough.'

Orla tried to smile, but things were getting wavery.

'It's okay, we gave you a sedative. You might be a little bit fuzzy. You're a bit bruised and you have some glass cuts, but you were really lucky, you haven't broken anything.'

'Your English is really good.'

'It should be. I was born in Castlereagh.'

Ah shit, Orla thought. Everything seemed a little distanced from reality, disassociated from the real world. She could get used to this; it was a bit like being very, very pissed.

The nurse was taking her pulse, Orla's wrist gripped

by cool, tiny fingers. *Father Phillip Eno*. She tried not to giggle and failed. She responded to the raised eyebrow. 'This is good stuff you've given me, seriously.'

The nurse nodded, professional.

Orla started to remember. 'What was it? What happened to us?'

A moment of confusion passed across the girl's features. 'Oh, you mean the bomb. It was a bomb. At the shopping centre.'

Orla was still trying to process that one when the curtain twitched again and a male nurse came in. He was dark-skinned and smiling, his manner professional and clipped. 'Ah, so you're awake. Orla O'Carolan, isn't it?'

The girl smiled reassurance. Orla struggled with the torpor. 'Yes, yes it is.'

'Here, your bag. We took your ID from it to admit you.'

Orla went to reach for her bag, but the sight of the cannula in her hand stilled her. The Asian girl took the purse and laid it down on the bedside cabinet for her.

He was garrulous, holding onto the curtain. Orla dully noticed he was wearing silicon gloves. She hated the things, all that powder inside them. She could never figure how people wore them all day. 'We got in touch with your father. He's coming to get you. He was very worried. Apparently you're supposed to be on a farm in Tipperary.'

That was true enough. Orla fought down a wave of strange, fuzzy-edged panic. What would Da say to all this? How could she even start to explain herself? There was something else, nagging at her battered consciousness like a forgotten word.

'And the police want to talk to you as soon as you're well.'

Uncle Pat. Oh Jesus. Oh God. Orla struggled to get her breathing under control. How did she get into this?

He twitched the curtain. 'Well, I've got to get on. Mary here will look after you.'

'Do you feel up to eating something?'

Orla shook her head. 'I could use a coffee though. My head's fuzzy.'

'That'll wear off soon enough. Sugar?'

'Please.'

The nurse stood and smoothed down her uniform. 'Coming right up.'

Orla watched her through the curtain then grabbed for her bag. Sure enough, the little blue Nokia was in there, five missed calls from Pat. The nurse returned. 'They'll bring your coffee in a tick.'

Orla dropped the mobile onto her bed. Mary took her unresisting hand. 'Right. I'm just going to remove the cannula. This won't hurt.'

A tearing sensation and a jab of pain, then Mary was swabbing the back of Orla's hand with an alcohol soaked cotton wool pad. She laid a plaster across the little wound and bruise. 'There.'

Orla flumped back into the pillow. Despite her panic and confusion, lassitude crept. She wanted to ask about Róisín, but Mary had stood and was smiling down at her. She didn't have the energy to call up.

'Get some rest. I'll let them know you're not up to it for now. I'll come back in a little while.'

She slipped through the curtain. Orla tried to make her traitorous mouth work, her fingers grasping for the rectangle of blue and silver plastic. She slipped into the darkness instead.

A Decent Bomber

Pat gave up hammering on the door of Orla's hotel room and slid the card key into the lock of his own. He shucked off his coat and lifted the handset by his bedside to call reception. He was stilled by a momentary sensation of disorientation, the ground under his feet fleetingly liquid. It was a feeling he knew well. He braced. The explosion was close by. The dull blossoming of its report reverberated in the streets outside. The window shook.

Pat pulled aside the net curtain to see the ball of black cloud rising above the rooftops, billowing up to meet the dull grey cloud hanging over the city. He rested his forehead against the cold glass, eyes screwed shut. *Just like the old days.*

He counted to ten. He wanted to pinch himself but he knew well enough this was real. He muttered 'Fuck' and watched his exhaled word fog the glass. He felt old and helpless and stupid. He opened his eyes and considered the roiling cloud's rise. The urge to action hit him, any action.

'Reception.'

'Hi. I'm looking for Orla Shaughnessy?'

'I'll just check for you sir.'

She put him on hold. Bathroom music. The black smoke was fading into a smudge across the overcast sky. The rise and fall of sirens echoed across the city.

'She's doesn't appear to be in her room, sir. Can I take a message?'

'No, that's fine.'

He called MacNamara. Orla used to tease him about knowing phone numbers for people, but back in the day that's what you did. People weren't icons on a screen then, they were people. Well, numbers at least. He missed her. Sirens sounded across the city as he listened to the ringtone.

'Brian MacNamara.'

'It's Dan Breen. Howya?'

'Jesus. You can't call me like this.'

'Didn't I just?'

'Look, not now. It's a bad time. You should know the police are after you, Pat. You're a wanted man. I can't be found talking to you. I have to go.'

'The call's made and logged, Brian. The damage is done. Listen to me for a second.'

'Pat, give yourself up. The police know you're behind the bombs. They're going to hunt you down. Times have changed. It's different being on the lam these days, there are cameras everywhere. They'll listen to you if you walk in of your own free will.'

'The hell they will. You're not thinking straight. There's a bunch of African fellows dancing around Belfast waving guns and bombs and PSNI is looking for *me*? They'll be as good at listening as they are at looking.'

'Pat, I have to go—'

'Hamid, the Libyan. Remember him?'

'Libyan? What Libyan?' MacNamara stuttered. 'Oh, you mean the Gaddafi fellow?'

'That's him. Whatever happened to him?'

'What the hell's he to do with anything?'

Another set of sirens, closer. Pat lifted the base of the phone and wandered over to the window to peer down at the street and the wash of blue lights.

'What happened to him?'

'He married an Irish girl, opened a shop, the Free Africa Bookshop or something. Settled down. What's it matter?'

'You sent us in to do for him and changed your mind at the last minute. You decide doing a favour for Gaddafi wasn't worth it in the end?'

'This is a telephone conversation, Pat. I never spoke to any Gaddafi in my life.'

'Big, is it, the trough you and Sean are looking forward to?'

'Now, Pat—'

Pat cut the line. *What a useless bastard*. And then he felt bad, because MacNamara hadn't deserved that. Pat called directories for the number of the Free Africa Bookshop and was rewarded with the number for the Free Africa Information Bureau instead. The number rang out. He tried again.

Sirens whooped past the hotel. Pat twitched the netting to see two white PSNI Range Rovers and a fire engine pass by in the street below. The number rang out. Pat kicked the holdall under the bed and pulled his Crombie from the chair. He slipped it on as he left. He closed the door behind him. The Glock sat deep in the greatcoat's pocket. In the lift he unhooked it from the lining and held it nestled in the cloth, laid straight against himself. He squeezed the short grip, the sensation oddly reassuring. He realised there was a camera and he looked like he was playing with himself. He withdrew his hand and crossed his arms.

Striding through reception, he stopped and caught the eye of the blonde behind the desk.

'What was the big bang, do ye know?'

She smiled. Red lips, blue eyes, peach skin. 'A bomb, they say, sir. The Victoria Centre.'

'And that's something to smile about, is it?' He watched the expression fade on her face for a second before he turned and barged out of the front door into the damp streets. Sirens were still sounding from all around, the pall of smoke had faded into the sluggish clouds.

Bathed in the orange light of the car park, Pat dug the keys out of his coat pocket and got into the Polo. The pistol in his pocket dug into him as he sat and he pulled it out and slipped it into the glove box.

He pulled out into the road, the wipers sloshing away across the screen. He turned left onto Bridge Street and a tailback, tapping the wheel as he waited. The cars ahead inched forwards. He craned to see what the problem was but there was a big van two cars ahead. The right lane moved and he was about to try and hustle into it when the van moved and he saw the cars were being turned around. He was momentarily frozen by indecision. The gap in front of him opened up and the car behind beeped him. The blare of the horn attracted the attention of the two cops at the roadblock.

Pat pulled up to them, winding down his window and gesturing at their white Range Rover. 'What's the problem?'

'Morning, sir. There's been an explosion at the Victoria Shopping Centre, I'm afraid. The whole area's cordoned off while the first responders do their jobs. I'll have to ask you to turn around.'

'A bomb, was it?'

'Can't rightly say, sir. Can I ask you to turn back?'

'Sure, sure. Thanks.'

'Pleasure.'

Pat turned the car, a tight three-point. He was just about to straighten up when the copper tapped on his window. He managed not to jump and wound it down with what he hoped was an appropriate look of puzzled surprise.

'Your brake light isn't working Sir. Driver's side.'

Pat cursed silently. 'I'm sorry I hadn't noticed.'

'People rarely do. Just so you know. Have a nice day.'
'Thanks.'

Funny, his pulse was normal. Pat was settling back into old ways. The thought was discomforting, somehow. The traffic was bad everywhere now, tailbacks from the roadblocks starting to gridlock the area. Pat struck out for the Westlink, trying to bypass the bad-tempered jams, but the going was slow to grinding.

Pat tried not to think about the bomb, his bomb, going off in a shopping centre. He'd forgotten so much, but would never forget the time he'd had to walk through the aftermath of a device gone off in Camden. He was usually out of the way before they went, he just made the things and other, invisible hands placed them. This one should have been put in a bin outside the Kentucky in Oxford Street but they'd screwed things up. He had got caught in the crowds as the police cleared Camden Street and Pat, trying to get out of the press and still be inconspicuous, watched it go up. The same stupid thought kept turning over in his mind *the wrong Kentucky*. Glass flying, a man thrown into the air by the blast. Women shrieked. The crowd turned animal and people kicked and clawed their way free of the others, the urge to flee sending them in all directions.

Pat had stood and surveyed the fallen. A wee girl with blood streaming down her face stared back at him, her face blank and uncomprehending. She was blonde and tiny, maybe four years old. Her white dress had little roses on it and was streaked crimson. Her leg was cut open; the lips of the cut curled back and red flash gaped. She was crying.

She was utterly alone. Pat wanted to get away but his own legs betrayed him. The wee girl wiped blood from her left eye and stared at her gory hand. She screamed, a high-pitched, repetitive howl. A woman ran to the child and scooped her up, held her and comforted her. Blood spattered from the tip of her shoe onto the street and Pat wondered how much of it there was in a person that small. The sounds of the street rushed back, shouting and sirens, people yelling and, from somewhere, the futile shrill of a police whistle. Pat wheeled and strode away from his handiwork, tears streaming down his face.

It wasn't remorse, mind. The British had killed Pat's own baby, still nestling in his lover's womb. Her red hair fanned out, her pale hands splayed to ward off the weight of the earth. The anger had sustained him through his years in prison and Brian MacNamara had talked him into going to London and taking the fight right back to their heartland. Pat joined the London active service unit. He was too hard back then to feel remorse. But it was all too easy to be hard when you only had to deal with the concept of your actions, not the brutal reality. He allowed his humanity to drain away and just leave the hardness. He was helping other people's babies to die like his own, but he was never going to bring his own baby girl back by hurting others.

Girl.

They'd only found that out when they did the post mortem.

He'd never told her, but Orla was named for his dead fiancé on account of her hair being red. Mikey had made Pat want to cry when he did that, and he'd always been inordinately fond of the girl.

Caught up in his thoughts, Pat almost didn't notice the purple scooter four cars behind him, but as it slipped through the traffic it caught his eye and he remembered one behind him at the roadblock in the city centre.

He pulled off the Westlink onto the ramp. The scooter

stayed on the main road, blonde hair poking out from under its rider's helmet. Pat relaxed as he approached the big double circle of wire mesh that decorated the roundabout ahead of him.

Pat jumped at the vibration and ring of the Nokia in his pocket. A car beeped him and he realised he'd let the car wander across the road. He straightened the wheel and delved in the deep pocket for the damn handset.

This time when Orla woke, the disorientation was only momentary. She was in hospital. She tried flexing her arms and legs. No pain. Her head throbbed, though. She called out, 'Hello?'

The nurse, Mary, pirouetted through the curtain. 'Are you feeling better now?'

Orla nodded. 'Yes, thanks.'

'That's great, because to be honest we need the bed. Do you think you can stand up?'

Orla pushed herself up to a sitting position and slid around to sit on the side of the bed. Her head swam and she paused to let things settle down.

'Your clothes are here on the chair. I'll give you a couple of minutes to get dressed. Can I tell the police you'll talk to them now?'

'No.' what was she going to say to them? She needed to find Róisín and get out of here. The mobile was in her bag on the floor. Mary was observing her. 'I'm not ready for that. Not yet. Can you tell me where they've taken Róisín?'

'Róisín?'

'Yes, Róisín MacManus. She was with me. In the explosion.'

The nurse's face clouded. 'I don't know. Let me find

out while you get your things on.'

'Thanks.'

The curtain draped closed and Orla dived for the mobile. Another wave of dizziness hit her as she tried to pull her clothes on and she sat heavily on the chair.

She tried to keep her voice low. 'Uncle Pat? It's me.'

'Orla, where for the love of God are you?'

'Hospital. There was a bomb.'

'At the Victoria Square. I know. Why? Were you there? Are you hurt?'

'Yes, I was there. No, I'm not really hurt. They put me in a bed but they want it back now.'

'Which hospital is it?'

'I don't know.'

'Ask someone.'

'I can't. I'm in this cubicle and the police want to talk to me.'

'Is there a table at the bedside?'

'Yes.'

'Open the drawer. Look in the bible.'

She slid open the drawer to find a Gideon bible and, sure enough, it was stamped in indigo ink, *Do not remove. Property of Royal Victoria Hospital, Belfast*.

'The Victoria. How did you—'

'I'm just cute like that. Hold on, I'm coming to you. I'm about ten minutes away. And don't speak to anyone. You hear me? Anyone.'

Orla finished pulling on her t-shirt. It was splashed with rusty stains and she grimaced as she wondered whose life's essence was soaked into the cotton. Her jeans were similarly spattered. The curtain rings clinked and she glanced up to meet Mary's brown eyes and drawn lips. She tried to stand to meet the news, but her body failed her.

'I'm sorry, love. Your friend is dead.'

Orla pushed forward, her mind a silent scream. *No, you don't understand she wasn't my friend. She was so much more than that, you couldn't even begin to imagine. She showed me something about myself I held back. She ended my confusion and showed me the truth I denied myself. She made me whole. She brought love to me and taken me to heights I never imagined in a few days that changed my life. I wanted her to be with me, alongside me. In me.*

She pitched forwards, hitting Mary as she flailed for support and crashed to the ground. Her stomach rebelled and stinging bile forced its way into her throat and mouth. She heaved, on her hands and knees, her tears dropping into the puddle of puke on the shiny floor.

Pat scanned the A&E waiting area but it was packed, busy and urgent. He tried not to get in the way as he searched for her beacon hair. The nurse at reception had said she'd be here, but for the life of him he couldn't…

'Uncle Pat! Over here!'

He loped over. 'Are you okay?'

She was pale, even for Orla. Her hair was wet at the ends. She smelled of soap and toothpaste. 'Yes, fine.'

'Well, you look terrible. Come on, we'd best move on out of here.' He offered her up his hand and she took it.

The voice turned them both around. 'Orla?' Two PSNI officers stood behind them, Laurel and Hardy. One fumbled for his radio, the other smiled, a tight, professional grin.

'Yes. Is there a problem?' Orla was too brittle. The officers stiffened.

'We just wanted to chat to you for a second.' He turned to Pat. 'Can I ask who you are?'

'Her uncle.'

The two made eye contact. Pat slid his hand into his pocket to grab the butt of the Glock. Just as fat man was raising his hand, Pat whipped the pistol out at them. 'Take your fucking hands down.'

Confused, both men raised their hands and stepped back. The fat one caught a trolley full of instruments with his heel and flailed for balance. He grabbed at his pal who struggled indecisively, unsure if he could lower his hands, pulled down by the weight of his colleague. They crashed to the floor, the trolley spilling a cloud of bandages, sharps and bottles across the shiny floor.

'Fucking *ludramans*. Orla! Move!'

Pat half lifted, half dragged her away. They hobbled down the ward together, shocked expressions all around. They burst through the swinging doors and Pat slipped his pistol hand under his flapping coat. Orla was like a deadweight and he urged her on: 'Orla, come !'

'She's dead.'

'Not now. Fuck, not now. Come along, will you?'

A male nurse stepped into their path, his hands held out to block them. 'Can I help you?'

The resolution surged through Pat. He hit out, a scything blow with the Glock in his hand. It caught the guy across the cheek, snapping his head back and driving him to the floor. Orla stumbled and Pat shouted at her, 'Orla! Jesus, move!'

The swing doors banged open, a cry of 'Stop! Police!' and Laurel and Hardy were there, stabbing guns around them. Pat let loose a shot and it reverberated through the stairwell, a puff of plaster and chip driven out of the ceiling above the coppers' heads. They ducked and Pat drove Orla with him down the stairway, firing a second wild shot to keep the busies' heads down.

They sprinted through reception, Pat waving his pistol and yelling at people to move aside. Screaming, the crowd jostled to avoid them. Stumbling out into the cold, he pulled her to him as she faltered.

They made the car park. He shot out the camera. Seven rounds left. Orla was keening and he tried to reassure her, pulling her to him as he dragged her through the clean rain to the car. He bundled her into the passenger seat.

It wasn't that Orla felt numbed by events so much as cheated. Everything she'd been brought up to believe was right was wrong. She was being hurled from tragedy to disaster with such sickening pace she hadn't even had time to think about who she was, let alone where she was.

Now, sitting in the wheezing Volkswagen Polo and speeding down the Westlink, she huddled into her denim jacket and gazed along the spattered rust trails on her jeans. So much blood had been spilled, every drop a vital part of a living thing. People, animals, all. Some of these burgundy marks would be Róisín's blood. Orla toyed with the idea of sucking the cloth to take some little remnant of Róisín's being into herself so they could be joined again, for just a second of realised sensation. A tiny sacrament.

They could have lived a whole lifetime together. Sixty, seventy years even. They could have grown old and crotchety or maybe would have flared and burned like fireflies, a brief summer of passionate heat before winter's cold. She would never know. But for her Róisín would always represent her awakening.

For however long *always* was to be.

Uncle Pat had the radio on for the news. And sure enough it came, the voices excited and urgent. Terrorists, bombs, suspects. Orla missed the words, they blurred into a series of barks. She was kissing Róisín and feeling that moment of completeness. Tears came again, stinging her eyes. Her throat burned as she tried to cry quietly, burying her miserable face against cold glass and plastic. The radio faded. Pat's hand squeezed her shoulder.

'Orla, it's okay. We'll get you back to the hotel and settled. You've seen too much danger. It's time to go home, love.'

Truth be told, she surprised herself with the violence of her reaction. 'No. I want to see this through. They killed her.'

The weight of his hand lifted as he steered around the roundabout into the North Road. 'Killed who?'

What to tell him? What to say? She'd been burning up with ways to broach the subject, but looking back at then, whenever *then* was, she'd hardly known the man. He had been her Uncle Pat before *this*. He was her rock and safety net, the gentle man who loved farming and animals and who had inspired her to take up her university course, dedicate her life to the land. Now he was a killer with a lifetime's history of murder and imprisonment and somehow being a dyke didn't seem such a big deal anymore.

'Róisín. My girlfriend, my partner was killed in the explosion.' Grief bowed her.

'Jesus, Orla. I'm sorry.' She glanced up at him through the curtain of her hair, but he was distracted, checking the mirrors and glancing around nervously. 'I didn't know you had a friend in Belfast. Had you known her long?'

Three weeks. A lifetime. 'A while.'

'Okay, we have to get out here. We're dumping the car.'

'Here?'

'Yes, here. We've been on Candid Camera and it's time we left the stage. We can take the bus back into town.'

'There are cameras on the buses, too.'

'It'll be a while before anyone finds this, let alone thinks to check bus cameras. We'll be long gone by then. Come on.'

Pat locked the car. Orla shivered. He wrapped his arm around her and she burrowed into his warmth and comfort. They left the car park and walked up the Ormeau Road. 'We'll have to get you some clothes. There can't be that many blood-stained redheads in Belfast right now.'

'This blood is all I have left of her.'

Pat halted and turned to face her. He lifted her chin with his finger and she found herself blinking back tears again, looking into his quizzical brown eyes. 'When you said girlfriend...'

She gulped. 'I meant with a capital G.'

He searched her face for a few seconds before nodding. He folded her into his embrace and she cried into the lapel of his greatcoat while he stroked her head and murmured Irish endearments. She wanted to curl up in the dark and warm and never have to face the world again but a distant siren forced her back to reality. She pulled away. 'I'm sorry, Uncle Pat. It's just—'

'Hush now.' He wiped her cheek. 'Right now you look like you could use a meal and a sleep, girl.' He put his arm around her shoulder and they marched together up the Ormeau Road towards the bus stop.

Chapter Eleven

It was past nine and the office was still buzzing. Boyle sipped his cold coffee and rubbed his chin. Stubble. It had been a long day of mayhem and despite being given access to any resources he needed, Boyle was no closer to tracking down Pat O'Carolan.

They had O'Carolan's car. That one had been Mary's triumph. She'd led the team reviewing CCTV from the vicinity of the hospital and had picked up the green Polo and traced its progress along the Donegal Road but they had lost it up the Ormeau Road. A team from C3 and a bunch of uniforms was sent out and had turned up the car dumped in the golf club car park.

'It's supposed to be a red Bedford van according to the plates,' Mary told him, straining against her blouse as she leaned over his desk. 'Dublin have a record of a stolen green Volkswagen Polo, they're checking the engine and chassis numbers. They also found a burned out Daihatsu which was registered to O'Carolan.'

'Just out of curiosity, who was the stolen Polo registered to?'

Mary sat back and thumbed through her printouts. 'One second, I've got it somewhere. Here. Vincent Byrne's his name.'

Boyle pulled his keyboard toward him. 'That rings a bell. Let's just run the little darling through Niche, shall we?' He twisted the screen so Mary could see it as he keyed in the name. 'And hey presto, he's got form. IRA. He was in the nick same time as O'Carolan. Ask Dublin what they've got on Byrne, would you? And nice work, Mary. Very nice work.'

She was back within fifteen minutes. Boyle finished up his call with the head of corporate communications. She was talking before the phone was back on the hook. 'Byrne's a naughty boy. Petty crime, handling stolen goods, several counts of TDA. And he's got an long history of violent crime, IRA associated.'

'Ask them if they could bring him in. And thanks, Mary.'

Her scent was still in the air when Boyle picked up the handset to call McLoughlin. He idly picked through the sheaf of printouts Mary had left behind as he waited for the phone to answer. McLoughlin was, of course, at home. Boyle cursed and made a mental note to call Fiona and let her know he was going to be late.

'Boyle. What's the news?'

'We've got his car, at least. It belonged to a Vincent Byrne in Dublin but was reported stolen. Byrne goes back with O'Carolan, they spent time inside together. I've asked our friends down south to pull him in for questioning.'

'But where's the man, Boyle? Where's the man?'

'We've got officers out talking to everyone we can think of who might have been associated with him. We've done a full check of hotels and our guys have moved on to guest houses. I've just been speaking to corporate communications. We want to go to media, splash his picture, if you're okay with that.'

'We still think he's travelling with the girl in tow? Has someone talked to her family?'

Boyle felt his armpits prickle and his stomach knot. How could they have overlooked that? 'Actually, no. It's a good point.' He kept his voice casual.

'It's basic policing, Boyle. You're all becoming too fond of your technology toys.'

'I'll get onto it right away.'

'Release him to media. No coverage of her until the family's been informed. See if they can get her mother to make an appeal for her return or something.' Boyle heard a woman calling 'dinner' in the background. 'Right. Have to go. Good work, Boyle. Tie up the family thing though, will you?'

He'd been let off the hook big time. 'Yes, sir.' *There, you arrogant old bastard. There's my thank you.*

Boyle got home to find his dinner in the dog. It was past ten and he hadn't called, of course, what with the call to Dublin to ask them to inform the O'Carolan family that their daughter had gone AWOL in cahoots with her gun-wielding uncle. Yes, he'd send someone down to be with the team who would see the family in the morning. No, he had no idea of where she was or indeed whether she was safe. He had nothing to give them other than the news she was in trouble.

And now here he was standing in his kitchen at home while Fiona, who was holding a half-full bottle of red wine and waving an empty glass in his face, raged at him.

'You didn't even call. The food was ruined. Not just yours, mine too. I don't believe I waited for you. I should have known. It's not as if you don't do it all the fucking time, is it?'

'Fiona, look—'

'No, you look. You're selfish, Boyle. It's not about your job or the hours you have to work keeping the world a safer place for people like me. It's about you being a thoughtless bastard whose sole predatory purpose in life is his own fucking gratification.'

Even angry, she was lovely. She'd filled out a little in her thirties, but it had given her a softness that enhanced her big eyes and yet her triathlete's musculature still caught the light when she moved. He stared back at her until she turned on her heel and walked out of the kitchen. There was already a bottle in the bin.

Boyle made a ham sandwich and took a beer out of the fridge. He wandered through into the living room to join her on the sofa, but she got up when he sat down. The second bottle clattered into the bin. She washed the glass and put it on the drainer and then her feet bumped upstairs. Boyle sat and gazed at Sky News for a while, eating his sandwich. He slipped the plate into the sink and got another beer. Sport, now. The headlines came up at eleven. They started reporting on the Victoria Square bombing and he couldn't watch it. He sat drinking his beer and watching his blurred reflection in the dead screen.

When he got into bed, Fiona curled around him and kissed his neck. He was asleep seconds later.

Boyle's mobile woke him. Ewan Bates. He flicked on the bedside light and Fiona grumbled, twisting over and pulling the duvet onto herself. It was two in the morning.

'What the fuck?'

Bates' voice was taut. 'Suspicious activity in the Cathedral Quarter.'

'What's that to do with us?'

'We thought it might be O'Carolan, but there've been a couple of reports of a number of armed men. HMSU's already down there and deploying.'

'Fine. Coming.'

Boyle twisted off the bed and pulled his clothes from

the chair, hopping into his jeans and unhooking his holstered G17 from the back of the cupboard door. Fiona sat up, bleary-eyed, her hair in disarray. He admired her dark brown nipples in the half-light. She crossed her arms.

'Avert your gaze, you dirty bastard. Where you going to now? It's two o'clock for Christ's sake.'

'Cathedral. Shooters reported. Catch you later.'

'Don't be an arse, Boyle. Keep your head down.'

He bent to kiss her and left, his arm caught in the sleeve of his bomber jacket.

Boyle pulled up by the turn from Bridge Street into Waring Street where Bates was waiting. Bates was Good People. Boyle's view of humanity was generally binary and very few people indeed made it into the same category as Ewan.

Bates handed him a Kevlar gilet and Boyle pulled off his leathers, fastened the vest and pulled his jacket back over it. He checked his holster.

Bates' breath misted in the cold air. 'HMSU are all set up and standing by.'

'Bill Cameron?'

'Yep. He's around somewhere. Ah, talk of the devil…'

Cameron had headed the Headquarters Mobile Support Unit, the SAS-trained division of C4 special operations since Boyle had first joined C3. He was in his fifties now, wiry and fit with grey hair and laughing blue eyes. 'Boyle, you handsome young bastard. Is this your mess we're looking at?'

'I'm hoping not, but I have a nasty feeling it might be. Your guys all set?'

'Ready as we'll ever be.'

Tucked around the corner were two Range Rovers, armed police in black flak jackets waiting arrayed along the glass-fronted restaurant on the corner. Two men were crouched in firing positions either side of the road facing towards the Premier Inn. There was a black Lincoln parked outside the hotel.

'Shots fired?'

'No. That Lincoln apparently pulled up about half an hour ago, pedestrian saw six men. Apparently they were waving a gun at the staff member inside to unlock the door. I've got men on the back entrance and a team trying to get roof access.'

Two muffled gunshots fired in rapid succession inside the hotel. Screaming broke out, followed by the rip of machine gun fire and shattering glass.

'Oh fuck. Move in, now!'

Boyle raced down the street, his pistol already in his hand, Bates at his side as they took cover behind the Lincoln to gain clear sight of the reception area. A black-masked figure stood framed in the light, legs apart and a machine gun fitted into its shoulder. A clear shot. The HMSU team hesitated and Boyle took it, the Glock 17 bucking in his hand. His palm was sweaty on the grip.

More gunfire inside the hotel. Boyle dashed through the doors, Bates and Cameron behind him.

The floor of the bar area was strewn with prostrate figures. Tables and chairs had been upended. The night manager lay by the reception desk, his dead features blue and distended. One stiff hand still clutched ineffectually at the noose dug into his puffy neck. Some of the prone figures in the bar area were moving. One, a man, was slapping his arm on the floor and keening, his back arched. Boyle left them for the uniforms behind him to look after. Cameron signalled to have men fan out across the ground floor. Boyle ran for the stairs as more shots were fired above, a burst of machine gun fire alongside single rounds. Shouting and screams, more gunfire.

Hugging the wall, his gun jabbing in front of him, he made it to the first floor. The doors were open and the rooms empty. Most doors were undamaged. Presumably the guests were taken down to the bar by the gunmen. *Looking for someone*. Boyle took the next flight of stairs. Now doors had been forced, again the rooms were all empty. Bates and Cameron joined him on the floor. He stabbed his finger upwards and they followed him as he crept up the stairs. From the mouth of the stairwell he could see the bedroom doors on this floor had been shot open and there were bodies on the carpeted corridor. It was eerily silent. He peered out but there was no movement on the corridor. He stepped away from the stairwell, scanning the corridor with his gun.

The sound behind him was tiny but in the silence and tension it roared. Boyle wheeled to face a black-masked man with a machine gun at his hip. Boyle knew he was too late as the man's body tensed. Two shots cracked from behind Boyle. The man's shoulder and head exploded in a spray of blood and matter. Thrown against the wall by the force of the bullets, the body left a dark streak as it slid to the floor. The machine gun clattered. Boyle spun to confront the shooter. A large man, pistol in hand, stood framed at the end of the corridor. He nodded briefly at Boyle and darted into the bedroom doorway beside him.

'O'Carolan! Give yourself up!' Boyle knew his shouts were futile. He beckoned Bates up out of the stairwell and inched along the wall up the corridor. All of the doors had been forced open; every room contained a slumped figure or two. The smell of cordite and iron was sickening, but there was something else sweet underlying it. People lost control of their bowels when they died like this.

The bodies in the corridor were all wearing balaclavas and gloves, bandoliers and machine guns slung around their necks. They were all dark-skinned, Africans and maybe Arabs. The last two doors at the end of the corridor had escaped being forced open.

Boyle shot the lock of one, Bates the other. Boyle dashed to the open French window. Outside the city lights reflected off the wet street and the glittering wet steel gantry of the fire escape. There was no sign of O'Carolan or his niece.

Fuck it. Boyle slammed his palm against the wall.

Forensics were moving in, uniforms securing the street outside and Boyle was reduced to the role of a spectator to the clean-up. Bewildered-looking survivors were being escorted back to their rooms by sympathetic officers to collect their belongings or helped out to the waiting ambulances. The seriously wounded had long ago been whisked away. The co-ordination of the effort was impressive, Boyle had to admit. Flashes outside marked the arrival of the media and Boyle winced as an older lady with blood on her forehead cowered at the bursts of light.

He had spoken to a few of the survivors himself when he and Cameron's team had picked them up, dusted the glass shards off them and helped the intact to sit and give first aid to the wounded. He was proud of the team, they'd held it together brilliantly until the uniforms and paramedics had taken over.

Bates had stood watching them dragging the bodies to

the luggage room, his skin pale with a cold grey sheen Boyle had seen before.

'Ewan. Snap out. We've got to help the living.'

'Christ, John, look at what those mad bastards did here. Nothing justifies this. Nothing.'

'It's grim right enough. I've never seen such a bad scene in my life, I'll admit. But you need to keep moving, stop yourself freezing up or you'll be no help to me or to them come to think on it. Get a shift on.' Boyle grabbed Bates' shoulder and shook it. 'Cop on, man.'

Bates regained his focus as Boyle pummelled his shoulder. He smiled. 'I'm fine. Honest. Thanks.'

Boyle and Bates worked alongside Cameron and the team from HMSU, encouraging them and lending a hand wherever they could, lifting dead-weights and comforting sobbing relatives and still-uncomprehending lovers. One young couple had spent their last night in each other's arms and Boyle had to find tissues from the box behind the bar for a young officer after she helped the surviving boyfriend limp out to the ambulance.

Boyle hiked up the hotel's stairs, feeling for all the world like an old man, a pair of silicon gloves limp in his hand. He was tired inside and out. They had the assumed name and credit card O'Carolan was using from the hotel's front desk records but it gave him no pleasure. He reached the third floor where the bodies of the Africans were still lying. O'Carolan must have done for the lot of them and Boyle found himself grudgingly acknowledging the feat. The guy was in his sixties and all.

Forensics hadn't made it up here yet. Boyle pulled on the gloves and knelt by the nearest African, black boots, jeans and a polo neck, a balaclava covering his face. The unflinching eyes stared at the ceiling. Boyle pulled the wool back to reveal a handsome young face, flared nostrils and clean shaven. Three holes were punched in the man's chest. His pockets were empty. Boyle would let forensics invert them and analyse the fluff and other detritus that pockets collected, but the jeans seemed brand new. He leaned down and sniffed at a leg, confirming his hypothesis even as he realised how incongruous he looked if anyone should turn a corner.

He straightened up and wandered over to the next African. He left the balaclava where it was: the man had clearly taken a shot to the head and the wool was likely holding things together in there. Again he patted the corpse down and came up with nothing. He continued his grim survey.

The last of the six bodies was more Arab than African under the balaclava. His skin was a light brown, and he was fine featured. Boyle's hand felt a bump in the jacket over the still heart and slid inside to the pocket. He pulled out a wallet, tan leather worn smooth with use. Boyle carefully opened it out. Credit cards. An ATM card. Four twenties and a five. A photo ID for a company called Contania which Boyle had never heard of. The dead man's name was Mohammad Muntasir. He was more handsome in death than he was on the photo ID. Boyle slid the wallet back and dragged himself to his feet. The adrenalin buzz had given way to intense weariness. Sick of the sight of bodies and the stench of blood and filth, he staggered to the stairwell and slid down along the wall as he plodded back down to the reception area in search of an evidence bag.

The buttons on Detective Superintendent Wayne McLoughlin's uniform sparkled as always. Boyle wondered if The Great Man's mousy wife polished them for him. Or perhaps he stayed up late into the night, rubbing at those huge epaulettes and dreaming of parades and salutes. Her name was Geraldine, the wife. Boyle had met her at drinks after some conference or another. She had looked up to her husband with doe eyes and Boyle had to fight a strong urge to shake her awake.

But McLoughlin had the floor and the team around Boyle didn't move a muscle as they gave the chief their attention, some thirty men and women in black uniforms sitting on chairs and the edges of desks. Displayed on the screen behind him were photographs of the six dead Africans. They had been cleaned up by the pathologist before the images were taken, but one had lost most of his right cheek, the grim sight Boyle had avoided when he left the man's balaclava on.

'Five of the men are Afro-Caribbean, names unknown. One is a Briton of Libyan ethnicity, a Mohammed Muntasir. They were travelling in a hired Lincoln SUV. We're currently engaged in getting CCTV footage and a copy of the card and ID used to hire the car. Any progress on the rental company, Myers?'

'It's Sunday, chief. Their duty manager's trying to get hold of the general manager. But it looks like Muntasir hired it two weeks ago.'

'Light a fire under them.'

'Chief.'

McLoughlin pressed his clicker and the slide changed to an image of Muntasir's Contania ID. 'Forensics have very little to go on. Muntasir is the only positive ID we have so far, the others carried nothing except guns. Those guns,' McLoughlin's eyes sought Boyle, 'were taken from a looted IRA cache which somehow escaped decommissioning.'

There was a rustle and low murmur around the room. Boyle scanned the audience, noting the tight lips and frowns, the accusing stares between colleagues. He marvelled at how suddenly trust built up painstakingly over almost two decades could be eroded. How fragile the peace they had taken so willingly for granted.

'Five of the men carried AK-47s, one of them had an Uzi which he was using to cover the guests they herded into the bar when DS Boyle intervened.' All eyes on Boyle, who had been dreading this attention since the briefing started. 'In total, we have sixteen civilian wounded, five dead. Four guests and the night manager. Three of the wounded are in a critical condition, two more still under observation. It's amazing there weren't more casualties, forensics have so far noted a total of two hundred rounds fired. Most of those were on the third floor where there appears to have been an intense firefight between the terrorists and a third party. Our mystery man was heavily armed and a skilled marksman according to forensics. It looks like he was the man the attackers were there to find, staying under the assumed name of Shaughnessy. His name is in fact Patrick O'Carolan and he is a former Provisional IRA bomb maker and active service unit member.'

A murmur around the room, one voice raised enough for Boyle to hear his 'Fucking hell.' McLoughlin paddled the air with his palms. 'Calm down, calm down. This is O'Carolan.'

The slide advanced to show a big, smiling man. He was bushy-browed, his hair starting to recede. He had a strong jaw and brown eyes, a tuft of hair poking up from the top of his soft-collared checked shirt. Behind him was a green corrugated barn. Rust streaks ran down its side.

A voice called out, 'He looks like a fucking farmer!'

and was rewarded by a rumble of laughter around the room.

'Thank you, Pearce. That's precisely what he was until a week ago. O'Carolan served eleven years in the Maze, where he earned himself the sobriquet of 'Swan' because of his habit of obsessively making small paper swans. It was because of that very habit we were able to link him to the Forestside Shopping Centre bomb. This first device we think was constructed purposefully not to detonate. We have reason to believe that O'Carolan was pressured to make a number of these devices by a group linked to a Somali terrorist and extortionist organisation known as Al Shabab. The group has demanded a ransom of one hundred million pounds be paid by Her Majesty's Government. We will of course not negotiate with terrorists.'

He's got them now, thought Boyle. You could hear a pin drop.

'How many?' The same man, Pearce, a rangy, tousle-headed youth with prominent front teeth and a cheeky grin. 'How many devices... bombs?'

McLoughlin scanned the room, *ah you shit* Boyle waited with the rest of them, *you're working it for the last drop of drama so you are*.

'Six. We understand there were five suitcase devices in all, each packed with five kilos of Semtex and there are three of these remaining in the wild, as it were. They also have a car bomb, mounted in a white Toyota HiAce van, consisting of some eight hundred pounds of explosive. They're out there somewhere, ladies and gentlemen, and we have to find them before more lives are lost. This is highly confidential, the media has not been informed of the scale of the issue and will not be until we have a solid handle on this. We are reporting our progress directly to

A Decent Bomber

the Home Secretary. So please, keep the information within this group. DS Boyle will take you through the operational planning. Good day.'

Your arse, thought Boyle bitterly as he smiled his thanks to McLoughlin and turned to face the room. 'Right, boys and girls, this is how it's going to work…'

Boyle glanced across at Mary Dwyer sitting in his passenger seat. He'd picked her up from her place up in Whiterock. She was wearing uniform, which surprised him on a Sunday morning. 'They're expecting the police,' she'd said as she caught his look getting into the car.

Boyle drove through the quiet streets, dragged back to the past by the woman in his car. Mary Dwyer and Boyle had a fling the year before he met Fiona. It was on and off in days, a whirlwind affair that came out of nowhere and went back there almost as fast. The time in between was spent in a riot of underwear and panting, groping and enthusiastic rutting that still occasionally threw up vivid memories when Boyle least expected them.

They'd both moved on since, but Boyle had retained a healthy respect for the girl from Leitrim who'd moved North to escape small town life. She was brunette, tallish with straight hair brushing her shoulders. She was curvaceous, constantly battling her weight. Her frank, startlingly blue eyes could be unnervingly compassionate but then be a million miles away a few seconds later, forgetting all about you instantly. She was a dreamer, she'd told him and he had to admit she was, in bed at least, a highly creative girl.

While appreciating her professionalism, Boyle had usually avoided going out on assignments with her because of the history thing. Fiona didn't know about the fling with Mary. Boyle would avoid work socials with the tag 'bring your significant other'. Fiona seemed happy enough to stay away, in any case. For some reason she wasn't keen on beer-soaked quiz nights full of sweary coppers and their private in-jokes. Boyle would catch sight of Mary at those dos, usually at the centre of four or five admirers. And he'd feel guilty even looking out for her.

Boyle pulled his BMW up outside the big, new townhouse. 'This the place, right enough?'

Mary had tracked the regional manager of Contania down to his home, despite the security guard's reluctance to share information on a Sunday. Peter Bryce had taken her call and suggested they meet at his house as it was closer to Brooklyn House than the depot. 'That's it. Number eleven. Want me to lead?'

'Sure. I'll just be takin' notes, me.'

Boyle locked the car with his reluctant remote and hunched deeper into his leather jacket. He watched Mary's calves. He wondered how you wore a skirt in cold like this. Stockings, he supposed. She rang the doorbell and they waited, arms wrapped around themselves and their breath showing as puffs. Somewhere an ice cream van jingled and they both laughed. Imagine, in this weather. Ice cream.

The smell of Sunday roast rushed out of the door, answered by a trim-looking man in his late forties wearing a polo shirt and jeans.

'Hi, I'm Peter. Do come in.' His accent was BBC English.

Boyle followed Mary past Peter Bryce and they waited in the corridor for him to close the front door and lead the way. 'I'm Mary Dwyer, we talked earlier. This is DS Boyle.'

'Nice to meet you, DS.'

'Just Boyle.'

'Right, right. Well, we can go in here, we won't be disturbed. This way.'

They passed the kitchen door, behind it children's voices and the murmur of a woman being patient. The conservatory was surprisingly warm, the lawn beyond dotted with leaves. Bryce caught Boyle's scrutiny. 'It's been too cold and wet for gardening. Although that's a year-round thing in Ireland, isn't it?'

Boyle sat on a cream sofa festooned with William Morris roses. Mary sat next to him, her legs crossed towards Bryce, who flopped back in his armchair. 'How can I help you? It was something to do with Mohammed Muntasir, wasn't it?'

'Well, yes,' Mary's glance at Boyle and nod to Bryce was masterly stuff, thought Boyle. She was acting nervous and subordinate. She'd have him changing her flat tyre next. 'It was. I'm afraid I've not heard of Contania...'

'We're one of the leading multimodal transport and logistics companies in Northern Ireland, but I'm not surprised you wouldn't have come across us. We specialise in white label transport solutions, so you'll likely see someone else's logos on the containers or even the lorries. It's something we're changing.'

'What did Mr Muntasir do?'

'He was a loading supervisor. He was relatively new to us, joined about three months ago. I had personnel email his file over. She wasn't too happy about having to go in today, tell the truth. Here, there's not very much there I'm afraid.' Bryce leaned over and handed Mary a memory key with a white on blue Contania logo on it. 'A relatively new hire, a good worker, passed through his probationary period. Nothing remarkable.'

Mary pocketed the little gadget. 'Thank you. Do you have any other new staff who are…'

A frown passed across Bryce's pale features. 'Muslim? Or Arab?'

She was smooth as silk. '…associated in any way with Mr Muntasir?'

'Not that I'm aware of, but I suppose you'd have to ask down at the Depot. We have over two hundred staff and I'm not familiar with them all. You won't get anyone today, there's just a skeleton crew working in despatch. But you can go down in the morning and speak to Bill McFadden, he runs the shop.'

Boyle leaned forward. 'If it were more urgent than that?'

'Bill's usually up a mountain somewhere at the weekends. I doubt you'll raise him. Can I ask, what precisely is Mr Muntasir supposed to have done?'

Boyle stood and Mary followed suit. After a moment's hesitation Bryce joined them. Mary put her hand out to Bryce. 'Thank you for your help, Mr Bryce. It's appreciated.'

'So what has he done?'

'We're just making enquiries,' Boyle smiled. 'We'll let ourselves out.'

The front door clicked behind Boyle as the cold hit him. The smell and warmth of Sunday roast was gone. Ahead was just a cold leather car seat.

'Waste of time, that.' Mary turned, her hair swinging around to frame her smile. 'But we've nothing better to do on a Sunday, have we?'

'I can think of plenty.' Boyle clicked the car.

'Fancy getting a drink?' Mary's gaze across the roof of the car was steady.

'Sure,' said Boyle, his heart pumping and his mouth dry.

Chapter Twelve

Orla woke in a sweat, having dreamed of Róisín. It was bitterly cold and her neck was killing her. The morning light was silvery-grey and she shifted against the unfamiliar lumps under her, the cloth drawn around. It wasn't her bed. The disorientation made her reach out. A car door. A car seat which didn't quite fold back flat. She rubbed her eyes.

Oh God. Pat stole a car last night. The Rover's windows were all misted up. She turned and stretched carefully, wrapping the nest of jumpers and her scarf back around her where they had fallen away.

Pat shifted, a big lump on the driver's seat, his legs squeezed under the wheel. 'Jesus.' A thump as he hit the wheel with his elbow. 'Orla? What time is it?'

She checked the dashboard clock. 'It's seven. I'm freezing.'

'Christ on a bike. It's cold enough.'

He was pale and bleary-eyed, his chin dark with stubble. He pulled himself upright on the wheel, squirmed to pull his chair up. Orla opened the door and stepped out, the fresh air cutting and filled with earthy scents. Cold it may have been, but leaving the fuggy car was a relief. She listened to the birdsong, the sunlight starting to stream through the branches of the trees around. Where the light fell, the ground sent up slow tendrils of mist.

Pat's door creaked open and he grunted as his feet hit the ground. 'We'd best get moving.'

'Moving? Where to? Where can we go after that…?' The memories came flooding back. Orla lurched for the roof of the car, clutching at the cold metal as the urge to retch hit her empty stomach.

Pat danced around the bonnet of the Rover to reach her. He folded her in his bear hug embrace.

'Ah, come on. I told you it was going to be rough. Let me take you back home, it'll be fine. You'll be safe, then. I'll take the blame, Mikey will be fine. Eventually.'

To her horror, her throat was burning and tears started to well up. She screwed up her face buried in his shoulder and tried to hold it back. 'I-I can't go back.' She fought for control, to force the words out. 'They know who I am, they came for me before and they'll come again. They'll hurt Ma and Da. Anyone in the way. Christ, you saw them last night, how they…'

He hushed her and rubbed her back. She heard pigeons in the woods but the morning's peace was ripped apart by the memory of the night before.

She had been fast asleep when she was woken by Pat hammering on the door of her room and sounds like doors slamming. Blearily she resolved them into gun shots. He shouted at her. 'Get dressed, Orla. Quickly now.'

She pulled on her clothes and yanked her door open. Pat pulled her into his room. He was holding a pistol, an obscene sight. 'Go behind the bed. Do not move for anything, you hear me?'

He killed the light and stood by the door, waiting. The shouts and banging grew closer. Orla peeked above the bed, her eyes adjusting to the darkness and the sodium light from the street picking out Pat standing in wait. The pistol was poking out of his belt and he had a snub-nosed machine gun slung over each of his big shoulders. His holdall was a dark lump by his feet. *An angel of death. My uncle Rambo.* She suppressed the urge to laugh and almost yelped in shock as a fist hammered on the door of the room next door. Pat must have had his door off the latch because he didn't make a sound as he moved, whipping it open and bounding into the corridor.

The machine gun fire roared, hammering percussions that made Orla fling up her hands to block her ears. Pat was hurled back into the room by a cascade of whining bullets that smashed plaster and plucked splinters from the door frame. The lights in the corridor snuffed out. He dropped to his stomach, pulling spare clips from his holdall and smacking them into place. The silence was broken by the sound of a man groaning. A single gunshot snapped in the street outside. Glass tinkled. Pat sloughed off the right hand machine gun and laid it on the floor, reaching for the pistol from his belt. He slid to the doorway and poked the gun into the corridor, firing short bursts with the automatic as he shot single rounds with the pistol. The returning fire died out and silence reigned again. Orla cringed. Pat got to his feet, reached for the spare machine gun and inched out into the corridor. Orla choked on the stench of the smoke billowing from the open doorway. Gunfire barked, strobing muzzle flashes like lightning in the dark corridor.

Pat careened back into the room, kicking the door shut behind him and throwing the two machine guns into the holdall. 'The window, quick.'

Orla jumped up and pushed the sliding door to the balcony open, Pat behind her and taking her arm as they clattered down the steel treads of the fire escape. Running after him through the multi-storey car park, Orla had felt a surge of elation.

Now, surrounded by the sounds of the morning countryside, the tears were abating. *Not feeling so clever now, girl.* 'L-last night…'

'Hush, Orla.'

'Y-you insisted on the room at the end of the corridor.'

'I did, aye.'

'Because it was next the fire escape.'

'Yes.'

'You knew they'd come?'

'I didn't, no. But old habits die hard.'

She pushed back from his shoulder, leaving glittering moisture on his greatcoat. 'How many?'

He pulled the hair from her eyes. 'Six, far as I could tell.'

She smiled up at him. 'It's okay, Pat. I'm getting used to it already.'

'Please God, don't ever say that again. It's no small thing, Orla. It's not a game.'

She bit her lip. He patted her shoulder. 'Come on. Let's find ourselves a greasy spoon. I'm starving and I can't think on an empty stomach.'

'What then?'

'I don't know. We're on the lam and that hasn't usually ended well for me in the past, tell the truth.'

The Mullingar Grill was just off the Dargan Road and popular with lorry drivers waiting for the ferries. Clinking mugs of tea and plates of fried breakfast slid across the counter with comforting regularity. Black and white photos of brewery drays, harvest scenes and cloth-capped lads standing outside Croke Park were framed on the beige, tea-splashed walls. A big TV screen drooped cables down the wall. The stained Formica tables and battered chairs were all part of the charm but the food, as

Pat could well attest, was good. Sipping his tea, he stole a glance at Orla as she finished her breakfast roll. She had borne up well, but this was no caper for a girl. He wished there were somewhere he could take her and know she'd be safe until this was all over.

If Mikey even knew the danger she had been in. Jesus, *was* in, he'd lose his brother, he knew. They'd never speak again. Christ, they'd had their fallings out back in the day, especially when Pat had come out of Long Kesh and arrived at Mikey's with nothing but a bag of clothes and the stench of disinfectant in his hair. MacNamara had already fled, his car turning the corner at the end of the road as Mikey opened the door.

Pat gazed at the surrealist masterpiece on the plate in front of him, a swathe of yellow egg and a spotting of grease reflecting the lights, bean sauce mixed with HP sauce brown, a white whorl where he'd mopped up with his toast. He should have known, of course. Mikey hadn't been at the front gates to pick him up, MacNamara had done the honours. So why had Pat expected some sort of prodigal son performance when he had turned up on the doorstep of the little council house? Mikey had pulled him into the back room hissing that he didn't want his young family dragged into Pat's politics and his murder.

He'd told Mikey it was over, that he'd learned his lesson. But his brother had looked into his eyes and what he'd seen had disgusted him. Mikey had been right, Pat had to admit. He'd been glib and lied through his teeth. Fair enough, the great 'Cause' had sent him to the edge of insanity, pushed him into years of humiliation and institutionalisation. But truth been told, he'd spent his time inside reading, learning about Fidel, Che and Karl. There were other struggles against injustice and he came out fiercer than when he'd gone in. MacNamara had channelled that anger like the pro he was and talked Pat around. He'd gone on to make bigger and better bombs. The biggest. The best. Ever.

And that's when he'd woken up. When he'd walked away and refused to go back. When the human cost of idealism had truly hit home. The big bombs scared him because of how they made him feel. Powerful, decisive, sexual even. He'd felt the rush of his heroin and had the sense to finally, turn his back on the drug. After Docklands he'd gone back to Ireland to stay on Grannie's farm. Mikey wasn't talking to him and she was the only member of the family who'd have him. Broken, silent Pat and his love of sitting up on the bog, folding wee swans and watching the sun move across the sky that glorious August.

The farm was a mess when he got there. Grandpa had died two years past and the old lady was mourning him still. The herd was down to about three head and two of them had mastitis. Pat had stayed to clean up the place a little and, day by day, she had rallied.

And then, of course, he found her cold in her bed that Sunday morning when he would normally have driven her into town to Mass. Her will left the farm to Pat and caused a sharp row with Uncle Maurice and his wizened little shrew of a wife, whose Expectations had been dashed. And Pat had become a farmer. A simple Irish farmer.

They set off the second big bomb without him. He watched the pictures on the news. *I made that.* Now it was going to happen again. Someone else was using bombs he'd made. And when they set off the big one, the one in the HiAce, Pat knew there'd be no warning, no chance to clear the town centre before the blast wave struck.

He was dragged back away from the past by Orla

shaking his shoulder. 'Look!'

It was the news, a presenter with a headscarf around shoulders crested by tumbling blonde hair. She was framed by a night-time crime scene, blue lights flashing across the white front wall of the hotel, streetlights picking out PSNI officers and paramedics.

The strapline read 'Terrorist Outrage in Belfast'. Pat glanced around the café but nobody else was watching the screen. Turning back to it, he saw a photo of a younger Pat O'Carolan. Looking up at the screen, Orla was open-mouthed, shaking her head. The strapline had changed to 'Dissident IRA suspect'.

Her green eyes flashed. 'The bastards. There's Africans all over the place blowing people up and shooting them and they're looking for *us*?'

'Me. At least they didn't have you up there. Come on, we need to get out of here before someone sees us.'

They stole out of the café into the cold, sunny air. Pat pressed the Rover's remote and dumped into the driver's seat. Orla clambered in. 'Where are we going to go now?'

Pat shrugged. 'That's not an easy question. We should check in somewhere and lie low, but we have to assume that the credit card I got from Vinny Byrne is no use anymore. I'd get the hell away from Belfast, but there's a man I need to see.'

'Let's go and see him, then.'

Pat opened his mouth and then closed it. He put the car into drive. 'Fine.'

'Who's the man?'

'I was on the way to him yesterday when you called me. Odd chap by the name of Muntasir. Hamid Muntasir. He's Libyan, married to an Irish girl back in the eighties and settled down here. He runs a bookshop on the Lisburn Road. He's the only link between the

A Decent Bomber

Provisionals and Africa I can think of.'

Orla's mobile rang in her pocket. She pulled it clear and examined the screen. She held it out to Pat in her open palm, shrugging at him.

'Hello?'

Pat's chest tightened at the sound of the smooth voice. 'Mister O'Carolan. Perhaps we need to talk.'

'How did you get this number?'

'Oh, your car dealer friend was very co-operative.'

'And what might you imagine I would want to talk to you about?'

'You are becoming famous, Mister O'Carolan. The media has become very interested in you. Soon they will be interested in your niece's family. As are we. The choice for you to make is between you and them. If you talk with us, you will live and so do they. There is the hard way, of course, but that would not bear thinking about for you, I would say.'

'Okay, so talk.'

'Not like this. You will meet me. Tomorrow morning at 9 o'clock. Belfast Central Railway Station, platform four. The waiting room. You will be alone and unarmed.'

The line cut. Pat stared at the mobile in his hand, rubbing the side of the little handset with his thumb.

'So? Who was it?'

'Him. The Accountant. He wants to meet. I don't need any Libyan monkeys. I just got called by the organ grinder himself.'

'MacNamara.'

'Brian. It's Pat O'Carolan. You okay? You sound like

shit.'

'Jesus, Pat. I'm at Vinny Byrne's place. Jesus.'

'They got to him.'

'It's awful. They tortured him. They pulled his fingernails then cut out his tongue. The forensics guy said he was still alive when they did it. How did you know?'

'They told me. The Accountant just called me. He wants to meet. They've threatened Orla's family. I have little choice.'

'When?'

'Tomorrow at 9.'

'Come in, Pat. I'm with the police here. I can convince them, I know I can. We can work together on this.'

'They think I'm a terrorist, Brian. I've seen the TV.'

'I can talk them round. Let me call you back. Will you think about it if I can?'

'Sure, I've hardly got a grand choice ahead of me, have I?'

'I'll call you back on this number.'

'Ten minutes, Brian. After that I'm destroying this SIM. I'm not having them trace me through my number.'

'I understand. Bear with me.'

Chapter Thirteen

MacNamara picked his way across the crime scene, trying not to get in anyone's way. It wasn't easy, the place was festooned in alleyways of tape. Little markers scattered the ground and there were Gardaí CSIs in rustling Tyvek boiler suits everywhere you turned. Vinny Byrne's death had been anything but clean and MacNamara, still reeling from the damage done to his family, was ashen faced and fighting hard to keep his feet on terra firma as he tried to efface the images of blood spray and sprinklings of gore etched in his mind.

Before the drive with Boyle down to Dublin, MacNamara had taken Jean to see Simone in the City Hospital, but their daughter was in a medically induced coma and wasn't likely to be any way else until tomorrow. MacNamara had put his arm around Jean's quivering shoulder and she had twisted away from him.

He found Boyle smoking on the edge of Byrne's car lot, a sour look on his face as he surveyed the scene. MacNamara was breathless from the little dance he'd had to execute in order to avoid all the detritus. 'I've got a breakthrough. But you're going to have to work with me. To trust me.'

Boyle took a drag on his cigarette. 'That's a big ask. Far as I can see, you boys are up to your old tricks again. You're turning the clock back, so you are.'

'Look, forget the Union Jack for one second.' MacNamara's voice was trembling and he fought hard to maintain control. 'Forget your Da and my sister. They're in the past. My wee Riley's not even laid to rest, Boyle, and I'm down here with you because some bunch of mad

African bastards have murdered another innocent man, whatever lay in his past. And all those people in that hotel, and the people in the shopping centre – and I think I can help make it stop.'

'They're using your codes, your explosives. Your bomb maker.'

'Boyle, come on. You know what's going on here as well as I do.'

'Well, let's say for a second I don't. Let's just say I'm not so sure.'

'Listen, The Accountant has asked for a meeting with Pat O'Carolan.'

'So he can make them another bunch of bombs.'

'Pat called me, Boyle. I think he'd work with us. You just need to listen to him and trust him.'

MacNamara started at Boyle's bark of laughter. 'Trust him? He's about ten counts of murder on his head. I'll trust him when he's grippin' steel bars.'

'But that's the point, isn't it? You can have him behind bars or more people like my wee girl lying on gurneys in a mortuary.' MacNamara felt the tears come again. 'She was one of four innocent people, another five died last night and these bastards are going to do it again and again. The hospital's overloaded, Christ I should know I was there to see my own daughter lying in a coma because she got hit by a fucking nail bomb. She doesn't even know her child's dead.'

Uniformed officers grabbed MacNamara's arms. 'Now then, Sir. Calm down.'

'Listen to me Boyle.' MacNamara let the tension drain from his muscles. The hands on his arms relaxed. 'We're not as equipped to deal with this all as we used be. They're running rings around us and there's another four bombs out there, including the big one. Vinny Byrne is the third man they've tortured to death. Pat O'Carolan's the only one who survived an encounter with them. He's a lead, surely you can see that. Give him immunity and he'll work with us.'

Boyle gestured the men to leave MacNamara go. 'Those bombs were made by none other than your chum O'Carolan. You think I've got the authority or even the desire to grant him immunity?'

'He's been trying to undo what they made him do. He can help you.'

'What number did he call you from?'

'It's no use trying to trace it. You can have it, here. He'll destroy the SIM in,' MacNamara checked his screen, 'Four minutes.'

Boyle tapped the green icon and listened, his gaze on MacNamara. The phone was answered. 'No, it's not Brian. This is DS Boyle from PSNI. I think we might have met briefly last night.'

'You the guy in the Premier Inn?'

'That's right.'

'You're a lucky one, aren't you?'

'I'm not going to thank you. I'd rather see you locked up before indulging in any niceties.'

'I've been there before. I can't recommend the food. And I'm in no hurry to go back.'

'You might have thought about that before making bombs and murdering men.'

'Neither was by my choice.'

'A court will decide that.'

'Mister Boyle, I think we might have a situation on our hands a mighty bit more urgent than your courts.'

'I understand you have been in contact with the group

behind the bombings.'

'Hassan Ali Jaffar. They call him The Accountant. He's to meet me tomorrow morning on platform four at Central Station.'

'At what time?'

'Nine.'

'I can't grant you immunity.'

'Then you can go to hell. I did eleven years in Long Kesh, I'll not spend a day more in a prison. I've been a farmer these past twenty years and until these boyos came calling I lived a peaceful life. I've done nothing any other man wouldn't have. Come to think of it, I've done more to stop them than you have.'

'It doesn't make it right. There's laws.'

'You'll let innocents die for your laws. Let that be on your head.'

'Wait. Wait. I'll have to call you back.'

'Not on this number you won't. Make your decision now or not at all.'

'I don't have the authority.'

'Okay. I'll call you back in thirty minutes.'

Boyle handed MacNamara his mobile.

'Well?'

'He's calling back in thirty minutes. I don't know what the hell I'm to do now.'

'Call McLoughlin.'

'And tell him I want to grant immunity to an IRA killer?'

'Yes, if you like, you could tell him that.'

Boyle tapped a cigarette out of his packet and lit it, a grateful drag before he reached for his mobile. Clouds were starting to form and the sunlight was becoming patchy.

'It's Boyle. O'Carolan claims he has a meeting with

the leader of the group behind the bombings. He's suggesting we work together. I'm minded to believe he's genuine and he's our only lead outside a dead man's wallet. He wants immunity.'

'Out of the question.'

'He's our only hope of wrapping this up quickly.'

'He killed six men last night alone.'

'Known and wanted terrorists who are part of a gang which tortured three civilians to death and placed a bomb which killed four more.'

'A bomb O'Carolan made.'

'Under duress.'

'Besides, it's five. Five more. Simone Burnock succumbed to her wounds an hour ago.'

Boyle staggered. He twisted away from MacNamara and hissed, 'What do you mean succumbed? She only had a flesh wound. They said she was going to be okay.'

'Apparently there were complications.'

MacNamara had wandered away and was rocking an engine block buried in the wild grass with his foot.

'What complications? They said it was straightforward. MacNamara doesn't know about this.'

'You'll have to tell him.'

'What about O'Carolan?'

'Absolutely no question of it.'

Thanks a bundle. Boyle shoved the mobile back into his jacket pocket. He wheeled to face the Portakabin and punched it savagely. His hand screamed pain, his knuckles skinned by the textured finish. He leaned his head against the cold wall muttering 'Shit' to himself.

Nursing his knuckles, he strode over to MacNamara who was staring disconsolately at the bustling crime scene as the paramedics pulled the blue bundle on a stretcher out of the caravan, struggling to negotiate the rickety steps.

'Brian, you need to leave. It's Simone.' MacNamara turned to Boyle, his face crumpling as he saw Boyle's expression.

'No. For the love of God, no.'

'I'm afraid she's passed away. I'm sorry.'

MacNamara appeared ten years older, his eyes red-rimmed and his face lined. Boyle reached out a steadying hand which MacNamara went to push away but ended up clutching. Boyle walked him to the car and helped him drop into the passenger seat. Boyle took the wheel. 'Belt up, Brian. I'll get you there quick as I can.'

They were a little past halfway to Belfast when O'Carolan called.

'So, what's your answer?'

'Yes to your immunity. I'm with Brian MacNamara, his daughter was caught in the Victoria Square bomb. She's passed away. We're going to the Victoria Hospital now. You can meet us there and we'll go into Brooklyn House together.

'Deal. When?'

'Give us an hour.'

'Right. Listen…'

'What?'

'Nothing. Just give Brian my condolences.'

Pat and Orla sat in the car together, parked up on the side of the Lisburn Road. Pat was on the phone. Orla was gathered into herself, listening to the rumble of his voice but not the words. She wondered if you could just stop breathing, if it were possible to have that much self-control that you could kill yourself. And if she did, whether Róisín would be there waiting for her. If there was a *there*. And if you killed yourself believing in *there* and it wasn't there, what a waste. What a monumental error. But God, she ached to be with the gypsy who had woken her, to be at peace in the strong, soft arms.

Orla tried to remember Róisín but to her horror realised her memories were already becoming fuzzy. It wasn't her, anyway, it was what she had opened up for Orla. Her new self-awareness. *Christ, listen to yourself.* Orla tried to stop her mind buzzing, to think of something mundane. She picked at her fingernails. She decided she needed a shower.

Pat finished his call, grim-faced. Orla heard his last words. 'Condolences? Who's Brian?'

'Brian MacNamara's a guy I go back with. His daughter and granddaughter were in the Victoria Square bombing. They're both dead.

So's Róisín was Orla's first thought, which she realised shamed her. 'I'm sorry. He must be very unhappy.'

'We're going to meet him and this Boyle guy at the Victoria Hospital.'

Orla felt sick, a wave of heat and panic drew her under. 'No. Not there. I'm not going back there. I'll wait in the car.'

'Fine.' Pat shot her a glance and put his hand out to her. 'It's okay, Orla. It's okay. You'll be safe now.'

'What about you?'

'I'll be safe, too.'

Boyle loathed hospitals. He had no good memory of one, from childhood sickness through to the ruins of people he had encountered in his time as a copper. The rumble and squeak of rubber wheels on lino, the stench of disinfectant, the clinical efficiency of the staff – it all got on top of him and made him feel snappy and then invariably brutish.

The ICU duty nurse had taken them over to the room where Simone MacNamara was laid out. 'Your wife is there already,' she told MacNamara.

'I'll leave you to it,' Boyle muttered.

'No, come on in. If you don't mind.'

'Sure.'

Boyle followed MacNamara into the brightly-lit room. Jean MacNamara stood bowed over the young woman laid out on the hospital bed. The still face, eyes closed, was a grey colour Boyle knew all too well.

Jean MacNamara's veiny hands were balled at her sides. She whispered. 'All these years you did these things to other families and now it's come home to us. It's God's judgement. You have no right to mourn her.'

'Jean, Jean. Please, there's—'

Boyle cleared his throat. 'I'm sorry. For this.' He caught the venomous gleam in Jean MacNamara's teary eye.

'There's nothing you could have done.' MacNamara turned to Boyle. 'We just have to work to stop the people who did it.'

Jean MacNamara hissed. 'You did it.'

'Sorry, Boyle, my wife's a little distraught.'

'No. You can't paper over this with political platitudes. Your own daughter and granddaughter are dead at the hands of bombers, as others' families have suffered at the hands of the men you are so fond of playing your games with.' Her voice was quiet and she spoke to the figure on the bed, but Boyle heard the edge of madness in the high tremor. 'The explosives you brought to this country did this, explosives you intended to cause misery and loss to others. You might as well have killed her and Riley by your own hand. I want nothing more of you, Brian MacNamara. I won't have you in my house. My life. It's over. Thirty years and more of sham marriage end here. You've taken everything from me as sure as ripping it from the womb you plundered to put it there. I'll have no more. Go.'

'Jean…'

Boyle moved fast and caught her bony arms as she raised them to strike MacNamara. He restrained her with ease. She twisted and tried to bite him, her face a rictus. His mobile rang. MacNamara put up his hand.

'Let her go. It doesn't matter.'

Boyle stood aside and pulled the mobile from his pocket. Jean slumped over the body on the bed, racked by heaving sobs.

'What's the craic?'

'You're here?'

'In the car park. Blue Rover.'

Boyle glanced at MacNamara's broken-down face and the mortal ruins of his family. 'Be down in five minutes.'

Boyle strode down the corridor and barged into the interview room, a Starbucks in his hand. Mary Dwyer followed him, a little tray with four more takeaway cups and a pile of sugar and stirring sticks. MacNamara, O'Carolan and his niece all sat around the table. All three looked exhausted. MacNamara's eyes were still red from the crying and he was bent like an old man, his head down. The O'Carolan girl's mass of red hair was like a wild woman's fanny and she was pale, her skin almost translucent. The big man himself seemed tired but otherwise dead-on. His gaze up at Boyle was startlingly direct and there was a sense of absolute control to the man Boyle found disquieting.

He tried to sound breezy and confident. 'Okay, McLoughlin's agreed to the Central Station operation I've got all the resources I need. You'll go in wearing a wire and we'll have all the backup you need.'

Mary bustled around the table handing out coffees. She put a hand on Orla's shoulder, getting a wan smile in response.

Pat crossed his arms. 'You'll be right behind me, four hundred yards behind me, right?'

'Something like that. Now, what can you tell us about these people we don't already know?'

To Boyle's surprise it was the girl who answered, sweeping hair back from her face. 'They're part of Al Shabab, a Somali-based group. Their leader is a man they call 'The Accountant'. His name is Hassan Ali Jaffar.'

'You're pretty informed. And composed if I might say so.'

'We've had time to get used to the situation.'

Boyle turned to O'Carolan. 'They got the codes from Quinlan and the cache from Burke's. Then they contacted you using an old IRA code and asked you to make a bunch of nail bombs. And you did that without question because they gave you a code?'

'They weren't nail bombs. They must have packed the nails in afterwards. I made them not to go off, all bar one.'

'But you just went ahead and made them?'

'They took Orla. I had little choice. I tried to outsmart them, but they put a guard on me. The head guy doesn't get his nice city shoes dirty, he lets his boys do the spadework.'

'What's he like? This accountant?'

'African-looking, slim. Maybe five eight? Expensive

tastes, likes suits and shiny shoes. He's got a funny accent, a bit African a bit American a bit British public school.'

'Okay, so you made his bombs. You must have known they'd work out you had left a lead loose.'

'I'd never intended them to make it to the end of the lane, but just in case I did that so at least the first wouldn't go off and buy me some time to find them. They made me go up to a cache in a warehouse in Newry. They gave me an address to meet them, 24 Lusitania Gardens, and then they led me to the cache. I somehow doubt the house will still be occupied when you go there to take a look. We went back to the warehouse, Orla and I, to check. It was empty and had never been rented by them in the first place. I loaded up the explosives and detonators and they made me drive the HiAce back to mine. That's where I thought I'd get them, but they put a giant on me, a man called Yousuf.'

'The guy in the bog.'

'That's the one.'

'What did you do to him?'

'I got Orla's location from him. I built a wireless detonator into one of the bombs, the only active one, and tried to detonate the lot with a wee walkie talkie I had in the shed. It's all I had to hand. I hadn't expected them to leave me with fucking giant. By the time he was out of the way it was too late. They were out of range of the transmitter. It was only a kid's radio, I had nothing better to hand.'

'Why not contact us?'

O'Carolan's outbreak of laughter left him coughing, patting his chest and crying out, 'Jesus.' He regained his composure. 'Seriously, listen to yourself. Do you really think you'd have done anything other than lock me up and throw away the key? No, I had to go get Orla back.'

Mary leaned close in to murmur in Boyle's ear and his blood rushed at her perfume and the heat of her breath on his skin as she whispered, 'I'll run the names and addresses through PNC and Interpol and I'll get on to Newry about the address.'

Boyle shifted in his chair to relieve the awkward pressure of the inevitable result of her proximity in his kecks. He caught Orla's amused glance and played with his rustling Starbucks cup in silence before finally twisting around in his chair and fleeing, sending a surprised officer into the room to take down formal statements.

Boyle had managed to return to a state of normality by the time the typed statements were emailed to him. He had called a meeting of his resources and units for five o'clock to review the operation McLoughlin and he had pulled together. He was sitting in his office Googling *Al Shabab* when Mary entered. Boyle was bitterly regretting going for that drink with her. A straight, even rude 'no' would have saved him this descent down a slippery slope. He was with Fiona and there was no going back. He was happy, he had a partner who accepted the mad hours and pressures of his job. Not always with good grace, but it could be worse. Perhaps that meant they weren't spending much time together these days, but she was cool with it all and that mattered to Boyle.

'Mary, about—'

She cut into him, business-like. She layered printout onto his desk. 'It's a mess. Al Shabab is fighting a virtual war with the Kenyan government, they're as much into extortion and piracy as they are ideological terrorism.

They seem to use the one to fund the other and nobody much knows which their ultimate goal is. They're into maritime piracy and arms smuggling, the Interpol databases are crammed with references and mentions of them. There's so much there it's actually hard to get the core facts out of all the hype and fear mongering. The Newry warehouse location was broken into, the estate agent noticed four days ago and reported it to PSNI, but his last visit was the month before so they could have been there for ages. He's had no approaches from Africans interested in the property. Lusitania Gardens was owned by an Irish couple living in Dubai and rented to an English national of Libyan origin called Mohammad Muntasir. The guy from Contania.'

Boyle nodded. 'And what have we managed to dig up on him? Muntasir?'

'His full name was Mohammed Muntasir. His father ran a bookshop and small press called The Free Africa Information Bureau. Mohammed had travelled four times to Kenya in the past two years. And once to Lebanon and then Cyprus. It's likely he travelled from there to Libya or perhaps Palestine. The trail ends there. He doesn't seem like a Cyprus sun seeking holiday kind of guy from this profile'

'So we have a Libyan connection.'

'It gets better. Muntasir's father originally travelled here as Gaddafi's liaison man with the Provisionals. He was responsible for overseeing the Libyan end of the shipments of Semtex and arms from Libya back in the eighties.'

Boyle rocked back in his chair. 'Jesus, but that's dynamite…' He realised too late and Mary burst into laughter. 'Stop it, I didn't mean…'

He jumped up, his finger wagging but her laughter

was infectious. She was standing by him, her breasts lifting and falling, a joyous eruption. She wiped her eyes, her mouth open and breathless. Their eyes connected and Boyle's heart leapt. Jesus, he was like granite down there. A fucking jack-hammer of a boner.

He tore his gaze away, found focus on the floor and shook his head. 'No. Mary. No. I can't.'

The stillness of her uncertainty turned to hurt. He knew she was his, that he could reach out to her softness and she'd melt. His hand was halfway to her breast, poised in mid-air. Boyle turned on his heel before he betrayed himself.

Pat O'Carolan was alone in the interview room, playing with the digital recorder, when Boyle arrived. He didn't seem like he had a care in the world, which annoyed Boyle for some reason. He kicked the door shut. 'Where's the girl?'

'Oh, Orla?' O'Carolan smiled. 'Gone to find sandwiches from the canteen. It's alright, she had a peeler with her.'

'We've informed her family as to her whereabouts. Your brother wants to kill you. We've had a *Gardaí* protection team assigned to them.'

Pat considered that one for a second. 'Fine.'

Boyle paced the room. 'A quick question for you, maybe a strange one.'

'What?'

'Do you know any Palestinians or Libyans? Here in Belfast, I mean.'

Pat nodded, fidgeting. 'I do. I was thinking of paying him a visit. My old mucker Hamid.'

'Right, and who's Hamid when he's in his tent?'

A Decent Bomber

'Hamid Muntasir,' Pat leaned back in his chair. 'He came over here in the eighties in the first rust bucket full of guns they sent over to us. I didn't know him then, I was inside. But I met him after I got out, when he'd settled down here. He'd met him a nice *cailín* and decided to stay. Cheeky bastard claimed political asylum from the Gaddafi regime and got it. And of course he was working for the old sod all along. I'd forgotten all about him until a guy I know happened to mention him.'

'Vinny Byrne?'

'They got to him, didn't they?'

'Oh, yes.'

Pat ran his hand back through his hair and drew a long breath, letting it out in a sigh. Boyle waited. Pat glared up. 'He's dead, right? That's what you're telling me?'

'You went to see him the other day. He fixed you up with, what,' Boyle counted on his fingers, 'a car, a credit card some cash and a pair of mobiles.'

'Okay, you win. I'm impressed, Sherlock.'

Boyle shrugged. 'Not too hard to figure out. You're driving a different car. We ran the number plate. You were staying under an assumed name at the Premier Inn. And of course we recovered Orla's mobile from the crime scene. The Gards found your Daihatsu. It got torched. Like Byrne, really. Sorry,' Boyle paused, because all great comedy is about timing, 'about the Daihatsu.' He glared at Pat, who was in turn staring at the table top. 'Were you close, then? You and he?'

'We went back.'

'And it was him mentioned Muntasir to you?'

'Aye. We both knew him, back then. Most of us did. He cut something of a dash.'

'A Libyan in Belfast?'

'Exotic, right enough. Once he'd settled he became like an ex-smoker, he was a one man opposition to Gaddafi's regime. He set up a bookshop and published pamphlets about Gaddafi's downfall and sold kaftans and king sized Rizlas to the hippies.'

'Wouldn't Gaddafi have tried to do for him?'

'Possibly. But I assumed he'd done a deal in return for his silence.'

'How you mean, you assumed so?'

'You didn't get told things you didn't need to know.'

'But you made the bombs, surely you'd be in on that?'

'No. Someone else got the stuff, I just made do with whatever they gave me.'

'So why were you thinking of going to see him?'

'The mosque didn't exactly get the result I was expecting, he was the only other lead I could think of to that sort of thing. Africa. All that.'

'You were at the mosque? You know about the—'

'Yes, I was there. I was to go back later in the evening and he was going to give me information. They got to him first.'

'I'd say they did. So the gunfight was you? That and an aggravated assault on police officers at the Victoria? Shots fired in a hospital? You've been leaving something of a trail behind you, Mister O'Carolan.'

'Tell me about it.'

'I talked them out of charging you for the hospital stunt, but only for now. They'll come back to it later.' Boyle slapped his hands on the table and stood up. 'I've got an operation to put together. We booked you into the Hilton under the name of Smith. I've two plain clothes will stay with you. They'll be discreet. But I'd appreciate if you'd hand over the firearms you have. You've caused enough trouble with them.'

A Decent Bomber

'No. I'll take your protection, but leave me mine.' Pat, too, got to his feet. He towered above Boyle, who met the unflinching brown eyes and the resolution in the craggy face. They stood facing each other in the silence. Boyle nodded. 'For now, then.'

It had been a busy afternoon. McLoughlin had insisted on checking the arrangements in place at Belfast Central station. Boyle met him at the entrance. McLoughlin was looking uncomfortable in a tweed jacket and jeans. He had only ever seen the man in uniform. The jeans were a bit baggy-arsed, tell the truth. Sort of Dad-jeans. They were generally pretty discreet, wandering around behaving as much like the other travellers as they could while they went through their planned locations, approaches and exits. Boyle even bothered to have a city map with him so he could appear convincingly lost.

The station was busy, commuters starting to make their way home. The Tannoy rang out, echoing across the open spaces. Trains lined up, filling with their cargo of weary workers.

Boyle raised his voice over the Tannoy. 'So we're tight. Every entrance is covered. The second we catch sight of any African, we've got him on camera and there's a sniper on him. I'm asking you to authorise deadly force.'

McLoughlin raised an eyebrow. 'You think it'll come to that?'

'They've been pretty deadly forces themselves so far. I don't expect them to play any more nicely now.'

'What about the public? I don't want people put in harm's way.'

Boyle struggled not to let his incredulity show. It was,

after all, bad for business. 'We've got evacuation procedures in place; ambulances will be close by parked in two discreet locations where they won't seem incongruous. A number of officers are tasked with taking a pure public safety role if anything does happen. Generally, I'd say we're good.'

McLoughlin halted and turned to Boyle. He put an avuncular hand on Boyle's shoulder. Boyle managed not to flinch at the touch.

'Authorised. Good job, John. I'm not best pleased you ignored me on the issue of extending immunity to O'Carolan and I won't pretend that I am. But for what it's worth, I think you probably made the right call. Don't make a habit of countermanding me in future, though.'

McLoughlin gave his shoulder a couple of pats for good measure and walked away, leaving Boyle in a state of half-fury, half-wonderment.

Boyle's last task was the C3 section briefing. The heads of the uniform sections were there, as well as his team of intelligence officers. They'd play a plain clothes role, mostly surveillance and management. It was a long and detailed planning session with a lot of questions and answers.

Boyle called a halt, finally, and wrapped it up. 'That's it, ladies and gentlemen. We all know who we're reporting to, who to escalate to if something seems out of place or if it all goes tits up. I'll say this one last time; the people we're expecting at this rendezvous are deeply unpleasant and quite happy to use deadly force. There's a hundred million quid ransom resting on this, as well as God knows how many innocent lives, so we've got one chance to get it right. There are no heroes and there's no place for departmental or inter-force point scoring or rivalry. We've all got to get this right. And I, for one, know that we're in safe hands. Now fuck off home and get a good night's kip.'

He gave them the thumbs up and they gave him a cheer and then the room broke up as they rushed the exit, chattering.

It was dark outside and Boyle, kicking a stone down the street as he reached his car, reflected bitterly on yet another working Sunday.

Chapter Fourteen

Pat was impressed by the plain clothes officer who took them to the Hilton and saw them checked in. She was pretty, efficiently friendly and had the whole thing down pat so you almost wouldn't notice you'd been put precisely where she wanted you all along. If they'd had a few more of her back in the nineties, it'd have been game over a lot sooner, he mused.

They stood under the big red architectural pillar in the hotel's swanky reception waiting for Orla to get her card key issued. Boyle had arranged a suite for them both, paid for by the British taxpayer, which amused Pat no end. The staff were curious, despite themselves. Any bags sir? No they only had hand luggage thank you, and Pat had become yet more interesting to the receptionist. Surrounded by sweeping white marble and arcs of glass, Pat tried not to gawp.

Pat turned to the officer. She was brown-eyed and had laughter lines, perhaps in her early forties but Pat could never really get ages. 'Can I ask your name?'

'I told you, it's Breda.'

'Your real name.'

'That's Breda, too. Breda Fitzsimmons.'

'Well, it's nice to be protected by you, Breda.'

She glanced at the holdall at his feet and back up at him with a raised eyebrow. 'A pleasure.' Orla turned away from the reception desk and Breda led the way to the lifts. 'Right, let's get you to your rooms.'

Orla looked as tired as Pat felt. 'I'm famished. Where can we get some food around here?'

Breda hit the button. 'I think room service is probably

the best option.' She held open the door. 'Here we go.'

They were silent in the lift, Orla slumped against the back wall, pale and playing with the ends of her hair. Breda stepped out first and gestured them to follow. She stood aside as Orla slid the card key into the door of the suite and followed them in. Pat caught a glimpse of the harness under Breda's leather coat as she hoisted out her mobile. The room was modern, beige walls and rugs, dark wood flooring and big windows with a view across the scattered lights of the city.

Orla shrugged off her backpack and flumped down on the sofa to read the room service menu.

'Club sandwich and a coke,' Pat threw at her as he hefted his holdall into the master bedroom. Breda called out. 'There's a Brian MacNamara at reception.'

Pat poked his head back into the living room. 'Can they send him up?'

Breda nodded and Pat grinned thumbs up at her before kicking the door shut behind him and peeling off clothes that felt stuck to his skin. He felt every year of his age, trying to ignore the hairy, pale bulk in the wall length mirror. The shower heated up and Pat stepped in, opening up little pots and unwrapping wee soaps until there was nothing left but a pile of plastic wrapping swirling about in a race for the plug hole. Stepping out, he wasn't sure what he smelled like but he felt better and anything would have smelled better than Pat pre-shower.

He shaved with the hotel disposable and managed not to tear his face open, which was a bonus. Wafting out of the bathroom back into the bedroom, Pat pulled his jeans and t-shirt off the floor and dressed. He wrenched open the door. 'Ta da!'

'Orla's gone to get a shower,' Breda smiled. She had unbuttoned her coat and sat back in an armchair, her leg over the arm of it. Her harness was fully visible, including the pistol in the pocket stitched across her belly. She caught his glance and lifted two fingers, sighted down them and shot him.

Brian MacNamara was sitting on the sofa. He seemed dead beat, his eyes red and his sago-skinned face lined and sombre.

'Brian.'

'Pat. I'll not stay long. I'll look after Orla in the morning. Boyle didn't want me to but I insisted. It's the least I can do and I want to do something, anything than just stand by as those bastards undo everything we've worked for.'

'I heard about Simone. I'm sorry.'

'I've just come from Sean Driscoll. It's mayhem down there. The word is out we're responsible for the Victoria Square bombing. There are riots in the streets, a pub's been petrol-bombed and two lads are dead and another shot in the legs. The Unionist crazies are baying for our blood and even the moderates are calling for explanations we can't give.'

'Well, how about telling them the truth?'

'It's not playing so well right now. We don't even know what the truth is. There's a lot more riding on bringing this bloke in tomorrow morning than what they've done to my family. Or what's left of it.' MacNamara got to his feet, his shoulders slumped.

'At least you have Jean.'

MacNamara stared at Pat, his drawn face bleak. 'No, Pat, that I don't. She's left me. She wants nothing to do with a murderer who's had the comeuppance God had in store for him and which has been brought down on her head by him.'

Pat was stuck for words, his mind trying not to think

things like *it was your fault for marrying a Presbyterian* but failing. He stepped forward, his mouth open to at least force his brain to say something, but MacNamara waved him away and turned away to the door.

'Forget it, Pat. I can try and right my house once we stop these African boys from tearing our city apart. And you know something? It's twenty years too late, but you were right all along.'

'What's that?'

'Sean Driscoll's a flaky bastard. I'll see you in reception at half seven tomorrow.'

MacNamara closed the door behind him. Breda laughed softly, contempt distorting her face. 'You can sing that.'

'You know him? Driscoll?'

'Not personally. I just see him out now and then kissing babies.'

The doorbell rang and Breda swung up off the armchair to get it. She stood aside for the room service trolley. 'Just leave it there, thanks.'

Pat signed off the bill, regretting he didn't even have a fiver to give the waiter. Breda stood by the door and let the man out. She closed the door after him and went over to rummage in her handbag on the coffee table.

'I'll leave you to it, so.' She fished out an old-fashioned looking mobile. 'Here, this is a Tetra handset. Hit this button here and you'll be talking to the whole protection team. There are two of us here in the hotel and four more outside. I'll be in the room next door. I'll come for you at seven in the morning.'

She put her hand up to his cheek and stroked it with her thumb, smiled sweetly at him and left. Pat stood staring after her for a few seconds and then the smell from the trolley reached him. He strode over to Orla's room and banged on her door. 'Food's here.'

Whatever she said, it just came across as a muffled something. Pat didn't wait and lifted the plate cover to reveal a club sandwich and fries. He took the plate and his coke over to the dining table and unrolled the tight wad of cutlery. There was tomato ketchup. There was mayonnaise.

Pat got stuck in. If you learned one thing in prison, it was eat what you can when you can. The lesson never really leaves you, he thought, happily shaking salt over his fries.

Pat woke with a start, the dream still fresh in his mind and his hands clutching at the duvet. His pillow was wet, but a chill lay on him. He was disoriented for a second, thrown by the big, super-soft duvet and plumped up pillows. *Hotel. Belfast. Meeting with Somali terrorist at nine. Christ on a bike. Business as usual, then.*

He rolled over and checked the bedside clock. It was just gone three. He lay back and stared up at the ceiling, the vividness of the dream-memory slowly dissipating. He had been young again, full of energy and throwing himself at life like a lunatic flinging himself against a padded wall. She was everything a girl could be, vivacious and cheeky, beautiful and fresh as a summer's raindrop. She and Pat had lain together in the long grass, bees buzzing as his hand slid up her dress and her legs opened for him as their tongues entwined.

They had gone at it like rabbits all summer. Pat had never known happiness – or lust – like it in his life. Then the day she had been all serious-faced, her hesitant 'Pat, I have something to tell you' and he *knew* before she licked her lips, before she opened her mouth. The only thing he felt when she had spoken, her fearful eyes awaiting his reaction, was all-consuming joy. They talked about how they were going to act through the scenes when they told their parents and the daft old priest giving them a dressing down and they didn't care because the three of them had so much ahead of them it would make you want to burst.

Until the nervous kid in fatigues at the checkpoint was the one who pissed her off one time too many and she refused to stop walking for him when he shouted at her to halt. Pat was halfway to her, crying out her name, begging her to see sense and turn back for the wee man. The swans on the sluggish river took flight at the shot.

Her name was Orla, the never-to-be mother of Pat's child. She was a redhead. Pat's brother Mikey named his daughter for the young woman who died on the tarmac by a checkpoint, a baby girl struggling in her cooling belly.

The tears came to Pat again, lying in his hotel bed. He scrabbled on the bedside and blew his nose noisily. An old man wrapped up in events too young for him, a lifetime wasted when a moment went wrong. Pat smacked himself over the head with the remonstration, twisting it in his mind, hurting himself so he couldn't possibly face sleep anymore and lay on his back with his eyes wide open and mouthing her name, the hot moisture coursing down his temples onto the pillow.

He woke again at six and wondered what the hell had been going through his mind in the night to make him punish himself with the past like that. Knowing well he was about to walk into something he'd never encountered before, something dangerous and – in its way – important. He hated the thought the moment it occurred to him. Pat had never been about his own importance, yet MacNamara's talk about the unravelling of everyone's fragile confidence meant this meeting could well save the peace.

Christ, man, get a grip! Would you ever listen to yourself?

It was still dark outside. The streetlights reflected in the puddles. Pat padded back to the bed and rolled himself up in the duvet like a sausage roll. The room was warm and he felt like just telling them all to go to hell, he would stay wrapped up like a wee Irish chrysalis and emerge an emerald butterfly. He stretched out to pop on the bedside lamp. There was a Hilton notepad by the bedside and he tore off the top sheet and set about folding it into a delicate paper swan, his trembling fingers steadying as he immersed himself in his task.

The doorbell woke him. He flung out his arm and a cascade of little paper swans tumbled over the lip of the mattress to the floor. He scooped and plucked them into the bin and pulled on the heavy hotel dressing gown, stumbling bleary-eyed through the living room. He pulled open the door and stood aside automatically to let the room service trolley through. Breda followed behind it, wearing a t-shirt and jeans under her waist-length leather coat. It was open to show the lightweight harness she wore, radio handset and gun tucked into pockets set in the webbing.

'Morning hotshot. You're looking like shite.'

Pat pulled a face at her. 'Didn't sleep so well. What's all this?'

'Breakfast. The condemned man eats a hearty meal. You can shit, shower and shave after.'

A Decent Bomber

'What time is it?'

'Just after seven.' Breda signed off the bill and let the waiter out.

Pat banged on Orla's bedroom door, rewarded with a muffled howl of outrage. He tried the handle and pushed the door open. 'Get up! Breakfast!'

Breda had set the table from the trolley and was already carving her way into a massive fry.

'Jesus, you didn't hang about.'

'That's me, quick, see? I'm a reactor, I am.'

Pat paused, bacon hanging in mid-air, dripping falling onto his toast. 'A what?'

'A reactor. I'm a fast Breda.'

'Yer arse.' Pat scraped butter onto his bacon-fat toast and poured himself a cup of tea. Orla appeared in her dressing gown, tousle-haired and grimacing in the light. Pat glanced up at her and tried not to remember the ancient history that had kept him awake. Today was about facing the future, uncertain though it may be.

'Come on, get some food.'

'How can you eat at a time like this?'

Pat laughed, fried egg wobbling on his fork. 'When you've been truly hungry, girl, you'll learn to eat what you can, when you can. Come, eat, so.'

Breda poured tea for Orla as she gathered herself into the chair, pulling her hair back from her face. 'Did you sleep okay?'

'Like a log,' Orla picked at the fry, helped herself to toast. 'I nearly drowned in that duvet, though. How the other half live, eh?'

Breda grinned at her. 'You're going to be with Brian MacNamara this morning. He'll take good care of you but he'll make sure you're both close by. Pat, Boyle's coming at eight to wire you up and fill you in on any last minute details. I'll be with you up until you're on the platform. Once you're there, I'll stick as close by you as operationally prudent.'

'Fine. Pass the marmalade, would you?'

If Pat had been twenty years younger, they'd have made a nice family, he reflected as he poured more tea. Well, apart from the fact mummy was wearing a gun.

Pat sat back, his hands on his belly. 'God, but that hit the spot. Right, I'd best get cleaned up. I'll leave you girls do the plates.'

Grinning at Breda's growl, Pat flapped to his bedroom in his hotel slippers. He washed and shaved, taking care not to nick himself with the hotel razor. He used an electric one usually, left behind a million years ago in a Tipperary farmhouse. It was hardly worth it, the stubble was only light after last night's shave, but then sluicing himself in hot water and drying off with a warm, soft towel, Pat felt a good shave, like a good fry, was a luxury only a man who has served time can truly appreciate.

As he was dressing the doorbell sounded, the hubbub of voices outside rising. The unreal world of the Hilton was starting to become the real one of preparing to meet a deadly terrorist and Pat felt short of breath. He reached into the holdall and pulled out his Baby Glock, testing its action before sliding in a magazine, pocketing a spare and shoving the gun into his greatcoat pocket.

He walked out into the living room with his coat over his arm to find Breda with MacNamara, Boyle and two PSNI constables. Big though the suite was, it was feeling crowded.

'Orla's freshening up,' Breda looked up from browsing her iPad Mini and smiled in response to his raised eyebrow.

Boyle shook his hand. 'Right, so. We'd best get you

miked up. Everything's in place, we've got plain clothes units covering every approach to the station and two profiling teams already in the station. We've two men covering platform four with full line of sight. We've fixed cameras around the station and doubled up the operators so we don't miss a mouse. It's going to be a breeze.'

'You're a fine man, sure you are, Boyle. Ain't everything a breeze from half a mile away?'

'Here. Try this on.'

Pat dumped his coat on a chair and took the padded black gilet Boyle held out to him. He slid it over his shoulders, a good fit. It had a pocket stitched across the front for a pistol.

'That's handy,' Pat smiled. He reached into his coat and pulled out the Glock, slipping it into the pocket in the gilet. The magazine fit neatly into a pocket to the left.

Boyle froze at the sight of the gun. He caught Pat's eye and his lips tightened. 'Okay, so. I didn't see you had that. This is your radio. It's one-way, we can hear you but you can't hear us. We can't afford to risk an earpiece. This is the off switch, please be so kind as to remember it if you go for a piss, we can live without the sound effects. For the love of God, if you do go, remember to switch it back on again. Here, put your coat on.'

Boyle clipped the slim black unit into a stay set into the gilet. He fed the cable up from the radio to a small barrel-shaped microphone which clipped to the gilet by Pat's armpit. Boyle buttoned Pat's coat and stepped back. 'That's grand. We've been making a bit of a fuss about you in the news media, so your man has no reason to believe you'll be working with us. In fact, you're an armed and dangerous terror suspect and the public has been warned to stay away from you at all costs. Don't go scaring any grannies. Whatever this Hassan Ali Jaffar wants, promise him it. Try and get him to talk about their network, assets and operations. But just agree with him and let him go. Once you're clear, we'll move in on him. If anything looks wrong, shout and hit the deck. The snipers'll do the rest.'

'Snipers, is it? You're not messing around, Boyle.'

'Dead or alive, Pat. That's a fact. Now, don't lose this.'

'This?'

Boyle handed over the slip of card. 'Your ticket to Victoria Station. Platform four at Belfast Central is the Larne line, comes down through Carrickfergus to Victoria Street.'

Orla joined them. She'd changed her clothes and found makeup from somewhere. Pat wanted to tell the PSNI boys to get their eyes off her, which was just the adrenalin, but there was no doubt she was attracting attention. She handed a small bag to Breda, which explained where the makeup had come from.

'Are you all set?' He asked her. Her small nod and troubled glance made his heart want to break and he reached out and pulled her to him. 'It'll be alright, *mo chara*, we'll get this out of the way and start again. You just see.'

'Let's move out,' Boyle opened the door. 'We're cutting it fine.'

They drove through the early morning streets, the traffic thick, tyres swishing in the wet. Pat sat in the front, Boyle driving and talking on his hands free to various units.

Boyle glanced at Pat. 'We've been monitoring the area closely since yesterday evening, particularly with an eye to any surveillance or watcher activity.'

'Any joy?'

'Well, this morning we've managed to trace two prostitutes and a kerb crawler.'

'Impressive. That's pretty early.'

'You'd be amazed at the things we see.' The radio buzzed. 'Hang on. Boyle.'

The voice on the hands free speaker was deadened by the radio. 'Can we get a sound check please boss?'

'You're on stage, Pat.'

'Right, so. There's this American tourist in Belfast and he's minding his own business right enough, you know, just walking around and taking in the sights, like, when he feels a gun pushed into the very small of his back and a voice says "Are you Protestant or Catholic?" and so yer man thinks fast on his feet and says, "Neither buddy, I'm Jewish." And the voice says, "Well, would you cop for that? I must be the luckiest fucking Arab in Belfast." How's that?'

Boyle grinned and the voice on the radio was laughing. 'That's just fine. Good luck, sir.'

'Well I'll be jiggered. That's the first time a Peeler's ever called me sir and not made it sound like he was talking to a dog.'

'Let's hope it's not the last.' Boyle pulled up in front of a long line of taxis. 'Here we are. Good luck. Breda will pick you up from here.'

Pat got out of the car and glanced back to check MacNamara and Orla were still behind. She waved through the car window and he smiled for her. Breda appeared at his side, her arm in his and sweeping him along. 'Pat? Is it yourself? Pat O'Carolan? Well I never! It must be, what, five, six years? Where have you been hiding, you lovely man?' They passed through the automatic doors from the street and on into the station building. 'Come on, you can buy me a coffee. How's everyone back home? Still the same? Don't tell me Mary Ryan still has that bicycle shop on the high street, it must be a lifetime since she could ride a bike, mind you know what they said about her and bikes when she was younger, not that I'd have any time for auld slander like that, you know yourself.'

Arm in arm, they strolled into the terminal, Breda keeping up her tide of mad banter. Pat peeped at his watch, eight fifty. They headed for a café advertising cooked breakfasts scrawled on floor-standing chalk boards, something Pat didn't need on account of having just had one and wanting to throw it up, actually, his stomach was that tight right now. Breda made great show of installing him at a table before going to get coffees. A man in the queue let her in. He wore a Gabardine, a newspaper folded under his arm. The haircut gave him away. Peeler.

She was back in a flash with the coffees, loads of milk in his. 'How did you know?'

'Asked Orla, 'course. Now, you can chat with me like an old friend, but have the odd glance at your watch and then stand up at about five to and make your apologies, say how nice it was to bump into me and leave promising to stay in touch.'

'Ah, Breda, if I were only twenty years younger.' Pat checked his watch.

'I'm fifty this year, don't be giving me yer auld *plámás*.'

Pat raised an eyebrow. 'Sure, you don't look it. Shouldn't you be settled down instead of running around with guns?'

'You can never be too old,' she waggled a finger at him, 'to be running around with guns. Are you not a prime example yourself?'

Touché. He was about to think of something witty to say back to her when she pressed a hand to her ear, nodding. 'Okay, Boyle's got everything in place and he's ready. Time to go, Pat.'

She threw back her head and laughed. She stood with him, put her hand on his shoulder and kissed his cheek. A light perfume with a hint of sweet melon. Heading for platform four, he glanced back to see her standing and waving at him. He waved and turned to stride across the concourse towards platform four. The Larne train, was it? He checked the board, sure enough, due in at five past nine, coming in through Carrickfergus and Jordanstown. So would his man be on the platform waiting or come in on the train? Pat felt in his pocket for the ticket Boyle had given him, humming Carrickfergus because he was nervous and it would maybe give the lads listening in a laugh. The Jordanstown bomb wasn't one of his and he was glad. For all he had on his conscience, a woman dead with her baby unborn wasn't on it. The thought brought her back to him, the moment she fell and her whispered words as her eyes flickered away into unseeing reflections of the dark sky. And the beat of the swans' wings as they fled.

He flicked his ticket at the inspector and walked onto platform four, singing under his breath.

I wish I was in Carrickfergus, only for nights in Ballygrand.

I would swim over the deepest ocean, the deepest ocean for my love to find,

But the sea is wide and I can't swim over, neither have I wings to fly.

If I could find me a handsome boatman to ferry me over to my love and die.

He remembered the microphone. Ah, feck 'em. They

could do with a good tune to cheer 'em up.

The platform was almost empty, a young woman with a pierced lip and nostril, purple hair and panda-eye makeup, a pensioner couple leaning into each other to better hear whatever it was they had to say. Not an African in sight. Pat leaned against the glass window of the empty waiting room and glanced at his watch. Dead on nine.

He was coming on the train, then. Or not at all.

'Lads, the bastard's only late.' He whispered, leaning down so his head was in his hands and nobody could see his lips moving. He pushed away from the wall and paced the platform. Two men in suits walked past him as he turned back towards the turnstile. They didn't look like plain clothes, but then that was the point in any case, wasn't it?

Pat checked his watch again. Three minutes past nine. He wondered if they could hear his heart on the radio, because he certainly felt the thumping in his chest. Ten past, he'd bail. They hadn't even talked about a no-show as a possibility.

People were starting to gather in anticipation of the train. A mother pushed her baby buggy up the platform; a young couple were wrapped in each other and laughing at their private jokes. Pat tried not to scan the rafters for the snipers.

He heard the rails singing before he spied the yellow and blue flash of the engine's nose in the distance. The tannoy announced the arrival of the oh nine oh five from Larne at platform four. More people were pushing their way up the platform now as the train approached.

Pat peeped at his watch. The train was a minute early, miracle of miracles. He felt lonely vulnerable and filled with the intense desire to be sitting by the range and tickling Kirstie's ear as he listened to the news.

The train juddered to a halt, the screech of brakes and a hiss of air as the doors slid open. Breda shouting his name turned him. She was racing toward him. Fear made her face ugly. Behind her, Boyle clattered to a halt and stood off.

Breda ran square into him, hitting him a second before the blast wave.

It had been Mary's diligence made all the difference. When 'Big' Bill McFadden had reported for work at Contania's Jordanstown depot, eight thirty on the nail as always, he had found her waiting for him by the front door. She'd decided to go in mufti, flashed her ID at him, dropped Peter Bryce's name and smiled sweetly. McFadden was a burly smoker in his fifties, hair thinning around the temples and a lantern jaw with a disapproving mouth. He carried a paper under his arm. He peered at her ID and took a last puff of his cigarette before grinding it out with his heel.

'Peeler, is it? Right, well you can tell me about it over tea. No tea, no talk. Right?'

'Sounds good to me. Lead on.' Mary scurried alongside the loping man. 'You don't look like a mountaineer.'

'Why?'

'We wanted to talk to you yesterday. Bryce said you'd be up a mountain.'

'That's just his English way. I help my brother farm his sheep at weekends. I'm amazed ye got him out of bed the weekend. You'd not find him getting up for church, that one.'

It wasn't until they'd pushed into the canteen and slid

two mugs of brown tea onto the worn table, one sugared, that McFadden slapped his newspaper down and gave her the benefit of his blue-eyed, bushy-browed glare. 'So what can I do you for? Or have you come to do for me?'

'Mohammed Muntasir. He worked for you.'

'Worked? What do you mean by that? He's still on the payroll, far as I know.'

'I think you can take him off. He's dead.'

McFadden's jaw was out, his hand raised. Mary's words stilled him and he let his hand drop to the table. 'Well, is that a fact? How, may I ask?'

'He was one of the gunmen in the Premier Inn terror attack.'

McFadden tapped the newspaper. 'This?'

Mary nodded. She waited as he scanned the lurid story. She sipped at her tea. It was the wrong mug and she grimaced at the cloying sugar.

'Well, that's one for the books alright.' McFadden let the paper drop and sat back. 'You'd never have thought it. Something wrong with that tea, young lady?'

'Sugar.'

He tasted his tea and screwed his mouth up in disgust. He reached across the table and pulled sachets out of the little plastic holder, tore them open and stirred the flow of sugar into the mug. He tried the tea again and smiled. 'Better. He was new, just passed his probation. Good lad. Libyan. You'd never think he was… well, you know. One of *them*.'

'Mister Bryce mentioned he was new. Did he have any known associates here?'

'Well, his brother. It was Karim suggested Mohammed for the job when it came up.'

'Karim?'

'Our head of despatch. He's been here these past, oh,

two, three years. We took him on as a despatcher but he's bright and a hard worker. He's done well for himself.'

'Can we speak with him?'

'Sure. Hang on.' McFadden delved into his overcoat pocket and tapped his mobile. He hooked his mug and drank as he waited. 'Rang out. No answer. Odd.'

'Where does he work?'

'Right here in the depot. Come along, let's see where he's got to.'

McFadden zipped up his coat and picked up his mug of tea. Mary pulled her bag from the chair next to her and followed him out of the canteen. They walked past lines of containers, the blue corrugated sheds loomed either side of them, the beeping of reversing pallet trucks and roar of engines all around. McFadden's tea steamed in the morning air. They rounded a corner into a busy yard. McFadden stopped a man in a boiler suit and shouted above the noise. 'Karim around?'

'Haven't seen him today. Try the office.'

Mary struggled to keep up with McFadden's stride. They walked into a red brick 1960s building, the warmth a welcome contrast. 'Anyone seen Karim?'

McFadden put his mug down on a desk. He looked worried. 'Let me just check. He pulled out his mobile again. 'Hi Joan, it's Bill. Did Karim Muntasir clock in today? Sure, thanks. No, I'll wait if it's all the same.' He turned to Mary, the mobile tilted away from his ear. 'He's not had a day off since he joined. He should have been supervising the skeleton crew yesterday. He gets a day in lieu, usually takes a Friday.' The mobile squawked. 'Sorry Joan. Right you are. Thanks.'

McFadden laid the mobile down on a desktop, his face clouded. 'He's not clocked in since last Thursday. He took his day off Friday, didn't pitch Sunday and hasn't clocked in today. Is he one of them too, then?'

'We don't know for sure, but I think I'd like to have a look at his desk.'

'No, wait up a wee bit. You understand the situation here? If he is, he's had access to pretty much every container that's ever been through Belfast, by road or rail.'

'Rail?'

'Sure. This facility backs onto the main line out of Belfast here.'

Mary stared at McFadden. 'Right. Give me just a second, would you?'

She walked back out into the cold and called Boyle.

Boyle had joined Breda at her table in the café after she'd seen Pat off to his platform, his hands curled around a paper take-away mug of coffee. 'How's it going?'

'Fine. He's a brave man.'

'He's a former IRA bomber who did time in Long Kesh and don't you forget it.'

'Jesus, Boyle. Did you never think of forgetting as an option?'

'Never.'

His mobile rang and he answered it, his eyes widening as he listened. He nodded, twice, said 'Thanks' and hung up.

'Sounded interesting.'

'One of the Premier Inn gang worked for a company called Contania. Turns out his brother was head of despatch there. They handle most of Belfast's container freight and their terminal backs onto the railway. So we have a terror suspect with a stash of bombs and a national road and rail distribution network. It's a fucking nightmare.'

It hit Boyle with awful clarity. Afterward, he could never quite work out how he'd made the connection, but Pat's whispered voice in his earpiece complaining that there was nobody in the waiting room and the train was coming triggered the thought of Contania's depot and trains slowing to pass the freight yards. He leapt to his feet, hitting the table and hurling the coffee onto the floor. The container burst and splashed dark liquid.

'Christ, Breda. The train! Come on!'

Boyle sprinted across the concourse, his legs pumping as he shouted into his radio, 'Clear the fucking platform. Clear platform four.'

He slammed into the platform entrance and pushed away, hurtling towards Pat and then faltering as the immediacy of the bomb hit him. Where would it be? Which carriage? It wasn't a freight train, it was a passenger train. Breda was ahead of him, shouting. The world went into slow motion, Pat turned towards Breda, his face a mask of surprise. She hit him like a rugby player, a foul tackle with her arms around his chest to bring him down. They rolled.

Boyle threw himself down as the train erupted, a huge burst of energy splitting it down the platform side and throwing out a dark hail to shatter the windows of the rooms along the platform. The sound hit him a moment before the concussion wave, which slammed him against the station-master's cabin, the crash of glass smashing above his head and the evil zings of shrapnel. Boyle felt tugs at his leg, his arm. Still the smash and tinkle of shattering glass, the low roar and a burgeoning mushroom of black smoke and orange flame roiling into the graphite sky above the train. Screams rang out and Boyle uncurled himself, his shoulder pulsing agony. He examined himself, shallow cuts to his arms, a ruined jacket and shirt. A deeper gash in his leg. He pushed himself up to a sitting position against the blue office wall, surveyed the scene in front of him. There was detritus all over the place, the carriage had split open like a joke cigar, jagged teeth of framework and aluminium skin curled back from the flaming maw. There was a thick haze in the air, bodies lying further up the platform, at least one figure on its feet but stumbling blindly. Pat and Breda were nowhere to be seen.

Boyle's throat was raw from the smoke. He barked into his radio, 'Ambulances, fast. You hear me?'

'They're already on the way. You okay?'

'Minor. A lot of casualties here. I lost O'Carolan and Breda.'

'We're on the way.'

Police officers were already streaming out onto the platform, stooping to assess the bundles on the ground. Sirens keened in the distance.

Boyle rose painfully to his feet and staggered to support himself against a railing. He surveyed the scene of carnage along the platform, the cries of the wounded ringing out from inside the train. Medics were rushing through the smoky haze.

Two figures walked up the platform towards him, arm in arm. A man and a woman. The man was limping, the woman supporting him. Boyle's throat was dry. 'Breda? Where the fuck'd ye go?'

'We fell off the platform. Damn near killed ourselves.'

Boyle tried to laugh, but it just came out as a croak.

Chapter Fifteen

Waiting in the Belfast Central Station car park, Brian MacNamara had given up trying to be cheerful and breezy in the face of Orla O'Carolan's contempt. The silence was oppressive and his memories crept up on him. The rain pattered down, the dark sky and parked cars reduced to impressionistic blobs by the streaks and pools of water on the windscreen.

Simone's first day at school, the tears at the gate. Sleepovers and princess parties. The time she'd stepped on a nail in the park. It had gone straight through her foot, dirty and somehow medieval looking. She had screamed blue murder. The ambulance had been sent for, MacNamara gripping her pale hand as they jabbed her arse with the tetanus shot. Winning the Irish dancing. He'd been proud fit to burst that night. The day he'd caught her smoking and the row after. And the dark days, when she'd gone to the bad and it had grown cold between him and Jean. His white wedding turned into a white marriage. Simone came back, in the end, righted herself and made herself into a success, a woman of substance. MacNamara had been so proud of his girl but Jean had never really come back to him after the trouble with Simone. The distance had grown and she had become angry while he had tried to please her to the point where he knew he was being pathetic.

'Please stop doing that.'

He took his hand from the dashboard and let it rest on his leg. Christ, and the wee one. Riley, a lifetime ahead of her, cut down. Maybe Jean had been right. Maybe it was being brought home to him because they had done this to other families in pursuit of The Struggle.

The ground seemed to become liquid for a split second. Orla turned to MacNamara. 'What was–?'

The echoing blast answered her. She craned to follow the rising pall of black smoke through the window. She reached for the door handle. His hand on her arm stopped her. 'No. Stay here. We don't know what's happening in there.'

She flashed at him. 'Pat's in danger, that's what's happening.'

'Pat's got a whole army of police looking out for him. Wait.' MacNamara reached for the Tetra handset Boyle had given him. 'MacNamara here. What's going on?'

'There's been a bomb on the train at platform four. Hang fire until we assess the situation.'

She shrugged her arm away from his grip. 'My Uncle's in there.'

'And my daughter's dead. But we need to hold on and let the professionals deal with this.' He regretted the words the second he'd uttered them. It was his problem, not hers. He'd have to learn to grieve alone.

The radio crackled. Boyle's voice husky, coughing. 'Okay, there was a bomb. Pat's safe. We're bringing in ambulances and backup. Stay put for now.'

'Okay, understood.'

MacNamara turned on the wiper and swept the window. Orla had opened her side window to get a better view, the smoke rising above the station, a black column against the heavy sky.

'I'm sorry about your daughter. She died in the shopping centre bomb, didn't she?'

Yeah, the one your Da made. MacNamara was surprised by the violence of the thought. He'd have to find an outlet for all this anger and bitterness or he'd burst. He felt the tears well up and couldn't trust himself to reply to her. He turned aside and wiped his eyes, trying to steady his voice. 'Yes, yes she did. Her and my granddaughter both.'

He almost missed the movement. A man doubled up, running between the rows of cars. He was in black, his face covered. Two, three dull cracks sounded, the dark domes of the cameras overlooking the car park entrance shattered.

MacNamara made his decision, rebelling against his initial impulse to lay low and hope whatever it was would pass over. He threw the radio at Orla. He twisted the key in the ignition, the engine kicked into life and he watched the figure jinking between the cars halt and turn to them. He hit the accelerator and wrenched at the wheel to stop the car spinning on the wet tarmac, its rear veering as they lunged towards the exit. Orla screamed as the back window shattered. Distant shots cracked and bullets thudded into the car's bodywork. They made the gate, MacNamara almost lost the car again as he careened right into the main road, cutting across the junction and almost hitting a transit van. Its horn blared. Orla struggled against the inertia system to pull her seat belt down. She shouted into the radio, 'We've left the car park, they're shooting at us. Can you hear me?'

'Hi Orla, it's Breda. Calm down a second there. Where are you?'

'Where are we?'

MacNamara snapped, 'Albert Bridge.'

'Coming onto Albert Bridge.'

'Take it handy, we'll try and get a car after you.'

MacNamara slowed, checking in the mirror. A squad car was turning in front of the station. Its siren wailed, shrieking above the clamour of others echoing across the city. MacNamara looked for somewhere to pull over, his eyes drawn back to the mirror as tyres squealed behind them. A red Mercedes barrelled into the main road from the car park area, its headlights shimmering on the tarmac. It started to spin and straightened, its engine howling. Orla turned to see what the noise was. She screamed in his ear, 'Go!'

She scrabbled for the radio in her lap. 'Breda? Breda? There's a car chasing us. A red Mercedes.'

'Hold on there, we've a car after you now.'

MacNamara floored the throttle, bracing against the spin and cursing the big saloon's cumbersome engine as the car behind gained on them. He manoeuvred around an outraged Yaris and risked a glance in the mirror. The squad car pulled alongside the Mercedes, an officer waving it down out of the window. The answering burst of automatic gunfire threw the man back against his driver. The police car swerved, lost control and ploughed into the side of an oncoming Rover, climbing up and twisting in the air, a moment of balletic grace before it came crashing down and the car behind the Rover reamed into it. Glass burst in a corona around the two cars, panels distorting and the air filled with the screech of grinding steel.

Orla screamed into the radio, 'The police car crashed. They shooting at us. Please for the love of God do something.'

'There's a car behind them now, we have other units on the way. Hold in there, Orla, it's going to be okay.'

MacNamara pulled out to overtake the lorry blocking the road ahead, oncoming cars blaring their horns and swinging aside. His wing mirror shattered against an oncoming van looming too close for comfort. Another burst of automatic fire sounded from behind, a cluster of dull impacts on the car's body. The junction ahead split the road for a right filter and MacNamara took the filter lane. He pulled back beyond the traffic island, trying to beat the lorry before the other side of the junction. He moved across too soon and hit the lorry with his rear bumper. The heavy horn boomed as the driver tried to pull aside and lost control, jack-knifing and sliding into the traffic island, mowing down bollards, railings and lights and sliding to a stop sideways to the road.

The lorry almost blocked the entire carriageway. It would have bought them safety and time to get away from the car pursuing them, but the junction was wide, a full seven lanes in all. Orla was huddled up and crying beside him as MacNamara watched the Mercedes negotiate its way around the wreckage they had left behind them, driving the wrong way up the opposite filter lane.

The next junction was all red lights. MacNamara slowed, tracking the Mercedes' race towards them in his mirror. He flicked into the right filter and pumped the throttle, slamming the wheel left at the last second and sliding to miss the kerb of the planted central reservation. His hope they'd slide on the slick road was dashed, the driver behind was skilful and had a more powerful car to boot. It was close behind them and the flat crack of shots was answered by impacts studding the Peugeot's ruined bodywork.

Orla sobbed into the radio. 'Please, Breda please, where are you?'

MacNamara glimpsed the little blue building to the left, Ulster Unionist Party on the sign and Union Jacks hanging from the big brick building next to it. The scrollwork 'Orange Hall' above the ornate doorway. He barely had time for an ironic thought, the lights ahead were orange turning red. Both lanes were blocked by stopped cars. He swung into the oncoming traffic and ran the lights, horns and smoking tyres as a van slid to avoid him, the impact of the car behind hitting it and sending it spinning. The van caught them a glancing blow.

'Orla? Orla? We've got you, we've got visual. We have a helicopter up now. There are patrols coming to you. It's going to be okay.'

Still the bullets smacked into the bodywork. A bullet hit the windscreen, starring it momentarily before the whole surface crazed into opacity. MacNamara balled his fist in his coat sleeve and punched the window out. Splinters of safety glass flew as the windscreen collapsed onto the dashboard, showering them both with fragments.

The whump of a helicopter punctuated the constant rise and fall of sirens. MacNamara wanted to cry with relief at the sight of flashing lights ahead of them, a blockade of squad cars with their yellow and blue checked markings pulled up across the road. Armed police ran towards them.

The volley of automatic fire from behind had the police ducking behind their cars. MacNamara gasped at a tattoo of heavy blows played across his back. He tried to move, but he felt leaden, weighed down. The world was made of candyfloss, woozy and indistinct. With a sick feeling he looked down at his crimson chest. He vaguely heard Orla's screams, but they were like distant seagulls as he stood on the cliff top watching the yacht with its white sails full of the wind crossing the white-capped waves toward him, come to take him away to Simone and Riley.

*

A Decent Bomber

Orla fell out of the door of the car to the wet tarmac, grazing her palms. The radio tumbled into the footwell, Breda's voice squawking her name. Gunshots and breaking glass, shouting and her own sobbing breaths – a megaphone voice, 'Armed police. Drop your weapons.' An answering angry bark of automatic gunfire from nearby.

An urgent voice. 'It's alright love. You're going to be fine. Stay here with me for the minute, they're still shooting.'

She lost track of time, lying on the wet tarmac and listening to the man barking into his radio. Sirens everywhere, men shouting out to each other. The crack of a gunshot and then the bass rhythm of the helicopter. She looked up and there it was, black against the graphite sky almost directly above them. She recoiled at the sight of Brian MacNamara slumped against his car window, his shirtfront crimson with his life's blood. Two more policemen joined them, pulling at her. She tried to help but the tension had left her muscles and she just flopped around in their arms. They half dragged, half carried her away. Her face was raised to the sky, cold raindrops on her skin. Róisín gone. The world turned mad.

There was a whooshing sound. More shouting all around her. The sky lit up, the black bee-shape blew apart, a great flowering of rolling flame and boiling black smoke. The men next to her shouted 'Christ' and they dropped her. Just like that. She fell to the pavement, her hands out to ward off the impact. She rolled onto her back to feel the rain again, to see the fireball slowly drop from the sky.

It looked beautiful, in its way, Róisín. You'd have loved the way it went into slow motion. Ah, but I wish you were here with me to see this. I wish you hadn't left me the way you did. I wish I wish I were a fish.

Breda and Pat sat in the deserted railway station coffee shop. Medics were helping people walk outside to the ambulances. Waiting rooms had been turned into triage stations. Armed officers covered all the doors and forensics teams were working on the rubble-strewn platform. The tannoy was silent. Despite the painkillers they'd given him, Pat's bruised leg was hurting horribly. Breda had a takeaway cup of coffee. She'd gone foraging behind the counter while the medics were tutting over Pat's bruises.

Boyle joined them. He was limping himself. 'Right. They've got Orla, they're bringing her here now. She's fine, a little rattled. It's a huge mess altogether. Brian MacNamara's dead. Three bullets in the back, the poor bastard. And we lost a helicopter with two men in it.'

Pat was glad to be sitting just then. He gripped the table. Only Jean was left of the whole family. It seemed impossible.

Breda put her coffee down. 'So what's the good news, Boyle?'

'Oh, I have some of that, right enough. We dropped all four of the fuckers.'

Pat looked up from regarding his hands in time to see Orla running towards them. He leapt to his feet and caught her, pale-faced and dirt-stained, and hugged her to him.

Boyle finished growling into his radio. 'Breda will take you back to the hotel and you can get cleaned up. We've got fourteen confirmed dead, over fifty injured.'

*

A Decent Bomber

A storm had whipped up, blustery winds and unrelenting rain sloshing down. Pat and Orla dashed across the car park, following Breda to her blue Mini Cooper. The hazard lights flashed. He wrenched open the passenger door, chivvied Orla in and dived out of the rain himself. The drops hammered on the bonnet as Breda reversed. His leg hurt.

Pat shook the raindrops from his coat sleeve. 'Soft day.'

'Nice day to be sitting in the Hilton drinking cups of tea, at any rate.'

They joined the traffic, slowed by the fierce rain. The water tumbled along the gutters.

'Breda, I don't want to go back to the hotel.'

'Tough, Pat. That's where we're headed. You heard the man's orders.'

'There's someone I need to go see. Someone who might be able to help.'

'I can't take my eyes off you, Pat. I'm supposed to be protecting you, remember?'

'So come with us.'

'Against orders.'

'Break the orders.'

'Oh, that's a smashing idea. Why didn't I think of that? Sure, I'm in a fierce tear to end my career.'

'Look, this whole thing is rooted in the past. That's where I'm from, the past. Sure, I thought I could leave it all behind me, but I was wrong. They wouldn't let me retire. Now, the Boyles and McLoughlins, they're concerned about the future. And fair play to 'em. But there's someone I need to go and talk to about the past.'

They pulled up outside the Hilton. Breda acknowledged the subtle nod from her colleague sheltering inside the glass front doors.

'And how are you intending to go about all this? A time machine?'

'In a manner of speaking. I want to find Emily Patterson.'

'Emily who?'

'In the early eighties we did a deal with Gaddafi. We the IRA, I mean. He wasn't a big fan of the Brits and let's say we found us some common ground there. He offered to supply us with whatever we needed to win our independence. Guns, explosives, money, whatever. No strings attached. We're looking at hundreds of tonnes of stuff, literally. There was so much of it, we had problems finding ships big enough to take it all. Gaddafi sent a bloke over to make sure we made good on the deal, a man called Hamid Muntasir. Hamid found life in Belfast a great deal more to his liking than Tripoli and settled down with a nice Irish lass. They opened a bookshop on the Lisburne Road.'

'Emily Patterson.'

'He settled down here with Emily, applied for political asylum. His timing was perfect, we had a falling out with Gaddafi.'

'So nobody paid him a visit.'

'We were asked to, sure enough. My unit was given the job. Then they changed their minds. The message reached the gunman as he was about to pull the trigger.'

'I have the strangest feeling I know who the messenger was.'

'Well, now, I have the strangest feeling you're wrong. I was the gunman. So, how about it?'

She shook her head disbelievingly at him. 'One visit. Then we're back here. And Orla stays here.'

'No.' Orla leaned forwards and put her hand out to Breda's shoulder. 'Don't put us apart again, Breda. I'm safe with Pat.'

'See? I'm a knight in shining armour.' His hand on the door handle, Pat pushed out into the rain. 'Okay. Hold on, I'll be back in two minutes.'

He ignored Breda's cry of protest and dashed to the hotel doors, startling the man in a suit gazing out at the weather. He pulled his card key out in the lift and strode up the corridor to his room. He swiped the lock and shoved the door open, half expecting to find a scene of chaos or a gunman facing him. The little 'do not disturb' sign fluttered. The room beyond was precisely as he had left it. He pulled his battered holdall out of the cupboard and slung it over his shoulder.

Walking across reception, he felt eyes on him. The suit was still there, looking uncertain. Pat tipped a forelock at the Peeler and shouldered open the glass door. The holdall clanged against the glass and Pat winced but kept moving into the rain. He slung the holdall into in the back of Breda's Mini.

Breda, Pat would have to admit, looked less than impressed. 'What the hell is in that bag?'

'Just some stuff.'

'Boyle said you were carrying guns.'

'Self-protection.'

'I'll provide the protection. You can't just go around with bags of guns anymore. This is Belfast after the peace, you understand?'

'There's no before or after. Peace is a process.' Breda's lips tightened and Pat opened his palms to her. 'Ah, come on, look, these boys are serious. They kill people. I've been the one has stayed alive so far and I don't intend to be a sitting target for any man.'

Breda searched Pat's face. She nodded. 'Fine.' She put the car in gear and pulled away from the kerb. 'Where to?'

'Lisburne Road. The Free Africa Information Bureau, it's called. And thanks.'

Boyle banged into his office in Brooklyn House and flopped into his chair. His leg hurt. The stink of burning and blood was still in his nostrils, probably in his hair and clothes. That'd be right, to be stinking of death. Ewan Bates came in carrying two mugs of coffee.

'Here. Thought you might use this.'

'Cheers. Thanks, Ewan.'

'They've posted a video. The big secret's out. I sent you an email with a link. McLoughlin's in a fury. The Chief tore him a new one. Guess the Home Secretary bust his balls. Funny how it's always all about the big monkey hitting the little monkey hitting the tiny monkey.'

Boyle pulled the keyboard over to himself. 'Nobody's hit me yet.'

'Give it time.'

Cupping his hands around the warm coffee, Boyle waited for the system to come to life. 'I can't believe they actually brought down a helicopter.'

Bates sipped his coffee. 'Did you see it?'

'I was dancing around corpses and body parts in the station. Heard it, though.'

'The fireball just stayed suspended up there in the sky, it seemed like for ages.' Bates put his mug down. 'It's lucky there wasn't more damage when it landed. I'd love to see the insurance claims, "I was shopping at Lidl when a burning helicopter landed on my car." Will go down well.'

'There were two good men in that thing.'

Bates lowered his head. 'You're right. Sorry.'

A Decent Bomber

'Where the hell did they get an RPG from?' Boyle scowled. 'Don't answer that. We know.'

'Do we? We found the launcher and it's a Croatian RPG-22, same as was used back when the Real IRA hit Mi6 headquarters.'

'What are you saying, that it didn't come from one of Driscoll's precious caches?'

'Or that there are links between the Real IRA and our Partners in Peace.'

'I don't even want to think about that right now. We've our hands full as it is. Here.' Finally the machine loaded and Boyle clicked on Ewan Bates' link.

Bates came around the desk to see. Boyle set it to play full screen and sat back cradling his coffee. Martial music, men in balaclavas. The usual stuff.

A black man in a balaclava filmed green screen, standing in front of a photograph of the wreckage of Belfast Central Station. 'Your government has been misleading you. Two days ago we offered a chance to avoid today's unfortunate events.' The video cut to grainy CCTV footage of platform four as the train came in. 'The offer remains open. A further tragedy will inevitably take place if our reasonable terms are not met.'

Boyle paused it. 'How the fuck did they get that? Did they have a camera placed there? Ewan, get someone up on those rafters and find out how they did this. Check what security we've got on the CCTV files for the station.'

Bates snorted. 'Already on both.'

'The lives of these people have been cast away by your government. Their blood is on the governments hands. More blood will be shed. We are Al Shabab. We do not make empty promises or lie. Meet our terms. That is your only choice. There will be more tragedy, more mothers shedding tears, if you do not. In twenty four hours there will be another explosion and more inevitable loss of life if our request is not met.'

'Jesus wept.' Boyle stared at the screen.

Bates walked back around the desk and picked up his coffee. 'I'll see what they found in the station. You might want to call McLoughlin.'

Boyle nodded and reached for his phone. 'Monkey time.'

The dark green shop front was faded, the gold paint proclaiming this to be the home of the Free Africa Information Bureau had all but peeled off, leaving a faded ghost of former glories. The mullioned windows were smeared with some long ago attempt to clean them. Stacks of faded books were almost invisible behind the dusty patina. Pat pushed open the door and a bell jangled. He stood aside for Breda, who entered the shop with her nose twitching at the mixture of musty book, stale cigarette smoke and neglect in the air.

The counter was at the back of the shop, a doorway behind leading to a curl of steps, books piled up on them.

Heavy footsteps sounded. 'Hang on. Coming.'

Breda stalked the shelves of books, scanning the tatty spines. Pat watched her mouthing the titles, a look of awe on her face. Emily Patterson rounded the stairs and landed on the wooden floor. Pat had known Emily before he'd gone to jail and met her once more when he came out. He wouldn't have recognised her in a million years. Back then she had been blonde, plump-breasted with legs like a gazelle's stretching away from the scandalously rucked hot-pants she was so fond of wearing. Before 'her Arab' she had been something of a local fixture. Her hot-pant days were clearly a lifetime behind her; she must have weighed twenty stone. Her blue eyes were couched in fat, her cheeks a maze of broken blood vessels. The greasy hair was tucked under a headscarf which she twitched at with fingers like sausages. She squinted at Breda then back at Pat. Her eyes widened.

'For the love of God, if it isn't the little brave soldier.'

'Hello Emily. It's been a long time.' Pat smiled at her, shy in the face of the change to the woman he once knew. 'This is Orla and this is Breda.'

Emily's slow eyes flicked behind Pat. Her mouth opened soundlessly. Her eyes were wide. Pat glanced around at Orla, who was clearly perplexed by the woman's reaction to her. 'What is it?' Orla asked.

Emily staggered and grasped for the countertop. 'She… she…'

Pat smiled, realising the source of Emily's confusion. 'Emily, meet my niece Orla.'

'For the love of sweet Jesus. Your niece is it? She's the spit of—'

'Yes, I know.'

Emily recovered herself. 'Well, whatever it is you want, we haven't got any.'

'Libyans, Emily. I'm after getting me some Libyans.'

'There's nobody here. They've gone, left. Days ago. And good riddance to 'em.'

They sat upstairs in the little front room drinking tea from china cups and eating Lyle's Golden Syrup cakes. Emily rolled around offering sugar. She settled down in a large rose-patterned armchair with a wheezy sigh. 'It's funny, but I thought it would be the polis or maybe even something nice and handsome from MI5 would come looking for him. I didn't expect you to turn up.'

Breda fished out her ID. 'I'm a police officer, Mrs Muntasir.'

'Emily. Or Patterson, if you please.' Emily's gaze flicked between Breda and Pat. 'She know what you do in your spare time, Pat?'

'I'm a farmer, Breda, have been for twenty years and more. Until a bunch of African lads came knocking on my door. Where's Hamid?'

'Hasn't been here since last week. Upped sticks and gone. I always said he would one day. Last five years he's been a stranger to me. He's been lost in some African fantasy. He never forgave Gaddafi, you know?' She unpeeled a green foil packet and slid the golden cake into her mouth, chewing contemplatively. 'He took my boys away.'

'You've seen the news?'

'They shouldn't have published that picture of Mohammad. That wasn't kind. It's no way for a mother to find out.'

'The police didn't inform you?'

'Like I said, I've been expecting them. But you're the first here.'

'Were you aware of any terrorist activity before this?'

Emily struggled to control her tea cup, swallowing convulsively and reddening. She put the cup down on the side table, her hand wobbling. 'Jesus, don't do that. Terrorism? *You* asking me about terrorism? Oh, that's rich, that is.'

'I retired, I told you.'

'Well, if you mean scared young men waving guns in my face until his pals pull him away, no, not in almost thirty years. If you mean that mad wee Somali bastard, well, that's different.'

'Somali?'

'The Accountant, they call him. Hassan Ali. He came around here dangling liberation for the Libyan people in Hamid's face, like a cat with a dead canary. Only Hamid's got a hard on for canaries, hasn't he? Especially dead ones called Gaddafi.' She turned to Breda. 'Arabs bear a grudge for a lifetime and more, believe me.' She unwrapped another cake and bit it in half. 'He took Mohammed with him first. Came back for Karim, then. I never let him take Marwan. They both went and joined the good fight. Mohammed came back mad and, just, all *wrong*. Karim came back quiet as a funeral parlour. Never said a word, but his eyes were different. Scared. Of course, Marwan never forgave me. Mind you, neither did Hamid.'

'Came back? From Libya?'

'They all went off to join the glorious people's Islamic revolution. I never heard a word from Hamid for the first six months, then he came back brown as a nut and all fired up with stories of how we were going to live in a new world. I've never seen him like that before, him with his Messianic Zeal on him. He took Mohammed back with him, was gone for just over a year. Then he came for Karim. He didn't stay around longer than two weeks. He had Hassan Ali with him that time, like a little black shadow. All smart suits and nasty intentions, that one. Hamid was always easy led on, but it was tragic, the way he worshipped Hassan Ali.'

Breda had folded her foil wrapper into a line and wrapped it around her finger. Pat stopped fiddling with his own wrapper and put it down on the coffee table when he'd realised a swan was starting to take shape. Breda leaned forward. 'Did Hamid have a study or a workroom of some kind?'

'Yes. They'd lock themselves up in there all night.'

'Do you mind if I take a look?'

'Third door on the right. Help yourself.'

Breda slipped out. Pat took a pull of tea. 'When did he come back? From Libya?'

'For good, you mean? Oh, not until last year. Not from Libya, though. Syria. They'd moved on. The revolution was going to spread across the whole Middle East, then light a fire in Europe. They had a new Cordoba and everything. I'd lost him by then, of course. I just cooked and cleaned up.'

Pat saw the fat tears well up and slide down her rosy cheeks, spreading moisture on the folds in her neck as she pulled at a foil wrapper. They sat in silence until Breda returned. 'Okay, I've called Boyle. There's a support unit and a forensics team on the way. Emily, we're going to take a closer look at Hamid's things, there are computers and bank accounts and all sorts we're going to need to examine to find out what's been going on. I'm going to have to ask you to come with us and give a statement if you wouldn't mind.'

The thought hit Pat from nowhere. 'So where's Marwan?' He asked Emily, who had gone back to fiddling with her headscarf.

Her gaze flitted around the room. 'Marwan?'

'Your youngest son. The one who never went to Libya with Hamid. Where is he?'

'I don't know, do I?'

Well, what happened to him?'

'Nothing happened to him. We fell out when I wouldn't let him go with Hamid, but he settled back down again. He found himself a nice girl, they met at the Islamic Centre. They were married in February. Hamid wasn't there for the wedding, 'course. He was travelling abroad.'

'So where is he now?'

'I told you, I don't know. I'd say he'd likely be driving.'

Sirens sounded in the street outside. Breda waited in the doorway, frozen on her way down to meet the support team. Pat shook his head to clear it. 'Why driving?'

'Because he's a driver. That's what he does. He drives a lorry. Long distance. For a company called Contania.'

Breda stilled, wide-eyed. 'Christ.'

Getting Emily out of the flat above the bookshop was a mission in itself. The forensics team had arrived and started to strip down the computers and files in Muntasir's workroom. Orla was wandering downstairs in the bookshop with Breda. Emily insisted on bringing four retail packs of golden syrup cakes with her. She fussed down the stairs in front of Pat. Emily would go down to the station to give her statements in a Range Rover. As Breda had pointed out quietly to Pat, you wouldn't get Emily into the Mini.

Breda was waiting by the door with a rangy policeman. 'Emily, this is constable Pearce, he'll drive you down to Brooklyn House. We'll be right behind.'

'Here,' said Pearce. 'I'll take those from you.' He reached out for the boxes, then led the way out of the bookshop. Orla followed Pat out. The rain had let up but it was dark and Pat shivered in the cold. He buttoned his coat.

Pearce slid the boxes of cakes onto the back seat and opened the passenger door for Emily. She gripped the top of the door. Pat caught the movement in the upstairs window of the house opposite a second before the muzzle flash. There was a single gunshot, flat in the night air. Emily's head hit a sickening crack off the roof of the Range Rover and she collapsed onto the road, a red wash blossoming across her chest.

Pat shouted, 'Orla, get inside!' He ducked behind the Range Rover and dashed across the road, his hand pulling the Glock from the gilet he still wore. The front door of the house was red-painted wood and Pat charged it with his shoulder, crashing into it and splintering the lock. He kicked it fully open. The gunman was halfway down the stairs facing the front door. He raised the rifle he was carrying.

From behind him, Breda shouted 'Down!' Pat dropped to the floor as her shots rang in his ears. He sighted up from his position lying on the floor. The gunman limped up the stairs, hit in the leg. Pat fired but missed as the man fell onto the landing and crawled out of sight. He got to his feet and started up the stairs.

Breda caught up with him and pulled on his shoulder. 'No, Pat. I can't let you go up first. I'm supposed to be the protection.'

'I'm not going to argue about it Breda. Come on.'

A gunshot echoed from upstairs. Pat surged up the worn steps and barged into the bedroom where a man in a balaclava lay on the floor, the top of his head missing and the wall and ceiling sprayed crimson.

Breda pulled on blue gloves and went through the man's pockets. 'Nothing. How many of these bastards are there?'

'One less than there was, I guess.'

Chapter Sixteen

Boyle sat on his desk and dialled home to Fiona. It was dark out and he was tired. His head was killing him. It's not every day at work a chap gets bombed, after all. He waited for her to pick up, kicking the leg of his desk.

'Where the hell are you? We're supposed to be going for a drink with Kieran and Pam tonight. You promised you wouldn't forget.'

'I didn't.' He lied. 'You know I'm on a case.'

'He's the one client keeping me going. And we cancelled on him twice before. And you fucking know this really matters to me.'

'Calm down. There'll be other times.'

'There won't Boyle. There simply won't.'

'Get a grip, Fiona. It's just a drink.'

'Don't tell me to get a grip. Don't tell me what to do. Fuck you, Boyle.'

'I don't need this.'

'You self-centred sod. I've got fifteen minutes until we're supposed to be meeting my biggest client and his wife for a pleasant evening out and you're ditching me? Is that why you're calling?'

'Look, Fiona…'

'No. No more. I'll take Roddy.'

'I can make it back in—'

'Forget it, Boyle. Seriously, forget it.'

She hung up. He sat on the edge of his desk, staring at the screen and willing himself not to fling the fucking mobile through the window. Roddy. That baying, superior English wanker.

Boyle rang her back but she didn't pick up. It went to

voice mail and he cut the line. Fuck her, at any rate. He screwed his eyes shut and tried to will it all away. Truth be told, he was knackered and the pounding was getting him down, despite the fistful of Nurofen he'd popped earlier. Under the impressive-looking bandage was a nasty bruise and a couple of minor, if bloody, flesh wounds. He'd live. There was nothing left to do here; the building was pretty much deserted.

He tried Fiona again, no reply. This time he left a message. 'Fiona, look, I'm sorry. Call me back. I can be there in time, the day's done. I got a bit knocked up today and maybe I'm not thinking straight. Call me when you get this, love, yeah?'

He thumbed the mobile and let it drop to the desk. There was a half-bottle of Jameson somewhere in his filing cabinet and he was halfway to it when his office door burst open. Mary was bright eyed and triumphant.

'I've got it!'

Jesus. 'Got what?'

What was it about women? The second he'd opened his mouth, Boyle regretted his asperity but the hurt was already reflected in her face like a slap. She'd brought him a mouse and he'd kicked her. His head throbbed. 'Sorry, Mary. The archive?'

Her excitement carried her through the moment. 'Yup. Muntasir had three sons. He took them to Libya to fight against Gaddafi, at least he did two of them. He hated Gaddafi big time, a man on a mission. It was payback for the eighties.'

Boyle fished in the cabinet and found the bottle and the two cheap branded glasses that had come with it. A Christmas gift he'd never got around to taking home. Tell the truth, he'd always quite liked the idea of the copper with a bottle of scotch in the office, although they'd throw the book at him if they'd found him drinking.

'Here, Mary. Join me in a guilty pleasure.'

He plonked the glasses on the desk and twisted the bottle cap.

'I don't drink whiskey.'

'Ah, ye will, ye will. Go on, go on.'

She took the glass from him and sipped. She winced.

'So what does that tell us about Muntasir?' He gulped fire and gasped appreciation.

'It's not easy. The Historical Enquiries Team was broken up and getting hold of anyone who knows how this deep archive stuff works is hard. And the Internet thinks the world before 1996 doesn't exist. But I got it. All of it.'

'You're the best, Mary. You know that.'

'He came over from Libya when Gaddafi sent a first shipment to the IRA. He was supposed to check everything was handled properly, but he was always flaky. We brought him in, but had nothing on him. There are his interview notes from 1985. He was written off as an émigré nut. We logged trips to the mainland, MI6 logged trips to Cyprus and Libya from Heathrow and nobody put two and two together.

Boyle shook his head. 'How did we not spot this?'

She wore a white blouse over a black lace bra and Boyle looked up an instant too late to avoid catching her expression. Her eyes widened. 'Sometimes we miss the obvious.'

She leaned into him a little, checked his eyes and leaned again. Her breath was sweet with whiskey but her lips were cool. Her tongue was wet as it met his and curled around it. His hand found her shoulder, the other her breast and the tight little knot that pressed against the cloth. He slipped his hand inside and pinched it.

Her hand slid between his legs, grasped him and pulled at him through his trousers. A twist and she'd unzipped him, her cool fingers finding his heat. He tried to pull back, to push her away, but her downward tug made him rear to meet her hand's sweet pressure. She held him, pulling at her underwear and then dropped onto him with a suddenness that made him bark out. She melted around him and he thrust into her joyously.

Breaking into their low-voiced, sweaty laughter, the insistent clangour of Boyle's mobile finally forced him to move and break the magic of their nuzzling.

'It's Breda. I'm with Pat O'Carolan on the Lisburn Road. There's been a shooting and—'

Boyle snapped. 'Why call me about it? I'm off duty.'

'It's at Hamid Muntasir's house. Above the bookshop. We were taking his wife in when a sniper hit her. We've hard disks and records to go through. Muntasir had three sons, two of them were radicalised in Libya.'

Mary was licking his ear, the touch warm and infuriatingly lustful. He hardened again. 'Look, what didn't you understand? I'm off duty.'

'That's no way to lead a team. We've got a crisis here and—'

'I'm off fucking duty. End of.'

He thumbed the red icon and dropped the handset onto the desk. He turned to Mary, his voice serious. She was moving against him and mewling in his ear. 'Not here. We need to get out. There's a pub down the road has rooms. Come on.'

'Will you get me drunk, Boyle?'

'I'll drink you meself, so help me God.' He hoisted her off his knees, saw her to her feet and prised himself back into his trousers with some difficulty while she ran her thumbs down and around to straighten her knickers.

She caught his eyes on her and leered. 'You'd better be thirsty, Boyle.'

Pat felt every year of his age as he pushed against the glass door into the hotel's lobby. Breda bustled behind him, her solicitousness crowding him. Emily Patterson's gore was wiped away, but the rose leavings still stained his shirt. Orla was heavy on his arm, floppy with fatigue.

'There'll be officers on duty throughout the night. I'll catch you in the morning.'

'Thanks, Breda.'

'It's nothing. Look after my girl.' She patted Orla's cheek, drawing a wan smile. The lift door closed on her smile. Pat leaned on the wall of the lift.

Orla rubbed her eyes. 'Who was Emily talking about? When she first saw me?'

'Oh, that's a long story, *mo grá*.'

'Tell it me.'

The lift opened and Pat led the way out, his holdall banging against his bruised leg, forcing a grunt out of him. They went into the suite and Pat shouldered his bedroom door open. He slung the holdall clanking into the cupboard and popped open the minibar. 'You want something?'

'A coke.'

'Here.' He handed her the can. He took two Red Label miniatures out and dashed them into the tumbler sitting on the sideboard. The fiery spirit brought tears to his eyes. *Come Day Go Day, Glad in me heart it's Sunday. Drinking buttermilk all the week. Whiskey on a Sunday.*

'So, tell me.'

'I'm trying to.' Pat sipped his whisky. 'Right. A million years ago, when the world was younger and I was even younger than that, I fell in love with a girl. She was an Irish girl, in every sense, and we loved each other more than you can possibly imagine. She was my life and we were to marry. But she was a red-head and had spirit enough for ten women and one day when a silly young man at a checkpoint told her to stop, she didn't listen. And he was nervous and badly trained, trigger-happy and immersed in a culture of oppression and fear of the people he had been sent to protect from themselves.'

'He shot her.'

'That he did. He shot her through the chest and killed her in front of my very eyes and he took away my Orla. When you were born, your father gave her name to you. Because she died carrying my child. Our child.'

Orla was on her feet, her eyes filled with tears and she ran to him and put her arms around him and he put his hands on her back and felt the sobs running through her. A few seconds later, the tears came to him, too, and they cried together.

Boyle unlocked the front door. The morning was still dark. He looked into the living room and kitchen but Fiona wasn't there. He took the stairs two at a time. She was in the bedroom, sitting cross-legged and dressed on the bed.

He'd rehearsed it a hundred times. 'Hello, love.'

She didn't reply, just stared at him. He held her eye for a few seconds, but broke away. 'There was a bombing. At Central Station. I had to work late.'

She was still silent, her face impassive and her eyes steady on him.

'I was in the office past midnight. It didn't seem fair. I thought it best to get a room.' He waited for her to say something, the silence oppressive and weighing down on him. 'Come on, Fiona, you can't just sit there saying nothing. It's hardly an adult approach to take.'

The word when it came was a whisper. 'Liar.'

Boyle mustered himself for a spirited defence, but she repeated it louder and again until she was screaming and launching herself at him and her hands pummelled his chest and face. He grappled for her wrists, but she was fit and strong and her furious punches rained on him as she screamed 'Liar' at him. Boyle had his arm back to let fly at her when she stepped back. Her eyes on his were dead and she sneered at him. 'Get out. Get out now.'

'Fiona—'

'Don't bother. You stink of her, Boyle. You didn't even wash, you animal. Get the fuck out of my house.'

Boyle nodded and stepped back out of the bedroom. 'Fine.'

He bowled down the stairs, paused at the bottom, shrugged and pulled on his shoes. He walked out onto the dark street and stood by his car. Sure enough, his clothes came flying out of the bedroom window.

Everything comes to he who waits, Boyle thought. He scooped the clean clothes up and bundled them into the boot of his car. Driving up the street, he realised he had nowhere to go and a wave of self-pity washed over him. He let the road take him, driving aimlessly as the first grey of morning light started to appear.

Boyle's mobile rang in the cubbyhole in the centre of his console. Ewan Bates and eleven missed calls before him, apparently.

'Boyle. It's Ewan. Where you been? McLoughlin's been trying to get ahold of you and he's hopping mad.

He's called a briefing meeting for nine.'

Boyle checked his watch. Seven. Time to clean up, anyway. 'What's the big deal?'

'The shooting.'

'What shooting?'

'Jesus, Boyle, where have you been? A woman was shot last night by a sniper as Breda and O'Carolan were bringing her back to Brooklyn House. She was a connection to the terrorists. They got the guy who shot her, turns out it was her own son.'

'Okay, fine. I'm on the way. Get coffee. A lot of coffee.'

Boyle hadn't slept more than a couple of hours and Fiona was right, he stank. But it was, he reflected as he sniffed his fingers, a rather fine stink.

Pat wasn't usually much of a drinker, he'd maybe have the odd nip or a hot whiskey on those nights when the cold really sunk its teeth into you. But last night he'd trashed the minibar and the constant buzzing on the doorbell that woke him was, to say the least, unwelcome. He pulled on the white hotel dressing gown and shuffled to the door in his white hotel slippers.

'Jesus, Breda. You could've knocked.'

She had tied her auburn hair back and wore a red leather jacket and dark jeans. She looked fresh and, well, vibrant. And he felt like shite.

'Breakfast in ten minutes? We've been called into a briefing meeting at nine. They've picked up Marwan Muntasir from his number plates.

'What time is it now?'

'Seven thirty.'

'You're kidding me. Okay, give me twenty.'

'Fifteen.'

'Fine.'

Pat closed the door on her and shuffled into the bathroom, where he kicked off the slippers and respectively shat, showered and shaved. As he admired the end result in the mirror, looking a great deal better for the clean-up but perhaps a little lined and maybe a wee bit dark around the eyes, the doorbell buzzed again. Pat reached for his shirt. 'Coming, coming. Jesus give a man a break.'

They arrived at the meeting room at Brooklyn House in plenty of time. They'd had breakfast together. Not for the first time it struck Pat how the three of them came together like the family he could have had. Breda had fussed over Orla, who would sink into long silent reveries and come out of them looking bleak and devastated.

Pat hadn't wanted Orla to come to the meeting, but she wouldn't be left on her own and Breda couldn't be pulled two ways. They had both tried to cajole her into accepting another protection officer, but Orla had been adamant. Which, Pat had to admit, she'd always accomplished very well indeed.

Boyle, pale and unshaven, was already there, huddled in conversation with a Slavic-looking copper but broke off when they arrived. If Pat thought he was looking a little ragged around the edges, Boyle looked like the wreck of the Hesperus.

Boyle's face darkened as he rounded on Breda. 'What the hell happened last night?'

'You didn't care then, why would you give a shit now?'

Pat stepped between them. 'Enough.'

'What, you're a peacemaker now?' Boyle sneered.

Pat lifted his finger. 'I'm not Brian MacNamara. Watch your tongue.'

McLoughlin barged through the door backwards, holding a coffee balanced on a tablet. Behind him was a policewoman in uniform. She was as pale as Boyle and Pat caught her wild glance across the room at the man and the flash of hunger he returned her.

'Thank you for coming.' McLoughlin pointed at Orla. 'What's the girl doing here?'

'She's with me.' Pat rumbled.

'This is hardly appropriate—'

Orla's voice rang like flicked crystal. 'The girl has a name. It is Orla O'Carolan. And she's going nowhere.'

McLoughlin glared at her, looked to Breda for a reaction and shrugged. 'Fine. Right, ladies and gentlemen, we have little time so I'll try and be brief. We are in pursuit of one Marwan Muntasir, the third son of Irish citizen Emily Patterson and Hamid Muntasir, a gentleman of Libyan origin who sought asylum and settled in Belfast in the mid-1980s but who appears to have returned to Libya with his two eldest sons, fought against Gaddafi's regime and come back here with some very unsavoury Somali friends in tow. Would that be right, Boyle?'

'About the long and short of it, yes.'

'Marwan is not only the youngest of the Muntasir boys, he's the only one surviving. The sniper who killed Emily Patterson last night was in fact Karim Muntasir, their second son. You can see the sort of people we're having to deal with here,' McLoughlin looked around the room for effect. 'They are willing to cut down their own mothers in cold blood and have as little respect for their own lives as they do for others. Marwan Muntasir is currently driving a container lorry, which is what he does as a trade. We're tracing him using ANPRs and very low key surveillance.'

Pat cut in. 'ANPRs?'

Boyle growled. 'Automatic number plate recognition cameras. They digitise number plates so they can be tracked and analysed. Muntasir's currently on the A12, it looks like he was holed up somewhere in the country towards Newtownards. He holds a booking, in his own name, on the half ten crossing to Cairnryan from Port of Belfast. We can expect him to be alert to any changes in routine; he's a regular on that crossing. We're playing things very low key indeed. The camera team will track him in. We have a team waiting at the port. We could do with you down there to get positive ID.'

'Why me?'

'You knew his ma and pa as young people. You should be able to recognise him. We could use the extra corroboration. We don't have a clear image of him. And if we go in, we're going to be going in hard. A mistaken ID would be disastrous.'

'What about his passport photo?'

McLoughlin answered. 'It's scandalously out of date and almost useless.'

'Fine, then.' Pat threw up his hands. 'If that's what it takes. Are you sure he has the bombs in that container?'

The silverware glittered on McLoughlin's epaulettes. 'We haven't the faintest clue. But this is the only lead we've got. Any other questions? Right. Let's go.'

Boyle was trying to leave the room and catch up with Mary when McLoughlin called him back. 'Boyle, one moment.'

He held back reluctantly, watching the door close off his escape.

'Where the hell were you last night? You didn't pick up your mobile, your home number wasn't answering. We have a major security issue and Ms Fitzsimmons claims you refused to take her call.'

'I was off-duty. I hadn't slept in 72 hours. I was hardly an asset, believe me. Ewan has done a fine job in my stead.'

McLoughlin scowled. 'The temptation to make the arrangement permanent had occurred to me.'

'Will that be all?'

'That is all.'

Boyle found Mary at her desk. Just the sight of her provoked an instant reaction. Her total lack of inhibition, carnality even, stirred him. The image of her astride him last night came back. She had slowly explored his body, pressing the bruises and squeezing the scratches on his chest and arms, making him buck with the pain she so clearly enjoyed inflicting as she held him on the trembling verge with her languorous, clenching thighs. He focused back on the present and her softening eyes met his gaze. He watched helplessly as she raised a hand to her breast.

'Fiona threw me out.' He croaked.

'I hope it was worth it.'

He considered that one for a second. 'Yes.'

'Well, I have a flat-mate, so you can't stop at mine.'

'I'll find somewhere sure enough. Later?'

'Later.' Her finger travelled up to her moist lip and Boyle fled, walking crab-like in the open plan office to try and mask his condition.

Pat left Orla with Breda in the warm office at Belfast Harbour's Terminal Four and followed Boyle and Ewan Bates back downstairs. They wrapped their arms around themselves as they stepped out into the cold, Boyle striding ahead of Pat and Bates. Pat caught up with him as they crossed the car park towards the growing lines of cars and trucks waiting for the ferry in the loading lanes. They came to a nondescript building. Boyle led up the steps, held the blue door with its 'Harbour Police' logo on it open for Pat to enter. 'Here we are. The glass is one way. You'll be able to see our friend on camera as well as in person. We'll have ID'd him in any case, but you may be able to give us just that little extra bit of confidence. When this goes up, if we got the wrong man, my balls may as well be hanging in a liquidiser.

'I'd be pleased to throw 'em in meself.'

Boyle grinned. 'I'd say you would, too.'

Pat scanned the room. Screens showed camera shots of the approaches to the port, the line of lorries waiting for the boat. Officers scrutinised the images, tapped at keyboards and brought up new angles constantly. He noticed one was tracking a single vehicle. 'Sir. This is him now.'

Pat watched the lorry approach and stop at the checkpoint. The operator changed the camera view, zoomed in. *Jesus, but he was the spit of his father*. He watched Marwan Muntasir laugh with the officer at the checkpoint. He was easy, used to the routine here. Pat thought back to old Hamid and how he would court popularity with little thoughtful gestures.

'I'd have said he was identical to his dad when he was

younger. Even his manner. They know him well, here, don't they?'

'So I hear,' Boyle replied. 'He's a regular. Maybe as frequent as weekly.'

'They like him.'

'That's the way they tell it. Charming, easy guy. Does little favours for people.'

'Hamid was the same when I first met him. You'd wonder how he got mixed up with a gobshite like Gaddafi. He's your man for sure. I'd have no doubt on that. But any one of these guys could have told you as much.'

'I've got a thing for horse's mouths.' Boyle reached for his radio and his thumb on the side of it whitened a second. 'Go.'

'That it? One word?'

'We like to be efficient in the modern force.'

Pat watched the scene unfold on the other side of the window. It looked surreal, slow motion. The black-uniformed figures in helmets and armour seemed to materialise out of nowhere. Pat's gaze was torn between the multiple angles playing out on the bank of screens and the sight in the glass in front of him. Marwan Muntasir's hands were up, men now hanging into his cab pointing carbines at him. The door was torn open and Muntasir pulled out and pushed to the floor, cable tied behind his back. Pat watched the men shouting, jostling the supine figure.

He's lucky to be alive, Pat thought. They get over-excited, nervous. And the safety's off on all those guns. Like my Orla. That's all it takes. One nervous guy, one split second.

He turned away from the scene and fought the urge to throw up his Hilton breakfast. Orla falling, the child who would never cry inside her as her eyelids fluttered and she told him she loved him and the raindrops fell onto her cold face and splashed on unblinking blue eyes.

'You okay, O'Carolan?'

'Fine. Never better. I'm off back to the girls.'

'Suit yourself. Bates, can you make sure Mr O'Carolan doesn't do a runner on us?'

The urge to slap Boyle hit Pat. Bates' hand on his shoulder was gentle. 'Come on, Pat. Leave him to it.'

Pat stared out of the hotel room window, across the grey shimmer of the Lagan and the city beyond. Sunshine was breaking through the cloud here and there, forming spears of light dappling the grey cityscape. The drive back from the port to the hotel was quiet, Pat being in no mood for small talk. They were all tired and Orla had withdrawn into herself increasingly, despite Breda's little reassurances and encouragements. She had announced she was going to get some sleep and left them in the living room of the suite. Breda set the kettle to boil.

'You want tea?'

Pat turned away from the city. 'Please. Two sugars.'

'Penny for them.'

'I wish I'd been let alone to my farm, Breda. The past is nagging now and I'd put it behind me all these years.'

'I'm worried about Orla. She's awful quiet.'

'She's been through a lot. Too much. I wish I could send her back to her Da.'

'Why don't you?'

'She'd never forgive me for calling him. And he'll never forgive me for all this.'

'Maybe you should grasp the bull by the horns. Now they've got Muntasir, it's all over, isn't it?'

'Hamid's still on the loose and so's The Accountant, Hassan Ali. And we don't know how many more of Hassan Ali's crazies are out there.'

Breda handed a mug to Pat. 'It's only a matter of time. Careful, that's hot.'

Pat jabbed at the remote. He caught the porn channel, two pink figures squirming briefly on a bed before he thumbed it again, glancing at Breda to see if she'd seen the fleeting image but she was immersed in her wee iPad. Thankfully he found the BBC. He stood, the mug frozen in his hand, as the ticker announced 'Irish Terror suspect Patrick O'Carolan helping police with enquiries'.

'Breda, why the hell am I on the telly?'

'Search me. Turn it up.'

The presenter was in his forties, a receding hairline and jowls, all solemn-faced. 'A couple and their two children have been killed when their house caught fire in the early hours of this morning. Anthony and Caroline Mackey and their two young children Simon, five and Katie, eight, "didn't stand a chance" according to firefighters in Manchester who attended the blaze, which was quickly brought under control. Neighbours were woken by an explosion and the unusually fierce flames. Investigations are underway to find the cause of the fire. Police have arrested the man behind the two bombings that have killed eighteen and injured over a hundred and thirty in Belfast. Former IRA bomber Patrick O'Carolan is currently helping police with their enquiries. More arrests are expected in the investigation into the attacks. Two more cases of foot and mouth have—'

Pat killed the sound. 'Arrested, am I? Jesus, that's outrageous. You know fine well I'm not involved in these bombings.'

'Calm down, Pat. You may not be responsible, but

you are involved. There are cases to be answered, including three dead men in the South. You're going to have to face the consequences of that. You might not have been formally arrested, but there'll have to be a process, indemnity or not.'

Pat stared at Breda in disbelief. There was something else, something nagging at him beyond his anger at the way they'd used him. 'No way. No bars.'

She put her hands up. 'Not my call, hot shot. I'm just here to stop you getting yourself killed.'

Her radio handset chimed and she turned away to talk into it, avoiding Pat's furious glare. 'No, I don't know. No. What the hell are… hang on.'

The anger left Pat as he saw her bewilderment. She held the handset away from her as if it were on fire. 'It's the team down at reception. There's a Michael O'Carolan down there and he's about to be arrested for affray. He's hopping, Pat.'

'It's okay, Breda. Tell them to stay away from him. I'll go down to him.'

'Want my 2p worth? Bring him up here. It's less public, more controlled and your environment.'

'Fine, you just earned 2p.'

Breda barked into the handset. 'Send him up. I'll meet him at the lifts.' She held up her hand to quell Pat's protest. 'I can maybe calm him down a little before he gets here. It can't hurt.'

'4p.'

She grinned at him and winked, slipping the iPad into her big, lumpy handbag. Somehow the room seemed less alive after the door had slammed behind her, leaving Pat to worry about what he was going to say to Mikey. There was one thing he knew for certain: this wasn't going to go well. Thank Christ Orla had taken to her bed. The raised voices in the corridor came closer and Pat steeled himself. The door opened quietly enough, Breda using her card key. Mikey pushed past her, his face puce. He was moving fast and Pat realised this was going to get physical. He raised his hands. 'Mikey, hold up there. Mikey!'

The punch was wild and wide. Pat stepped back, his hands held out. 'Please, Mikey.'

Mikey flung another wild punch and Pat only just got his chin back far enough to stop it connecting. He felt the wind of its passing.

Breda took hold of Mikey's shoulders from behind and he wheeled to lash out at her. 'I really do not believe you want to do that,' she deadpanned. She held his gaze and his shoulders until the taut muscles relaxed and the fight went out of the man. Mikey turned to Pat, tears in his eyes and his face ugly with hate and crying, his white hair combed over and his chest hairs poking up through the checked shirt he wore under his tweed jacket.

'She's my fucking *daughter*. How could you do that to her? To us?'

'I did nothing, Mikey. I tried to protect her.'

'By setting bombs? Have you completely lost the head, Pat? Is that it? You're maybe not right or something? Tell me, we can get help. Let the police know where she is, please God.'

'Mikey, what have they been telling you? They know where Orla is. She's in her room. She's sleeping peacefully.'

Breda let go of Mikey's shoulders. He looked around at her for corroboration and she nodded and smiled. 'Orla's fine, Mr O'Carolan. Come on and sit down now and we can maybe tell you more about what's been going on.'

A Decent Bomber

Mikey felt his way along the arm of the chair and lowered himself into it. Pat handed him a glass of scotch from the minibar and took one himself, sitting opposite. 'I'll tell you a story, Mikey. But by God you'd hardly believe it.'

Breda sat between them with a diet coke in a glass.

They were on their third whiskey by the time Pat finished talking. Mikey hadn't interrupted once and now turned to Breda. 'Is this true? All of it?'

'As much as I know of it is true. There's a lot I hadn't heard before, but it all makes sense.'

'And what about Orla?'

Breda's tough features relaxed. 'She's a peach, Mr O'Carolan. But she's been through a lot and it's weighing on her. She's young and resilient. And she's followed the course she thought was right. I think she's going to be fine. In time.'

Mikey clutched the arms of the chair and pushed himself up. 'Well, that's all well and good but she's coming home to her family now. I'm sure you meant well enough, Pat, but I'd appreciate if you never see my daughter again. Or, for that matter, any of my family. I'm sorry, brother, but you have lived a life I cannot in all conscience condone. And I won't have my children exposed to danger like this or to ideologies like these. You spent eleven years in prison for your crimes and I thought you had served your time, learned your lesson. But there are three more deaths on your hands and God knows what part of the blame for these bombings you bear for having made the bombs, regardless of whether you thought it was for Orla. You should have gone to the authorities rather than take the law into your hands. If you had been fighting for anything, surely it was that sovereignty and the rule of law gives us a chance to live our lives in peace?'

'No.'

Mikey wheeled, gripping the sofa. The quiet word unbalanced him entirely. Not for the first time, Pat wondered how Orla got that resonance of glass into her voice.

'I'll not go with you. I'm staying with Pat, seeing this through. You had no right to come here like this, shouting and demanding on my behalf. I'm a grown woman. I'll make my choices.'

'Orla, you…'

'I said no. The one thing Pat left out was that I was in love with a woman called Róisín McManus and she died in the Victoria Square bomb. I have unfinished business.'

'You can't be serious, Orla. Listen to yourself.'

She said nothing, her solemn face calm and her radiant green eyes steady on Mikey, who was sweating so much it was coming through the tweed under his arms. He stared wildly at Breda and then turned to appeal to Pat, his hands held palm up.

'It's her choice, Mikey. I'd rather she be safe with you and Anne, but it's her choice.'

Mikey clenched and flexed his hands, his mouth working. Pat saw the fear and the hate that brought and, yes, the resentment in his brother at the way his own daughter had chosen Pat over him. He advanced to embrace Mikey, but his brother stepped back. 'Get away. I'll have nothing more to do with you. Either of you.'

'Ah, come on, Mikey —'

'No. She's no daughter of mine from this day on. And you can go to hell, too, Pat. Anne was right, I was a fool. And sure enough she was right when she said I would live to regret naming our baby girl for a dead woman. Good luck to you.'

'Fuck, no, Mikey…'

But Mikey was striding for the door and Orla was bringing her hands steepling up to her face and Breda was reaching for her and Pat was hitting the wall with the palm of his hand and wishing the world would simply go back to the way it was when he was milking fifteen head of cattle every day and worrying about how the rain would make the lower field too boggy again.

Chapter Seventeen

Boyle ducked under the low lintel of the door leading into the little two up two down terraced house. It was dark inside and he paused to look around, old frying in his nostrils and a child's crying coming from upstairs.

Latifa Ghazalla Muntasir pushed open the door to the front room and gestured Boyle in, her eyes downcast. She wore a *shayla* and a crushed air Boyle found profoundly depressing. The air in the room was stale, florid brown furnishings with big dark wood arms. The carpet was peach, with raggedy-edged cut pieces laid down in front of the seats. A coffee table bore garishly wrapped sweets, a big crystal ashtray and a gold-trimmed plastic tissue holder.

'Please, sit.' She gestured to the sofa and sat herself, her knees held to one side by her clutched hands.

'Thank you. I only wanted to ask a couple of questions. I won't take much of your time.'

Her shy smile lit her wan face up, the lines around her downturned mouth disappearing and her quick glance at him reminding him of Princess Di playing the coquette for the media and their cameras. 'Please, you are welcome. Have you seen my husband?'

He was minded to lie to her but that quick glance flashed at him again and he was suddenly desperately sorry for her. 'I have. He was well.'

Her eyes stayed on her hands. 'Good. I am sure he is being... protected.'

Boyle wanted to leave, then and there. No questions, no examination. Just flee. The picture of Marwan Muntasir in that damp-stinking, dark room, cable tied to a chair while the two 'specialists' from MI5 screamed abuse at him was fresh in his mind; he had come straight from the interrogation, which was now into its eighteenth straight hour. Muntasir was incoherent, begging and sobbing his heart out. Sure, he was being protected very well indeed.

Marwan's lorry and the container he was pulling had been torn apart at the seams. Nothing smaller than a match-head could have made it through that search. And it was clean. The most interesting thing they had found was traces of rolling tobacco and hash deep in the crease of the passenger seat.

The door was pushed open and a small child stood holding a tatty-looking knitted rabbit. A white-haired lady in a floral house-coat hobbled in, her hand brushing the child's matted hair, a little custard glass of tea in the other hand, which she placed on the coffee table in front of Boyle. There was a little green packet on the saucer, a Tate and Lyle's syrup cake. Her gaze stayed on the floor as she turned away, her hand on the child's shoulder. 'Come, Selim.'

'Baba?'

'Not yet. Come.'

Latifa raised her face to glance nervously at Boyle. She licked her lips and he was horrified at the quickening in himself. She saw it and averted her gaze. 'You wanted to ask some questions.'

'What was Marwan's relationship with his father like?'

She frowned at her hands. She was wearing black stockings under the long dress, flat shoes. 'They were not friends. Abdel Hamid wanted Marwan to join him in his war against Gaddafi but his mother wouldn't let him. He was closer to his mother. God have mercy on her soul.'

'How did you meet?'

'Marwan?' She glanced up at him. Her Shayla slipped and she ran her finger around its edge to pull it back into place and tighten it. 'In the bookshop. A student friend had stumbled upon it and told me of this collection of books about Libya and Africa. Marwan was looking after it. We started talking. He was a funny, kind man. I loved him from that moment. I hated his father and so did he. Maybe I hated him because Marwan did. I don't know.'

'Your family is from Libya?'

'Yes. My father died when I was young, before I came here to study. My mother came to live with us here.' She allowed herself a tight smile. 'We are British now.'

'When did he last see his father?'

'Four weeks ago. I told the police this.' Her quick eyes met his again and there were tears in them. 'He had nothing to do with Hamid and his stupid war against Gaddafi. Marwan never went back to Libya like the others. He is innocent man.'

Boyle sipped the tea for something to do. The little green cake packet slid down into the saucer and he placed it on the coffee table. The tea was warm, fragrant and sweet. Latifa brushed at her tears and pulled her shayla around her. The child upstairs had stopped crying and the little glass clinked on its saucer.

'Why did they meet? Marwan and Hamid?'

She sniffled, reached across for a tissue and wiped at her nose. She clutched the little white ball of paper on her lap. 'They argued. Hamid came to the house in the night. He wanted Marwan's van and Marwan refused him at first. He became angry and so Marwan gave the keys to him. And then he left and we have heard nothing of him. *Khalas*. The end.'

'His van?' Boyle had read the officers' transcript of

their visit to Latifa Muntasir and there had been no mention of a van.

'Yes. He had a van he used for the car boot sales. Marwan worked at the weekends selling things when he was not driving. At the car boot sales. He rented it to friends. It was white. And old.'

'Did you tell the police about this?'

'No. They were asking where Marwan was, not where his van was.' She patted at her nose with the tissue ball.

'Do you know the registration?'

'I have papers. One moment.'

Boyle contemplated the green packet. He hadn't eaten in a day. He pulled it open.

'We kept them for Marwan's mother.' He hadn't heard her come back into the room. She slid a copy of a registration application across the coffee table. 'The cakes.'

Boyle folded the form and slipped it into his inside pocket. 'Thank you, you have been most helpful.' He stood.

'My husband is innocent. Please let him go.' She implored, her pale upturned face lit by the window reminding him of the Virgin Mary.

Boyle smiled, nodded and let himself out, glad of the rush of fresh air. He pulled the creaky iron gate to behind him and latched it. He stood in the street a moment, savouring the open air. He stabbed the key fob at the BMW, rewarded on the third attempt. He called Mary Dwyer.

'Mary, it's me. Listen, I need you to trace this vehicle. It's a white Toyota HiAce registered to Marwan Muntasir. ALZ 2321.'

'On it. Boyle?'

'Yes?'

She cut the line. He guided the car along the road, fidgeting in the seat to adjust himself. Even that one word from her had got her the reaction she'd doubtless wanted.

By the time Boyle had got back to Brooklyn House, the two MI5 attack dogs had been pulled off the remains of Marwan Muntasir by the arrival of a fussy but effective little lawyer from a Belfast-based human rights group. Ewan Bates followed Boyle into his office.

'Nice one on the HiAce. It crossed on the same ferry Marwan Muntasir was booked to go on.'

'Shit.'

'Driven by one Emil Patterson.'

'Hamid in other words.'

'Seems that way. We're looking back over the CCTV files.'

'So Marwan is culpable.' Boyle wriggled out of his leather and dumped down on his chair.

Bates shrugged. 'Or it's coincidence. What would he be up to with a clean lorry?'

'Riding shotgun for Pa. Distracting us so Hamid got a clean run through.' Boyle shook his head. 'Did you get the vehicle details over to the mainland?'

'Yes, they've got crews out with roadblocks at Lockerbie and Gretna, but we're likely too late. Cumbria have got cars out to every major nodal point but if he's made it past Carlisle, we've lost him, basically. It's touch and go.'

Boyle smacked the desk. 'Under our noses, the fucker.'

Mary Dwyer burst into Boyle's office. 'They picked up the van on a camera outside Dumfries. It looks like he was following B roads all the way. He only slipped up that once.'

'So that's it. We've lost him.' Boyle slumped back in his chair. The tiredness was overwhelming him now.

'Unless Marwan knows what his dad was planning.'

Boyle ran his hand back through his hair. 'And he'll tell us, will he? Because those two goons from five were our best chance to get anything out of him. Now we have to play nicely he'll just be laughing in our faces.'

'Still, it's worth a try.'

'Be my guest, Ewan. Let me know if you get anywhere. I've got to grab some shuteye.'

Bates left. Boyle dragged himself to his feet and pulled his jacket on. Mary was looking at him strangely. 'I'm serious, girl. I'm knackered. Here.'

'What's this?'

'It's a copy of the key to room twelve at the Devonshire for when you knock off.'

Her eyes flashed wickedly. 'And what if I'm washing my hair tonight?'

'I'll take you over the basin.'

'You know the way to a girl's heart, don't you, Boyle?'

He opened the door and stood aside for her. She brushed up against him and squeezed him fleetingly as she passed. He had to take his jacket back off and drape it in front of him on his way out of the office.

Pat had left Orla in Breda's care. 'I have to go see a man. I won't be long. But I think I might have something.'

'Something like what thing?'

'An old memory I need to check on.'

'How do I know you won't skip on me?'

'Jesus, Breda, you know by now. Orla's the most

precious thing I have, more so now than ever. I'll be back for her.'

'And I thought it was me you'd come back for.'

Pat had replied 'Aye, and maybe that.' Before even thinking. The memory of Breda's blush had him grinning in the back of the taxi cab.

They pulled up outside the smart house in Carmichael Gardens. The taxi driver was young, spotty and painfully thin, a real gurrier, thought Pat. 'Would you mind waiting a while?'

'No problem. I can wait all day. It's on your tab.'

'Right you are. Back in twenty minutes or so.'

Ringing the doorbell, Pat was surprised to be greeted by the great man in person. 'Sean Driscoll, as God is my witness.'

'I'm sorry, I don't think I've had the p... Pat? Pat O'Carolan?'

'Himself.'

Pat hadn't expected the fatted calf, but he also hadn't expected Driscoll to blanch and stagger quite like that, either. Driscoll fought for breath. 'Well, well.' He grinned weakly. 'This is a surprise.'

'Shall we go inside, do you think?'

'Yes, yes, of course. Come in Pat. Well, imagine after so many years.' Driscoll waved him in and Pat waited for him to close the door and lead the way. Driscoll pushed past him in the corridor with indrawn breath and a nervous grin. 'This way, this way.'

Pat walked into the living room. It was ornate and neat, a maroon carpet and floral decorations on the sofa set, mahogany furniture. He couldn't remember Driscoll's wife's name.

'Please, do take a seat. A drink? Will you take a whiskey?'

A Decent Bomber

'No, thanks.' Pat stood looking out of the window through the net curtains. 'Nice house.'

'Thank you, Pat. Now how can I help you?'

'Remember a fellow name of Anthony Mackey? Headed up the Manchester ASU as I recall.'

'Ah, Pat, I wouldn't know anything of that, now.'

Pat moved fast, his hand grabbing Driscoll's tie as his other darted a vicious double jab into Driscoll's paunch. He pushed the dead weight of the man back into one of the flowery armchairs. Driscoll's face was puffed and crimson. For a second Pat thought he'd overdone it and Driscoll was having a heart attack but the man drew a huge shuddering gulp of air. He pushed himself back in the chair as if trying to escape Pat through the back of it.

'Stop pissing about, Sean. This is important. Anthony Mackey. Still in Manchester?'

Driscoll nodded. 'Y..yes.'

Who from the London ASUs are still there? Patsy Logan? Con Connolly?

'Both. Both are.'

'You have contacts for them?'

'Yes.'

'If you'd oblige, Sean.'

'In the study.'

'Get up.'

Driscoll scrabbled out of the chair, his hands grasping at the arm. He hobbled out of the room, Pat following him. Opening the door at the end of the hallway, Driscoll went to his antique style desk and slid open the drawer. There was a painting of the 1916 rebellion hanging on the wall behind the desk and for some reason it offended Pat. Perhaps because he had a very low opinion of Sean Driscoll indeed, always had, and didn't think him fit to even share the room with pictures of the giants on whose shoulders Driscoll was presuming to stand.

Driscoll had reached into the desk and pulled out a revolver, which he was pointing shakily at Pat. For all he knew it could be a starter's pistol. Driscoll stepped out from behind the desk which, Pat considered, was the stupidest thing he had seen done in while. Pat strode forward, knocked the gun aside and hit Driscoll in the face. The blow sent the man reeling back into the bookcase, which tottered and threatened to come down on top of him. Pat pulled him away and shoved him into a chair.

Ruffling through the contents of the unlocked drawer, Pat found a black leather-bound address book. Sure enough, it contained the names he knew so well and had tried so hard to forget: Jim Slattery, Con Connolly, Logan, Kennedy and the rest. Pat slipped the book into his pocket.

'Any caches over there still?'

Driscoll's nose was bleeding and he was trying to staunch it with his handkerchief. He shook his head and Pat took a step towards him.

Driscoll wailed. 'Yes. Yes there are.'

'Where?'

'Mackey and Logan. The rest are gone.'

'What do they have?'

'Mackey just has a few guns.'

'And Logan?'

'G… grenades. Some guns.'

'Did either of them know Abdel Hamid Muntasir?'

'The Libyan? Yes, they both would have from back in the eighties.'

Pat leaned down and picked up Driscoll's gun. To his surprise, it was actually loaded. He flicked the safety off and fired into the ground. It made a deafening racket in the enclosed space. Driscoll spasmed and cried out.

Pat slid out the magazine and thumbed the bullets as the spring delivered each to the top. They fell to the soft carpet, ringing out as they struck each other and bounced. 'You know what? You need to get rid of this, like you should have got rid of all those dumps, including the one you had me sitting on all those years.'

Pat threw the gun aside. Driscoll was whimpering in the chair, blood on his chin and smeared on his crumpled shirt.

Pat closed the front door behind him. The skinny kid took a last drag of his cigarette and flicked the butt into the gutter. He got into the taxi. Pat climbed into the passenger seat.

'What was that noise?' The driver started the engine.

Pat turned slowly to face the youth. 'What noise would that be, now?'

'In there. Sounded like a gunshot.'

'Yes,' Pat smiled sweetly at him, 'that was indeed a gunshot. Take me to the Hilton, if you please, driver.'

His reddened knuckles hurt. Massaging them, he pulled off a flap of skin from one left by the impact with Driscoll's teeth. He caught the driver's nervous sideways glance. Pat sat back and enjoyed the silence.

It was dark and Orla was watching rubbish on the TV in the suite, curled on the sofa still in her dressing gown. She glanced up as Pat came in and her dull gaze fell back to the screen. The sliding door to the bedroom was open and Breda beckoned him in.

She pitched her voice low. 'I'm trying Pat, God help me I am, but she's just folded into herself. It's not that we're strangers, her and I, because we're not. We get on.

But she's just in her own world now.'

Her breath smelled of mints. Pat reached out to her and let his hand rest on her warm shoulder. 'She's safe. There's time for everything else as long as she's safe. Listen, I need you to get in touch with Boyle. I know what they're doing.'

'The Africans?'

'They're using our old active service units in the UK like they did here. They're burrowing into our past like maggots in old flesh. I know where they're going next. Tell him. Get him to come here. I need to talk to him. Fast.'

She nodded. 'Fine.'

Pat pulled the sliding door to the bedroom shut behind him. He strode over to the TV and hit the button. Orla swung her legs off the sofa. 'Hey!'

'We need to talk, *mo chroí*.'

She shook her head. 'No. There's no point.'

'Listen to me. I'm not the brightest button in the box but I've just spent thirty-odd years doing what you're doing now. You can't shut yourself away and wait for the memories to die because they just hang around until something new comes along and replaces them. The hurt goes away after a while and you realise it's actually your life and you're best living it rather than mourning the things you did wrong or that were done to you. You move on. You're feeling pain and hurt. I know how that feels.'

Orla stared at the blank screen, then closed her eyes. Her fists were clenched and Pat leaned into her as the tears came. He held her. 'It's okay, Uncle Pat. It's okay. I just feel a bit lost.'

'And alone.'

'Yes.' She glanced at him. 'And I shouldn't, right?'

'Mikey will come around. He was just sounding off. He was right to be angry, I mean he thinks we're sitting in a Tipperary farmhouse looking after a herd and drinking tea and then he cops us on national TV as terror suspects.

Orla's smile was a fragile thing of wonder to Pat. He wanted to frame it, to freeze the moment and keep it for all eternity because it was a moment of hope and pleasure against a backdrop of so much pain and death. That he would ever see a gun again, let alone have to use one. He turned away from her so he wouldn't spoil her moment with his bleak face.

Breda opened the sliding door. 'Okay, Boyle will be here in an hour or so.'

'Right. Let's go downstairs and get something to eat. I don't know about you two, but I need a change of scenery.'

Breda cast her gaze to the girl curled on the sofa. 'I think we all do. Come on, then.'

Boyle joined them as they sat around the leavings of their meal in the charmless, empty restaurant. He pulled up a chair and glanced around the group. They were all of them tired, himself included although to be fair he was hardly taking things easy on the Mary front. He had torn himself away from her voluptuous wickedness and left her in bed in the warm little room above the pub. At least he'd managed a few hours' exhausted sleep before she had slipped into the room and woken him with a lingering kiss before stripping and sliding into the bed, her smooth skin burning hot against his.

'Coffee?'

Boyle jumped. He turned to Breda. 'Yes, God yes.'

Pat O'Carolan leaned forward. 'Boyle, listen, they're going for the London ASUs, the active service units. They're doing what they did here. That fire in Manchester was at the house of an old army hand, Anthony Mackey. He had a small cache of weapons. They're on the way South.'

'How do you know that? About Mackey?'

'Saw it on the news and put two and two together.'

'The cache?'

'A birdie told me.'

O'Carolan's gaze could be disconcertingly direct. Breda was busy ordering coffees in the background. Boyle shrugged. 'That's circumstantial. You've no proof.'

'We need to go over, Boyle. I know the men they're targeting. I go back with them. They'll talk to me.'

'Just give us the contacts and we'll take care of it. No more vigilante stuff.'

'That won't work and you know it.'

Boyle fought to suppress his irritation. 'What we know is we know our jobs, Pat. We deal with incidents every hour of every day. If you have information that will help us, I'll be pleased to receive it. But I'm not going to let you play Rambo all over the mainland.'

Breda's mobile rang and she answered it with a 'Hang on a second.' Her eyes widened and she mouthed a silent swear word. There was wonder and fear on her face as she caught Boyle's eye. 'There's been another bombing. London.'

O'Carolan was about to make his point but the words stilled him. Breda waved at the waitress. 'Excuse me, where's the nearest television?'

'In the lobby.'

Breda wriggled along the settle. 'Come on.'

Boyle followed her into the lobby, Pat and Orla

behind him. Breda called out to one of the receptionists. 'Can you turn the sound up on this?'

The ticker said it all. Harrods blast five dead. Breda had the TV's remote. The presenter's voice came out of nowhere, blaring before she found the volume button. '...feared terrorist group has released a video claiming responsibility.'

O'Carolan's hand was on his shoulder, pulling him around. 'Boyle.'

Boyle tore his gaze from the burning darkness on the screen in front of him. O'Carolan had found his reason to be allowed to go to London. Boyle nodded at him. 'I know, I know. I'll call McLoughlin now.'

Pat had poured himself a whisky when Boyle rang on the suite's bell. He opened the door. Orla was on the couch, watching CNN's coverage of the Harrods bombing. 'Well?'

'McLoughlin hated the idea. MI5 loved it. We fly in the morning. Breda will look after Orla.'

'Grand. What time?'

'I'll come for you at eight. Okay?'

'Sure. Thanks.'

'Goodnight.' Boyle shambled off down the corridor. He turned. 'One thing.'

'What?'

'No guns.'

Pat nodded and closed the door. He lifted the glass and sipped the warming liquid. Orla's voice turned him.

'Please don't leave me behind, Uncle Pat.'

'I have to Orla. It's insanely dangerous. Mikey was right and the least I can do now is make sure you're safe. Breda's a good woman; she'll look after you well.'

'Please.'

'No.' He drained his drink. 'I'm going to hit my *leaba*. Goodnight.'

'Please.' That small, silvery voice again.

Pat slid the bedroom door shut.

Chapter Eighteen

Pat was no happy flier at the best of times and this wasn't the best of times. The 737 bucked and yawed as it cut the murky cloud above George Best Belfast City Airport. Boyle was sat next to him and smelled of Axe and women's perfume. The plane gave a particularly dramatic heave and Pat muttered, 'Jesus Christ.'

Boyle regarded him. 'You a religious man, Pat?'

'Right now, yes I bloody am. I hate these yokes.' He stared broodily out of the window at the water streaming in runnels over the wing and reprised his leaving that morning.

Orla had been in tears as Pat abandoned her, their table scattered with the detritus of breakfast, golden flakes of croissant, little glass pots of jam and tomato stained plates. Pat had polished off a full fry. The place mats had sun motifs and exhortations to have a nice day. He clattered his cutlery on the plate and took a last sweet mouthful of tea.

'Right, I'm off. Take care, you two.' He swung himself to his feet, pivoting on the chairback.

Orla shrugged off Breda's arm around her shoulder and tried to follow Pat but Breda was made of sterner stuff than that. 'Come on, Orla. You must realise it's for your own good.'

'I'll scream the place down.'

'You go right on ahead.' Was the last thing Pat heard as he strode through into the lobby to reclaim his bag from the concierge. Boyle was waiting by the front desk. They had a black SUV to take them to the airport, a luxury Pat had never before experienced. He had wanted to wave regally at the whey-faced passers-by.

Reaching the terminal they were whisked through security by the two suited men who met them at the kerbside. The suits, Pat couldn't help noticing, were wearing shoulder holsters.

The Baby Glock and his two spare magazines stayed un-scanned and therefore undisturbed, nestled in the roll of his spare jeans at the bottom of his bag. As his mammy so often told him, he who never tries will never succeed. Boyle's gun, on the other hand, travelled in the hold boxed and tagged as per regulations.

The plane broke through the cloud into the blue. Pat gazed out over the cloudscape and thought about Orla. She had been through too much and it had been his fault. Mikey was fair mad, too. Last time they'd argued like that it had been years before they reconciled. So much had happened and it all started with that smooth African voice on the phone and its accented pronunciation of *Darn Breen*.

There was no fire in the recollection, no passion, just a mental statement of fact. The African was a dead man and he would die by Pat's hand. For the herd, Kirstie, Orla's girl and the others. Pat would end it the only way it could, should, possibly end.

The seatbelt sign turned off.

Orla's girlfriend. Jesus, where do you put that? He hadn't really considered it, possibly because he hadn't wanted to, possibly because things had been mad altogether. If that was what Orla wanted, that was fine by Pat. Truth was, he had been avoiding thinking about it. He hadn't even acknowledged to her that he understood; that Róisín had been her… partner. There'd be no child for her to leave the farm to, mind. He wondered about how she would live on a farm with another girl. The nights. Jesus, don't even start thinking about that stuff. That's way wrong. Pat shifted in the confines of his shiny blue leather seat.

Boyle was amused. 'You okay there, big man?'

'Fine.' Pat muttered. 'Never better.'

He watched the drinks trolley being prepared. They were sitting in the third row and it wasn't long before Pat was saying 'Whisky on the rocks.'

Boyle raised an eyebrow. 'You're starting early.' And then responded to the steward's raised eyebrow with 'Gin and tonic please, pal.'

Pat pulled the little foil packet he'd been handed open and dug into a strange mixture of candied fruit, nuts and chocolate. It passed the time well enough, but he'd have preferred a pack of peanuts.

'Here.' Boyle had raised his plastic beaker to Pat. 'To success.'

'Fair play,' Pat wondered what Boyle's idea of success was. 'Success.' *And you'll likely try and arrest me if I succeed the way I want, you bastard.*

It was raining in London and Pat watched the tendrils of moisture stream across the window as the perimeter fence flashed past and they bumped to a landing. The last time he'd done this was back in December '95. He was to spend Christmas away from home for the first time in his life and he remembered how that touchdown had been, the mixture of fear and excitement that had him wiping the palms of his hands on his jeans as they had taxied to the terminal. Meeting the lads. The stacked bags that amounted to almost two tonnes of weed-killer collected in a London warehouse, unveiled for him in a moment of revelation and awe one cold winter's day, the low laughter of the three of them as he goggled at the immense haul. It had blue doors, the warehouse. Beyond that he hadn't had the faintest clue where the place was. But, God, the sacks and sacks of Ammonium Nitrate piled up in there, the result of three years gathering and hoarding. They had travelled all over the country, a sack here, ten sacks there. Never too much, never the same place twice. A couple of sympathetic farmers lending a hand.

Pat shook his head. Too many ghosts these days. Twenty years on a farm to bury them and now they were rising up from the ground like a black miasma to curl around and choke him.

The plane lurched to a halt and passengers leapt to their feet, crowding the aisle and shoving at each other as they brought bags down. Mobiles peeped and wolf-whistled and people eagerly scanned their little screens. Boyle handed Pat's bag over to him, sitting looking out of the window at Heathrow twenty years ago.

It hadn't been so bloody wet back then.

The doors opened and people shuffled for the exit. Pat slid across the seat and an Asian man let him into the press. 'Thanks.'

His bag banged against his leg as he joined Boyle, who'd been met by a suit. They walked up the airbridge together, turning left when the other passengers went right. There was no security, but there was a stark white-walled little room with a white table and steel-tube white plastic chairs around it. They were shown in and left to their own devices. 'What's going on?'

'We're waiting for my gun.'

'Do you like it?'

Boyle frowned. 'What, my gun?'

'Yes.'

A Decent Bomber

'You rakin' me?'

'Straight question.'

Boyle considered it, his leather jacket shining in the harsh light. 'Yes. On the balance of it, I do. What of it?'

'Nothing,' said Pat, leaning back in his chair, hands folded over his tummy. He felt oddly giddy. 'Nothing at all.'

The door banged open. A tall brown-haired guy in the ubiquitous dark suit was framed in it. Now there's a word, thought Pat. *Ubiquitous*. You could roll that in the mouth like brandy, so you could.

'Shall we, gentlemen?'

Shall we what? Sing the Angeles? Pat followed them out and down the corridor. And then they were in arrivals and Boyle was chatting to another suit and Pat just tagging along for the ride except there was another, more discreet suit, off behind them to the right. He felt herded.

No scanners, no fuss. Just through like that. It was a marvel, really. Pat remembered smoking as he waited in security, way back then. Smoking. Jesus. Sideburns and big collars. Smoking. And girls in hotpants.

Why were they always black? The cars? Pat ducked into the BMW and settled into the leather seating as Boyle chattered with the driver. The muscle sitting to his left was silent and Pat stared out of the window, enjoying the sight of London in the rain. Such a change from Belfast in the rain.

Twenty years back, a rickety van and a sweating kid driving. Chewing gum and dragging deeply on his fag. How did we even do that? Back then? Chew and smoke?

Too many questions. Pat tried to focus on the here

and now, but his recollected past was clamorous. MacNamara's long, pointless lecture about necessity. Taking tea in a terraced house with Martin and the bearded bloke; fags and bacon sandwiches. And them pretending not to know him, what he was doing, but then clapping him on the back as he left as if they'd known him a lifetime. Our great mate Pat.

The loneliness afterwards. The damage. Deciding that was it. Enough.

How much was enough? Too many questions.

They checked into a Travelodge. Sort of like the Premier Inn, Pat reckoned. He'd barely had time to dump his bags before Boyle was calling on the bedside phone, urging him downstairs. They had a meeting, apparently. Pat was tiring of meetings. He flicked through Driscoll's little black book and called Patsy Logan using the wee blue Nokia. He plucked an apple from the complimentary fruit bowl as he listened to the ring tone. The apple's flesh was grainy.

'Logan.'

'Patsy. It's Pat O'Carolan.'

There was a pause then an explosion of laughter. 'Sweet suffering Jesus. Pat O'Carolan. Where the hell have you been all these years?'

'On a farm. How about you?'

'Ah, you know yourself, living life in the big city. Gettin' by. Raising a family.'

'You've settled, then.'

'Settled? I'm working myself to death. I've two kids and a wife to keep.'

Pat smiled at that. 'So whereabouts are you these days?'

A Decent Bomber

'Wandsworth. Are you in town?'

'Yes, I got in just this morning.'

'What, is there a convention of old timers going on or something?'

'How do you mean?'

'Hamid, the Libyan fellow, called me up just a while ago wanting to catch up.'

Shock stiffened Pat. 'When?'

'Just an hour ago or so. He's on the way over here.'

Pat was urgent. 'Patsy, listen to me. It's important. Get out, now. Have you family with you?'

'Are you messin' Pat? There's nobody home bar me.'

'I'm deadly serious. Get out, stay away from the house. Hamid's behind the bombings in Ireland and the Harrods bomb, too. His lot have already killed three of our lads. I'll meet you. Is there a pub or something where we can find you?'

'There's a place by the common, a pub. Called The Hope. Who's "we"?'

'Give me a while.' Pat almost forgot to ask and kicked himself for being old and slow. 'What's your address?'

'68 Honeywell Road. Pat, tell me you're serious about this.'

'He killed Mackey.'

'I saw that on the news. So it wasn't an accident?'

'Murder, Patsy. Pure fucking murder.'

Boyle was pacing around in reception when Pat got downstairs.

'Where the hell have you been?'

'Talking to an old friend. I was right, they're targeting our old ASUs. Hamid is on his way to a house in Wandsworth right now. 68 Honeywell Road.'

'How?'

'Fellow called Patsy Logan. Hamid called Patsy earlier, arranged to go over to his place.'

Boyle pulled his Tetra handset from his bomber jacket. 'It's Boyle. We have a location for them. 68 Honeywell Road, Wandsworth. We think they're on the way right now. Yes, we'll meet there.'

'Come on,' Boyle urged Pat. 'Meeting's postponed.'

The car was waiting outside. Pat settled back into the smell of leather. The muscle wasn't there, but the driver looked capable enough and was, a peek over the front seat confirmed, wearing a shoulder holster. Boyle sat in front as they pulled away into the traffic.

'Where to, guv?'

'Wandsworth. The address is 68 Honeywell Road but we need to take the last few yards on foot. It could get rough.'

The driver fiddled with his GPS. 'About twenty minutes.'

'Can we do it in less?'

Pat was shoved back into the leather. Boyle was jabbering into his radio, swiping map images on his mobile. 'There's a school there, yes. I understand... Two at the end of the road... All plain clothes, right? No, of course no sirens or squad cars...'

They were moving fast now, weaving through the traffic. Pat admired the driver's unflurried skill. 'You do a lot of this, driver?'

'Been a bit quiet recently, hasn't it? A nice change, this. Like a bit of action, me. And the name's Michael.'

'A good Irish name. I'm Pat. Nice to meet you.'

'You the IRA chap, then?'

'Retired, Michael. I'm a farmer by trade.'

The driver chortled. 'A farmer, are you? A long way

from the country here, mate.'

'Oh, I don't know. There's a lovely sward of green over there.'

'That's Clapham Common. You'll not find any cows on that. Hang on.' He paused, his finger to his ear. 'Right, right. Cheers.' He turned to wave at Boyle, interrupting the flow of his conversation on the Tetra handset. 'We got parking around the back of the school. There in two minutes.'

Boyle nodded. 'Thanks. You ready, Pat?'

'Can I have a gun?'

'No. Guns is for big boys only.'

The driver swung the car left. 'Okay, that's us here.'

'Great, thanks. Can you keep Pat here covered?'

'Pleasure. I've got your back, Pat.'

'That's kind of you, Michael. It's my front I'm worried more about.'

Scrambling out of the car, Pat found himself facing a tall shaven-headed fellow wearing a blue jacket and jeans. He was hard-looking, a military type and his handshake was an iron grip. 'I'm Peter. We've got your friend Logan safe and sound.'

Boyle shook hands. 'Family members?'

'Rounding them up now. Mr Logan's getting a little bit restive, so it might be an idea if Pat here has a word with him.'

Pat snorted. 'Well, you can understand he might be a bit nervous at having the busies take him in and rounding up his family. Given his previous experiences.'

Peter's laughter was cut short. He inclined his head, touching his ear. 'Okay, we have contacts. Four of them, approaching from Northcote Road. Logan will have to wait. Come on, this way.'

The kids were out on the playground of the school,

their high voices clamorous.

'Do you have a team inside the house?' Boyle asked Peter.

'Yes. They'll answer the door. There are two more groups in position across the road in the Honeywell Road Estate. The second the door opens, they'll go in.'

'I'm not so sure that's a good idea. They're an awful trigger-happy bunch.'

'We've deployed SAS and their orders are shoot to kill. We're not planning on giving the bad guys much time to react.'

There was a hint of Hollywood hero to Peter that Pat found unsettling.

'Okay, this is far enough. The house is along there on the right, just past that play area you can see. Here.' Peter handed a little pair of binoculars to Pat. 'Your guys are coming up the street now. Recognise any of them?'

Pat focused. One figure was strolling up the road, the other three hung back in a huddle. 'That's Hamid alright. I'm surprised there aren't more of them, though.'

'Why would there be more?'

Hamid stepped off the street. The doorbell's ring sounded faintly. Two shots rang out and then a volley.

A voice rang out 'Drop your weapons!'

Uniformed men poured out of the housing estate, but a hail of accurate fire came from the three men still in the road. Machine guns at their hips, they moved back towards the front door. The soldiers took cover and returned fire.

Boyle and Peter started running and Pat followed with Michael the driver by his side. Michael had pulled his gun out. The children's voices on the playground were screaming now. All four of them took cover behind a van parked on the side of the street.

'So what now?' Pat asked.

Peter peered beyond the van, then back at him. 'We leave it to the professionals.'

'Have you got the back of the house covered?' The question earned Pat a stare of withering scorn from Peter.

The gunfire grew sporadic, punctuated by children's screams and teachers' shouts. Sirens sounded in the distance. Pat was beginning to loathe the noise of the things. Life had become a series of whoops and yeaows. The firing died down. Men's shouts echoed down the street. There was quiet from the direction of the school.

Peter cupped his hand to his ear. 'We're clear. In we go.'

They ran down the street towards the house. Three soldiers lay spread out on the tarmac; a fourth was sitting up against the wall, wounded. He was being given water by another. A soldier waved at Peter and beckoned them into the house. Pat recalled the smell of his dead herd. All that blood made the air smell of iron. Inside, the house smelled the same.

Hamid Muntasir was lying in a pool of blood on the white-tiled kitchen floor. He was still breathing, pluckmarks on his front oozing to join the pool. He'd grown a beard and his hair was flecked with white, but otherwise he was the man Pat had known back in the late eighties. The heavy-lashed eyes fluttered open and his brown eyes focused. Pat knelt, avoiding the pooling blood.

'So. Pat O'Carolan. Is this heaven, then?'

'The closest thing to it, *habibi*, it's Wandsworth. Where's this Accountant? Hassan Ali Jaffar?'

'I can't tell you that.'

'You're dying, Hamid. Emily's gone. Only Marwan is still alive. Tell me.'

'As you say, I have lost everything.' He coughed. 'I

have no reason to help you.'

'You do. You can help me because it doesn't matter. Jaffar can detonate every one of those bombs and make videos until he bursts, the government won't pay a penny. And once he's run out of my bombs, where's he going to go? He can't make his own. You're not very good terrorists, Hamid. You might have made good insurgents but you don't have the staying power, the organisation or even the political will to cut it fighting against a real government. You're only any use in failed states. So you'd be as well to tell me to avoid the pain and suffering he'll cause when he surely fails.'

'Bravo,' Muntasir croaked. 'Now go to hell.'

Pat grabbed at a kitchen unit and pulled himself to his feet. He shrugged at Boyle. 'It's no use. He's not going to tell us anything. He can stay here and die.'

'Works for me. However, the army medic's here and insists on treating him. He might even live.'

'Fine. Show him in.'

A croak. 'Pat.' A weak beckoning of two fingers.

Pat knelt again, careful to avoid the spreading pool of blood. 'What?'

'Emily. *Shou* gone?'

'Karim shot her. She was talking to the police.'

Muntasir turned his head to Pat. He grimaced, his dry lips trembling. 'He did well, then. She betrayed us.'

'You loved her once.'

'A gazelle I loved, not the hippo.'

Pat breathed deeply. 'Jesus, but you've got an awful gob on you for a dying man.'

'I have been silent for long time.' Muntasir winced. A faltering smile lit up his face. 'Ah, you remember back then? When we were all crazy with Gaddafi and his guns?'

'I do, at that.'

'Gaddafi, the black bastard.' Muntasir clenched his fist. He tried to move his trembling arm but didn't have the strength. 'You were kind to me. Back then. They sent you to scare us, to hurt me and you didn't.'

Because the order came not to Hamid, not because I loved you.

'True enough. Fair play to me, then.'

'Hassan Ali is a greedy man. I thought he was for Libya, but he is for Hassan Ali.'

'Even I could have told you that, Hamid.'

'Marwan. He is alive?'

'Yes. He's being interrogated. His wife misses him.'

'You believe Hassan will fail?'

'Yes, I do.' Inspiration came to Pat. 'And so do you.'

'So. Take him, then. He's using your warehouse.' Hamid coughed and his tongue was bloody. His brown skin was pale and there was a tinge of blue to his lips. Not long now, Pat thought. 'Mackey never sell it.'

Anthony Mackey's lockup. The one with the blue doors. More ghosts, then. At the precise moment Pat had the thought, Hamid Muntasir took a juddering, deep breath that scraped in his throat and left him as a gentle sigh.

Pat pulled the eyelids closed and stood. He washed his hands in the sink and stepped over the body and the crimson splash on the floor and tottered out of the ruined back door into the garden. He stood looking up at the cloudy sky and enjoying the cool, fresh air.

'It's been a pretty rough ride, hasn't it?'

Pat turned to Boyle. 'You can sing that.'

'What was that about warehouses?'

'Oh, he told me where to find Hassan Ali Jaffar. I think for no better reason than because he didn't have to.

Hamid was always a contrary little bugger.'

'So where is he?'

'Oh, no. Not this time, Boyle. I'm done with playing by your rules, being dragged around in swanky cars and told I can't play with the big boys.' Pat turned on his heel and strode back through the house, glass crunching under his feet.

Boyle danced through the wreckage behind Pat. 'I'll arrest you.'

Medics and forensics teams were arriving, the soldiers standing in groups in the road. Police had cordoned off the street. Pat reached the cordon. Boyle flashed his ID and they were let out. 'Arrest me, then.'

'You have no money, no credit card. You can't get anywhere without me.'

'Watch me.'

'Okay, fine. We play it your way. Whatever that is.'

'Right now, I just want to see Patsy Logan.'

Chapter Nineteen

Orla lay on the sofa and gazed at the ceiling. She thought about death and its finality, the abyss that awaits us all. And yet it comes sooner, the ending, to some. We're selfish; she looked over to the rain-flecked window lashed by the shower darkening the city. We only care about the dead because they've left us behind. We think we're mourning them, but we're not. We're mourning our own sense of loss and our anger at them for leaving us.

She wondered if Róisín had truly awakened something in her or if it had purely been about her unique feeling for one girl. Did Orla like women? Yes, on the whole, she probably did more than men. She wasn't in any hurry to test it. She still felt Róisín's loss like a bruise. You could forget it for a time, but if you pressed it, the pain comes back. And when Pat had left her alone for England, he'd pressed the bruise hard.

Breda was nice, but Orla didn't need sympathetic company. She needed to wallow, or perhaps the opposite. Action. Wallowing was easier on the balance of it. Breda was in the bathroom.

The idea came to her like a bucket of icy water. It exhilarated and shocked her. And she knew in the very instant it was the right thing to do. She jack-knifed off the sofa, slipped into the bedroom and pulled her things into her bag. Toiletries she'd just have to pick up on the way. She pulled on her jacket and went back into the living room, scribbling 'Sorry' on the pad by the phone and pulling the leaf off.

Breda's handbag was on the floor by the armchair. It

was like her; big and disorderly. Orla dipped into it, pulled out the purse and Breda's iPad Mini with its old fashioned rubber cover. She slid the Visa card out and flipped the notes from the pouch. She left her scribbled note in their place. She slipped out of the front door and ran as quietly as she could to the lift. She flicked the metal wall with her fingernail on the interminable journey down. As she burst out of the front door of the hotel into fresh air she was filled with an elation that all but threatened to paralyse her from sheer joy. She waved down a black cab that had dropped a woman in a black fur coat.

'The airport, please. George Best.'

'Right you are, love. But I'm not George Best.'

'Well, at least you'll be sober for the ride.'

She got her laugh. On the way, she used Breda's credit card and iPad to buy a ticket on the next BA flight to Heathrow. The iPad asked for a passcode and Orla remembered watching Breda using the little tablet to read the Daily Mail as they had waited around in the hotel room. She tapped 9999 and got through. Making the booking, she paused a second before hitting 'Confirm' on the website, a vague feeling of unease that passed like a bird's shadow. She regretted stealing from Breda, but what she was doing felt so *right*.

You have to focus, Orla told herself as she twizzled a coil of burnished hair around her finger, on the big picture. She looked out of the window at the grey town and the copper tresses reflected in the rain-spattered glass.

Orla paid the driver and hopped out of the cab and into the little airport building. She had a good two hours to kill before the flight. The BA check-in wasn't busy and yes, she had packed her bag herself. She was giddy, moving her weight from side to side. A little knee dance.

The check-in girl slapped her boarding pass up on the counter. Orla reached out for it but her hand was covered by another. It was warm and bigger than hers, with blue-painted fingernails.

'Did you think I came down in the last shower?' Breda's minty breath was hot on her ear and there was a hint of both authority and malevolence in her tone that made Orla tremble.

She wheeled around to face Breda's glower. Two uniformed officers stood behind her. 'Oh no, Breda.'

'What do you mean "Oh no"? You stole my cash, my credit card and my bloody iPad.'

'I had to get to Pat and I knew you'd try and stop me.'

'I spent a lot of time trying to do my best for you. Not my job, that's purely to keep you alive. But my best. I tried to give you someone to talk to, some hope because I felt sorry for you, the terrible things that have happened to you and yet you threw it all back in my face and stole from me. The only thing you've got going for you is that you're so utterly incompetent it's clear you've never done it before.'

'I... I don't understand.'

'I get a text every time my credit card's used, Orla. It took about two minutes to backtrack the transaction.'

'Oh.' Orla wanted to cry. Her great adventure had lasted a taxi drive and ended up in making someone she liked very much treat her with more scorn and contempt than she could ever remember.

Breda turned to the police officers. 'Thanks, lads.'

'Pleasure, Breda. Catch you around.'

'You-you're not going to have me arrested?'

'No. Come over here with me.'

Orla trailed Breda across to the ticketing desk. Breda held out her hand. 'Credit card, please.' She took the card and handed it to the assistant. 'To Heathrow, please. Same flight as this one, BA1417.'

'One way or a return.'

'Can you issue it as an open return?'

'No problem.'

Orla stammered. 'You're coming with me?'

'Well, you're clearly not for stopping put and I can hardly leave you toting my bloody credit card around Europe, can I? Now, I'll take the cash back while we're about it.'

Orla took the little wad of bills from her bag and handed them over. 'Sorry, it's minus a taxi fare.'

'There,' said Breda with an air of satisfaction. 'And this is yours.' She handed over a little Hilton cream paper notelet with the word 'Sorry' scribbled on it.

Orla and Breda sat on the bright red chairs in the espresso bar, gazing out at a FlyBe Bombardier taxiing, its propellers throwing up spray from the tarmac. The clanking and hissing from the espresso machine punctuated the low hubbub of conversation around them. The place smelled of coffee and cooking. It was all very ordinary and Orla liked that and took comfort from it. Breda cupped her coffee in her hands.

'Do you think Pat will find them?' Orla took a bite of warm Panini.

'Together with Boyle, as long as they can stop themselves from tearing each other's' heads off, I think he's got the best chance.'

'Why don't they get on?'

'It's a long story. Boyle's father was killed by the IRA. He's not a big fan.'

'I still find that whole Uncle Pat in the IRA thing a bit mad, to tell you the truth. We never had any idea about it. Thinking about it, I'm a bit pissed off with my Da, I feel he chose to keep something from us that actually mattered. It sounds too dramatic, but sort of living a lie if you know what I mean. When Pat first told me I was all over the place. To be close to someone all your life and then find they had blood on their hands, you know?'

'When did he tell you?'

'After I was kidnapped.' Orla crunched on the heel of the sandwich and licked her greasy fingers. 'I needed that.' Orla wiped herself on the crinkly paper napkin. 'You know, quite a lot's happened over the past few days what with one thing and another.'

'You seem to be taking it pretty much in your stride. You're very resourceful.'

Orla flicked her hair back. 'I've not really had many options, have I?'

Breda smiled. 'No, you haven't.'

'So what now? When we get to London?'

'I'll have to call Boyle and let him know we're there. I expect he'll flip.'

They stood together in the yawning, brushed steel expanse of Heathrow's Terminal Five. Breda had gone shopping in Belfast and had a carrier bag packed with toothbrush and toiletries. Underwear had been something else. They sold all manner of crap in those shops, but a pair of clean knickers was definitely not on offer. The one thing she actually needed.

Orla was pale, but a transformation had come over

the girl since Breda caught up with her at the airport. She had cheered up, seemed to have made her way out of the introspective torpor that had overcome her and Breda had enjoyed her company on the flight. Orla would surely break hearts. More than a few, Breda thought with a dry chuckle, when they found out she wasn't interested. Breda wondered if it were a phase as she held the mobile to her ear. She listened to the ring tone. She wasn't looking forward to this conversation, silently playing it out to herself on the short flight over.

'Boyle.'

'Hiya. It's Breda.'

'What's new?'

'Um, I'm at Heathrow with Orla O'Carolan.'

The explosion didn't disappoint. Breda held the handset away from her ear and Orla winced.

'What the fuck are you doing here? Have you lost your fucking mind?'

'She ran away. I thought it was best all round if she was close to her uncle.'

'Do you not think we've got enough on our fucking hands? You're supposed to be running protection, not playing nurse maid. Who paid for the flights?'

'I did.'

'Well don't think for one second you're claiming them. Jesus, what the hell am I supposed to do with you both now? Do you have a weapon?'

'Yes.' Breda had fretted over bringing it, the fuss of handing it over, waving her warrant card around and going through the additional security checks before having it tagged and put in the hold. Picking the gun up at Heathrow, feeling the weight of it back in her hand, she'd known it was the right thing to do.

'At least that's a small mercy. Right. We're staying at

the Travelodge in Vauxhall. You'd best get yourselves over there.'

'Okay. Thanks, Boyle.'

Orla put a hand on her arm. 'How was it?'

Breda grinned at her. 'Not nearly as bad as I thought. He must be going soft. Come on, we've got a hotel to check into. And I need to find some knickers.'

Michael the driver pulled the big BMW up outside a pretty–looking pub on the apex of a y-shaped junction. 'Here we go. The Hope.'

'Thanks. Boyle, I'll meet you back at the hotel.'

'No way. I'm coming in with you.'

'I told you, my way or the highway. The driver can show you the highway. Logan's already going to be spooked, and he won't talk with a copper in earshot.'

'We don't have to tell him I'm a copper.'

Pat had the door open and one foot on the kerb when he stopped and looked round at Boyle. 'Are you right in the head? You might as well have the word tattooed with your eyebrows as an underline. Wait here if you like, then. I won't be that long anyway. You okay to wait there, Michael?'

'Sure.'

Pat stalked across the pavement and into the pub. He blinked at the transition from daylight into the dark pub interior. Logan was sitting on a settle across the end of the triangular seating area away from the bar, a half full glass of Guinness in front of him. He was framed by two blue standard lamps. He caught sight of Pat and his worried face broke into a grin. Pat strode over and they pumped hands and grasped elbows.

'Well, by God, Patrick O'Carolan as long as I live. It's

been twenty years and more since I last saw that ugly face.' Logan held him away and looked him up and down. 'Christ, but you're still a big bollix.'

'It's been a while, Patsy, right enough.' Pat tilted his head towards Logan's drink. 'That's an idea. Another?'

'I will, Pat, I will.'

Pat went to the bar and ordered two pints, gratified the bearded young barman rested his Guinness. The English had come a long way, then, since back in the day. 'It's alright,' the barman said. 'I'll bring them over.'

'Thanks.'

Pat wandered back to Logan, who was draining his glass. He'd aged. He was silver-haired and his thin face was lined, the long, crooked nose and bushy eyebrows framing pale cornflower eyes. Logan's face had seen a lot of laughter, but Pat fancied there was also pain in there. His nails were long and, from the yellowed fingers, he was still a big smoker.

'I'm afraid they made a mess in the house. They say there'll be compensation and the like.'

'What do you mean, a mess?'

'I won't lie. There's glass broken, a load of bullet holes. The furniture's banjaxed. The front and back doors are off their hinges. A gun battle sort of mess.'

'Ah, fuck. What am I going to say to Trina?'

'Well, telling her to be thankful to be alive is a good start.'

'I couldn't believe it when they all arrived in here looking for me, Pat. I thought the game was up. Armed police, goons in suits with earpiece radios. I nearly shit myself.'

'I'm sorry. I tried to make sure you were safe and all.'

'Fair play. They tried to explain what was going on to me, but I was in shock. You'll admit, 'tis ironic, like.'

'Given the past? I know what you mean. But I haven't really had the time to enjoy the joke, tell the truth. Listen, I need a bit of help.'

'How are you wrapped up in all this, Pat?'

'Jesus, look now, Patsy. We don't have the time for me to even begin to explain. There's a bunch of lunatics going around setting off bombs. Not for a cause or anything, just for money. They've been using our networks to find the caches we hadn't turned over.'

'So that's what they were after.'

'What have you got?'

'Nothing. I ditched them ten years back. Drove them out into a forest south of Tunbridge and buried them. They were burning a hole in my conscience. I was scared the police would find them. I'd no appetite for doing time, especially after the peace deal. What was the point? I never told Driscoll.'

Pat sat back and marvelled. 'That there omission damn near got you killed, Patsy.'

'Here we go.' The barman placed the two pints on the dark wood. 'Cheers.'

'Cheers,' Pat took a long pull of the pint and licked the foam off his upper lip. He could use a shave, come to think of it. 'You remember Tony Mackey's lockup? With the blue doors?'

'Yes, of course. God, how could I ever forget that place? Two tonnes of that fertilizer stuff. The sight of them sacks, even. Stacked up to the rafters, they were. Jesus, but they were some bombs, Pat.'

Pat gazed down at the black beer in his hand. *Yes, Patsy and I've been the last twenty years trying to put them out of my mind. The bombs we made to tear out the heart of Docklands and the centre of Manchester. That snuffed out two lives and tore gouges out of countless innocents. And saw the end of my career so I could retire to become a murderer of conscience.*

'Where is it? Con Connelly took me there back then, but that was twenty years past. I haven't got a nonny where it is now.'

'Wembley. Linden Avenue. Never forget it, that place. I had a key to it myself at one time. I haven't seen Mackey since back then, either. I don't remember any post code though. Did we use them then?'

'Was Mackey sitting on a cache? In Manchester?'

'I wouldn't know, Pat. We never talked again, any of us, not after the Manchester bomb. Of course it was all over just after. We won, Pat. Imagine. God knows, it's a crying shame we never got brought together to celebrate that. What we did. Here. *Sláinte.* The Peace.'

'The Peace.' Pat clinked glasses but his mind was whirling around a thousand pounds of ammonium nitrate packed with Semtex-filled tubing to set it off. He, of all people, knew of the devastating effect of a device that size. Detonated in a busy city centre with no warning, it would kill hundreds. Maybe thousands.

It was the warning that did for him. To make a bomb capable of smashing a thousand windows is one thing. To be asked to hand it over and take no responsibility for how it was used, that was where he had finally broken. The botched Docklands warning had flung the broken remains of two men through walls and gouged shrapnel into the flesh of blameless people. Women, children had been caught in the path of that huge eruption and Pat had been powerless to help them. A political point, a bargaining chip. A tool. Every time he breathed in, he enjoyed a moment he had denied other men.

How many hours had he sat up on the bog looking at the blue hills and thinking of them? The faceless people whose lives he had savaged. Slapping a cow's arse and feeling the muscle move, the animal impulses of life transformed into still, cold flesh.

Fuck your peace.

Pat slid onto the back seat of the BMW. 'Okay, I think I know where our car bomb is. Wembley, Linden Avenue. There's a warehouse there belonged to Anthony Mackey. It's where the Docklands and Manchester bombs were assembled back in the nineties.'

Boyle twisted round in his seat. 'And how do you know that?'

'Little birdies, Boyle. Let's get going.'

'No, we do this properly. We have to plan our approach, ensure the proper resources are in place.'

'There's no time for all that. For pity's sake, the thing's packed with almost a tonne of explosive.'

'And you made it.'

'You don't think I've been regretting it every second since? Come on, Boyle. Move it.'

The car pulled away from the kerb. Boyle twisted to Michael the driver. 'And where the fuck do you think you're going?'

'He's right. There's no time. We can call it in, but there's no time.'

Boyle threw up his hands.

Breda knocked on the door of Orla's room. There was a puff of scented air, Orla stood in a white fluffy dressing gown with her hair in a towelled stack. 'Oh, hi. Come in. I thought I'd freshen up while I had the chance.'

'Sure, don't you smell only lovely? Get dressed, we're

going out. They've found a lockup in Wembley they reckon the bad guys are using. Boyle says we're to stay put but you know what? I'm bored of staying put.'

'Give me five minutes.'

'Meet you in reception.'

Breda went back to her room and checked her firearm and ammunition. She paced the room before taking the stairs down to reception. A thin-faced man was waiting at the reception desk. Breda peered out of the window at the traffic passing. The receptionist came out of the back room and smiled at him.

'Can I help you sir?'

'Mr Patrick O'Carolan, please. I believe he's staying with you.'

'He is, but he's out of the hotel at the moment. Can I leave him a message?'

'Can you give him this? Tell him Patsy Logan left it.'

Breda strolled over to the reception desk and held her hand out to Logan. 'Hi, I'm Breda Fitzsimmons, I'm here with Pat. Can I help?'

Logan shook her hand. 'He said he was staying here but I didn't have a number for him or anything. It's this, the key to the lockup he's interested in. I thought I had it somewhere. It's been sitting in a pot on my mantelpiece for twenty years. It was about the only thing in the house those bastards didn't break.'

Orla arrived in the reception area and Logan paled, his mouth dropping open.

'Are you okay?' Breda followed his stare. 'This is Orla O'Carolan, Pat's niece.'

'My God, but you're the spit of Pat's Orla. Gave me quite a turn. It's that red hair.'

Breda rang Boyle. 'We're coming over, we've got the key to the warehouse.'

A Decent Bomber

*

Anthony Mackey's lockup in Linden Avenue was one of three shabby double story warehouses in a cul-de-sac off the street of Edwardian terraces. All three had blue-painted peeling wooden double doors and cracked, dirty windows with a single door alongside. Pat remembered coming here all those years ago, the sense of dislocation of being herded around a big city you didn't know. Those doors probably hadn't been painted since. There was rubbish on the margins of the concreted forecourt area, a broken pram with tatty mildewed canvas hanging off its rusty hood, piles of rotting clothing and a collapsed plastic vegetable rack. There were several black plastic bin liners piled in the corner. The concrete was littered with damp paper sheets and shards of discarded plastic packaging.

Breda and Orla were sitting in a taxi at the end of the road waiting for them. Pat pulled open the door and flung his arms around Orla, who buried herself in his shoulder. 'Jesus, why did you come here *a chuisle*? You were safe in Belfast.'

Breda walked around the car and Pat hugged her. 'You should have stayed put.'

'Orla wouldn't have it any way but she was with you. I just followed her.'

'Well, stay here. This won't take long.'

'Here,' Breda handed him the key. 'A man called Patsy Logan brought this to the hotel. It's the key to the lockup.'

Pat took it. It seemed comfortably old fashioned, the brass cold in his hand. 'Thanks. Right. We'll be getting on with this.'

He strode towards Boyle, who was pacing cautiously

along the wall, his gun held in both hands, pointing down in front of him. Breda called to him. 'Pat.' He turned to her. 'Take care of yourself. I'd prefer to see you again.'

The courtyard area was silent, the swish of leaves in the wind and crackle of a crisp packet on the concrete the only sounds.

'Which one?' Boyle hissed.

Pat passed him. 'Middle. I have the key.'

Boyle's eyes lit up furiously as Pat pulled his Baby Glock out of his pocket. Pat shrugged to let him know his views on Pat having a gun were of no consequence whatsoever to him.

They crept along the warehouse frontage. Pat peered through the grimy window into the first warehouse but could make out little other than an iron walkway around the big space at mezzanine level. His heart hammering, he inched towards the middle warehouse, crouching to try and peek through the lichen-smeared glass without casting a shadow against the glass. He could make out nothing in the gloom beyond.

Boyle tapped his shoulder, signalling for the key with a twist of his hand. Pat handed it over, pushing his way to his feet against the rough brick wall. Michael the driver was standing off across the courtyard, his gun in hand. He returned Pat's wave with a wink. Sirens sounded in the distance.

Boyle stooped over the lock. He slid the key in and held it with both hands to turn it, grimacing in anticipation of the sound. The lock turned quietly and Boyle straightened, his face relaxing. Pat gave him the thumbs up and a grin. Boyle pushed the door open. The rusty hinge's screech stilled them both.

It was cool, dark and silent inside. The air was musty.

Chapter Twenty

Boyle slid through the half-open door, Pat behind him. The office to the left was abandoned, papers scattered on the battered desks and carpet-tiled floor. The corridor led to another office, the black-painted door at the end marked as a toilet. The metalled door to the right was ajar and Boyle pushed at it. Pat tried not to peer over his shoulder. The silence was deafening.

Boyle paused, his head cocked. Pat caught the stink of paint and thinners. Boyle looked back at Pat and touched his nose. Pat nodded. Boyle shrugged before pushing cautiously through the door, his gun held ahead of him. He stepped out onto the concrete floor. Picked out in the gloom by the light from the dirty window, was a blue HiAce van, newspaper stuck on its windows with masking tape.

The far side wall of the warehouse had a stairway leading up to a black perforated steel mezzanine gantry with a railing. It led around the walls of the warehouse to a steel-walled, half-glazed office above them. Pat peered around. The warehouse seemed bigger than it had looked from the outside. Boyle stepped out into the open floor of the warehouse, swinging his gun as he peered up into the space above, grimy neon tubes suspended from the high ceiling.

'Where the hell have they got to?' Boyle whispered.

There were two workbenches in a corner, a compressor beside them. Pots of paint were scattered on the floor. Pat breathed out, feeling light headed from having held his breath. 'I don't care. I wasn't particularly looking forward to their company.'

He paced over to the van and touched the paint. It had set. He checked the driver's side door handle, but it was locked. He picked at the masking tape and pulled the blue-sprayed newsprint aside. The van was loaded, just as he'd last seen it with its pallet of sacks.

He wandered around to the back of the van and checked the doors but they too were locked. Rounding the van, he saw Boyle stood by the workbenches, his gun held loosely. Boyle called out. 'It's like the Mary bloody Celeste.'

The burst of automatic gun fire from above knocked Boyle into the bench. Paint tins clattered to the floor as he fell, the roar of the shots echoing in the big space. Pat leaped behind the van for cover.

He called out. 'Boyle?'

The flat crack of shots sounded outside. Pat crouched to the floor and tried to get a glimpse of Boyle from under the van but he could only see the grey coated concrete warehouse floor. He didn't remember the rubbery coating from back then, the old days. The floor had been rough-surfaced, he could swear. That pattern you got by stippling it with the edge of a plank, like in his milking shed. The death of his herd came back to him, their life blood soaking into the rough ground.

He pushed himself to stand. He leaned back against the doors of the van and waited for his heart to slow. He tried to control his ragged breathing, to calm himself.

'Mister Pat.' It was the Somali. The rich, accented voice rang out in the expanse of the lockup.

Pat straightened, glancing left and right to check he was shielded from any line of fire from the gantry. He gripped the Glock tight in both hands. 'Mister Hassan.' He was glad his voice sounded a great deal more confident than he felt.

A Decent Bomber

'You have nowhere to go.'

Pat smiled to let his amusement carry into his voice as he called out. 'Right enough. But I have time, a luxury you don't.'

'You have been very troublesome, Mister Pat.'

'You have no idea how good it feels to hear that from you.'

'Your wireless detonator was most ingenuous. I admire your craftsmanship. We learned from you. A similar detonator is inside the vehicle you are hiding behind, but with a more powerful transmitter and receiver. It has an effective range of five miles. We repaired the errors in your wiring. You are very careless for a skilled man.'

'They'll gun you down the second you leave this place.'

'They are not here yet. And if they come before I am ready, I shall press this button and go to God. Imagine, I have your life in my hand.'

'And yours with it. You're in a hurry to die, are you? Press away, you African fucker. Go on, do it. There's no way out for you now. You're over, history. Hamid's dead, his kids are dead. Your buddies are gone. It's just you left.'

Pat felt rather than heard the careful footsteps on the gantry above and realised he was exposed. He pulled his hand back into cover too late. A burst of automatic fire reverberated in the open space of the warehouse. Bullets smashed into the Glock. They ripped the gun from his grip, breaking his fingers, the sickening snaps followed by a rush of agony. Pat cried out. His gun skittered across the concrete and was lost in the shadow under the van. He dropped to the floor, doubled in pain, his ruined hand gripped at the wrist by his good one. Blood pulsed onto the rubbery surface. He sobbed with the hurt of it, his legs kicking out at his flapping greatcoat as he scrabbled across the floor for cover, headed for the van's shadow like a cockroach caught in the light. A gunshot spattered the concrete, stinging his face and stilling his crawl.

He heard slow footsteps ring out on the gantry above. Hassan Jaffar came into view, his wooden-stocked automatic rifle trained on Pat. 'I should kill you now.'

'Do it. You'll never leave this place.'

The Somali laughed. He padded to the stairs and danced down them lightly, the AK-47 trained on Pat all the while. Pat suppressed the urge to scream with the pain in his hand, gritting his teeth as he struggled towards his gun. The expensive brown leather shoe crashed down on his ruined hand and Pat shrieked, flapping over onto his back to try and punch above him but the Somali stepped back. Pat gripped his hand, sobbing with pain.

'I have an idea. You shall die wonderfully, Mister Pat. Lying on your own bomb.'

Pat didn't see the kick to his head coming. His world burst into a flash of white followed by blessed unconsciousness.

Waiting in the back of their black taxi, Orla and Breda lapsed into silence. The driver hadn't spoken a word since they had picked up the cab outside the hotel. The windows had steamed up, blurring the figures of football fans walking past on their way down to the stadium. They were mostly wearing black and white scarves. Orla pondered the many hours she'd spent huddled in the seats of cars over the past few days. She closed her eyes

A Decent Bomber

and tried to blot out the memories which kept coming back to haunt her.

Breda's voice was gentle. 'How are you, love?'

'Tired, Breda. Tired like I'll never be able to sleep enough to feel normal again. What's with the mob in the scarves?'

'Newcastle fans. That's the Wembley Stadium down there at the end of the road.'

'Oh. It's the football today?'

Breda's glance was pitying. 'The FA Cup, yes.'

'What was that?' Orla straightened in her seat, reached for the window button. People had stopped in the street. The muffled, unmistakable sound reminded her of Pat executing his herd. Gunfire.

'Breda, we need to help them.'

'There's help on the way now. We can't get involved, we'll just get in the way. Trust me, Boyle knows what he's doing.'

Orla craned to listen. It sounded again, a peppering of flat cracks from inside the warehouse. 'Please, Breda.'

Sirens sounded in the distance. A group of fans gathered in the street by the entrance to the warehouses, nervous-looking and yet curious. Some were pulling friends on down the hill towards the stadium, others inching towards the warehouses and beckoning for company.

The driver turned towards them. 'You hear that? What's going on in there?'

Breda shrugged at him. 'Search me.'

'They haven't come out. Breda, we need to help them. Where are the police?'

'They're on the way, you can hear them. Just sit tight for now, Orla.'

She wrung her hands, glancing miserably at the

normalcy of the street with its groups of football fans.

A figure appeared on the first floor balcony around the garages, pointing a gun slung over his shoulder down and tracking right as a man appeared in the entranceway shouting 'Get back' at the uncertain bystanders. The gun in his hand bucked as he fired upwards but he was cut down by the spray of bullets from the roof. Concrete chips flew up in a cloud of grit.

Breda barged the taxi door open. 'Orla, stay here. Don't follow me.' She banged on the driver's partition. 'Look after her. Take her back to the hotel, can you?'

The driver was pale. 'Course, love. Rely on me, you can.'

Breda pulled her gun out of her handbag. The taxi door slammed and Orla twisted to watch her dart across the road, hugging the wall. Orla gazed fearfully up at the rooftop but couldn't see the gunman up there. Breda inched along the wall, out of direct sight from the roof, her gun held out straight ahead of her.

The taxi started to move and Orla hammered on the partition. 'No. Stop.'

Pat rose up from the darkness slowly. His hand felt as if it had been burned in a blast furnace and his head was in agony, throbbing waves of nausea washed over him. His wrists and mouth had been taped. He was in the back of the van, the pissy reek from the stacked sacks of ammonium nitrate was sickening and Pat fought to keep himself from retching, hit by the sudden terror of drowning in his own puke.

He jack-knifed away from the pallets, pushing his face against the base of the van's back door to try and get some fresh air. The door moved and Pat blinked in

A Decent Bomber

wonderment. *Fucking amateurs.*

He gazed around him, peering up at the piled plastic sacks of white pellets. He shifted to try and get a look at his bindings. His wrists were tightly wrapped, but his good hand still had movement in it. His legs were bound with duct tape over his jeans. He reached down to his belt, hooking the leather tongue with his little finger and pulling it free. He almost cried out with the pain as the movement of his good hand caught the swollen, purple flesh of his broken one. He managed to grip the belt between his fingers and pull at it so the prong loosened and fell away from the leather. His bad hand was visibly darker. He pulled open the fastener of his jeans, grunting with exertion and agony.

Pat kicked off his shoes and used the side of a pallet and his heel to catch the denim hem, pointing his foot, twisting his body and bucking to loosen the jeans around his waist. He stilled at a sound from the warehouse. He crabbed his foot against the denim, inching the trousers off. His foot was jammed by the tight duct tape, cramp starting to blossom in the arch of his foot. He pushed at the denim, his ruined hand leaving streaks of blood.

He pulled against the constraining tape, his foot coming free. He wriggled his leg out of the trousers and used his socked foot to hold the other trouser leg as he freed himself from his jeans. His swollen hand had stopped bleeding and had turned blue, which wasn't a good sign.

His discarded belt clanked against the metalled floor of the van. Pat froze. *Ah, shit.* He listened, trembling.

A door closed somewhere, faint but unmistakeable. The silence inside the warehouse yawned. The faint sound of sirens from outside. Breda's voice called out. 'Pat? Boyle

Pat's heart did cartwheels. He reached up to his mouth, pulled at the duct tape unthinkingly, wrenching it aside and ignoring the pain in his hand and the tearing around his lips. He cried out, his throat arid. 'Stay back! Breda? Stay back!'

Steps sounded in the corridor. Breda yelled, 'Pat? It's okay, they're coming. The —'

A man's voice cut across her, barking commands Pat couldn't make out. He kicked out at the van's doors and they flew open. He rolled and dropped, trying to screw around and protect his hand from the drop. He fell onto his shoulder, winded and pained, but following the plan, rolling as fast he could under the van. Undignified, panicked and keening with the pulsing agony from his hand, he hit out at the first sharp edge he could find in the dirty collection of steel members above him. The blow caught the duct tape against the muddy, rusty steel edge. Sobbing, he repeated the movement, tearing at the silvered mass.

Bullets tore at the concrete at the rear of the van, stinging chips flew but Pat was out of range for the moment. Three times he smashed his tied wrists up against the chassis member, forcing them apart to tauten the tape as the heels of his hands drummed against the cold, dirty steel.

His hands freed and flew apart, the glue tearing at his hairs unnoticed in the blast of pain from his damaged hand, the blood started to return to the half-necrotic flesh and a new wave of torment coursed up his arm. He arced, keening as the tattered ribbon of tape still stuck to his skin flapped around.

Pat flipped onto his stomach. His gun was there, resting by the front offside wheel. He crawled towards, hand and elbow. The gunfire stopped. The dust settled.

A Decent Bomber

Pat's left hand found the grip of the Glock. He glanced around at his floor-level view from under the minivan.

A door banged open. Pat curled around towards the source of the noise. Breda backed into the warehouse with her hands raised. Her pistol dangled loosely from her fingers. A swarthy man in combats with a shaven head and a wispy brown beard followed her, jabbing his AK-47 at her.

His thin features contorted. 'Drop gun. Drop now. Hear me? Drop.'

Shouldering the door's rebound, the gunman was distracted for a second. Pat moved fast, swinging his Glock around. The gunman's attention switched to Pat as his moment's indecision cost him dear. Pat took the shot, a middle-fingered double tap that found its mark despite Breda's wheeling around across his line of fire. The Chechen collapsed. The automatic rifle fired off, blowing holes out of the block wall. The man's body spasmed, his legs jerking.

Breda brought her pistol into her palm, recovering her balance to aim across the warehouse. More shots rang out. Pat rolled out from under the van to try and cover her, supporting himself on his elbows and firing wildly with his left hand across the rear of the van towards the opposite corner of the warehouse. His bullets tore holes in the van's skin. Breda was thrown back by a series of impacts. She crashed to the floor, dropping her gun and curling into a ball. Pat whipped around to face Hassan Jaffar as the suited man came into view around the back of the van. The shot took him in the arm before he could raise his gun. The strength went out of him and the Glock clattered to the floor. Blood pulsed down along his forearm as he collapsed onto his back. Hassan Jaffar stood over Pat, the AK-47 trained down on him.

The Somali gave a deep chuckle. 'An old man in his socks and underwear.' He held up a small black transmitter. 'The trigger.' He paused and cocked his head to one side. Sirens sounded loudly outside the warehouse, tyres screeching. 'I know it is useless now, that the game is over. But you and I shall go out together, Mister Pat, in a blaze of glory. We shall be liberated with a fireball to take our souls to heaven.'

'Or hell.'

'Perhaps for you, hell. For me, paradise.'

Pat winced at the hammering report of a shot close by. Hassan Jaffar's arms flailed wide as a crimson bloom showed on his chest. He staggered back. A second shot rang out, then a third caught his shoulder a glancing blow. He fell to his knees, a look of wide-eyed surprise on his face. His features turned ugly as he raised his hands to clutch at his front, the gun falling from his slackening fingers.

'That's for Róisín,' said the small, silvery voice of the red haired girl standing by Pat's feet.

Chapter Twenty-One

Pat laid the wreath on the neat black marble grave, crossed himself and stood at its foot listening to the birds and smelling the sweet air. Orla squeezed his good hand, the other was in splints and wrapped in bandage.

Orla searched his face. 'Was she really so beautiful? Your Orla?'

'She was. You're my Orla, too, you know.'

'Mum says Dad's adamant, he won't speak to me. He's written me out of his life. Even his will, she said.'

'I wouldn't worry about that. You've been in mine since you were born.'

'Really?'

'The farm's yours. I'll have to die first, of course.'

'Then I never want to have it.'

Pat sighed, the sun warm on his face, despite the coolness of the day. Ironically this corner of the cemetery was a sun trap. 'Anyway, Mikey will calm down. In time.'

Orla faced Pat. 'Did you seriously never come here before?'

'Never. I've spent a long time forgetting. Omitting, perhaps is a better word. The past can be stifling.'

The wreath was a circle of red roses framing a swan picked out in tiny white flowers. The gravestone was plain, the text cut into the stone etched in gold.

'I think I know what you mean.'

'Come on, we're keeping Breda waiting.' Pat turned away from the grave and led the way down along the gravel path.

Birdkill

ALEXANDER MCNABB

Robyn Shaw has amnesia, a recent trauma so great her mind has veiled her memory. When she starts a new life teaching at a research institute devoted to exceptionally gifted children, the last thing she expects is for those blocked events to be lying in wait for her.

Plagued by dreams of death and blood that threaten to overwhelm her, Robyn is fragile and vulnerable. When she meets student Martin Oakley plucking sparrows from the air and breaking their necks, she is pitched into a vicious battle that threatens her grasp of her own mind.

Attacked from without and within, Robyn struggles to maintain her increasingly tenuous hold on reality as journalist Mariam Shadid races to discover the dreadful secret buried in Robyn's past before her friend is consumed by insanity.

More at: **www.alexandermcnabb.com**

Also by Alexander McNabb

Olives – A Violent Romance

Beirut – An Explosive Thriller

Shemlan – A Deadly Tragedy

Birdkill

Available from Amazon in Kindle and in paperback from Amazon, Book Depository or local bookstores on order.

Also available as ebooks at iBooks, Barnes & Noble, Kobo and other fine online retailers.

A wee note

This book started because of a running joke: Sarah's Uncle Pat is a kind, mild mannered and gentle man who keeps a small herd of milk cows on his small farm up high towards the Cummermore Bog in South Tipperary. It always amused me to allude darkly to the arms cache he was doubtless sitting on – he was a keen enough Republican when he was a younger man.

I can only hope he'll forgive me for the terrible thing I have extrapolated from that silly gag.

My terrorist is your freedom fighter, and vice-versa. I've lived these past 30-odd years with the conflicts of the Middle East all around me – and along with them, the convenience of automatically dubbing the other side of any undeclared war or territorial conflict 'terrorists'. The PLO were terrorists, but they were fighting for a return to the land and homes taken from them by the likes of the Haganah and Stern Gang – both groups identified at the time – quite rightly - by the British as Zionist terrorists. The French resistance were heroes to us Brits, fighting the illegal occupation of their country, but terrorists to the 'other side'. And so it goes on.

The idea that 'terrorism' isn't quite that simple – isn't a bumper sticker thing - is why I wrote my first serious novel, *Olives-A Violent Romance*.

The largest bomb on the British mainland since WWII went off in June 1996. Over a tonne of explosive packed into a van did more than a billion pounds' worth of damage and tore the heart out of the British city of Manchester. Although nobody died, over 200 people were wounded alongside a devastating loss of property. They never did find the men who made and placed it.

This is a novel, a fiction. I hope I manage make some points in it about reconciliation. But my experiment in pitting 'real terrorists' against the chimera our government keeps waving in our faces today certainly wasn't carried out with the intention of glamorising any terrorism – that of the IRA or any other group. Whenever terror makes itself felt, whoever the victims are, it's painful and awful and results in senseless loss and human suffering. I don't think it's admirable and, not being a madman, I don't think it's a solution.

The image on the cover, incidentally, is an Easter Lily badge, traditionally worn by Irish Republicans in commemoration of the Easter uprising. It's a powerful symbol of Irish nationalism that remains divisive even today.

Thanks

Brian Webster created a Grooveshark playlist (back when you could do that sort of thing) which stayed with me throughout the writing of this book and jettisoned me back to deepest, greenest Ireland every time I needed to fly there in moments flat, even when it was 45 in the shade in Dubai and the sandstorms were blowing. I don't know if I could have done it without those tunes. It was a prodigious and wonderful list of brilliance, including Dropkick Murphys, Fight Like Apes, David Holmes, Japanese Popstars, Therapy?, The Stunning, A House, The Frames and so very many more.

Carrie Webster managed projects and people alike with typical panache, including introducing me to former IRA man, H block prisoner and Sinn Fein councillor Brendan Curran, who kindly gave of his time and insight: any idiocy regarding life in the IRA remaining in this book will be entirely mine and no result of his having kindly lent the fruits of his experience.

Katie Stine was, as always, a genius proof reader and editorial author-beater. Thanks go out to Derek Kirkup, Bob Studholme, Phillipa Fioretti, Pete Morin, Mita Ray and Micheline Hazou for their friendship, insights, comments and inputs on early drafts. And also to writerly pals Rachel Hamilton and Annabel Kantaria, always wonderful company in the booky journey, who gave me the final push to finish this when all seemed lost.

A group of people who have supported me tirelessly and

championed my books with inspirational zeal and great kindness have so far gone un-thanked, so it's time to right the wrong. To Isobel, Yvette, John, Chrissie, Mohammed, Cathy and the delightful and hard-working team behind the Emirates Airline Festival of Literature, the Dubai International Writers' Centre and Dubai Eye Radio's *Talking of Books* – my heartfelt thanks and gratitude not only for their encouragement on my own journey, but for the work that has seen so many new writers emerging, blinking, from the cultural wasteland that was and finding new inspiration to start their own explorations of the joys of writing – and reading.

Sarah, as usual, has put up with me throughout what has been – I'll freely admit – an unusually long and difficult gestation.

And, of course, thank you for reading this!

Interviews, book club notes and more at
www.alexandermcnabb.com

@alexandermcnabb